THE ROAD TO CULLODEN

THE ROAD
TO CULLODEN MOOR

Bonnie Prince Charlie and the '45 Rebellion

DIANA PRESTON

CONSTABLE · LONDON

First published in Great Britain 1995
by Constable and Company Limited
3 The Lanchesters, 162 Fulham Palace Road
London W6 9ER
Copyright © 1995 Diana Preston
The right of Diana Preston to be identified as
the author of this work has been asserted by her
in accordance with the Copyright, Designs and
Patents Act 1988
ISBN 0 09 474080 1
Set in Linotron Sabon 11pt by
Rowland Phototypesetting Ltd
Bury St Edmunds, Suffolk
Printed in Great Britain by
St Edmundsbury Press Ltd
Bury St Edmunds, Suffolk

A CIP catalogue record for this book
is available from the British Library

To Michael

CONTENTS

ILLUSTRATIONS

ACKNOWLEDGEMENTS

I have always been fascinated by the legend of Bonnie Prince Charlie, not least because of a family connection with the events of the '45. Antoine Walsh, the Anglo-French slave trader who supplied the Prince with the vessel that took him to Scotland and sailed with him, is an ancestor of mine. As a child I came across a collection of Walsh's correspondence with the Prince and with a network of Jacobite agents. The letters defined a strange world of spies and intrigue, ambitious schemes and elaborate plots, but also a world of disillusionment and heartbreak. From those pages I could trace the high hopes of Charles and his supporters in 1744 and 1745 through the bitter aftermath of Culloden to the Prince's decline and the end of the Jacobite dream. For me the story has an enduring mystique and I hope others find it as compelling.

It is difficult to know where to begin in thanking all the people who have helped me with this book. However, top of the list must be my husband Michael for his help with the research, his encouragement and for stopping me falling too much a victim to the spell of Bonnie Prince Charlie. I must also thank Vera Faith, Clinton Leeks, Neil Munro, Justina Binks and my agent Michael Thomas for their help and advice at various stages in the project. I would also like to thank the staff of the London Library for their efficiency and resourcefulness in locating the main source material.

Diana Preston

NOTE ON DATES:

Sometime before the '45, the continent of Europe adopted the 'new style' Gregorian calendar, whereas Britain used the 'old style' – eleven days behind – until 1752. All the dates in the book are given in the old style except for events on the Continent which, unless indicated otherwise, are new style. A good example is that in Rome Charles's birthday takes place on New Year's Eve 1720 (new style), but he celebrates his twenty-fifth birthday on 20 December 1745 (old style) as he retreats across the Esk back into Scotland from England.

NOTE ON QUOTATIONS:

On the few occasions where the eighteenth-century spelling and punctuation would, in my view, distract from the meaning or be confusing I have modernised them.

INTRODUCTION

'Unless you tear our hearts out and rip our breasts right open, you will
never remove Charlie from us until we are snuffed out. He is woven into
our souls . . .'

In Rome, in early 1788, an old man lay dying in the arms of his
illegitimate daughter. There was nothing heroic about his bloated
body and protuberant blood-shot eyes, nothing to suggest that
here lay one of the most charismatic and compelling figures in
British history – Bonnie Prince Charlie. To himself and to others
he was a failure. His great ambition, to reclaim the throne of
Britain for the Stuarts, had eluded him and the rest of his life had
been an embarrassing descent into wife-beating, paranoia, despair
and drunkenness. In those final moments his clouded mind may
have recaptured his glory days during the 1745 Jacobite Rebellion.
Perhaps, before his eyes dimmed forever, he saw himself young
and handsome again, his body 'formed for war', as he marched
at the head of his 'brave Highlanders'. Perhaps he wondered how
these events would be remembered, or if they would be
remembered at all.

In fact the story of Bonnie Prince Charlie and the '45 is one of
the most enduring. Two and a half centuries later the handsome
young hero still gazes at us from the labels of thousands of liqueur
and whisky bottles and tins of shortbread. This book tells that
story and in so doing seeks to explain the legend and why it has
such a special place in our folklore. How did a half-Polish prince,
born in Rome, who spoke English with a foreign accent, and
whose great undertaking ended in utter failure, become the celebrated 'Bonnie Prince Charlie' of the poems and songs? Why does
the 1745 Jacobite Rebellion still rouse such passionate emotions,
particularly north of the border?

The answer lies partly in the story itself which has all the elements of high adventure. Even at the time people acknowledged that it was extraordinary. One of Charles's officers described the '45 as 'one of the most memorable events that has distinguished the times we live in. Everybody knows that this Prince, with a handful of undisciplined men, made himself master of Scotland; – penetrated into the heart of England; – vanquished armies of regular troops in pitched battles; – and for several months engaged the attention and kept in suspense the fate not of Great Britain only, but of Europe.'

The story has two phases, each important in the creation of the legend. The first saw a series of dazzling successes, as Charles carried all before him and got within striking distance of London, causing a run on the Bank of England and panic among the capital's citizens. Yet it culminated in the disaster of Culloden, the last battle on British soil. It was the Prince's only defeat and his cousin the Duke of Cumberland's only victory, but its impact was devastating, shattering the Jacobite dream and ending the Highland way of life. Culloden soon came to symbolize an heroic but doomed cause.

However, it is the second phase of the story which cemented Charles himself so firmly into our collective memory his escape after Culloden and flight through the Highlands and islands have a powerful romantic appeal. It was full of hairbreadth escapes, drama and self-sacrifice. The stories of the faithful Highlanders – including Flora Macdonald – saving him at great risk to themselves and their families have become part of the folklore.

So the story of the '45 is truly the stuff of theatre and legends. It comes complete with heroes and villains. Bonnie Prince Charlie converts into the perfect hero, brave, handsome and chivalrous. 'Butcher Cumberland' makes an appropriately villainous foil, corpulent as Charles is slender, harsh as Charles is merciful, a libertine in contrast with Charles's virginal aloofness. Both transcend the centuries, larger than in life and one-dimensional, like characters from a melodrama. Others share the stage like 'gentle Lochiel', the Cameron chieftain, and 'Hangman Hawley', the suitably hissable Hanoverian general with a predeliction for the gallows. There are spies and secret agents, heroes and heroines – particularly Flora Macdonald and the beautiful and martial Lady Mackintosh to add the necessary romantic dimension. There is buried treasure and brave deeds. The sheer magnetism of the story has been cele-brated over the years by a mass of songs and poems and novels. The works of Robert Burns, Sir Walter Scott and Robert Louis Stevenson all helped to nurture it.

What initially fed the legend was the use of what we might now recognise as public relations techniques. Both sides – Hanoverian and Jacobite – understood the value of influencing public opinion, and Charles was particularly adept at it. From an early age he showed an ability to create the right image and mould audiences, individuals and groups to his will. When Charles arrived in the Highlands in 1745 he consciously used his good looks and charm to appeal on an emotional level, presenting himself as the saviour who had come to throw off the Hanoverian yoke from the shoul-ders of his oppressed people. He dressed in Highland clothes to show that he identified with the clansmen. He marched at their head and shared their hardships to show he was as tough as them. His tactics were so successful that he became their 'Tearlach' or 'Charlie'. It was they who gave him the epithet 'Bonnie' and called the period of the '45 'Charlie's Year'.

Charles also knew that he had to appeal to more than just the Highlanders. By his actions he was careful to emphasize his independence from foreign puppet masters, reminding others that he had come to reclaim his kingdom almost alone, with no foreign army, simply relying on the love and loyalty of his people. He also appealed to their pecuniary interests. He offered officers in the service of the 'foreign usurper' an extra year's pay 'if they joined their natural sovereign' and encouraged his followers – many of whom were in severe financial straits – to declare for him by offering to indemnify the income from their lands.

Charles did not have to begin his appeal to hearts and minds from scratch. Ever since his grandfather, James II, had been forced from the British throne in 1688, a vigorous propaganda machine had been churning out poems, pamphlets, songs and ballads. The very term 'Jacobite' derived from that period, based on the Latin for James 'Jacobus'. Each successive rising gave a fillip to this literary creativity giving Charles a well-established role to step into as the Prince from over the water, he who had been 'lang o'coming'.

The increasingly influential press was used as a weapon by both sides. There were some twenty newspapers and magazines in London alone, like the *London Magazine*, the *London Evening Post* and Henry Fielding's *True Patriot*, as well as several in Edinburgh and the other cities. The Hanoverian reporting of events took full account of the 'what's in it for me' factor. They wanted the English, Welsh and Lowland Scots to question why they should risk their growing prosperity under the unglamorous but constitutionally fettered Protestant Hanoverians for the chimerical emotional pull of a handsome young Stuart who was a Catholic and who believed in the divine right of kings. They gave dire warnings about the Rebellion's effect on trade. They were not above personal abuse, casting aspersions on everything from Charles's appearance to his sexuality and his motives, and vilifying the Highlanders. They horrified their readers with lurid tales of the Inquisition and reminded them of the Protestants burned at Smithfield in Mary Tudor's reign.

The *True Patriot* made the good citizens of England quake with descriptions of the Highlanders as 'savage Inhabitants of Wilds and Mountains . . .', adding with relish that 'Some thousands of them are Outlaws, Robbers, and Cut-Throats, who live in a constant State of War, or rather Robbery, with the civilised Part of Scotland'. It waxed lyrical about the Duke of Cumberland, claiming he was 'an Englishman in his Nature, as well as his birth'. The Jacobites on the other hand were all that was foreign and frightening, a compound of 'Highland Rapine, Italian Bigotry, and French Tyranny'. The *London Magazine* invited its readers to contrast the attributes of the Duke of Cumberland and Charles. 'In Years, Strength and Activity they were nearly equal; both too possess'd the same Constancy of Spirit, and both courted Renown with the same Ardour, but in different Ways. William, in Acts of Beneficence, had no superior; Charles, in the Practice of Tyranny, had no Equal. . . . William was celebrated for his Bravery; Charles for his Chastity. . . . The ruling Passion of Charles was to gain a Crown, and avoid a Coffin; He vied not in Honour with the Worthy, nor in Courage with the Brave; but was not inferior in Pride to the most Rapacious or in Falsehood to the most Perfidious: He lov'd the Men better than the Women; and yet, which is wonderful, the less he courted the Ladies, the faster they followed him.'

The Hanoverians did not have it all their own way in the campaign to discredit the Jacobites. Charles did his best to refute the most damaging allegations against him and the Jacobite press reported this. The public could read how he demonstrated religious tolerance by attending Protestant services; how he showed his humanity by his treatment of prisoners of war and care for the wounded; how he promised a free Parliament and emphasized his concern for ordinary people by ensuring that everything his army used was paid for and only imposing the 'rightful King's' taxes. However, as he discovered, in the Lowlands of Scotland and in England such reassuring messages cut little ice in comparison with the fierce diatribes of the Hanoverian papers.

After Culloden the attacks on Charles became less vitriolic. Charles's adventures during his five months as a fugitive fascinated readers and there was intense speculation about his whereabouts. The reporting became more sympathetic and human, portraying Charles as 'the young Adventurer' rather than a sinister Popish agent. As those who had helped him, including Flora Macdonald, were arrested, the details of his adventures leaked out and found their way into the press. Readers were riveted by the accounts of Charles escaping to Skye disguised as a maid. Trailing its next edition, the *London Magazine* promised 'We shall give some Account of his Escape and Adventures after the Battle of Culloden, in our next'. It told its readers what happened when Charles sailed to Stornaway. 'The Night proving very tempestuous, they all begg'd of him to go back, which he would not do; but to keep up the Spirits of the People, he sang them a Highland Song . . .'. Here we see the legend already in the making, the demon transforming into the hero of popular imaginings.

It adds a certain poignancy that Charles was able to read the accounts of his own adventures while he was still on the run in the heather. In particular he was moved by the accounts of the executions of the rebels. The Hanoverian newspapers reported fully on these, painting vivid pictures of the hangings, drawings and quarterings as well as the less barbaric deaths on the gallows and the block. The public were also touched by the courage and devotion to the cause of many who died. Their noble behaviour in their final moments and the fine sentiments of their speeches from the scaffold helped to soften the public's mood. They created images of steadfastness in the face of death and of men who believed they had a cause worth dying for, contributing to the growing romantic aura of the rebellion.

Another factor in the story's enduring fascination is the numerous accounts and memoirs written by participants and observers on both sides. The Rebellion was hardly over before men were putting pen to paper writing in explanation, justification and vindication, and with varying degrees of accuracy and veracity. On the Jacobite side the memoirs were legion. The authors all had their particular motives for writing and left vivid insights into what happened and what ultimately went wrong, written, of course, with the advantage of twenty-twenty hindsight. Rousing speeches at critical moments and confidential exchanges were recalled with surprising accuracy. Lord George Murray, who was the leading Jacobite general and who wrote extensive memoirs, candidly admitted that 'it is not an easy task to describe a battle. Springs and motions escape the eye and most of the officers are necessarily taken up with what is immediately near to themselves; so that it is next to impossible for one to observe the whole – add to this the confusion, the noise, the concern that people are in whilst in the heat of action'. Others were not so honest and seem to have been in several places at once and not just during battles. On the Hanoverian side men like Henderson, despised by the Jacobites as an ignorant little schoolmaster, dashed off highly colourful and partisan accounts while promising their readers 'the utmost Candour, the Strictest Impartiality'. Yet whatever the accuracy of these outpourings, they were gobbled up by an avid public. No previous event can have produced such an emotional outpouring of print, either in the immediate aftermath or in later years, or made such an impact.

The fact that the '45 failed and brought such dire repercussions on the Highlands is another key to the legend's emotional appeal. The savage repression – the 'long series of massacres committed in cold blood' and the measures to destroy the clan system – has never been forgotten. It was meticulously recorded by the Jacobite

Bishop Forbes who devoted his life to collecting eye-witness accounts for his great work *The Lyon in Mourning*. He bound the volumes in black leather and gave each title page a deep black border. He also attached 'relics' such as remnants of the garters Charles wore in his disguise as the maid Betty Burke, giving the 'Lyon' a holy and mystical quality.

The failure of the '45 hastened the diaspora which took the legend overseas. The Jacobite clansmen transported in punishment for their part in the Rebellion took it with them as part of their folklore. So did the Highlanders who emigrated of their own accord to seek a new life in the American colonies. As the events receded in time, so they created for succeeding generations an image of a golden age. The Jacobite legend is as strong today in some parts of Canada and America as anywhere in Britain.

The suppression of the Highlanders and the rapid fading of the Jacobite threat also meant that, from the late eighteenth century onwards, it became safe for the British establishment to embellish and romanticise Jacobite history. This process showed itself in the absurd outfit worn by George IV, the Duke of Cumberland's great-nephew, on a visit to Edinburgh in 1822, of a kilt, feathered bonnet and pink woollen tights to keep out the cold. It found its way into the tasteless tartan décor of Balmoral and into Queen Victoria's assertion that she was a Jacobite. Jacobitism had come to symbolize patriotism, honour, chivalry, romance – not revolution. It no longer caused dynastic jitters. Young ladies could choose from a number of genteel versions of 'Charlie Is My Darling' to trill away at in the drawing room. The images that would find their way onto the tins of shortbread and whisky bottles were fast taking shape.

Of course, in the Highlands themselves the legend lived on in a different and deeper way. The Gaelic songs and poems which descended from the '45 captured the poignant sadness of a past age. Tearlach was gone and 'Charlie's Year' was over, but neither would be forgotten. The story would always be inextricably bound up with the Highlands.

This book tells the story of 'Charlie's Year'.

CHAPTER ONE

'A FAR MORE DANGEROUS ENEMY . . .'

CHARLES Edward Louis John Casimir Silvester Severino Maria was born on a cold December night in the Palazzo Muti in Rome. The year was 1720 and it was New Year's Eve, a fact of enormous significance to the Jacobites who had crammed into the chamber to witness Charles's birth. As the lusty little boy's first yells rang out storms raged over Hanover, boding ill for German George on the British throne, and a shining new star appeared in the skies heralding a new era – or so the stories went. Whatever the case this was no ordinary event and certainly no ordinary baby.

Bonnie Prince Charlie, as we know him, was born right into the middle of his own legend. The celebrations were immense among the Jacobites and their supporters across Catholic Europe. The cannon of the Castello St Angelo in Rome thundered in royal salute while fireworks lit up the Roman sky. The Pope sent the pick of his relics to the happy parents together with 10,000 *scudi* – a sizeable sum. Bonfires were lit at Saint-Germain, and Versailles surpassed itself in jollity. Jacobite poets reached for their quills to pour out their emotions in dreadful, but heartfelt, verses, welcoming he who had been 'lang o'coming'. A provocative thanksgiving medal was struck hailing this tiny dab of humanity as the '*spes Britanniae*' – Britannia's hope.

Enemies to the cause, however, were apprehensive. One of these was Baron Philip von Stosch, Compton MacKenzie's 'expatriated Prussian Sodomite'. His less exotic code name was 'John Walton' and he was the principal Hanoverian agent in Rome. He had been prying into the Stuart family and supplying his masters in England with exactly the kind of reports they wanted. Having predicted that Charles's mother Clementina would never be able to bear any children, he had bribed the maids to check her dirty laundry for signs of pregnancy. Charles's birth was extremely public precisely to avoid the likes of Walton fabricating the sort of stories about babies smuggled in warming-pans that had dogged his father James's birth. Walton had to content himself with claiming that Charles was so deformed that he would probably never be able to walk. He also predicted with confidence that Clementina would never be able to bear another child – Charles's brother Henry was to be born in the spring of 1725.

So Charles was the centre of gossip, intrigue and speculation from the moment of his birth. He was also heir to a difficult legacy. The Stuarts had a dubious track-record as monarchs. Leaving aside the travails of his father (the Old Pretender), his grandfather (James II of England and VII of Scotland), and the execution of his great grandfather Charles I, a catalogue of misfortune stretched back into the middle ages. Robert III died of grief. His elder son was murdered and his second son James I, the poet-king, died by an assasin's knife. James II was killed by a bursting canon. James IV on Flodden field in 1513. Mary, Queen of Scots, was beheaded. Looking back the Stuarts seem like the Kennedys of their day – glamorous but curiously unlucky.

Charles's parents had had their own share of drama. His father James had been bundled out of England as a baby when his Catholic parents, James II and Mary of Modena, were forced to flee from Protestant William of Orange, the husband of his half-sister Mary, at the end of 1688. He had since lived in exile seeing the throne pass from William and Mary to his other half-sister Anne, and on her death in 1714 to his distant cousin George I, the first of the Hanoverians. Charles's mother, 'fair Clementina', was a heroine in her own right. This beautiful and elfin seventeen-year-old daughter of Prince James Sobieski of Poland was arrested on her way to her wedding with James in 1719. The villain of the piece was her cousin Emperor Charles VI of Austria who succumbed to English bullying and locked her up in the Schloss Ambras in Innsbruck.

She was rescued by a hot-blooded and daring Irishman, Charles

Wogan, who had encouraged James to choose her on the grounds that she was 'sweet, amiable, of an even temper, and gay only in season'. He disguised himself as a travelling merchant and gathered a small team of helpers – his 'Three Musketeers' – Gaydon, Misset and O'Toole. Mrs Misset, though about to give birth, and her maid Jeanneton came too, the one to act as a chaperone, the other to be a substitute for Clementina. Together they crossed the Rhine 'and declared war on the Emperor'. The scheme was to smuggle Jeanneton into Clementina's quarters and to remove the Princess disguised as the maid.

It had all the elements of romantic farce. Clementina duly disguised herself and escaped but proceeded to fall into a gutter so that dry clothes had to be found. In the confusion her jewels were left behind – no ordinary gems but crown jewels of England sent to her by James. O'Toole had to ride back cursing under his breath to retrieve them. He also did sterling work, once the alarm was raised, by luring the courier carrying the news into a tavern and entertaining him so well that he collapsed drunk under the table, mission forgotten. After a memorable journey of snowbound roads, plunging precipices, near starvation and flea-ridden inns, Clementina's companions – her 'faithful marmosets' as she called them – brought the young princess safely over the snow-covered Brenner Pass and into the Papal States.

At first all went well. James and Clementina were very happy together and the birth of Charles set a seal on their relationship. However, they were basically incompatible as time began to show. James was a gentle rather lugubrious character – the 'old Mr Melancholy' of the cartoonists and 'not always inclined to savour jokes or give himself up to gaiety'. Considerably older than his young bride, his various disappointments had made him philosophical. Attempts to regain the English throne in 1708, 1715 and 1719 had all come to nothing. Clementina, on the other hand, was excitable and volatile. As a child she had played at being Queen of England. While she loved James she longed for the glamour of the real thing rather than a make-believe court of displaced exiles. Rome fostered the sense of unreality with its hundred and fifty feast days a year, its gaudy carnivals and masked balls, its elaborate Papal rituals, its squalor and its magnificence. Like the

Jacobites', Rome's past was worthier than its present. As Clementina grew older she became progressively more unstable and obsessively religious, her attendance at mass and her penances growing ever more frequent.

The atmosphere of the Jacobite court did not help. With its factions of Scots and Irish, Protestants and Catholics, it pulsed with jealousy, intrigue and rumour. One moment hopes ran high, the next they were dashed. The anxious Jacobites constantly watched the political barometer in Europe scheming to take advantage of events and wondering where help might come from – France or Spain or maybe even Russia ... in short from any country with an interest in destabilising or merely embarrassing the British Whig Government. The Whigs were the upholders of parliamentary supremacy and toleration for Nonconformists. As such they had initiated the Hanoverian succession and abhorred the Catholic Stuarts with their strong adherence to the divine right of kings. Their name, originally used as a term of abuse by their Tory opponents, derived from a Scottish word for a horse-thief.

Charles was groomed from birth to play his part in all of this. Like his mother he was highly suggestible and had difficulty in separating reality from what he wanted to believe. This was not surprising since he grew up surrounded by courtiers ready to fill his head with all sorts of romantic notions, tales of heroism and the divine right of the Stuarts. They told him that the Catholic Stuarts were the rightful kings of Britain and that the Hanoverians were cruel unprincipled usurpers. Every decision about Charles's upbringing was carefully weighed. It was important that nothing was done which would exacerbate the divisions within the little court. Any sign of weakness or discord in this volatile camp would immediately be reported by the spies who buzzed about Rome's dusty streets like the *paparazzi* of today. Anything would be quickly analysed for its political significance, like the reports of three-year-old Charles refusing to kneel before the Pope in the Vatican garden.

The lady chosen as Charles's governess was Mrs Sheldon, a Catholic lady from a family of unimpeachable loyalty. She took charge of the royal baby in March 1722 and was firm and sensible about his various infantile ailments, including the weak knee joints which meant he could barely walk until he was nearly three. Under her care he made good progress. By the age of two he was talking well and by three he was already showing a liking for music. There is a delightful description of him at three and a half: 'He eats, sleeps and drinks mightily well. One can't see a finer child every way, neither can one wish him better in every respect than he is.' However, Mrs Sheldon had to contend with James who had firm views about his son's upbringing, fussed dreadfully and grew to mistrust her.

1725 saw a major crisis in the little Prince's household. James announced the appointment of the Protestant James Murray as governor to Charles and the Catholic Thomas Sheridan as sub-governor and dismissed Mrs Sheldon. Clementina reacted angrily to the dismissal. She saw no reason to get rid of her friend. Neither did she want her son taught by a Protestant. She also suspected that her husband was having an affair with Marjorie Hay whose husband he had recently made Earl of Inverness and Secretary of State and whose brother was James Murray, the Prince's new governor.

The cumulative result was a fit of emotional fireworks. In 1725, just before Charles's fifth birthday and just after the birth of his brother Henry, Clementina sought refuge in one nunnery and Mrs Sheldon in another. This all too public marital rift caused a sensation and was 'the severest stroke' to the cause in years, according to James's agent in Scotland. Clementina wept constantly and declared that her husband wanted to bring their children up as heretics. Rather than allow such infamy she would stab them with her own hands. She said she was afraid to return to James in case she was poisoned.

Hitherto the Stuart family had been a model of domestic happiness, particularly in comparison with the vicious feuding and loose morals of their Hanoverian cousins – George I had locked up his wife until her death for adultery, he and George II lived openly with their mistresses, and Frederick Prince of Wales, George II's son, was cordially loathed by both his parents. His mother later called her firstborn 'the greatest ass, and the greatest liar, and the greatest *canaille* and the greatest beast in the whole world' and said she heartily wished him out of it. There could not have been a greater contrast betwen the two rival houses, but now there was scandal in the Palazzo Muti. James blamed it on the 'malice and the finesse' of his enemies.

For Charles this was the begining of a disjointed time. Even as a very young child he had experienced Clementina's brittle nerves and now he was deeply upset by her withdrawal. Later, at the age of seven, he was to write a sad and telling little letter to his father, promising to be very dutiful to Clementina and 'not jump too near her'. In many ways his relationship with his highly-strung mother was a disaster for him. In later life he was to display many of the traits of a child who had suffered rejection, especially his inability to form close relationships and his insistence on unquestioning loyalty. He was also to show increasing symptoms of insecurity, depression and paranoia.

However, these traumatic events provided Charles with an early opportunity to exercise that famous charm which was to be such a factor in his life both as a weapon and a defence against the world. James decamped with his sons to Bologna where Charles was 'admired by all the nobility for his gallantry and wit'. His sixth birthday was celebrated with a sumptuous ball. It proved to be excellent public relations. So did the ball held in James's honour where the ladies of the Jacobite court danced in the Spanish style to win favour with the Spanish court who would no doubt hear about it. Yet it must also have been a strange and disconcerting time for the young Charles. He was lionised and petted by foreign courtiers who talked to him of a destiny it was difficult for the little boy to grasp. This destiny achieved a sharper focus in 1727 with the sudden death of George I. Charles saw his father scurrying off on a round of diplomatic missions to see how the land lay. However, much more important to Charles was the fact that Clementina arrived at Bologna in his absence to be reunited with her sons. The following year the family were at last together again in the Palazzo Muti.

Charles was growing up a sophisticated child but also a woefully under-educated and wilful one. His tutors struggled to teach him the rudiments but he found it hard to concentrate. Murray complained that it was impossible to get him to apply to any study. The Earl Marischal observed in 1735 that the Prince 'had got out of the hands of governors' and, according to the malicious Walton, the young Prince had in the same year actually been locked in his room for kicking and threatening to kill Murray. Whatever the case his Latin was awful and his spelling worse – 'God knows' came out as 'God nose' to James's despair. In fact, spelling was never to be his strong point. As late as 1744, the year before he set off for Scotland, he was writing to his father as 'Geems' and signing himself 'Charls P.'

Yet in all other respects he was the outward model of a young prince designed to charm. Handsome, athletic and strong he became an avid sportsman, as at home on horseback as on the tennis-court. He also showed a fondness for 'a Scotch game called goff'. His natural talent for languages meant he could speak French and Italian fluently, as well as English, while the royal performances on the viola apparently had the power to move great nobles and dignitaries to tears. He danced gracefully to the admiration of all who beheld him.

The development of this young hero was watched with alarm by the Hanoverian camp. His attractiveness was undeniable even to that consummate liar John Walton. Furthermore he was groomed from his earliest moments to become a prince to appeal to the English. James had decided that his 'brave, lusty boy shall be dressed and looked after as much as the climate will allow in the English Way; for though I can't help his being born in Italy, yet as much as in me lyes he shall be English for the rest over'. English was accordingly the language of the Jacobite court and the habits of the family were as English as possible, even down to the food. A traveller to Rome was surprised to notice that James only ate 'of the English Dishes, and made his Dinner of Roast Beef and what we call Devonshire Pye: He also prefers our March Beer, which he has from Leghorn, to the best Wines'.

Charles quickly learned how important appearances were. He also revelled in the adulation and the sense of his own destiny. His tutor Murray – by then Earl of Dunbar – described how 'Since he was 10 years old, his Majesty had admitted him to full confidence and with orders not to reveal anything to anyone. Which orders the Prince minutely observed. . . .' A Whig account went further stating that Charles had 'formed a Resolution of attempting the Recovery of the British throne' since the age of seven. If the young Charles hadn't been so charming his self-importance could well have seemed insufferable.

It became clear as Charles grew into his teens that his exuberant energies needed harnessing. At the age of thirteen he was sent to join his cousin the Duke of Berwick commanding the Spanish forces at the siege of Gaeta midway between Rome and Naples. It was his first real adventure. Charles travelled incognito under his father's old alias of the Chevalier de Saint George accompanied by Sheridan and Dunbar. Charles made a great impression. One day at court the cockade fell from his hat and a courtier refixed it in the wrong position. Seeing this, Don Carlos, son of the King of Spain and soon to be King of Naples, put it in the correct position. Charles thanked him effusively, promising to keep the cockade for ever in memory of his courtesy. Don Carlos, was 'perfectly ravished' with the 'lively and charming' young man and the French ambassador dashed off eulogies to the French court.

It was inevitable that Charles would also seek the opportunity to display his courage. The Duke of Berwick reported how: 'The Prince was scarce arrived when he entered the trenches with me, where neither the noise of cannon nor the hiss of bullets could produce any sign of fear in him . . . In a word, this Prince shows that souls born for great and noble achievements always outwing the commonsense of years . . .' Charles was suitably cool in his own comments about the danger, telling enchanted bystanders that 'the noise of the cannon was more pleasant music to him than the opera at Rome'.

To the alarm of his tutors he was soon carousing with the soldiers and officers who 'adored' the romantic young prodigy. Basking in all this Charles neglected to write to his mother. Neither did he reply to the letters sent by his deeply envious young brother Henry whose tutors had already complained of Charles's unkindness towards their charge.

It was enough to ring alarm bells with James and was a fore-runner of what was to happen to his relationship with his 'dear Carlucchio'. He wrote to Charles telling him off for not writing to his family and warning that if he did not cultivate the talents Providence had given him he would 'lose that good character which your present behaviour is beginning to gain you'. However, that 'good character' was gaining popular credence all the time. As one observer wrote: 'The Prince exceeds anything I was capable of fancying about him, and meets here with as many admirers as he hath spectators. When talking to this and the other person about their respective employments, one would imagine that he had made the inclinations of those with whom he conversed his particular study.' And all this from a fourteen-year-old. Walton wrote gloomily that 'Everyone says that he will be in time a far more dangerous enemy to the present establishment of the Government of England than ever his father was'. Charles clearly thought so too and was beginning to relish the power he had over people. The problem was how to apply it. At about this time he was painted by the Swedish painter Hans Hysing. The portrait shows a graceful boy – shrewdly clad in tartan.

However, in January 1735, following Charles's return from Gaeta, domestic tragedy struck. Clementina died aged only thirty-three, weakened by her excessive fasting. The pretty lively young girl who had escaped the clutches of the Emperor had become a wasted religious recluse, obsessed with self-mortification and pursued by phantom pregnancies and a craving for canonisation. Her death devastated James and her sons wept uncontrollably. Her body lay in state, embalmed and in the habit of a Dominican nun. Afterwards her body – minus her heart which was sent to the church of Santi Apostoli – was laid to rest in the crypt of St Peter's until such time as James was restored to his throne and she could be buried in Westminster Abbey.

James became even more melancholy and worried about Charles who seemed 'wonderfully thoughtless for one of his age' as well as 'very innocent, and extreme backward in some respects for his age'. Perhaps this was a hint about a lack of sexual maturity. Charles's sexual aloofness was certainly to exercise a powerful fascination for the Jacobite ladies who thronged around him during his Scottish adventure. Walton, mistaken as usual, passed on a report from agents in Rome that Charles was strongly attracted to women. Dunbar does not seem to have taken the advice of the dissolute Duke of Wharton to 'not only train the Prince for glory, but likewise give him a polite taste for pleasurable vice'. But there

was no psychologist in those days to explain that Charles's reti-
cence with women may have had deeper origins in guilt about his
parents' failed marriage, his disrupted relationship with Clementina and perhaps in a suspicion that his parents loved Henry more
than him.

Like many fathers of the age James decided that Charles would
benefit from making the grand tour. It turned into another public
relations success, thrilling the Jacobites and annoying the Whig
camp in Britain. Charles set off with Dunbar, Sheridan and a small
entourage in 1737 to visit the cities of northern Italy, this time
under the alias of the Count of Albany. Although he was supposed
to be travelling incognito he was fêted everywhere. In Bologna he
attended a public ball given in his honour by the Marquis of
Tibbia. In Parma he was lionised by the elderly and toothless
Dowager Duchess Dorothea who gave him a diamond encrusted
snuff-box and entertained him royally.

Apart from anything else he was a good-looking young man –
'tall, above the common stature, his limbs are cast in the most
exact mould, his complexion has in it something of an uncommon
delicacy; all his features are perfectly regular and well turned, and
his eyes the finest I ever saw'. Even allowing for Jacobite hyperbole
he was clearly both handsome and charismatic. He was also vain,
amassing great wardrobes of clothes and delighting in such garments as tartan jackets trimmed with ermine tails and gold braid.
He was an avid user of curling papers but worried about being
spotted in them. Whatever his coiffeur, by the time he got to
Venice he was openly treated as royalty. The idea that he was
incognito was laughable and a number of events were stage-
managed to show him off and annoy the British. The Doge was
particularly gracious, bowing to him when they met during the
spectacular ceremony of the Doge's marriage with the sea. There
were supposedly accidental encounters with the Elector and
Electress of Bavaria on board a Venetian galley when all were
masked, followed by a longer encounter in the library of
St George's convent before an audience of about two hundred.
Venetian high society welcomed 'the Prince of Wales' with open
arms and he danced till dawn to the anguish of his tutors. The
Venice visit was such a diplomatic coup that a furious British

Government gave the Venetian Resident in London, Businello, three days to quit England.

Their rage was a measure of Charles's success and he was exhilarated by it. Walton moaned that it was not so much the attentions being shown to Charles that was displeasing to the Hanoverian court as 'the manner in which the Prince receives them'. Poor Dunbar wrote to James that: 'As H.R.H. cannot enjoy the diversion of dancing with moderation, but overheats himself monstrously, I have refused a ball the publick here intended to give him tomorrow night, and have writ ... that he would accept of a *Conversazione*. ... The later he comes home and the more [need] he has of sleep, he will sit the longer at supper, so that it is not possible to get him to bed of an opera night till near three in the morning tho' he be home soon after one.' He was already showing signs of the stamina that would amaze the Highlanders during the '45.

By 1739 the Jacobites' prospects were looking up – Britain's overseas possessions were growing apace, heightening her rivalry with France and Spain. She was already at war with Spain. The following year saw the outbreak of the War of the Austrian Succession, with France and England squaring up on opposing sides and soon effectively, if not technically, at war with each other. Spies travelled feverishly across Europe exchanging coded letters in dusty back streets. A well-known Jacobite agent, William Mac-Gregor of Balhaldy, came to Rome in 1739 to argue that the time was ripe for a rising. James had heard it all before but sent Balhaldy to Paris to lobby the French court, together with his representative there, Lord Sempill. Unlike most Highlanders, Balhaldy's father had made money in business which meant that some Jacobites despised him. A contemporary, described him as 'the descendant of a cobbler, himself a broken butter and cheese merchant, a stickt doctor, a Jack of all trades, a bankrupt indebted to all the world, the awkwardest Porter-like fellow alive, always in a passion, a mere bully, the most forbidding air imaginable, and master of as much bad French as to procure himself a whore and a dinner'. However, such was the kind of back-biting that went on all the time in Jacobite circles and it augured poorly for their future chances of acting in concert.

Charles was in a fever of anticipation whipped up by Jacobite courtiers. The halls of the Palazzo Muti echoed with rumour and counter-rumour and passionate talk about shaking off 'the yoke of Bondage and Slavery' of the Hanoverians. The two crucial questions were whether James could look for tangible foreign aid, preferably from France, and whether the cause's friends in England and Scotland would rise. It was a 'catch 22' situation – before acting France wanted to be assured that there would be support for James in Scotland and England. Conversely, the Scottish and English Jacobites wanted to be assured of substantial foreign help before committing themselves. However, the reports coming out of Scotland at least sounded positive and in 1741 an Association of Jacobite leaders – 'the Concert' – had been formed. In the same year Charles wrote enthusiastically to the clans: 'I have received yours with a great deal of pleasure and see by the Plan which came with it the zeal and affection of those who propose it . . . I cannot without rashness say more but you may easily believe I long very much for the execution.' There is a suspicion that he was ready to endorse anything.

In 1743 the political balance tipped further in Charles's favour. The ninety-year-old French First Minister Cardinal Fleury, a fierce anti-Jacobite, died. Although he was not replaced directly, the pro-Jacobite Cardinal Tencin was now able to gain greater influence with Louis XV. (He also seems to have had a great personal admiration for Charles – he shocked Dunbar by commenting that the young prince had '*la plus belle. . . du monde*'. Dunbar refused to specify which part of Charles the cardinal thought was so beautiful.) In June of the same year the British assisted Austrian and Hanoverian forces in defeating the French at Dettingen. The British forces were led by George II, the last occasion a reigning British monarch was to take to the battlefield. His portly young son, the Duke of Cumberland, was also actively engaged.

This débâcle fuelled a French desire for revenge and Louis XV was persuaded by Balhaldy to invite Charles to Paris. He might at least provide a useful diversion for the British. As a veteran of so many disappointments himself, the invitation posed a real dilemma for James. On the one hand he had promised to let Charles go if the French King made a firm offer of support. On the other his intuition warned him, quite rightly, that the chances of success were slim and that French motivation was dubious. He did not want to expose his beloved son to unnecessary danger. He had much less faith than Charles in the optimistic statements of Balhaldy and other agents such as Lord Sempill. He was also wary of the promises of John Murray of Broughton, his impoverished twenty-eight-year-old secretary in Scotland – 'all his life a violent Jacobite' – about the strength of feeling there.

However, according to one account Charles 'never left teazing his Father . . . till he obtain'd his consent'. Ever conscious of appearances, poor old Mr Melancholy issued an optimistic Declaration of Regency stating that as there was a 'near Prospect of being restored to the Throne of our Ancestors' he was appointing Charles sole regent of his kingdoms. Yet he still had grave misgivings. How would Charles evade the network of secret agents and reach France in safety? The situation was fraught with danger.

James tried to instil some commonsense into the proceedings. As Dunbar commented, he 'realised the difficulties much more fully than the Prince'. There were many hazards to be overcome: 'The various vicissitudes of the war; the restrictions imposed by the plague . . . the great number of all sorts of vessels which traverse the Mediterranean; Rome itself infinitely inquisitive and everlastingly talkative'. It was entirely in character that, if anything, these dangers made the expedition all the more attractive to Charles who 'alone refused to be daunted and was ready to undertake it at any risk'.

In fact Charles's departure from Italy was carefully planned. It was also full of melodrama that fed the image of the dashing young Prince setting off to reclaim his own. The message was not lost in England. When his flight became known there a detractor observed sourly that it was 'entirely in the Italian strain. . . .'

Father and son parted in the pre-dawn hours of a bitter January day. Charles's supposed words to his father are part of Jacobite folklore: 'I go, Sire, in search of three crowns, which I doubt not but to have the honour and happiness of laying at Your Majesty's feet. If I fail in the attempt, your next sight of me shall be the coffin.' James's response was 'Heaven forbid that all the crowns of the world should rob me of my son. Be careful of yourself, my dear Prince, for my sake, and I hope, for the sake of millions.' In fact, James was never to see his son again, dead or alive, although both were to survive for many more years. Charles rode out to seek his destiny with as little thought of failure as any young would-be hero.

CHAPTER TWO

'A MAD PROJECT...'

THIS was the beginning of the adventure for which Charles had yearned. His body was certainly 'formed for war' since he had spent his boyhood years 'hunting, shooting, walking stockingless, all to harden himself for the campaigns that lay before his imagination'. The plot was cunningly designed to throw the spies off the scent – as early as 1741 Walton had warned that plans were afoot for Charles to 'play an important role shortly upon the world's theatre' and his every move was anxiously watched. Charles was to pretend that he was setting out on a hunting expedition to the estate of the Duke of Gaetano at Cisterna.

Only a few key players were in on the secret. Not even his brother Henry knew that it was all a sham as their little group trotted out into the snow. Everything had been arranged as normal with the usual hunting gear sent on ahead as well as the 'musical instruments for diversion in the evenings', indispensable in polite society. The night before Charles played cards, concentrating with admirable coolness, curbing the 'extraordinary joy' he was feeling inside. If anything he played with too much attention since he 'generally played quite carelessly and with a noble disregard for his losses, suitable to his high rank'.

The scheme was that Sheridan should pretend to have a fall and that Charles should slip away in the commotion. Everything was planned to the last detail, including Charles's black horse to help him blend into the darkness. It went like clockwork and as the others crowded around Sheridan, in his seventies and surely a bit old for such heroics, Charles removed his wig, slipped on a mask covering everything but his eyes and swathed himself in a dark cloak. A message was sent to Cisterna that he had met with a riding accident and was recovering at Albano. It was some days before the truth was out.

Charles doubled back northwards and made for the port of Massa which he reached safely, though it was not an easy journey. The roads at that season were treacherous with snow and ice and the horses he rode fell several times. From Massa he went by barque to Genoa and from there to Savona. Here something went wrong and he was detained. He was either put into quarantine against the plague or the savage weather conditions delayed him. Whatever the case the delay of six or so days was pretty galling to Charles 'after such a hasty dash from Rome to Genoa'.

Eventually he managed to board a felucca which slipped through the British fleet lurking in wait for him between Monaco and Antibes. From Antibes he went at break-neck speed to Paris, taking only five days and neither sleeping nor changing his clothes. His companions were exhausted but Charles, convinced he was on the threshold of great things, was bursting with vitality. 'If I had had to go much further I should have been obliged to get them ty'd behind the chaise with my Portmanteau . . .' he wrote home in jubilation. The situation looked promising and it was not surprising that 'a young Prince, naturally brave, should readily lay hold of it' and expect others to stay the pace.

What mattered now, though, was the reception he got from that beribboned, bejewelled and powdered demi-god at Versailles on whom his hopes depended. Louis XV's welcome was cordial enough, but he could not formally receive Charles while he was incognito which probably suited Louis's ambiguous motives well enough. However, the young Prince was happy at first, reporting to James that: 'I have met with all that could be expected from the King of France, who expresses great tenderness, and will be careful of all my concerns.' Yet young Lord Elcho who sought Charles out in Paris described a different scene. He found him all alone drinking tea at Lord Sempill's where he 'seemed very uneasy. He told me that the King of France had made him come, and had promised to send into England an army of ten thousand men, commanded by Marshal Saxe, who was to assemble and embark them at Dunkirk.' James, watching anxiously from Rome, was afraid that the French were thinking of reneging. He complained to Sempill. 'The promises of France are not to be reconciled with her negligent and indifferent behaviour to the Prince.'

The political situation was still very sensitive. France and England were not yet formally at war, despite supporting opposing sides in the war over the Austrian Succession. Reports about Charles flew furiously across the Channel. In the midst of the diplomatic to-ing and fro-ing the Hanoverian spymaster, Horace Mann, sent a description of the young Stuart to the Secretary of State, the Duke of Newcastle, which pictures a young man 'above the middle height and very thin. He wears a light bagwig; his face is rather long, the compexion clear, but borders on paleness; the forehead very broad, the eyes fairly large, blue [in fact they were brown] but without sparkle; the mouth large, with the lips slightly curled; and the chin more sharp than rounded.' This inaccurate and unflattering portrait was a measure of the concern about the young adventurer. It was also a measure of their concern that the British prepared themselves to face an invasion, assembling a fleet in the Straits of Dover under Sir John Norris.

The French invasion force Charles had described to Elcho did indeed appear to be mustering at last. Charles hurried to Gravelines, a small port about twelve miles west of Dunkirk, in readiness. He travelled under the name of the Chevalier Douglas and his only companion was the graceless Balhaldy, speaker of that dubious French. However, that did not matter – it seemed that his moment had come. Some seven thousand troops marched onto the French transports and Charles embarked with them. They carried the usual sort of proclamation for such a foreign intervention, eloquent about their wish to come in peace, shake off the yoke of a cruel foreign tyrant and restore the rightful dynasty.

However, as Sir Charles Petrie put it, 'as usual when a Stuart was about to put to sea, the elements took a hand in the game'. A violent rainstorm and high winds – 'Protestant winds' as some called them – put paid to the invasion. Those ships still in Dunkirk harbour were either smashed to pieces or thrown up on the shore. Most of the vessels which had already sailed sank with all hands. It was only by a seeming miracle that Charles and Marshal Saxe made it safely back to dry land. Meanwhile the French and English fleets had clashed at sea and the French had come off the losers.

That, as far as the French were concerned, was that. However, Charles did not realise this at first. He was too full of the sense of his own destiny to allow a freak of the weather to dull his optimism. Just a few days later he was writing to James that 'The little difficulties and small dangirs I may have run, are nothing, when for the service and Glory of a Father who is so tender and kind for me, and for the service of a countrey who is so dire to him. Thank God I am in perfect good health, and every thing goes well. . . .' Fine positive sentiments if misspelt in places. He was genuinely still quite cheerful: 'How severely soever he might feel it, he did not seem dejected; on the contrary, he was in appearance cheerful and easy; encouraged such of his friends as seemed most deeply affected, telling them Providence would furnish him with other occasions of delivering his father's subjects and making them happy.' Such infectious optimism was to be one of the chief weapons in Charles's armoury.

The hopeful young Prince continued to haunt the narrow streets of Gravelines though Louis was urging him back to Paris. Charles was still convinced that the expedition would proceed but his hopes were dashed in March when France at last declared war on England. This meant that the focus of French attention was now on defeating the English in Flanders. Marshal Saxe was despatched to the Low Countries and Charles was left alone to brood. In his bitterness wild schemes began to take shape – of sailing to Scotland alone or of fighting the Hanoverians with the French. He was talked out of these but was still desperate for action. Ignoring James's suggestion that he return to Rome, he went back to Paris to work out his next move. He was to spend more than a year trying to read the political tea leaves.

In England measures were being taken to contain the Jacobite threat. The Opposition introduced a bill making it a treasonable offence to correspond with the 'young Pretender' as he was called. The Lords strengthened the measure by voting for the confiscation of the estates of anyone caught doing so. Sir Robert Walpole, by then Lord Orford, made an emotional address, saying that it was the 'winds alone' that had saved Britain from an invasion and that the rebellion he anticipated would be 'fought on British ground'. Charles certainly still hoped so and was scheming accordingly.

At the beginning of June he had moved into a pretty little house in Montmartre and was studiously ignoring advice from his father that there was 'no remedy but patience and courage'. Indeed, patience was never one of his strong points. He continued to assure James that 'The K. of France kindness for me is very remarcable, by his speking very often about me, and saying that he regretted mitely that sircumstances had not permitted him to see me hitherto.' However, it was very irksome to him not to be able to go about in public and court the acclamation that he knew he could rouse.

Charles's lifestyle was, as always, expensive. Stuart household accounts for 1743 showed that while Charles ran through 31,198 *livres*, Henry spent only a quarter of that, and James himself an eighth. So it was not surprising that by September Charles was running out of money. To his chagrin he was forced to move to a few rooms in town which were 'but a hole'. He also complained that 'The situation I am in is very particular, for nobody nose where I am or what has become of me, so that I am entirely burried as to the publick, and can't but say but that it is a very great constrent upon me, for I am obliged very often not to stur out of my room.' But he retained a sense of humour: 'I very often think that you would laugh very hartily if you saw me going about with a single servant bying fish and other things and squabling for a peney more or less.' This wry wit frequently undercut the pomposity of some of his youthful pronouncements and remained with him through these early years at least.

It was an increasingly lonely existence, though, and Charles did not altogether trust the bickering members of the little Jacobite coterie clinging to his coat tails. Their advice was confused and conflicting and it was difficult to know what to make of the situation. He was glad to be joined by his old tutor Sir Thomas Sheridan who had had the burden of accompanying him on all his exploits since the siege of Gaeta. James had previously written that 'Poor Sheridan is not fit to exert himself very greatly.' He was going to have to. He found Charles broader and taller – the latter due to Charles's taste for the French fashion for two-inch heels.

Meanwhile Murray of Broughton decided in August 1744 to come to Paris and see for himself how things stood. He strongly suspected the likes of Balhaldy and Sempill of misleading Charles about further French assistance. They met for the first time in the stables of the Tuilleries. The Prince 'informed him that the French had been serious in the Invasion' and that he 'had the strongest assurances from the French King and his Ministers that it would be put into execution that Harvest'. However, when Murray argued that this was now highly unlikely Charles expressed his determination to go to Scotland the following summer 'though with a single footman'. However romantic, this was just the kind of wild scheme that James had been worrying about and which Charles was beginning to see as a serious proposition. The sad truth was dawning that he was nothing but an embarrassment to the French court. In later years he was to write that a blind man could have seen that the French were only making sport of him. But he could not bear the thought of returning to Rome. Also, he 'had heard much of the loyalty and bravery of the Scotch Highlanders . . .'. So Murray was despatched back to Scotland to test out opinion while Charles had another go at Louis, arguing that the Scots were ready to rise and only needed arms and a little help from the French to begin the campaign. Louis did not reply.

James, on the other hand, was writing regularly with worthy, cautious and affectionate advice as well as news of Rome, of Henry and even of Charles's dog Stellina. Charles's replies were less frequent and couched in vague but usually optimistic language. 'Whatever I may suffer,' he wrote to his father, 'I shall not regret in the least as long as I think it of service for our great object. I would put myself in a tub like Diogenes if necessary.' He barely acknowledged his brother's letters.

For Charles Rome was a previous life. The all-consuming question was when and how to get to Scotland, not whether he should go. Murray of Broughton, despite his subsequent denials, has been blamed for urging him on, advising him that he should 'come as well provided and attended as possible, but rather come alone than delay coming; that those who had invited the Prince, and promised to join him, if he came at the head of four or five thousand regular troops, would do the same if he came without any troops at all; in fine, that he had a very strong party in Scotland, and would have a very good chance of succeeding. This was more than enough to determine the Prince.' Charles was confident that he would be irresistible to the Highlanders as their true Prince come to rid them of the Hanoverians.

This idea of selfless Highland chiefs eager to follow their Prince in his noble cause is integral to the legend. But of course it was not quite like that. The general reaction to the messages brought by Murray of Broughton was alarm, even panic. As one Jacobite reflected in later years: 'The Prince's friends in Scotland were extremely uneasy, when Murray upon his return, told them that the Prince was coming without troops. They looked upon the success as doubtful even with some thousands of regular troops, but impossible without that support.'

The situation in the Highlands, and in Scotland generally, was a complex one too subtle for a young man who had never been there and had to rely on others for his information. The Act of Settlement of 1701 had ensured the Protestant succession in England. When Hanoverian George I came to the throne, those Scots who proclaimed his Stuart rival James sang a derisive little song:

> Wha d'ye think we hae gotten for our king
> But a wee, wee, German lairdie,
> And when they went to bring him home
> He was delvin' in his kail-yairdie [cabbage patch]

The Act of Union of 1707 which joined Scotland with England under one Parliament was seen as an act of betrayal by the Scots. However, as the century drew on different interests emerged in a society driven increasingly by economics rather than religion. The Act of Union brought prosperity to the Lowland towns. Glasgow, for example, was growing fast and becoming rich from shipbuilding, linen manufacture, the import of tobacco and other trade with the Americas. It was pretty much a Whig stronghold. There was a widening gulf between the trade-loving Lowlanders and the other half of Scotland's 1.2 million population who lived in the Highlands and whom the Lowlanders regarded as Gaelic-speaking 'ruffiens' with 'uncowth weapons' who lived by cattle stealing.

The latter charge was not without foundation. Cattle raiding was integral to Highland life going back to the pre-Christian era. The Highlanders did not regard it as common theft but as a tribal challenge. The practice became so institutionalised it gave rise to the English expression 'blackmail'. 'Mail' meant rent, so 'blackmail' became the name given to the levy of black cattle imposed by Highlanders on other clansmen in return for free passage through their territories. It also came to mean the protection money extorted from Lowlanders who were the frequent victims of the raiding parties.

The Highlanders were divided in their loyalties. Some of the clans were traditionally loyal to the Stuarts. Others followed the Campbells under the Duke of Argyll who abhorred the Stuarts and was a firm supporter of the Government. Religious differences were another part of the picture. Many Highlanders were staunch Roman Catholics whose religion was flourishing in the glens at this time if picturesque tales of hidden seminaries, babies christened in natural fonts in the rocks and warrior priests are to be believed. A large number, though not all, had been devoted to the Jacobite cause for over fifty years. In theory, at least, they could be expected to help Charles, though many were to hold back. Other Highlanders were Episcopalians and non-jurants who had refused to take the oath of allegiance to the crown. The Lowlanders and their natural Highland allies the Campbells were largely Presbyterian.

On top of these complexities was the fact that the earlier failed rebellions had left their mark. Many of those to whom Charles now looked for help had been 'out' in the 1715 Rebellion and consequently lost their estates. Some of these had since been pardoned and their property restored to them. It was asking a great deal to expect them to risk their lives and lands again. One who eventually agreed to do so was the middle-aged Donald Cameron of Lochiel – the 'gentle Lochiel' of the stories who proved one of the most admirable characters of the '45. He now wrote to Charles: 'having maturely considered his Royal Highness's resolution, he was of opinion that to land in Scotland without assistance from abroad might prove an unsucessful attempt: but as he was entirely devoted to the interest of the Royal Family, if he should land, he would join him at the head of his Clan.' Others reacted similarly. Though it was a 'mad project' they 'believed they could not hinder themselves from joining in his fortune'.

However, this was a long way from the whole-hearted commitment Charles was seeking. The situation was threatening to become deadlocked when another more shadowy group of players entered the stage. Lord Clare, who commanded one of the Irish regiments in the service of the King of France, introduced the Prince to a circle of wealthy Jacobite Franco-Irish shipowners. Chief of this group was Antoine Walsh, a forty-two-year-old 'very rich merchant of Nantes' whose family had a tradition of loyalty to the Stuart cause. His father had commanded the ship which rescued James II after his defeat at the Battle of the Boyne and brought him to France. They had subsequently made a fortune building ships for the French navy and in those other lucrative eighteenth-century pursuits of slave-trading and privateering. Walsh declared that 'my zeal for your cause has no limits and I am prepared to undertake anything where the service of your Royal Highness is concerned.'

To Charles, kicking his heels in Paris, running up increasing debts and chafing under the restrictions of his daily life, this was a godsend. He met other members of this influential circle, such as the Hegartys, the Ruttledges and the Butlers, and saw that they combined shrewd judgement with a wide network of contacts. Charles was soon plotting deeply with this group and the substance of their discussions was revealed only to a few. Such secrecy caused dissension and jealousy in the sensitive Jacobite camp, with Sempill complaining about 'a spirit of giddiness' and James becoming increasingly worried in Rome about what his son was up to.

He was soon to find out. The defeat of the British by the French, and in particular by their Irish Jacobite brigade, at the battle of Fontenoy in May 1745 convinced Charles that it was time to make his move. While he knew it was not 'easy to forsee if it will prove good or bad for our affairs', the defeat did mean that the British were under pressure abroad and that the country would be emptied of troops. News of the battle also struck a more personal chord. His young cousin the Duke of Cumberland had distinguished himself there – a veritable 'Caesar or Hannibal' as his admirers put it – and Charles wanted to prove his own metal.

The situation looked auspicious if only the French would help. The Hanoverian royal family were not good at courting popularity with their British subjects – George II preferred to be in Hanover while, on the very night that news came of the seven thousand killed, wounded or missing at Fontenoy, the Prince of Wales continued enjoying himself at the theatre to the rage of the London populace. Surely they would welcome a deliverer with open arms, or so Charles reasoned. He stepped up his arrangements and his appeals to Louis.

However, the King would not commit himself to anything unless he was given clear guarantees about the levels of support for Charles in England and Scotland. His resources were strained and in many ways the political situation had moved on. But it suited him quite well to have Charles causing his own diversion and he did nothing to stop the schemes of which his army of spies and informants must have told him. His position was pretty cynical. There is probably some truth in the later accusation of one of Charles's enemies (who hated the French even more than the Jacobites) that: 'The French Ministers began now to be well pleased to see Things take this Turn, hoping he would make a desperate Attempt himself, at much less Expense than if abetted by them. . . . In Public therefore, and even under their Hands, they opposed and discountenanced his Scheme for an Invasion, but privately applauded it, and expressed a vast Confidence in the heroick Disposition of the young Pretender. . . .'

The heroic young Pretender was very short of money by now. To finance his plans he pawned some of the famous Sobieski jewels and borrowed 60,000 *livres* from the 'old Waters' and 120,000 from 'the young one' of the Paris bankers Waters and Son. Walsh, Ruttledge and their friends were busy with the practical arrangements. Walsh had promised to find 'a little frigate, a good sailor, which I will cause to be ready as soon as possible, but on condition your Royal Highness will allow me to accompany him and share all the perils to which he may wish to expose himself'.

In the event Ruttledge chartered the *Elizabeth*, a worthy old vessel of sixty-four guns captured from the British in the reign of Queen Anne some years earlier, while the ship which was to carry Charles was indeed a 'little frigate' – the sixteen-gun *Du Teillay*

which Walsh had diverted from her normal run to Sainte Dom-
ingue or Martinique. Both were loaded with the muskets, broadswords and field guns which Charles had bought.

All that remained was some judicious letter writing. Charles
wrote 'in most engaging terms' to the King and Queen of Spain
asking for help in his gallant enterprise. He also wrote to Louis
and to James but took care that the letters should not arrive until
after his departure. The letter to Louis was a firm reminder that
Charles had only come to France at his request and it ended with
an appeal to his self-interest: 'I beg your Majesty most urgently
to consider that in upholding the justice of my rights you will be
putting yourself in a postion to achieve a stable and enduring
Peace, the sole object of the War in which you are now engaged.'
Charles's letter to his father was different in tone. He complained
about the 'scandalous usage' he had received from the French
court before making a poignant plea that 'Your Majesty cannot
disapprove a son's following the example of his Father; you yourself did the like in the year 15, but the circumstances now are
indeed very different by being much more encouraging, there being
a certainty of succeeding with the least help. . . .' Of course the
letter also contained some suitably heroic sentiments and is famous
for the stirring comment: 'Let what will happen, the stroke is
struck and I have taken a firm resolution to conquer or to dye,
and stand my ground as long as I have a man remaining with me.'

However romantic and chivalrous, this do-or-die approach was
not universally welcomed by his supporters. In Scotland when
Charles's intentions became clear 'every body was vastly alarm'd
at this news, and were determinded when he came to prevail upon
him to go back. . . .' It was true that at least eight chieftains had
invited him over and promised to raise their clans but all but two
of these had required certain assurances. Not unreasonably, these
included that Charles should bring a large number of French
troops, adequate supplies of arms and plenty of money. There
were frantic attempts to stop Charles from setting out or, if already
landed, to advise him to return, but the various letters and anxious
messengers never reached him. Even if they had it might not have
changed anything. Charles was shrewd enough to know that by
throwing himself 'naked into their arms' and thereby showing his

entire confidence in them he was making it hard for them to refuse him.

The preparations for his departure were as clandestine as his flight from Rome. The assembly point for his small party was Nantes. At Walsh's suggestion Charles disguised himself as an *abbé* and once again he assumed the name of Douglas. He and his companions took their roles seriously, 'lodging in different parts of the town and if they accidentally met in the street or elsewhere they took not the least notice of each other, nor seemed to be in any way acquainted, if there was any person near enough to observe them'. It was a suitable prelude to a desperate business, but one wonders whether the young Stuart really went unobserved as he flitted theatrically about the backstreets of Nantes. It is much more likely that it was all reported straight back to Versailles. A fishing boat took Charles down the Loire and he boarded the *Du Teillay* at St Nazaire around seven in the evening on 22 June (old style). She slipped out of the harbour in darkness to rendezvous with the *Elizabeth* at Belle-Île and Charles was soon 'a little seasick'.

Charles's companions on his journey have become known to history as 'the Seven Men of Moidart'. They were an ill-assorted and somewhat elderly cocktail of four Irishmen, two Scotsmen and an Englishman. A more unlikely group of men would be hard to imagine. There was William, Duke of Atholl (or Marquis of Tullibardine as the Whigs called him), nearly sixty years old and crippled by gout – on the actual day of landing he was so laid up with it that he could not walk. However, he had impeccable credentials having been out in two previous rebellions and the mere sight of Charles apparently brought tears to his noble old eyes. There was Aeneas Macdonald, the banker, who had been intending to travel to Scotland on his own but was persuaded to join Charles's party because of his powerful influence among the Scots. The sole Englishman was Francis Strickland, Henry's ex-tutor, who was much disliked and distrusted and ultimately dismissed by James. He died 'of a dropsy' before the campaign was over.

Then there were the four Irishmen. Firstly there was poor asthmatic indulgent old Sheridan, devoted to Charles but increasingly frail. George Kelly was a parson but also a born intriguer and *bon viveur*. He had been out in the '15, was involved in subsequent plots and spent fourteen years in the Tower for his pains before he escaped. His experiences had given him an eye for the main chance. Sir John Macdonald (or Macdonnell) was another elderly man. Having served in the Spanish cavalry, he was appointed 'Instructor of Cavalry' but spent much of his time carousing on a truly eighteenth-century scale. The last of the seven was John William O'Sullivan. Born in County Kerry in 1700 and initially trained for the priesthood in Rome, he was the only one with any claim to active military experience. He also had a preoccupation with drink – and in particular 'mountain malaga' – at critical points in the campaign, but he was a brave and devoted if sometimes inept follower.

In addition to the 'Seven' of the folklore there were others including a clerk, Duncan Buchanan, the Abbé Butler, who acted as chaplain to the group, Antoine Walsh, Michele Vezzosi, an Italian follower who had helped the Jacobite Lord Nithsdale escape from the Tower after the '15, and a former servant of Lochiel's, Duncan Cameron, who was able to act as a pilot.

This then was the little group that left Belle-Île on 5 July 1745. There was nearly immediate disaster when, just four days later, the *Elizabeth* and the *Du Teillay* had a chance encounter off the Lizard with a British ship, the *Lion, en route* to join its squadron in the Bay of Biscay. Captain Durbé of the *Du Teillay* described in his log-book how the *Lion* and the *Elizabeth* engaged: '. . . the Englishman had time to pass forward, and contrived so well that he fired all his port volley, which raked the *Elizabeth* fore and aft, and must have killed many and done her great damage, so that the Englishman got between our two ships, and fired from his starboard guns three shots, which passed between my masts; my sails were riddled with his small shot, so much that we did not fire, being out of range to reach him with our small guns.'

According to legend, Charles, 'uneasy as to the result', wanted to go to the *Elizabeth*'s help but Walsh refused and even threatened to have him confined to his cabin. The ship's log tactfully makes no mention of this piece of *lèse-majesté*. 'After the battle which lasted for the space of six hours', the *Elizabeth* was forced to turn back to Brest with her killed and injured. She had been carrying '... 700 men aboard, and also a company of 60 volunteers, all good men' raised by Walsh. The *Lion*, similarly mauled and 'like a tub on the water', limped back to Plymouth with her captain wounded and her master missing an arm.

At Charles's insistence the *Du Teillay* sailed on with her cargo of ageing musketeers. A fortnight later, as the little frigate approached the shores of Scotland's Long Island, an eagle swooped overhead. The Duke of Atholl turned to Charles and said: 'The king of birds is come to welcome your royal highness upon your arrival in Scotland. I hope this is an excellent omen.'

As far as Charles was concerned he had come home. He had little more idea of what awaited him than Sir Galahad at the start of his quest for the Holy Grail but he saw himself in much the same light. He was setting out with zeal, endurance and chaste devotion to recover the Grail of the British throne.

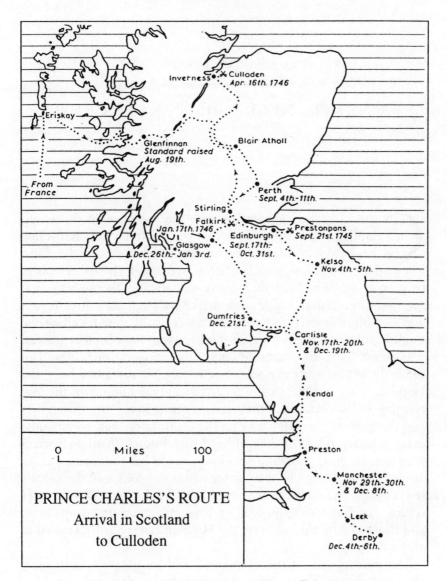

Inverness • ✕ Culloden
Apr. 16th. 1746

▲ Eriskay

• Glenfinnan
Standard raised
Aug. 19th.

Blair Atholl

From
France

• Perth
Sept. 4th.-11th.

Stirling •
Falkirk ✕
Jan. 17th. 1746
• Glasgow
▲ *Dec. 26th.- Jan 3rd.*
Edinburgh ✕ Prestonpans
Sept. 17th.- *Sept. 21st. 1745*
Oct. 31st.

• Kelso
Nov. 4th.-5th.

Dumfries •
Dec. 21st.

• Carlisle
Nov. 17th.- 20th.
& Dec. 19th.

• Kendal

0   Miles   100

• Preston

✕ Manchester
Nov 29th.-30th.
& Dec. 8th.

PRINCE CHARLES'S ROUTE
Arrival in Scotland
to Culloden

• Leek

Derby •
Dec. 4th.-6th.

CHAPTER THREE

'A NAKED, NEEDY, DESPERATE CREW'

CHARLES had grown up with the romance of the Highlands. The Scottish exiles of the Palazzo Muti had filled his head with tales of the loyalty and devotion of the clans. Yet as the *Du Teillay* threaded her way through the western isles there was no way he could really understand the society that awaited him. Tribal and feudal, driven by passionate loyalties, it was inexplicable even to the Lowlanders of the time let alone the English, to whom the Highlands might as well have been in Siberia.

Captain Burt, an officer of engineers travelling in Scotland in the early 1730s, left some revealing letters. He described how 'the Highlands are but little known even to the inhabitants of the low country of Scotland, for they have ever dreaded the difficulties and dangers of travelling among the mountains; and when some extraordinary occasion has obliged any one of them to such a progress, he has, generally speaking, made his testament before he set out, as though he were entering upon a long and dangerous sea voyage, wherein it was very doubtful if he should ever return. . . . But to the people of England, excepting some few, and those chiefly the soldiery, the Highlands are hardly known at all. . . .'

The perceptions of the Highlands and its people were nearly always negative. The scenery was described with words like 'dismal', 'horrid' and 'gloomy'. The people were a 'naked, needy, desperate crew, malnourished and suffering from the itch and savage in their behaviour'. '. . . . Ye clans live in a lawless manner' was the usual sort of sentiment. Henry Fielding went one further for propaganda purposes. In his magazine the *True Patriot*, launched to rouse his apathetic countrymen against the Jacobite threat, he called the Highlanders 'banditti . . . wildmen and savages', asserting that 'Some Thousands of them are Outlaws, Robbers, and Cut-Throats, who live in a constant State of War, or rather Robbery, with the civilised Part of Scotland'. As the rebels advanced he wrote increasingly lurid accounts of the Highlanders' savage and unsavoury habits.

But the society he afterwards admitted to maligning was a highly complex one with profound ideas about loyalty and chivalry, and the vanishing of its culture has become inextricably bound up with the romance of the '45.

So who were the Highlanders and where did they live? The true Highlanders inhabited the mountainous region north-west of the Tay. It was a wild remote world where wolves were hunted as late as the 1730s and a belief in magic still held sway. They spoke the Irish language – the tongue of the 'Gaels' or 'Gaelic' – and their way of life was rooted in the clan system by which they believed that they were descended from a common ancestor. 'Clann' in Gaelic means 'children', and they regarded the chief as their father.

An insult to one was an insult to all, and there were deep bonds. The chiefs protected their people, arbitrated in disputes and helped them in times of hardship. In return the clansmen had a duty to turn out and fight for him. The chief had powers of 'pit and gallows' over his people and if he was 'their idol' he could be a capricious one. An Englishman complained half in jest to his chieftain host that some of his clansmen had been rude to him. To his horror the chief immediately drew his broadsword and offered to cut off their heads. This was not the behaviour of the drawing rooms of Georgian England. Neither was the instant justice dispensed by a Clanranald chieftain to a woman accused of theft. He had her tied to the rocks by seaweed and left to drown.

To the eyes of outsiders the chiefs seemed an anachronism, brutish hangovers from the feudal middle-ages. This image was encouraged by the occasional scandal. For example, two powerful chieftains, Sir Alexander Macdonald of Sleat, the Lord of the Isles, and his brother-in-law Macleod of Dunvegan, tried to deport one hundred of their people to the American plantations for profit.

The ship was discovered and it was the subject of much shocked talk in the Lowlands. The two lairds had a difficult time weasling out of it but in the event escaped prosecution, which may have been a factor in their refusal to rise for Charles in the '45.

As Burt noted, people would not believe that Highlanders who lived by a different code, spoke a different language and wore different clothes could have any redeeming features. Yet he himself discovered '. . . a very high degree of intellectual refinement, entirely independent of the fashion of their lower garments, from the sight of which, and the sound of a language which they did not understand, their neighbours were fully satisfied of their barbarity, and inquired no further'. In 1746 some of the foreign officers who found themselves in Scotland were able to converse with the Highland gentlemen in Latin. They found that those gentlemen were at least as well if not better educated than themselves. They might have studied at the best universities in Europe – Paris or Rome perhaps – and have made the grand tour if they could afford it. They were well-read, good conversationalists, elegant dancers and drank the best, albeit smuggled, claret. Some admittedly, were a curious blend of the civilised and the savage like Coll MacDonell of Barisdale who had lines from Virgil engraved on his broadsword but was also the inventor of a fiendish torture device. It held its victim in a vice and propelled them towards a sharp spike aimed at the throat. Its capture by Government troops was quite a propaganda coup.

But what of these curious 'lower garments' that are referred to in such disapproving tones? The English accounts of the time are full of references to the near-naked state of the Highlanders and the immodest sight that could greet the eye on a windy day. The ordinary clansman wore a long plaid either pleated into a kilt or draped around his shoulders over a shirt. In battle the plaid might be cast off completely and they tied their shirt tails between their legs. The plaid was an all-purpose garment serving 'the ordinary people for a cloak by day and the bedding at night: by the latter it imbibes so much perspiration, that no one day can free it from the filthy smell'. However, the gentry of the clans were better attired. The chief, who was more likely to ride than march, wore tight-fitting tartan trews, a tartan jacket and waistcoat and a tartan plaid held on his left shoulder by a brooch. Like the tribal chiefs of many countries, the sign of his office was the eagle's feathers in his bonnet.

Travellers were struck by the hardiness of the Highlanders, living in such harsh conditions and apparently so ill-equipped by their clothing. However, it was a matter of honour among the clansmen to show contempt for hardship. A story was told that the laird of Keppoch, chieftain of a branch of the Macdonalds, was in a winter campaign against a neighbouring laird. He gave orders for a snowball to be laid under his head to help him sleep at night 'whereupon his followers murmured, saying, "Now we despair of victory, since our leader is become so effeminate he can't sleep without a pillow"!' There are many versions of this in the folklore but all making the same point – the Highlander was tough and bred to endurance.

This superhuman reputation certainly helped to terrify the English. They listened with alarm to tales of almost supernatural powers, of how the Highlanders coped with sleeping out in the hills in cold, dry, windy weather – 'they sometimes soak the plaid in some river or bourn; and then holding up a corner of it a little above their heads, they turn themselves round and round, till they are enveloped by the whole mantle. Then they lay themselves down on the heath, upon the leeward side of some hill, where the wet and the warmth of their bodies make a steam like that of a boiling kettle. The wet, they say, keeps them warm by thickening the stuff, and keeping the wind from penetrating.' When it rained they took to the water 'like spaniels', ringing out their bonnet 'like a dish-clout'.

Housing was primitive. Some of the chiefs might have very grand houses indeed, but the dwellings of other 'gentry' were often no more than simple cottages with earthen floors. Much later in the century Dr Johnson was to describe what it was like getting out of a comfortable and elegant bed in such a house and going straight up to his ankles in the mud of the floor. The ordinary clansmen's bothies were window-less hovels with a hearth in the centre of the room and the walls blackened by peat smoke. They were thatched, but not very efficiently, with turf, rushes, heather or straw. Sometimes a wattle and daub partition provided a second room which could be used to shelter livestock in bad weather.

Burt described the clansmen's life graphically: 'They have no diversions to amuse them, but sit brooding in the smoke over the fire till their legs and thighs are scorched to an extraordinary degree, and many have sore eyes, and some are quite blind. This long continuance in the smoke makes them almost as black as chimneysweepers. . . . the rain that comes through the roof and mixes with the sootiness of the inside, where all the sticks look like charcoal, falls in drops like ink.'

It was a precarious as well as a harsh existence and many existed on the brink of starvation. The availability of land was the problem. The chiefs had their own land but what mattered was the land they granted their tenants under leases or 'tacks'. The tacksmen, like Flora Macdonald's stepfather, were the gentleman farmers of the clans, next in the hierarchy to the chief. They were also the officers of the clan regiments and it was their job to bring out the clansmen in times of war. They farmed some of their lands themselves and sublet the rest to tenants. But they were essentially soldiers rather than farmers. Their agricultural methods were primitive and the land was hard to cultivate. Furthermore, there was not enough land to go round so that a number of families would try to support themselves on a piece of land sufficient only for one.

As in many other tribal societies, the women did the hard manual work – and there was much of it. In the islands there are even reports of them wading out with their husbands on their backs to the fishing boats to avoid their husbands getting their feet wet. Certainly, the clansmen could seldom be persuaded by Charles to carry equipment or dig trenches. To the English and the Lowlanders the Highlanders had the reputation of being an 'indolent, lazy people' when they were not out raiding cattle. But if they did seem to lack energy, 'lying about upon the heath, in the day-time, instead of following some lawful employment' it may have been the result of their diet. Burt described it with massive understatement as 'neither delicate nor opulent'. In the summer many survived on a diet of just milk and whey without bread, hoarding any butter and cheese they made until the winter. They even ate the 'braxy' mutton of sheep found dead on the hillside.

Coastal dwellers hunted whales for 'sea-pork' when they could get it. Come the winter food improved. Many beasts were slaughtered to provide barrels of salt meat which supplemented the butter and cheese, but bread was still scarce.

The Highland fairs provided a chance to barter but they were poor affairs with 'two or three hundred half-naked, half-starved creatures of both sexes, without so much as a smile or any cheerfulness among them, stalking about with goods . . . up to their ankles in dirt'. The goods were not appetising even by the standards of the day: 'the merchandise . . . is of a most contemptible value, such as these, viz – two or three cheeses, of about three or four pounds weight a-piece; a kid sold for sixpence or eight-pence at the most; a small quantity of butter in something that looks like a bladder, and is sometimes set down upon the dirt in the street; three or four goat-skins; a piece of wood for an axletree to one of the little carts, etc. With the produce of what each of them sells, they generally buy something, viz – a horn, or wooden spoon or two, a knife, a wooden platter . . . and carry home with them little or no money.'

Again, as common in tribal societies, a man's wealth was measured by the number of his cattle. These were the famous black cattle, small but sprightly and 'very good meat'. They were literally the life's blood of the poor clansmen. At the beginning of the winter some of the animals would be slaughtered and the meat salted away in barrels. The cattle that were spared for breeding purposes were bled alive. The fresh blood was mixed with oatmeal to make slabs of sustaining black pudding. This meant that by the time the spring came the cattle were so weak they had to be half carried back to the pasture.

However, it was not all miserable drudgery. The clansman had the security of belonging to a highly structured society. This was exemplified by the fact that the chief had his special retinue or 'tail' consisting of his 'henchman', his bard, his piper, his 'bladier' and his gillies. The henchman was the son of the wet-nurse chosen to foster the young chief as a baby. Nurtured with the same milk, he grew up side by side with his chief as his bodyguard, utterly loyal to him, sacrificing himself in battle if necessary. The bard was the chief's praise singer and genealogist. It was an hereditary post and on it depended a chief's hopes of immortality. However, the standard seems to have been variable. Burt described one who sang 'his own lyrics as an opiate to the chief when indisposed for sleep'.

The post of piper was also hereditary. He marched behind his chief into battle playing the wailing notes of the clan rant. He was one of the most important figures in the clan and jealous of his position. Burt describes an argument between a piper and a drummer over precedence, with the piper declaring 'and shall a little rascal that beats upon a sheep-skin, tak the right haund of me, that am a musician?' The bladier has been likened to the Mafia's *consigliere*, a lawyer chosen for his silver tongue in debating, capable of settling disputes because of his encyclopaedic knowledge of precedents and able to relieve his chief of a thousand onerous tasks. Lastly there were the gillies who carried the chief's weapons and baggage and sometimes the chief himself in wet or difficult terrain.

So these were the people in whom Charles was placing his trust. Fierce, proud, superstitious, loyal, a society of tribal warriors with long memories. The question was which clans would support him. He was coming with only a tiny retinue – there was none of the hoped-for foreign aid, no soldiers, no money, no weapons, just his emotional appeal as their lawful prince come to claim his own. However, at a conservative estimate there were over thirty thousand potential fighters in the Highlands. Quite enough to topple George from his throne if they were prepared to rise for him. Charles believed that he and his cause would be irresistible to all but the most hardened of his enemies and that those who would not join him would at least not fight against him.

Charles's first sight of Scotland came on 23 July as the *Du Teillay* threaded her way through the Outer Hebrides to anchor in the shelter of the island of Barra. Aeneas Macdonald was sent ashore to seek out his brother-in-law Roderick Macneil. He was rowed across to the castle of Kisimul but returned with grim tidings. The Macneil was away from home but worse than that was the news that the Government had arrested the chief of the Macleans of Mull, a leading Jacobite. It looked as if their scheme had been discovered before it had even begun. Sheridan and the

Duke of Atholl earnestly advised Charles to return at once to France, but he refused, backed up by Walsh. While the debate was still going on an immediate danger threatened. Captain Durbé recorded in his journal that 'as soon as our sails were set, we saw a ship tacking, her topsail close-reefed. The said ship is a big one. We take her to be a man of war.'

This required immediate action, and Captain Durbé made for a safer anchorage among the islands between Barra and South Uist. According to tradition the exact spot was An-t-Acarsaid Mhor, between Gighay and Fuday. However, on the afternoon of the 24th, it looked as if the larger vessel were making for the same anchorage, perhaps with sinister intent. Charles and his little party were hastily put ashore on the west side of Eriskay, a rocky islet racked by storms and owned by Alexander Macdonald of Boisdale.

And so the great adventure began – a hurried landing on a white wind-swept strand. The landing place is still known as 'Cladach a' Phrionnsa', gaelic for 'the Prince's shore'. It is said that a rose-pink convolvulus blooms there and only there because of seeds planted by Charles to mark his coming. O'Sullivan described Charles's first moments on Scottish soil less romantically: 'The Prince and his Suite set foot to ground ... fearing least that man of war, which we saw plainly was one, shou'd come into the harbor. His design was to go to Boisdale's ... house that was just on the borders of the bay, but it blew so hard, that it was not possible, and made the first land he cou'd. There was such a cruel rain, that he was obliged to stay in the first cabin he met with ...'

This 'cabin' was a small noisome hut belonging to one Angus Macdonald – typical of the smoky little hovels described by Captain Burt. Their first priority was to find some food, and the story goes that 'they catched some flounders, which they roasted upon the bare coals'. Duncan Cameron acted as the cook and Charles was mightily amused at his efforts: 'The Prince sat at the cheek of the little ingle, upon a fail sunk [heap of peats], and laughed heartily at Duncan's cookery, for he himself owned he played his part awkwardly enough.' When the time came for sleep Charles examined Sheridan's bed to ensure that the sheets were well aired out of affection for his indulgent old tutor. This annoyed

Angus who 'observing him to search the bed so narrowly, and at the same time hearing him declare he would sit up all night, called out to him, and said it was so good a bed, and the sheets were so good, that a prince need not be ashamed to lie in them.' It never crossed his mind that he was, indeed, entertaining a prince.

Charles certainly did not look like one. His beard had grown and he was still dressed in his abbé's outfit of 'a plain shirt, not very clean, a cambric stock fixed with a plain silver buckle, a fair round wig out of the buckle, a plain hat with a canvas string, having one end fixed to one of his coat buttons; he had black stockings and brass buckles in his shoes.'

There were other elements of farce that night. 'The Prince, not being accustomed to such fires in the middle of the room, and there being no other chimney than a hole in the roof, was almost choked, and was obliged to go often to the door for fresh air. This at last made the landlord, Angus Macdonald, call out, "What a plague is the matter with that fellow, that he can neither sit nor stand still, and neither keep within nor without doors?"' All his physical training could not have prepared Charles for the realities of Highland life but he was to adapt quickly and win a surprising reputation for hardiness.

The morning brought harsh reminders of how precarious it all was, with the realisation that some of the chiefs were thinking of reneging on their pledges to him. Alexander Macdonald of Boisdale came hurrying across the two mile stretch of water that separated Eriskay from South Uist with the sole purpose of telling Charles to go away. According to the stories the conversation was along the lines of 'You must go home, Your Highness' to which Charles replied 'Home? I am come home.' There was no doubting Boisdale's loyalty, but he was old and frightened and he was not going to risk everything for a cause which appeared to have no chance of succeeding. Furthermore, he brought categoric messages from Sir Alexander Macdonald of Sleat and Norman Macleod of Macleod that 'if he came without troops, that there was nothing to be expected from the country, that not a soul wou'd join with him, & that their advice was that he shou'd go back & wait for a more favourable occasion'. It was a bitter blow. 'Every body was struck as with a thunder bolt, as you may believe, to hear that sentence . . . especially from Macleod, who was one of those that said, he'd be one of the first that wou'd join the Prince, in case even he came alone. . . .'

Charles could not believe his ears and sent urgent messages to Sir Alexander. However, the reality of the situation was soon to be confirmed. Sir Alexander would not even agree to see Charles. Worse than that he and Macleod lost no time in writing virtuously to Duncan Forbes, the Lord President of the Council and the most important government official in Scotland, that Charles had arrived and that they had done their duty 'for the best'. They confidently asserted that not a single man of any consequence north of the Grampians would assist this 'mad rebellious attempt'.

However, Charles did not know this yet and assumed that these two great lairds could be brought to honour their obligations. He and his bedraggled little party went back on board the *Du Teillay* where 'it was strongly debated again, for his going back to France, but the Prince would not hear to it upon any account'. He had a passionate conviction that his faithful Highlanders would stand by him. Backed by Walsh and O'Sullivan he decided to sail to the mainland and try his chances there. On 25 July, St James's day, the *Du Teillay* arrived at Loch nan Uamh – the Bay of Whales – a sea loch running into the Sound of Arisaig between Arisaig and Moidart. Charles now prepared to launch his most powerful weapon – a charm offensive.

Aeneas Macdonald had been despatched the previous day in a small boat to fetch his brother, the laird of Kinlochmoidart. He now returned with him and also brought back Boisdale's elder brother Macdonald of Clanranald and a clutch of other Macdonalds. Next day Clanranald's son – referred to everywhere as young Clanranald – arrived and some emotional meetings took place.

One of the Macdonalds described their first encounter with their 'long wished for' prince. A large tent had been erected on the ship's deck 'well-furnished with variety of wines and spirits'. After a while a tall youth of 'a most agreable aspect' entered. He was plainly dressed, probably still in his clerical garb, but it was too much for the emotional Macdonald whose heart swelled 'to my very throat. . . . He asked me if I was not cold in that habite (viz.

the highland garb). I answered I was so habituated to it that I should rather be so if I was to change my dress for any other. At this he laugh'd heartily and next enquired how I lay with it at night, which I explained to him; he said that by wrapping myself so close in my plaid I would be unprepared for any sudden defence in the case of a surprise. I answered, that in such times of danger, or during a war, we had a different method of using the plaid, that with one spring I could start to my feet with drawn sword and cock'd pistol in my hand without being in the least incumber'd with my bedclothes. Severall such questions he put to me; then rising quickly from his seat he calls for a dram, when the same person whisper'd me a second time, to pledge the stranger but not to drink to him, by which seasonable hint I was confirm'd in my suspicion who he was. Having taken a glass of wine in his hand, he drank to us all round, and soon after left us.'

News of Charles's arrival rippled out through the western Highlands. Young Clanranald was sent to Skye with messages for Macdonald of Sleat and Macleod of Macleod. Kinlochmoidart was despatched to the Duke of Perth, Murray of Broughton, Donald Cameron of Lochiel and other Jacobite clans. As he was sailing over Loch Lochy full of his momentous news he met another boat carrying Bishop Hugh Macdonald, Roman Catholic Vicar Apostolic of the Highlands, who was returning from Edinburgh. He asked Bishop Hugh, 'What news?' When the Bishop replied that he had none to give, Kinlochmoidart shouted across the water, 'I'll give you news. You'll see the Prince this night at my house.' The Bishop asked what prince and when Kinlochmoidart told him is said to have replied, 'You are certainly joking . . . I cannot believe you.'

The next part of their exchange was a telling one. '"Then," said Mr Hugh, "what number of men has he brought along with him?" "Only seven," said Kinlochmoidart. "What stock of money and arms has he brought with him then?" said Mr Hugh. "A very small stock of either," said Kinlochmoidart. "What generals or officers fit for commanding are with him?" said Mr Hugh. "None at all," replied Kinlochmoidart. Mr Hugh said he did not like the expedition at all, and was afraid of the consequences.' To which Kinlochmoidart gave the famous reply, 'I cannot help it. . . . If the matter go wrong, then I'll certainly be hanged, for I am engaged already.' He was right – he was to be hanged, drawn and quartered for his pains at Carlisle in October 1746.

Bishop Hugh hurried to Arisaig to urge Charles to return until he could muster some foreign help. However, Charles was well prepared for that line of argument and knew how to turn it around to his advantage saying, 'he did not chuse to owe the restoration of his father to foreigners, but to his own friends to whom he was now come to put it in their power to have the glory of that event. . . . As to returning to France, foreigners should never have it to say that he had thrown himself upon his friends, that they turned their backs on him and that he had been forced to return from them to foreign parts. In a word if he could get but six trusty fellows to join him, he would chose far rather to skulk with them in the mountains of Scotland than to return to France.' He knew instinctively how to appeal to the Highlander's sense of honour and the Highlander's conceit.

But brave words were one thing. Firm promises of support were another. Young Clanranald's errand to Skye had been in vain. The news came back that Sir Alexander of Sleat and Macleod of Macleod were sticking to their guns that 'the P. coming without some regular troops, more arms and money, they were under no engagement to concur in the enterprise.' However, Charles continued to work on his emotional appeal. On hearing the news from Skye he turned dramatically to Kinlochmoidart's brother Ranald with a plea for help and won a famous declaration along the lines 'I will! I will! though not another man in the Highlands should draw his sword; my Prince, I am ready to die for you!' This emotional outburst 'which appealed so strongly to the feelings and prepossessions of a Highland bosom' as an early nineteenth-century writer put it, so overpowered some of the other Macdonalds, including young Clanranald, that they also swore allegiance.

Yet a far more spectacular and significant coup was to come. Cameron of Lochiel had pledged his support to Charles whether he came with foreign help or alone. His powerful clan – which could raise eight hundred fighting men – was famed for its loyalty to the Stuarts. Furthermore Lochiel's twelve sisters had married into a number of great houses so the Cameron influence was a powerful one. Charles was accordingly anxious to summon this blond warrior to Arisaig to ask him to honour his word. He came but with the greatest reluctance, convinced it was hopeless.

On the way he consulted his brother Fassefern who urged him not to see Charles, correctly anticipating the outcome: 'Brother, I know you better than you know yourself. If this Prince once sets his eyes upon you, he will make you do whatever he wishes.' He was proved right but Lochiel felt in duty bound to see his Prince. The story of their meeting is woven deep into the Jacobite fable and again, if it is to be believed, Charles knew exactly how to play his hand: 'In a few days with the few friends that I have, I will erect the Royal Standard and proclaim to the people of Britain that Charles Stuart is come over to claim the crown of his ancestors, to win it, or perish in the attempt; Lochiel, who, my father has often told me, was our firmest friend, may stay at home, and learn from the newspapers the fate of his prince.'

Lochiel's reply was just what Fassefern had been dreading. 'No,' he cried, 'I'll share the fate of my Prince; and so shall every man over whom nature or fortune hath given me any power.' Whether he really said anything so high-flown or not he was as good as his word. Despite his reputation as the 'gentle Lochiel' he did not scruple to burn reluctant clansmen out of their homes to force them out for Charles, nor to secure from Charles a guarantee of income equivalent to the revenue from his estates in the event of failure. His support was a turning point as the Jacobites all agreed – if Lochiel had persisted in his refusal to take arms the other chiefs would not have joined the standard without him and that would probably have been that. A Whig critic was complimentary about Lochiel as 'a very humane Gentleman' but was less so about the Camerons who he described as a 'lazy Clan, averse to Improvements . . . always ready to embrace every Occasion of Spoil'.

As it was, Lochiel returned to his lovely house of Achnagarry where he had been planting trees when the summons came. His friends noticed a 'deep sadness' and how he set about arranging his papers and affairs 'as a man does before setting out on a journey from which he was not to return'. Like others he seems to have sensed the inevitability of the events about to be played out. Alexander Macdonald of Keppoch also now pledged his support, afflicted by the same sense that there was no other option. Murray of Broughton observed shrewdly that 'nothing has so great an effect upon brave and generous minds as when a person appears to despise their own private safety when in competition with the good of their country.'

Convinced that the die was cast Charles sent away the *Du Teillay*. As Lord Lovat – a wily old fence-sitter who was willing to support whichever side would grant him the dukedom he craved, – observed, 'If he succeeds the whole merit will be his own; and if his mad Enterprise bring misfortunes upon him, he has only himself to blame.'

CHAPTER FOUR

'TEARLACH'

T HE *Du Teillay* had been hovering offshore in case of emergencies but it was necessary to cut this umbilical cord. Charles ordered her back to France and Antoine Walsh sailed away the richer for a knighthood and a gold-handled sword. He also carried a letter from Charles to his father exulting in the heroism of the Highlanders and affirming his passionate resolve to lead them to victory or to 'die at the head of such brave people'.

The ship's log shows the disquiet of Walsh and Captain Durbé about leaving Charles with just the gentlemen who had come over with him, 'two chiefs of the district, and with no more than a dozen men – these being all his companions'. It must have looked like suicide. However, Charles was cheerful about his prospects and set about his campaign for winning hearts and minds. He made Borrodale House his headquarters and became the centre of attraction for the neighbourhood with everyone 'without distinction of age or sex' crowding in to watch him. Overhearing a gentleman toasting the King's health in Gaelic, Charles immediately appointed him as his language master. Here was a willingness to learn that Charles had seldom displayed as a boy, but he knew the value of wooing his public, particularly as that public was proving worryingly fickle.

On 8 August he sent out appeals to the chiefs of the loyal clans to rally to the standard at Glenfinnan on 19 August. These included such stirring themes as his resolution to restore the King his father, or to perish in the attempt. He also offered an amnesty to those who had served the 'usurpers' from Hanover, provided they now swore allegiance to James, and he promised religious tolerance. He hoped such messages would strike a chord, but these were anxious days.

It may have been an act of consummate bravery to send away the *Du Teillay* but it was also a rash one. What happened at Glenfinnan would be crucial. Clanranald and his men set off along the shore to the rallying point, but Charles went by boat with the baggage to Kinlochmoidart where news was brought to him of the first Jacobite victory of the '45 – or skirmish to be more exact.

The governor of Fort Augustus had got wind that the Highlanders were 'hatching some mischief' and sent additional soldiers of the first Royal Scots regiment of foot to reinforce Fort William. What happened on 16 August was evidence of the Englishman's absolute terror of the Highlander: 'Within eight miles of Fort William stands High Bridge, built over the river Spean, a torrent . . . extremely difficult to pass but by the bridge. Captain John Scott . . . who commanded the two companies . . . was near High Bridge, when he heard a bagpipe, and saw some Highlanders on the other side of the bridge skipping and leaping about with swords and firelocks in their hands.' They were shouting and yelling and the soldiers 'were struck with such an accountable panic as with one consent to run off without so much as taking time to observe the number or quality of their enemy'. They retreated only to find themselves blocked on all sides by advancing clansmen. Keppoch, with his sword drawn, ran up to them and delivered the uncompromising message that if they didn't surrender they would be cut to pieces.

They laid down their arms at once. Lochiel arrived with a body of his Camerons and carried the terrified prisoners back to his house. Not a single Highlander had been hurt and it had really been an absurd victory: '. . . I can't help thinking that never accident of this kind showed more the extraordinary effects of fear than this, they had marched about an hundred miles and owned themselves greatly fatigued, yet after all upon seeing a triffling Enemy Idly throw away their fire without doing the least execution, and run twelve miles with incredible speed.'

The Highlanders were delighted with this early success which 'had no small effect in raising their spirits, and encouraging them to rebel'. Forbes, the Lord President, understood the propaganda value of this early victory and observed that it would 'elevate too much and be the occasion of further folly. Two companies of the Royals made prisoners sounds pretty well and will surely pass for a notable achievement.' It did.

Murray of Broughton joined Charles at Kinlochmoidart two days later. An anonymous letter had alerted him to the fact that Charles had landed in Moidart and he had set out at once armed with two boxes of proclamations and manifestoes and a small amount of weapons. Ever the operator, he despatched Rob Roy's son, James Macgregor to Edinburgh to mislead the Government with false reports of Charles's doings. As to be expected of a man who had arrived ready equipped with paperwork, Murray was appointed Secretary though he may have hoped for the more glamorous position of aide-de-camp. Whatever the case he was Charles's *éminence grise* and stayed with him until taken ill a few days before Culloden.

Together they planned the details of the great rendezvous that was to signal the start of the campaign. They also grappled with some of the logistical problems that would dog them throughout. The departing Walsh had thoughtfully intercepted two vessels laden with oatmeal to feed the clansmen. However, Charles could not prevail on his brave Highlanders to carry it to the rendezvous. They considered this to be manual labour and beneath them so that 'he could not procure one Boll of it to be carried. . . .'

At this stage of the game such stubborness did not worry Charles – he was on the eve of great events. On the evening of 19 August he was rowed up Loch Shiel full of anticipation. Glenfinnan at the head of Loch Shiel was a grand enough setting – in a narrow vale 'in which the river Finnin runs between high and craggy mountains, not to be surmounted but by travellers on foot' and ringed by lochs. He came ashore at eleven o'clock expecting the acclamation of thousands of devoted clansmen rallied by their chiefs. Instead he was greeted by a couple of shepherds in Gaelic. Apart from them there were only some companies of Clanranald Macdonalds – not enough to fight a battle let alone win a crown.

It was a dreadful moment and Charles withdrew into a hovel to think what to do. After a while Macdonald of Morar came marching into the glen with one hundred and fifty more

Clanranald men. With him came James Macgregor who, continuing his intelligence role, brought the welcome news that the Camerons were on their way.

Their arrival could not have been more dramatic or better stage-managed. Eyewitnesses described the distant wailing of the pipes borne on the wind. It was a war-pibroch and a fitting announcement of the arrival of the mighty clan Cameron. They advanced in two lines, over seven hundred men. They were a magnificent spectacle, but even better was the fact that between them marched the dejected red-coated prisoners captured in the recent ambush.

Charles was so 'elevated with the sight of such a clan' that he waited no longer to stake his claim. The elderly Duke of Atholl unfurled the silk standard and the double-sized flag billowed out, crimson and white. It was greeted by a storm of huzzas and 'schiming of bonnetts into the air ... like a cloud'. According to the stories a Gaelic poet recited an emotional address to 'Tearlach Mac Sheumais' – 'Charles son of James'. Atholl read proclamations from James appointing Charles his regent and declaring war on the Elector, after which Charles did what he was so good at. Looking every inch the young hero in the dun coloured coat, red-laced waistcoat and breeches that had replaced the scruffy abbé's outfit, he made a 'very Pathetick' speech which touched the hearts of his listeners even though many would not have known enough English to understand him. He talked about striving for their welfare and happiness as much as for his own rights. He talked about honour and the noble example of their ancestors. He promised to protect Protestants and Catholics alike. One can imagine the tears streaming down Atholl's face.

Not long after Charles's spirits rose even further as Macdonald of Keppoch strode proudly in with another three hundred men or so, 'clever fellows' of his 'hardy and warlike clan' and a small group of Macdonalds from Skye who had defied their chief and come to support their Prince. It was a moving occasion and men were seduced in spite of themselves to believe that there was a chance of success.

Other observers of this momentous occasion were old Gordon of Glenbucket a veteran of the '15 who had sold all his lands so he could devote his life to the cause. Like so many of Charles's supporters, Glenbucket was an elderly man reliving the glorious adventures of his youth. A contemporary described him as 'so old and infirm that he could not mount his horse, but behoved to be lifted into his saddle, notwithstanding of which the old spirit still remained in him'. He had been bed-ridden for three years but on hearing of Charles's arrival had risen Lazarus-like and hurried off to greet him.

There was also the celebrated Miss Jenny Cameron of Glendessary, a relation of Lochiel. This vivacious but definitely middle-aged woman was to be frequently and erroneously described as Charles's mistress. Jacobite memoirs made determined attempts to restore her reputation asserting that though she was handsome, with pretty eyes and jet black hair she was virtuous. She arrived, according to the stories, at the head of two hundred and fifty men. She was dressed in a sea-green riding habit, with scarlet lapels and gold lacings. The bay gelding she rode was also decked with green and gold. Those black curls were crowned with a velvet cap and scarlet feather and she carried a sword instead of a riding whip. According to one Jacobite, 'she was so far from accompanying the Prince's army, that she went off with the rest of the spectators as soon as the army marched; neither did she ever follow the camp, nor ever was with the Prince but in public, when he had his Court in Edinburgh.' But she was later arrested and became the subject of salacious gossip in the press.

Of course, this noble gathering in the glen was to be portrayed rather differently by the enemies of the cause. They painted a picture of fanatical popish ritual from the moment of Charles's landing on Scottish soil. According to one story, Charles threw himself on the ground and kissed it after which his confessor hacked a piece of turf and offered it to him, as James's regent, on behalf of the Pope. This was strictly on condition that he would see to 'the utter Extirpation of the Persons of Heretics' and persevere manfully with the same 'until the Blood of the Heretics shall be washed away from the Face of the Earth'.

The raising of the standard was portayed in a similarly sinister light: '. . . they erected their Standard with great Solemnity: The Priest first washed it all over with Holy Water, and blessed it, then a certain number of Ave Marys and Paternosters were said, besides

Prayers to the Saints; in all which Acts of Devotion, Charles distinguished himself with greater Zeal (if possible) than the Priests
themselves.'

In general, the news of Charles's arrival was greeted with a
certain amount of incredulity by the Government and its supporters. It seemed more bizarre than heroic to land with only seven
henchmen, and some were quick to see the fell hand of France
behind it. The adventurer Dudley Bradstreet, a rumbustious
character right out of the pages of *Tom Jones*, described the initial
reaction in London: '. . . there was certain Intelligence that the
young Chevalier was landed in Scotland, with seven Persons to
aid and assist him. In the Beginning, this weak Attempt was
despised by some, and alarmed others: Most of the King's Troops
were engaged abroad and his Majesty in Hanover, when this
Advantage was taken by the French King, who sent his occasional
Tool to employ some of the Forces of England at home.'

Cumberland's private secretary compared the exercise to a squib
set off by the French who did not care 'if it bursts, or in whose
hands, or about whose ears'. There was a greater inclination to
despise the attempt than to be alarmed by it in the early days. It
was this apathy that worried Henry Fielding and persuaded him
of the need to whip up patriotic fervour in the *True Patriot*. In
Edinburgh the reaction to 'the news frae Moidart' was amused
and rather patronising. The genteel *Edinburgh Evening Courant*
observed to its readers that their fellow-countrymen from the
Highlands were 'only a pitiful crew, good for nothing, and
incapable of giving any reason for their proceedings, but talking
only of tobacco, King James, the Regent, plunder and new
brogues'. Whig poets pompously predicted that the inexperienced
young Pretender would swiftly tumble:

> Like Phaeton, with pride elate,
> Unskill'd you soar too high;
> Like his, unpity'd too your fate,
> Hur'ld headlong from the Skie.

However, such sentiment did not prevent the Lords of the
Regency, appointed to govern during George II's absence in

Hanover, from offering a reward of £30,000 for Charles's capture. When Charles heard about it his reactions were mixed. First of all the price on his head was less than it had been on his father's. On the other hand this was now the middle of the eighteenth century. Surely, civilisation had moved on and 'in proportion as the world grew in Politeness they had done so in humanity, that it were unjust to call the ancients Rude and Savage, &c., when no example could be given of their taking so mean and unmanly a way to get rid of their Enemy.' Yet, on the assumption that any of his supporters would stoop so low, he joked that he might consider offering thirty pounds for George. In the end, though, he was persuaded to match the offer pound for pound. The Government also sent immediate orders that all the British troops garrisoned at Ostend should re-embark at once. There was truth in the observation that 'such as knew the Highlanders were justly afraid'.

Meanwhile, the ceremony at Glenfinnan 'was followed by a general Housaw, & a great deal of Allacrety'. Morale was riding high with much toasting of the King's health in brandy and a general air of excitement and expectation. O'Sullivan described how Charles used the occasion to demonstrate that chivalry which helped establish him as a romantic hero. He saw that the captured soldiers were well-treated and given good sleeping quarters. (The Highlanders, as was tartly observed, had to make do with sleeping in the fields.) Captain Scott, who was wounded in the shoulder, had already been paroled shortly after his capture by Lochiel who was 'shocked with the barbarity' of a refusal by the old governor of Fort William to send the garrison surgeon to treat him under a pass of safe conduct.

Charles now freed another officer, Captain Swettenham, who had been captured in a separate incident and was 'recon'd a very good engineer', on the condition that he would promise not to take up arms again for a year and a day. Charles was genuinely merciful but as a tactic it worked brilliantly. 'This officer behaved very gallantly, he frighten'd the Governors of the Garrisons he past by, and even Cope [who had the grand title of Commander in Chief of all the forces in North Britain]. For he told 'um all, that the Prince had six thousand men, & that neither armes or mony was wanting to 'em; he gave every where the most favorable account that cou'd be given of the Prince's personne and activety. It is said the Ellector sent for him when he arrived at London, & asked him, what kind of a man the Prince was, he answered that he was as fine a figure, & as clivor a Prince, as a man cou'd set his eyes on, upon which George turned his back, & left him there.' The other officers were released conditionally a few days later but 'behaved basely', returning to their colours at the first opportunity.

As one of Charles's officers later wrote, Glenfinnan 'was, properly speaking, the beginning of the Prince's expedition'. By any standards Charles had already succeeded remarkably. With little more than personal charisma he had managed to spark a rebellion that was embarrassing at the very least to his enemies. As his father wrote to Louis, 'I knew absolutely nothing about it, but . . . I frankly admit I cannot help admiring him.'

Instinct told Charles that audacity must continue to be his chief weapon. He decided to push south and seek out his foe. His aim was to engage Sir John Cope, before the Government could call up reinforcements from Flanders. Hearing that Cope was preparing to march north for Fort Augustus he sent appeals to some of the clans between Glencoe and Glen Garry asking them to join him in marching to meet Cope.

A few days later he and his half-naked, ill-equipped little army set out. He again had problems persuading the Highlanders to do heavy work. This time it was weapons, ammunition, pick-axes and shovels rather than grain which had to be abandoned since 'the Highlanders could not be prevailed upon to carry them on the shoulders, but there was no other method of transporting them in this rugged country.' However, Charles determined to show them what he was made of. He marched on foot with his men the whole way to Invergarry. All that training in Italy was paying off to the extent that he walked sixteen miles in boots, 'and one of the heels happening to come off, the Highlanders said they were unco' glad to hear it, for they hoped the want of the heel would make him march more at leisure.' He halted at Invergarry Castle, the stronghold of the Glengarry Macdonalds, and sat up late with his chiefs discussing which route to take.

A messenger struggled through that wet and stormy night bringing word from old Lord Lovat. Lovat was a dubious ally. He had excused himself from coming out for Charles on account of his age and ill-health, but this did not prevent him from offering his advice. This was that Charles should march north to Inverness. Charles, however, listened to the advice of others and decided to continue south to seek out Cope. He was not to know that Lovat was also busily corresponding with the Lord President Duncan Forbes and describing him in highly unflattering terms as 'a mad and unaccountable gentleman'. Neither did he know how closely his every move was being watched. Lovat's spy even recorded how the next morning Charles put on Highland dress: 'the young forward leader called for his Highland clothes; and at tying the lachets of his shoes, he solemnly declared that he would be up with Mr Cope before they were unloosed.'

The route the Prince picked lay over the wild Corrieyairach Pass but Charles and his Highlanders crossed it 'like lightning'. Hearing that Cope was to camp that night at Garvamore, 'the Prince marched directly to him, with a design to attack him wherever he met him.'

Cope, on the other hand, was not having much luck. Unlike Charles he had plenty of weapons but no one to use them. As he advanced northwards with his force of two thousand he heard to his dismay from the Hanoverian Duke of Atholl and Lord Glenorchy that they had failed to raise a single man to fight for the Government. As he marched gloomily on he was plagued by desertions and sabotage. Bags of grain mysteriously burst open and his horses were stolen. Captain Swettenham, full of his experiences at Glenfinnan, brought the unwelcome news that the rebels now controlled the Corrieyairach Pass.

Instead of advancing to Garvamore, Cope veered off 'in the greatest hurry and disorder to Inverness, so that he left the Prince peaceable possessor of the Camp of Garvamore & nothing to oppose him from thence to Edinburgh'. So Charles found the way to the Lowlands open without a fight and was understandably 'quite surprised' by this turn of events. Some deserters from Cope's army were brought into the camp and delighted the Highlanders with vivid descriptions of how Cope's men were 'very much fatigued and frightened'. What delighted them even more were their descriptions of all the baggage and horses waiting to be looted so that 'there was nothing to be heard but a continued Cry to be marched against the Enemy.' The chagrin was considerable when Charles made it clear that the priority was to strike south for the soft underbelly of the country and leave Cope to his own devices for the present. He was pressured into allowing a small raiding party to attack the barracks at Ruthven but was 'not at all disappointed' when it failed, as he had predicted, through lack of assault ladders and other equipment. His military judgement was vindicated.

He would have been intrigued to know how all these events were being perceived south of the border. There it appeared that he had given Cope the slip and not vice versa. Horace Walpole wrote: 'The confusion I have found, and the danger we are in, prevent my talking of anything else. The young Pretender, at the head of 3,000 men, has got a march on General Cope.' These numbers were an exaggeration. Charles did not yet have two thousand men. However, he gained one important recruit in Cluny Macpherson whose reluctance to declare for Charles resulted in him being kidnapped from his house and brought to him. Cluny made a virtue out of necessity, declaring that 'an angel could not resist the soothing, close applications of the rebels' and promised to raise his clan.

The little army marched confidently into the Duke of Atholl's own country. It was an emotional moment for the elderly and asthmatic exile. His brother James, recognised by the Hanoverians as the legitimate duke, had fled at the rebels' approach. Murray of Broughton painted an extraordinary picture of the 'men, women and children who came running from their houses, kissing and caressing their master, whom they had not seen for thirty years . . . an instance of the strongest affection, and which could not fail to move every generous mind with a mixture of grief and joy'.

An interlude of rare luxury followed for Charles as the Duke played host at Blair Castle. Charles charmed Atholl by attempting to drink the healths of the chiefs in Gaelic – he was quickly developing that 'slight taste for wine' that was worrying his father – and by only partaking of those dishes 'supposed to be peculiar to Scotland.' He was also careful to show himself to the Highlanders who clustered around the hall, anxious for a sight of their

Prince. What seems to have struck Charles most about this magnificent old house was its well-tended bowling green and his first
taste of a pineapple.

This was a welcome halt for his troops as well, after the chal-
lenging pace set by their young leader. It was the first time that
the men 'could properly be said to have had bread from the time
of their rendezvous at Glenfinnan, having eaten nothing but beef
roasted on the heath, without even bread or salt, during their
march thither'. This interval also gave Charles an insight into the
character of the men he was commanding. When he reviewed his
forces he discovered that some of them had disappeared out of
pique at not being allowed to follow after Cope for plunder. They
had to be cajoled and threatened before they would return.

A few days later Charles moved on to Lude where he danced
minuets and Highland reels to the delight of his admirers. According to legend the first reel he asked for was the aptly named 'This
is no' mine ain House'. He had a powerful effect on his hostess
Mrs Robertson, 'who was so elevate when about the Young Pretender that she looked like a person whose head had gone wrong'.
But, as his female admirers were so often to discover, his mind
was on other things. Now he was poised for his first real coup.
On the evening of 4 September he entered the city of Perth to
claim it for the house of Stuart.

It was a perfectly staged event. The citizens of Perth who
thronged the streets in some bewilderment saw the personification
of the Jacobite dream. Charles rode at the head of his troops, a
vision in a suit of tartan trimmed with gold lace. The people
'dazzled by his appearance, hailed him with loud acclamations'.
His father was proclaimed King at the Cross to the cheers of the
Jacobite supporters and he was appointed Regent. He did his very
best to endear himself to the populace, displaying 'great cour-
teousness of manner'. Spies might report that his only support
came from those 'who had little to lose, Bankrupts, Papists, and
such as were outlawed by Church and State' who resorted to Perth
'as to an Asylum', but there is no doubt he was on a roll. He
boasted to his father that 'I have got their hearts'.

He now gained some further and very important adherents in
the form of the Duke of Perth, Lord George Murray, Lord Ogilvy,

Lord Strathallan and Lawrence Oliphant of Gask. Lord George Murray, brother to the Duke of Atholl, was the most significant of these and was pivotal to the campaign from the moment he bowed his knee to Charles. The Athollmen called him 'duine firin-neach' meaning 'true or righteous man'. Like so many others he was a mature man who had been out in earlier risings. Pardoned in 1725 he had set about repairing the family fortunes and had become a friend of Duncan Forbes. He was risking everything by following his Prince. But like Lochiel he was a Jacobite by convic-tion and could not fail to respond to this call to do his duty. Also like Lochiel, he did it with a heavy heart, unlike the excitable young men whose eyes were dazzled by the glamour of the cause.

It seems that Charles was openly suspicious of Lord George and his links with the Government from the outset. However, in deference to his military experience he appointed him joint Lieutenant-General, together with the Duke of Perth who had narrowly escaped being caught and locked up in his own castle before he could join the Jacobite forces. Charles tried to achieve a *modus vivendi* between the two by giving each of them the same number of men in battle, alternate command of the left and right wings and supreme command on alternate days. O'Sullivan was appointed Quartermaster.

The first priority was money – Charles had apparently entered Perth with no more than a guinea in his pocket. He and his advisers decided to appoint collectors to gather money from the city of Perth, and other neighbouring cities like Dundee, on the grounds that it was a legitimate activity for the lawful King to levy excise money. Ever mindful of appearances Charles even went to call on one Perth dignitary to explain the levy he was imposing on the city. However, this backfired a little. His zealous Highland attend-ant was disgusted to see the bailie wearing a large wig while Charles stood bareheaded. He seized it and jammed it on Charles's head exclaiming that: 'It was a shame to see ta like o'her, clarty thing, wearing sic a braw hap when ta very Prince hersel' had naething on ava.'

More generally the levying of taxes was deeply resented by the town dignitaries, but it meant that the Jacobites could claim that they did not plunder the countryside, despite reports to the contrary. The Whig press were quick to describe and to invent events in which wild Highlanders ravished the countryside not to mention its people. However, a Government spy acknowledged that at Perth Charles's men 'keep good discipline and pay for everything', except apparently for Keppoch and Glengarry's men who were harder to control. To counter the charges about Papism Charles was careful to attend an Episcopal service in Perth. It was a strategy he was to follow in other cities to rid himself of the spectre of religious intolerance.

Charles was comfortably lodged in a house belonging to Viscount Stormont 'one of whose sisters is credibly said to have spread a bed for his Royal Highness with her own fair hands'. During the few days he was in Perth he found time to attend balls, though it was remarked that he offended the ladies 'by the shortness of his stay'. He was preoccupied. Time was of the essence and he and his chiefs needed to decide on their next move. It was agreed that Edinburgh must be the goal. The psychological advantage of taking the capital would be tremendous, and it might encourage the French to send the reinforcements that Charles still hoped for. However, this could not be achieved if the army was not properly provided for. It was a well-known fact that if the Highlanders were not adequately fed they would melt away to look for their own supplies. Lord George ordered all the bakers in Perth to bake loaves for the Highlanders and he had knapsacks or 'pokes' made for them to carry the bread in as they marched.

In fact Lord George 'took charge of everything, and attended to everything'. He drilled the troops at Perth, which required particular techniques. He later wrote: 'It was told me that all Highlanders were gentlemen, and never to beat them. But I was well acquainted with their tempers. Fear was as necessary as love to restrain the bad and keep them in order. It was what all their Chiefs did and were not sparing of blows to them that deserved it which they took without grumbling when they had commited an offence. It is true that they would only receive correction from their own officers; for upon no account could the Chief of one clan correct the faults of the meanest of another. But I had as much authority over them all as each had amongst his own men ... At any time when there was a post of more danger than another [I] had more difficulty in restraining those who were too forward than in finding those who were willing.' In other words they were jealous, touchy, temperamental and needed careful handling. They would take almost anything from their chiefs, including being burned out of their homes to raise them for the Jacobite standard, but no one else exercised authority over them without their consent.

Lord George was equal to the challenge of the Highlanders. Neither did the Duke of Perth cause him much difficulty. Educated at the Scots College in Paris, the Duke had an over-fondness for attempting to speak broad Scots, but he was a brave and unassuming man who gave way to Lord George's stronger personality and greater experience without rancour. 'About 34 years of age, six foot high, of a slender make, fair complection and weakly constitution', his weak lungs were said to have been caused by his chest being crushed by a barrel when he was young. He was good natured and affable, if not overly intelligent. His tastes were for horse-racing and a quiet country life but he was not to enjoy these again.

Lord George was destined to fall out with Charles who, nurtured in a world of rumour and intrigue, listened to ill-founded warnings about Murray's allegiances and in particular about his friendship with Duncan Forbes. However, any friction in these early days was as much to do with Murray's bossiness as with any more deep-seated doubts Charles had. Charles was quite honest about what he expected. At their very first meeting he explained 'it is the obedience of my subjects I desire, not their advice', but he never succeeded in making Lord George behave with due humility.

On 11 September the Jacobite army, enriched by its new recruits, and now numbering some two thousand four hundred men, marched out towards Dumblane. The clansmen apparently seemed 'extremely fatigued with this march, which could only be imputed to the good quarters and plentiful diet which they had had at Perth, and their being so many days without exercise'. For all his strictness Lord George had let the Highlanders grow soft.

But to the population of Edinburgh they were as terrifying as ogres. Panic spread at the news of their approach, even among the dragoons who were meant to defend the city. The fact that Cope had thought it prudent to evade Charles had begun the rot. 'The citizens had previously looked upon the insurrection as but a more formidable sort of riot, which would soon be quelled and no more heard of; but when they saw that a regular army had found it necessary to decline fighting with the insurgents . . . it began to be looked upon in a much more serious light.'

From Dunblane Charles intended to march to the Fords of Frew and there to cross the Forth. Passing by Doune an incident ocurred 'which showed that he was at least the elected sovereign of the ladies of Scotland'. He stopped at the house of a Mr Edmonstone where all the gentlewomen of Monteith had assembled to see him pass. He gallantly drank to the health 'of all the fair ladies present' who begged the honour of kissing his hand. One of the ladies decided 'it would be a much more satisfactory taste of royalty to kiss his lips, and she accordingly made bold to ask permission to pree his Royal Highness's mouth. Charles did not at first understand her homely language, but it was no longer explained to him than he took her kindly in his arms, and kissed her fair and blushing face from ear to ear; to the no small vexation, it is added, of the other ladies, who had contented themselves with a less liberal share of princely grace.'

He reached the Fords of Frew to find no one to dispute his crossing. Colonel Gardiner's dragoons who should have been defending the river had fled in sheer panic – 'those doughty heroes, who had hitherto talked of cutting the whole host in pieces as soon as it approached the Lowlands, now thought it proper to retire upon Stirling.' It was a critical moment for Charles who 'in crossing Forth may be said to have passed the Rubicon; he had now no rough ground for a retreat in case of any disaster, and being entered into the low country must fairly meet his fate.' But he had no doubts about the strategy and plunged into the historic waters of the Forth. Fielding was quick to distort this heroic picture by reporting that in his eagerness he slipped and had to be preserved by one of his lieutenants 'who at the hazard of his own Life, rescued him from the Waves'.

Having crossed without incident Charles decided he must press on and take Edinburgh before Cope could get there. He bypassed

Stirling Castle, unmoved by the cannonball that fell near him and reputedly observing that 'the dogs bark but dare not bite.' On 14 September the Jacobites took Falkirk and Charles dined that night at Callandar House with Lord Kilmarnock. The Earl's affairs were desperate and his property was in imminent danger of being seized. It seemed to this handsome young aristocrat that a successful Jacobite campaign would be a good way to repair the family fortunes. He had another motive as well for throwing in his lot with Charles. After a wild and misspent youth he had married an ardent Jacobite, Anne Livingstone, and she implored him to come out for the Prince. Her passionate entreaties coupled with increasing pressure from his creditors clinched it. His reward was to be death on the scaffold, but all this lay in the future while the present looked promising.

Kilmarnock told Charles that Gardiner's dragoons had fallen back on Linlithgow and intended to defend the bridge there. Charles sent Lord George ahead with one thousand men to attack them. Hungry for action, he wanted to go himself, 'but the rest of the men declared they'd all march if he did, so was obliged to stay, to contain the rest'. But when they arrived the birds had flown, retreating towards Edinburgh. So Charles took possession of Linlithgow unopposed on 15 September.

Mindful that it was a Sunday he sent messages that the citizens would not be disturbed in their worship 'notwithstanding of which, the Minister either left the Town, or declined preaching, to enduce the ignorant vulgar to believe that if he had, he would have been insulted and persecuted'. That night Charles slept in a small farmhouse, having ordered his army to be under arms by five o'clock next morning ready to advance on Edinburgh.

The good citizens of Edinburgh received their first communication from Charles the next day. It was a judiciously worded summons to the provost and magistrates to fling wide the gates and receive him into the town. He promised to preserve their rights and liberties but made it clear that if there was any opposition he would not be answerable for the consequences.

This put the city dignitaries in a quandary. They had been trying to organise the city's defences but it had been a farce. The provost was 'so slow in his deliberations, backward in executing things agreed. He fixed upon a dismal signall – the ringing the alarmer or fryer bell – to call the volunteers or the burgers, and this was a public intimation to the rebel friends within and without the city. The volunteers had old crassey officers. . . .'

But what of the regular troops to whom the burgers would naturally look for protection? There had been a complete fiasco which became entrenched in the folklore. Gardiner had fallen back on the little village of Coltbridge, just outside Edinburgh where he had joined up with the other regiment left behind by Cope in the Lowlands, commanded by Colonel Hamilton. His mood was not improved by the arrival of Brigadier Thomas Fowke to take command of the two regiments. Gardiner complained that his men had been 'harass'd and fatigued for Eleven Days and Nights', that they would be massacred if they stayed where they were, but that he did not care as he would soon be dead anyway. He was a strange character, a reformed rake who had suffered a religious conversion during a liaison with a married woman.

In the light of this rather negative view of things, it was decided to fall back to Leith Links where the two regiments could shortly join up with Cope. However, before the weary, dispirited dragoons could be galvanized into action there were reports that the Jacobites were advancing. Tradition has it that the alarm was sparked off by a dragoon who had tumbled into a disused coalpit and whose cries for help were mistaken for the savage yells of the advancing Highland hordes.

Whatever the cause, the effect was electric. The whole party immediately broke up, and commenced a retreat, not to Edinburgh, but to the open country beyond. In what was afterwards styled the 'Canter of Coltbrigg' the soldiers rode off in full view of the citizens. The Jacobites exulted and the Whigs despaired at this ignominious flight which 'spread a panick thro' the City'. The only soldiers left were those in Edinburgh Castle and they were sitting tight.

Hence the uncertainty of the provost and the magistrates. There were scenes of 'civic pusillanimity' with would-be defenders, including one sick old man who insisted on guarding the Netherbow Port in his armchair, arguing furiously with those who wanted to throw in the towel.

The authorities sent a deputation to Charles to ask what exactly was expected of them. Murray of Broughton spelled it out – they must open the gates of the city, deliver up the arms of both the town and the garrison, together with any ammunition and military stores. However, the dignitaries continued to play for time, hoping that Cope would come to their rescue. But their scheming was pretty transparent and the Jacobites' patience was wearing thin. As the deputation's great cumbersome carriage came rolling back into the city after yet another parley, the Jacobites took their chance: 'The coach brought them back to Edinburgh, set them down in the High-Street, and then drove towards the Cannongate. When the Netherbow Port was opened to let out the coach, 800 Highlanders, led by Cameron of Lochiel, rushed in and took possession of the city.'

And so, as Murray of Broughton observed, Charles became 'master of the Capital without shedding a drop of Blood. . . .'

CHAPTER FIVE

'A RESOLUTE RAGE'

T HE city drew its breath as the Highlanders surged in with drawn sword and target, the savage impression heightened by their 'hideous yell and their own particular manner of making an attack'. Uncertain what resistance they would face, the clansmen raced through the narrow streets to seize the city's guard-house. But their behaviour was restrained and the Jacobites were able to record with pride how civil and innocent it was 'beyond what even their best friends could have expected'. Not that their opponents saw it like that. To their outraged eyes these wild-looking men were just verminous scum. One Whig sourly recorded, 'I entered the town by the Bristol port, which I saw to my indignation in the keeping of these caterpillers. A boy stood with a rusty drawn sword, and two fellows with things like guns of the 16 century sat on each side the entry to the poorhouse, and these were catching the vermin from their lurking places about their plaids and throwing them away. I said to Mr Jerdin, minister of Liberton, "Are these the scoundrels [who] have surprised Edinburgh by treachery?" He answered, "I had rather seen it in the hands of Frenchmen, but the devil and the deep sea are both bad."'

There was worse to come from an anti-Jacobite viewpoint. One of the Highlanders' first acts was to seize the heralds and *poursuivants* who were essential ingredients of any great ceremonials. At midday they were marched out to the Market Cross, magnificent in their 'fantastic but rich old dresses'. Ringed by watchful Highlanders, they proclaimed James as King. The usual manifesto and commission of regency were then read out to the excited crowd. It was the sort of scene beloved of Victorian artists, with women leaning from their 'lofty lattices' in the High Street waving white handkerchiefs in an ecstasy of loyalty. Even more picturesque, Murray of Broughton's beautiful wife sat on horseback near the cross, in a white dress, drawn sword in her hand, distributing white cockades to the populace. The Highland guard 'looked around the crowd with faces expressing wild joy and triumph; and with the license and extravagance appropriate to the occasion, fired off their pieces in the air.' The wailing of bagpipes rose over the hubbub with a loyal pibroch. Charles's critics bemoaned as a 'commick fars or tragic commody' but there was a dignity and magnificence about those moments.

Charles's arrival was the icing on the cake. Nobody could deny his handsome appearance and regal bearing when he rode to the ancient palace of Holyrood House later that day. His entry into Perth had only been a dress rehearsal for this triumphal progress. Now there was something messianic about him as the crowd pressed close trying to touch the boots on his feet or the bridle of his horse. His most hardened enemies had to admit that 'The figure and presence of Charles Stuart were not ill suited to his lofty pretensions. He was in the prime of youth, tall and handsome, of a fair complexion; he had a light coloured periwig with his own hair combed over the front; he wore the Highland dress, that is, a tartan short coat without the plaid, a blue bonnet on his head, and on his breast the star of the order of St Andrew. Charles stood some time in the park to shew himself to the people; and then, though he was very near the palace, mounted his horse, either to render himself more conspicuous, or because he rode well, and looked graceful on horseback. . . .' To the Jacobites he was like Robert the Bruce. The Whigs looked at him with more jaundiced eyes – they found him 'languid and melancoly' and concluded that 'he looked like a gentleman and a man of fashion, but not like a hero or a conqueror'.

On reaching the Palace of Holyrood he dismounted and walked slowly towards the great doors of the palace of his ancestors. An even more theatrical event then occurred. A gentleman stepped out of the crowd, drew his sword, and holding it aloft walked up the stairs in front of Charles. This was James Hepburn of Keith, a grizzled veteran of the rebellion of 1715 and an inveterate opponent of the Act of Union, regarded as the very model of a true Jacobite gentleman.

There were jubilant scenes that night. The crowd surged about the streets and huzza'd every time Charles appeared at the windows. People of fashion came to the palace to be presented, including Jacobite ladies avid for a sight of their hero and the chance to kiss his hand. Dr Alexander Carlyle was to describe in his autobiography how a well-informed citizen told him that two thirds of the ladies in the city were Jacobite supporters. However, Charles shied away from them for all his polish and chivalry. His officers were surprised that he always seemed embarrassed to be with women and excused it on the grounds that Charles was unused to female company. Looking back over his childhood they were probably right, but whatever the cause, the prince's aloofness only seemed to increase his appeal. He was the personification of the heroic young warrior bent on his quest to the exclusion of earthly pleasures.

Not that there had been much fighting yet. As contemporaries observed, the remarkable fact was that he had taken Edinburgh – a city of some forty thousand people – with hardly a drop of blood spilt. But what kind of a city was this that had fallen so easily into his waiting hands? Captain Burt had found it magnificent with its handsome stone-built houses. However, he had a few problems with the standards of hygiene. Given that the eighteenth century was not the most fastidious of times they must have been appalling. He described dining in a tavern where the cook was 'too filthy an object to be described' and where another Englishman suggested to him that if the cook were thrown against the wall he was so greasy he would stick to it.

Even worse health hazards were to be found out of doors as Burt described graphically: 'Being in my retreat to pass through a long narrow wynde or alley, to go to my new lodgings, a guide was assigned me, who went before me to prevent my disgrace, crying out all the way, with a loud voice, "Hold your hand." The throwing up of a sash or otherwise opening a window, made me tremble, while behind and before me, at some little distance, fell the terrible shower.' He blamed this 'great annoyance' on the very high buildings, sometimes ten or even twelve storeys all crowded close together.

Daniel Defoe was similarly struck with the sanitary arrangements, wondering whether the people of Edinburgh 'delighted in Stench and Nastiness. . . . In a morning, earlier than Seven o'Clock, before the human Excrements are swept away from the doors, it stinks intolerably; for after Ten at Night, you run a great Risque, if you walk the streets, of having Chamberpots of Ordure thrown upon your Head. . . .' It was a problem that had not been solved some fifty years later when Dr Johnson described with his customary relish 'Many a full-flowing perriwig moistened into flaccidity'.

However, such grossness did not intrude into the noble apartments of the Duke of Hamilton in Holyrood House where Charles was considering his next move. He had been joined before entering Edinburgh by young Lord Elcho who had first made Charles's acquaintance when he was making the grand tour in 1740. James had made them stand back to back to measure which was the taller and he had watched Charles in the Villa Borghese playing a 'Scotch game called goff'. When Elcho later returned to England he was such an elegant dandy, or 'macaroni', in the language of the day, that he was booed and hissed in the streets of Rochester with cries of 'Down with the French dog'. He was now a welcome addition to Charles who made him his aide-de-camp and discussed with him the battle to come. The encounter Charles had been waiting for was not far off. Hearing that Cope had disembarked his army at Dunbar on 17 September and was advancing towards Edinburgh he famously exclaimed 'Has he, by God?' in the best laconic tradition of the British military.

The great question was how to arm his Highlanders properly. His opponents had been quick to note their eccentric weapons as they stood at the Market Cross, in particular the superannuated old guns, 'some tied with puck thread to the stock, some without locks and some matchlocks'. Much of their remaining armoury consisted of little more than pitchforks, scythes lashed to poles and some old Lochaber axes, although some had the longswords which the Government had tried to confiscate in the aftermath of previous rebellions and which had been hidden deep in the thatch of their houses or in the peat.

There was not long to remedy this. A proclamation demanding

the surrender of firearms in the city yielded some powder and ball and about twelve hundred muskets, some serviceable, others 'indifferent'. Collecting any other weapons they could find or patch together, the Jacobites prepared for their first real trial of strength. They also sought out 'Clothes, Shoes and Linens, of which they were in great Want, the most part having nothing but a short old Coat of coarse Tartan, a Pair of Hose, much worn, coming scarce up to their Knees, their Plaids and Bonnets in the same Condition'.

Charles joined his troops at Duddingston where it was agreed they would march on Cope without delay. On the morning of 20 September the men assembled to the sound of the bagpipes and Charles called his chiefs to his side. There was palpable excitement in the camp as Charles addressed them. Like the diligent secretary he was, Murray of Broughton described the scene. He shows us Charles, exhilarated and confident, drawing his sword and proclaiming that he had flung away the scabbard and how with God's assistance he did not doubt of making them a free and happy people, prophesying that 'Mr Cope' should not give them the slip as he had in the Highlands. As the messages reverberated through the lines there were hoarse cheers and those ragged bonnets were flung in the air.

A Highland army on the march must have presented quite a spectacle. An old lady described in the 1820s what she witnessed that day. The amazed young girl saw the Highlanders stride by, 'with their squalid clothes and various arms, their rough limbs and uncombed hair, looking around them with faces, in which were strangely blended, pride with ferocity, savage ignorance with high-souled resolution'. Even allowing for the language and sentiment of the nineteenth century writer who recorded her memories, it must have been a remarkable sight. Of course she had words of praise for Charles: 'Our aged friend remembers, as yesterday, his graceful carriage and comely looks – his long light hair straggling below his neck – and the flap of his tartan coat thrown back by the wind, so as to make the star dangle for a moment clear in the air by its silken ribbon. He was viewed with admiration by the simple villagers; and even those who were ignorant of his claims, or who rejected them, could not help wishing good fortune and no calamity to so fair and so princely a young man.'

With Lord George Murray and the Lochiel Camerons at its head the army moved quickly. Charles and his leaders believed that Cope was heading to Tranent, planning to face them on the moorlands to the west of it, and they raced to capture the high ground before him. However, Cope decided to strike north towards some low ground between the villages of Preston and Seton. It was a shrewd move. The stubble fields in which he drew up his men were protected to the north by the sea and to the south by a ditch and morass. It was difficult to know how best to get at him. The Chevalier Johnstone, a young Jacobite officer who wrote a detailed account of the '45, was full of gloom, seeing 'no means of attacking him without visibly exposing ourselves to be hewn in pieces with dishonour'.

There were other problems as well. At this inopportune moment fierce inter-clan rivalry threatened to undermine the whole operation. The point at issue was who should fight in the place of honour on the right. Charles had become aware of this ticklish problem very early on. At Perth he had made the diplomatic suggestion that the problem be settled by the drawing of lots. This proved fine in principle, but less so in practice. To their chagrin the Macdonalds now drew the left-hand position, while the Camerons and the Appin Stewarts who had chosen to fight together won the coveted place on the right. The Macdonalds balked at this, loudly asserting their traditional right to fight in the place of greatest honour. Lochiel solved it by suggesting that if there was no action on that particular day, he would willingly yield his post to the Macdonalds on the next, notwithstanding the agreement.

Another sign of the tensions within the Jacobite camp was the row which now took place between Lord George Murray and Charles. He had deployed a detachment of Lord George's men to block off Cope's retreat in case he tried to give them the slip and make a dash for Edinburgh. It was sound enough strategy but caused Lord George to scold him like a school master. O'Sullivan recorded in disapproving tones how Lord George 'asked the Prince in a very high tone, what was become of the Atholl Brigade; the Prince told him, upon which Lord George threw his gun on the Ground in a great passion, & Swore God, he'd never draw his sword for the cause, if the Brigade was not brought back. The Prince with his ordinary prudence, tho' sensible of the disrespect, & too sensible of the consequence it may be of, gave orders that the brigade shou'd come back, but Lord George who was brought to himself, by Lochiel's representation as it is said, prayed the Prince to send the brigade to their first destination.' In the event this does not seem to have happened and there was no real reconciliation between the two, even if later that day they appeared to be 'great at cup and can' together. Instead it marked the beginning of an open breach that was to grow wider and ultimately prove fatal to the aspirations of both men.

However, in spite of these problems Charles was in good spirits the evening before the battle. He went to dine with two companions in the principal inn in Tranent. It was a poor place but he apparently 'condescended to enter it, and accept of its meagre hospitalities'. Unfortunately the inn-keeper's wife had hidden every bit of pewter she had 'for fear of the wild Highlanders'. She was now faced with the embarrassment of a royal guest and no dishes or cutlery. All she could manage was two wooden spoons to be shared between the three of them. They ate their supper of soup and meat with some difficulty and Charles afterwards provided himself 'with a portable knife and fork for the exigencies of his campaign'.

That night Charles called a council of war at which it was decided to attack Cope at dawn. The Highland army wrapped themselves in their plaids and lay down on the prickly, stubbly ground to sleep as best they could before the coming battle. Although, as the *Caledonian Mercury* had been recording, the weather that September was the finest for decades, the evenings were growing chill. That night a cold mist was rising which 'without doing any particular injury to the hardy children of the North, was infinitely annoying to their opponents'. Not only was it uncomfortable for those unused to bivouacking in these conditions, but they had to be on the alert against a night attack. Cope lit great fires around his camp to warm and comfort his men and he planted pickets all around. However, it was a sign of his nervousness that he sent his military chest and baggage away to safety under a strong guard.

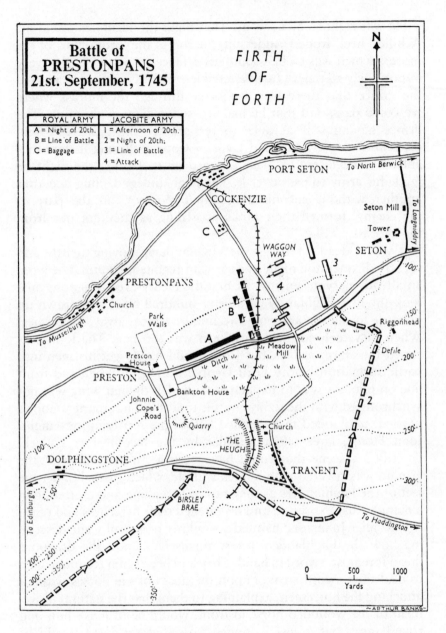

Battle of PRESTONPANS 21st. September, 1745

ROYAL ARMY	JACOBITE ARMY
A = Night of 20th.	1 = Afternoon of 20th.
B = Line of Battle	2 = Night of 20th.
C = Baggage	3 = Line of Battle
	4 = Attack

FIRTH OF FORTH

PORT SETON

To North Berwick

COCKENZIE

Seton Mill

Tower

SETON

WAGGON WAY

PRESTONPANS

Church

Park Walls

Preston House

PRESTON

Bankton House

Johnnie Cope's Road

Quarry

THE HEUGH

Church

TRANENT

DOLPHINGSTONE

BIRSLEY BRAE

To Edinburgh

To Musselburgh

To Longniddry

Riggonhead

Defile

Meadow Mill

Ditch

To Haddington

0   500   1000

Yards

~ARTHUR BANKS

He was right to be nervous. That night the Jacobites found his Achilles' heel. Robert Anderson, the son of the 'proprietor' of the morass which was Cope's southern defence, came to Charles 'very opportunely to relieve us of a terrible embarrassment. He assured the Prince that there was a passage through the morass where we could pass, and that he had crossed it daily in shooting. The Prince having sent at once to reconnoitre the passage, found his report correct, and that General Cope, believing it impraticable, had neglected to place a guard on it. During the night he made his army to pass over it. The Highlanders defiling one after another without encountering any opposition on the part of the enemy, formed their ranks according as they got out from the morass. . . .'

It was a deadly tactic – the Highlanders, moving swiftly and silently through the night in their clan regiments, outmanoeuvred an already nervous enemy. At first the bleary-eyed dragoons mistook the first Highland line, twelve hundred clansmen drawn up in battle formation and only two hundred paces away, for bushes! When they realised their mistake it was too late. The look-outs raised the alarm at last, but Cope could barely get his men into battle formation before Lord George hurled the Highland front line on him. As was to happen at Culloden the left wing was not synchronised with the right, but this time it did not matter. Cope's untried, unblooded men quailed before the terrifying onslaught. John Home, later taken prisoner by the Jacobites at Falkirk, described a scene that could have been a Zulu attack: '. . . the ground was covered with a thick stubble, which rustled under the feet of the Highlanders as they ran on, speaking and muttering in a manner that expressed and heightened their fierceness and rage.'

Chevalier Johnstone painted a similarly powerful scene describing how the Highlanders threw themselves upon the dragoons 'head foremost, sword in hand. They had been often recommended to deal their sword strokes upon the noses of the horses without attacking the horsemen, explaining to them that the natural movement of the wounded horse in front, would be to make him bolt round; and that a few wounded horses at the head would be sufficient to throw a whole squadron into disorder, and without their being able to remedy it. They followed this advice with exactitude, and the English cavalry were immediately in disorder.' So were all of Cope's forces.

He had put his infantry in the centre with the 13th Light Dragoons on the right and the 14th on the left flank. A conventional deployment against an unconventional enemy. The 'hideous shout' of the attacking clansmen completely unnerved Cope's naval gunners who fled followed by the 13th Light Dragoons who had not managed to fire one shot at their attackers. The 14th scarcely did better, holding their ground for a mere thirty seconds under an assault from the Macdonalds in their cherished place on the Jacobite right wing. In their wild flight the dragoons actually rode down the artillery guard. The infantrymen in the centre thus found themselves unsupported with the Highlanders in their midst. Those who could took to their heels. The general level of resistance was summed up by Murray of Broughton who doubted 'if such behaviour merits the name'.

By the time Charles arrived with the second line 'the rout was total'. He had wanted to lead the battle charge but had been overruled by his chiefs who pointed out that if he fell, victory or defeat would be all the same to them. So he charged with the reserve, some fifty yards behind. Leaping the four-foot-wide ditch that bordered the morass he slipped and fell to his knees. Chevalier Johnstone grabbed him by the arms and pulled him up, but was startled by the expression on Charles's face. He looked as if he feared it was a bad omen. But one glance at the stubble fields still wreathed in the early morning mists showed that his victory had been absolute and his confidence in his Highlanders' fighting skills justified.

He had grown up with the warrior-legends of the clans. He knew that the whole system was based on the chief's right to call out his men and on their duty to follow. The clan system provided a natural hierarchy so that every man knew his place in the battle order. As Charles had already discovered the place of honour was on the right and was hotly contested. The chieftains and their tacksmen led, the clansmen followed according to their rank, with the poor 'humblies' at the back. The humblies were so called 'from their wearing no covering on their head, but their hair, which at a more early period they probably matted and felted'. The common tactic was to advance within range of the enemy, discharge the guns and then fall to the ground until the enemy had returned fire. Then, while the enemy was reloading they would leap up and charge, yelling their clan motto. This yelling was particularly unnerving to the English troops.

To young, gullible and untried soldiers a Highland charge must have seemed terrifying, like being attacked by dervishes. So would the method of raising the clans which was done by a fiery cross carried in relay across the wild terrain with each runner shouting the name of the rendezvous to the next. There were also still strong rumours of pagan ritual and witchcraft in the Highlands of the eighteenth century. All in all, it was probably the Highlanders' terrifying reputation as much as their tactics on the day which gave them such a convincing victory in a battle which had lasted no more than ten minutes.

Charles was deeply impressed, writing to James that it was 'one of the most surprising actions that ever was'. Some of his men had been well-armed but others had had to improvise, attaching sharpened scythes to the ends of long sticks and thereby creating 'a most murderous weapon'. Some had fought with only sticks in their hands. Nevertheless, they had overwhelmed the enemy with their 'incredible impetuosity', capturing between sixteen and seventeen hundred prisoners including seventy officers. Charles's own casualties were probably no higher than fifty. This filled him with confidence for the future. Rather too much so according to young Lord Elcho, who described how 'The Prince from this Battle entertained a mighty notion of the highlanders, and ever after imagin'd they would beat four times their number of regular troops. . . .'

The Highlanders did not pursue their fleeing enemy very far, being more concerned with plunder. However, there is no doubt of the blind terror of the Government troops and the pitiful ease with which they were captured. They were described as 'on the plain like a flock of sheep which after having run away, gathers together and begins to run again when seized by a fresh fear'. A single Highlander 'from a rashness without example, having pursued a party to some distance from the field of battle . . . struck down the hindermost with a blow of his sword, calling at the same time, "down with your arms!" The soldiers, terror-struck, threw down their arms without looking behind them; and the High-lander, with a pistol in one hand, and his sword in the other, made them do just as he pleased.' The carnage on the battle-field had unnerved them – it was a blood-soaked 'spectacle of horror, being covered with heads, legs, and arms and mutilated bodies'.

The accounts also show Charles's humanity. He insisted that there was proper medical treatment for the wounded of both sides. He and Lord George Murray were in complete agreement on this, and messengers were sent off to Edinburgh to fetch more surgeons. There was also the question of how to bury the dead. The High-landers refused to bury the enemy dead, neither would the locals. Charles wrote to James: 'Those who should bury the dead are run away, as if it were no business of theirs. My Highlanders think it beneath them to do it, and the country folk are fled away. How-ever, I am determined to try if I can get people for money to undertake it, for I cannot bear the thought of suffering Englishmen to rot above the ground.'

Charles's first experience of real war seems to have left him in reflective mood. He was also aware of being closely observed by friend and foe alike, and that his behaviour would be widely reported. One of his officers described how although 'nothing could be more complete, or more important, than this victory; nevertheless, the Prince did not seem to be much elated with it: he had a livelier sense of other people's misfortunes than his own good fortune. . . .' He even issued orders that there was to be no public celebration of the victory on the grounds that he was 'far from rejoicing at the death of any of his father's subjects, tho never so much his Enemies . . .'

As the news filtered south it was met with outrage. The *London Magazine* carried a speech by the Archbishop of York three days after the battle which bristles with indignation: 'It was some Time before it was believ'd, (I would to God it had gain'd Credit sooner) but now every Child knows it, that the Pretender's Son is in Scot-land; has set up his Standard there; has gather'd and disciplin'd an Army of great Force; receives daily Increase of Numbers; is in the Possession of the capital City there; has defeated a small Part of the King's Forces; and is advancing with hasty Steps towards

England.' On the very eve of the battle Horace Walpole had written to Horace Mann about the strange turn of events: 'There never was so extraordinary a sort of rebellion ... banditti can never conquer a kingdom. On the other hand what can't any number of men do that meet no opposition ...'

The propaganda machine was furiously at work on both sides to present the battle in the best light. While Charles's chivalry and humanity were being woven into Jacobite folklore, his enemies tried to diminish or traduce it. One virulent anti-Jacobite, Henderson, who was a master at the High School in Edinburgh and published his history of the rebellion in 1748, painted a callous picture of Charles lounging among the corpses on the battlefield and enjoying a hearty meal of cold beef acompanied by a glass of wine. Murray of Broughton angrily rebutted this calumny by a 'little ignorant School master who has pretended to write the history of an affair of which he could be no judge, but when people will act above their Sphere they must be allowed to stuff their performance with whatever suits their confined fancy best, tho at the expense of truth'. Another account thundered away about make-believe cruelties 'which the Rebels (as 'tis generally Said, under the command of Lord Elcho) inflicted on Some of the troops after they had ask'd quarter' and which were 'dreadfully legible on the countenances of many who Surviv'd it'. It was alleged that Colonel Gardiner, who had gloomily but correctly predicted his own demise, was hacked to pieces in sight of his own home, Bankton House, after asking for quarter. Conversely, a Jacobite broadsheet contrasted remarks made by Charles before the battle calling on the 'Assistance of God' with Cope bloodthirstily promising his men 'eight full hours ... pillage' in Edinburgh after they had defeated the Highlanders.

Poor old Cope became a general object of derision. To the Jacobites he was the general who had been caught napping by their brilliant young hero. As they marched into England's heartland, tradition says they sang the famous ballad celebrating his defeat:

> 'I' faith,' quo' Johnnie, 'I got a fleg,
> Wi' their claymores and philabegs,
> If I face them again, deil break my legs!

So I wish you a very gude morning.'
Hey, Johnnie Cope, are ye wauking yet?
Or are your drums a-beating yet?
If ye were wauking I would wait,
To gang to the coals i' the morning.'

Chevalier Johnstone says Cope escaped by placing a white cockade on his head and arrived at Coldstream to be greeted by Lord Mark Ker, one of a family 'who had long had hereditary claims to wit as well as courage', with the acid remark that 'he believed he was the first general in Europe that had brought tidings of his own defeat'.

Others were not much kinder. Henderson scolded Cope who 'either from a natural Incapacity, or from his Apprehensions of the People he had to deal with, very poorly executed his Orders'. Later writers were equally acerbic, even those who were not pro-Jacobite. An article in the *Quarterly Review*, possibly by Sir Walter Scott, asserted that, 'He was, in fact, by no means either a coward or a bad soldier, or even a contemptible general upon ordinary occasions. He was a pudding-headed, thick-brained sort of person, who could act well enough in circumstances with which he was conversant, especially as he was perfectly acquainted with the routine of his profession, and had been often engaged in action, without ever, until the fatal field of Preston, having shown sense enough to run away. On the present occasion, he was, as sportsmen say, at fault.'

So were some of his men if the tales are to be believed. There was one sly story about how two of his volunteers were sent to watch the coast road to Musselburgh. However, they were seduced from their task by the discovery of 'a snug, thatched tavern, kept by a cleanly old woman called Luckie, who was eminent for the excellence of her oysters and sherry'. The two bon vivants fell into the hands of the Jacobites and narrowly missed being hanged for spies.

However, it was horror not humour which prevailed in England in the immediate aftermath of Preston Pans. The press carried lurid stories of women exposed naked at the Market Cross in Edinburgh and then butchered. Pamphlets poured onto the streets of English towns prophesying every sort of atrocity. Clergymen denounced Charles as a snake in the grass in the pay of the Pope and the King of France. In Scotland his enemies remained largely silent but his supporters churned out poems, pamphlets, ribbons and medallions celebrating their triumph. The *Caledonian Mercury* praised Charles to the heavens. He was toasted as the prince who slept rough with his men, sharing all their hardships and able to eat his dinner in four minutes and defeat the enemy in five. Until this point Charles had just been the romantic symbol of Scotland's past struggles and hopes to come. Now he had stamped his own mark on the Jacobite legend which from this moment became peculiarly his own.

CHAPTER SIX

'I AM RESOLVED TO GO TO ENGLAND'

T H E Battle of Preston Pans changed many things. Charles had left Edinburgh an untried adventurer with a seemingly undisciplined rabble at his heels. He returned as the conquering hero. The victorious Jacobite army marched back into the capital to the sound of pipes and drums. The trophies of war – the captured cannon and the colours seized from Cope's dragoons – were paraded before the cheering crowds that clustered around the lower gate and along the main streets. At the end of the long column stumbled the prisoners of war, still numbed by events. Chevalier Johnstone described this triumphal march through the city with cynical hindsight, especially the huzzas of the populace, 'always equally inconstant in every country of the world'.

Charles's achievement was remarkable. As Murray of Broughton wrote, the success of that one day at Preston Pans – or 'Gladesmuir' as the Jacobites now called it in deference to an old prophesy of Thomas the Rhymer that 'In Gladesmoor shall the battle be' – had rendered the Chevalier entire master of Scotland. The only exception was the forts of Edinburgh and Stirling and four small garrisons in the north.

However, Charles knew that these were not yet the days of wine and roses. His position was precarious and his success was only a first step towards the prize on which his heart was set – England. In the meantime he had to consolidate his gains and show his fitness to rule. As part of that process he assured the Presbyterian clergy that they were perfectly free to preach and got a flea in his ear. A deputation arrived to ask whether they might mention King

George in their prayers. Charles assured them he would take no notice of anything they said and probably meant it. One of his supporters, Lord Kilmarnock, when quizzed about Charles's religious tendencies on the eve of his execution, said he was convinced Charles had no real concern for any outward profession of religion, perhaps as a reaction to his mother's religious mania.

Despite this, some clergymen still refused to conduct their services 'pretending fear of insults and the like'. One who did go ahead prayed: 'Bless the King – Thou knowest what King I mean; may the crown sit long and easy on his head. And for this man that is come amongst us to seek an earthly crown, we beseech Thee in mercy to take him to Thyself and give him a crown of glory.'

However, such acts of defiance were limited and the Government was worried. Duncan Forbes took a wry look at the euphoria sweeping the Jacobite camp and those who now began to cling to its coat-tails, observing that 'All Jacobites, how prudent soever, became mad; all doubtful people became Jacobites; and all bankrupts became heros and talked of nothing but hereditary rights and victories; and what was more grievous to men of gallantry, and if you will believe me, much more mischievous to the public, all the fine ladies, except one or two, became passionately fond of the young Adventurer and used all their arts and industry for him in the most intemperate manner.'

Charles certainly exploited his physical magnetism but he was careful that his behaviour was seen to match it. One of his adherents described how even those 'whom interest or prejudice made a runaway to his cause, could not help acknowledging that they wished him well in all other respects and could hardly blame him for his present undertaking'. In particular it was his 'good nature and humanity' which made such an impression on people's minds. This is a highly partisan view of Charles but there is no doubt that many hardened Whigs found something to admire in the conduct of this romantic young Prince, 'flushed with victory', even if they could not support his ambitions.

The Prince was as careful to court public opinion as any modern politician. He issued a proclamation that any soldier or person connected with his army found plundering from 'the good people of Edinburgh' would be executed. This edict was only partially successful. One night six Highlanders broke into a house near Edinburgh and apparently got more than they bargained for. The house belonged to 'a very mortified Gentleman, remarkable for his great Charity, Piety and abstemious Life, who lay every Night in his Coffin and Winding Sheet. The Highlanders having secur'd what Arms were in the House, set a Guard on the Servants, and pack'd up all the Plate and Linen they thought they could carry off. The Chamber where Mr – lay, was without Furniture, and the last thing they visited as they were going off, having lock'd the Servants in a Room, seeing the Coffin, they concluded a Corpse was inclos'd in it, and that it might have a good Winding Sheet, thought it would be a Pity to leave it behind them; they therefore, with a Design of taking what the dead Man would never miss, remov'd the Lid off the Coffin; on which Mr – raising himself up, they were struck with such a Panick at his ghostly Appearance, and imagining that the Devil had taken Possession of the Corpse, and that he would have them next, they all took to their Heels, and Mr – running after them to the Door, at their rushing out fasten'd it upon them, though the Precaution was needless; for they fearing the Devil would take the Hindermost, never look'd back, or slacken'd their Pace until out of the Sight of the House; their Terror was so great that they left all their Plunder behind. . . .'

There were many more credible, albeit less spectacular, complaints of looting and petty pilfering. Murray of Broughton was not entirely justified in claiming that 'there is no instance in the history of any times in whatever Country where the Soldiery either regular or irregular behaved themselves with so much discretion, never any riots in the Streets, nor so much as a Drunk man to be seen.' However, Charles and his commanders were remarkably successful in keeping order and some of the thieving was undoubtedly done by opportunists who stuck a white cockade in their hat and went freebooting.

Finding billets for the army was another problem which needed careful handling to avoid alienating the townspeople. Charles and his chiefs did their best to ensure that the 'Burgesses and people of fashion were not harassed with common fellows for their guests.' The Highlanders were partly encamped at Duddingston and partly billeted on 'publick houses and people of low rank' in the suburbs and outlying areas of Edinburgh. What the people of 'low rank' thought about this arrangement is not recorded.

If there was apprehension among some of the citizens of Edinburgh as they waited on events, it was mild in comparison with the reaction in England to Charles's success. At last the country was waking up to the danger. Catholics, English and foreign, were ordered to leave the area ten miles around London on or before 19 September and subjected to harassment. To some like Lady Isabella Finch these measures were not stern enough. She reflected with pleasure on how 'our epicures and coxcombs' would be able to manage without their continental cooks and *valets de chambre* and decided that if she had a say in Parliament she would tax every family who had French servants as a punishment for harbouring 'such wretches in the heart of our island at a time when they will have such opportunities of doing mischief'.

All over the country clergymen thundered from their pulpits about the bloodthirsty intentions of the Roman Catholic church, warning their congregations that whatever Charles might say and however 'honest and good-natur'd' he might be, Rome and France would force him to be 'perfidious and cruel'. He was but a tool of Rome. Virulent articles painted bloodcurdling pictures of what Rome might have in store: 'She damns all who are not of her horrid communion, and murders, or would murder, all that she damns; witness her universal practice and constant massacres at Paris, in Ireland, her crusades against the best Christians, the daily fires of the Inquisition and the burning in Smithfield, especialy under Queen Mary. Be warned O Protestants; continue what ye are; Christians and freemen; your all is at stake, Liberty, Property, Conscience; abhor the Harlot and oppose the tool of the Harlot.'

The newspapers brimmed over with reports of 'loyal' and 'humble' addresses to his Majesty King George. Loyal Associations were formed and subscriptions raised to keep out the Popish horror that threatened from the north. They were interlarded with references to Crécy and Agincourt and the glorious Protestant Princess Elizabeth who had routed the Catholic Armada. Those who had been criticising the Government thought again. They discovered it was not Hanoverian George they had been objecting to but his ministers. The wife of a former Tory MP wrote to another Tory in October 1745 that 'I have been in deadful frights about the rebellion, but the zeal and unnanimity that has appeared in all ranks of people in supporting our happy constitution in Church and State has given me inexpressible satisfaction and dissipated all my fears; and hope when we have recovered this shocking sceane a more pleasing one will present it self to our view which will be lasting and hope make the king's crown sit easier upon his head many, many years. For he must now see t'was not him we cavelled at, but his ministers and I hope a mutual confidence will for the future be t'wixt king and people. . . .' The Quakers contributed flannel waistcoats for the troops, apparently inspiring one soldier to avow in verse that he would 'fight for those whose creed forbids to fight'.

This rising panic was whipped up by skilful Whig propaganda. In the London theatres the national anthem was sung with an additional verse:

> From France and Pretender
> Great Britain defend her
>   Foes let them fall;
> From foreign slavery,
> Priests, and their knavery,
> And Popish reverie,
>   God save us all.

Captain Dudley Bradstreet described with relish how the city buzzed with rumours of fiendish plots, including one to seize the Tower of London. This, of course, the gallant Captain was able to put a stop to by his cunning and bravery.

Jacobite supporters and Roman Catholics who were supposedly afraid of open insurrection were accused of trying to cause a run on the Bank by their wretched 'little artifices'. A story went the rounds of how 'a well-dressed rascal came into a Coffee-house about Seven in the Evening, and cry'd out, We are all undone, for the Bank is Shut up! Yes, reply'd an old Gentleman. It is always

Shut up two hours before this time of day, for fear of such Rogues as you. Upon which the Rascal quitted the Coffee-house.'

Charles and his Hanoverian cousins were soon engaging in their own war of words. King George had returned from Hanover at the end of August at the news of Charles's landing. In the middle of October he addressed both Houses of Parliament and called on their assistance in suppressing the 'unnatural rebellion' which had broken out in Scotland. When Charles heard that Parliament had been summoned, he issued a proclamation warning that anyone who obeyed the summons would be guilty of treason and rebellion and would not be pardoned under his general amnesty. He also took the opportunity to declare that 'the pretended union' of England and Scotland was at an end and to accuse the Hanoverians of bringing misery on both countries.

He followed this up with a further proclamation which was a personal appeal to his subjects, laying bare his intentions and his aspirations. He promised freedom of religion and that Parliament would review what could be done about the heavy burden of the National Debt. He warned them against the lies in the weekly papers, ringing with 'the dreadful threats of popery, slavery, tyranny and arbitrary powers'. He also gave them a sense of the sacred quest he was pursuing. 'I, with my own money, hire a small vessel, ill provided with money, arms or friends; I arrived in Scotland, attended by seven persons; I publish the King my father's Declarations, and proclaim his title, with pardon in one hand, and in the other liberty of conscience, and the most solemn promises to grant whatever a free parliament shall propose for the happiness of the people. I have, I confess, the greatest reason to adore the goodness of Almighty God, who has in so remarkable a manner protected me and my small army through the many dangers to which we were at first exposed, and who has led me in the way to victory, and to the capital of this ancient kingdom, amidst the acclamations of the King my father's subjects. Why then is so much pains taken to spirit up the minds of the people against this my undertaking?'

While the rhetoric flew the Government in London counted their blessings that Charles had not invaded at once after Preston Pans. Charles had actually gathered his commanders around him on the battlefield that very day and proposed they march immediately to Berwick, where Cope had fled, as a prelude to an invasion of England. However, he was dissuaded on the grounds that they did not yet have enough men and it would be better to wait in Edinburgh while they built up the army. One of the problems was that many clansmen were already melting away to their homes with their booty. A fine example of this was the elderly Robertson of Struan who left for home immediately after the battle riding in Cope's own personal carriage and magnificent in Cope's chain and furlined nightgown. Chocolate found in Cope's carriage was soon on sale as 'Cope's salve'. Within a few days of the battle Charles's army was down to only about fourteen hundred which meant that at least one thousand had disappeared. It might, indeed, have seemed a 'Don Quixote expedition' as his enemies were fond of calling his army, if he had headed straight for England. On the other hand, Charles knew that delay would only make his enemy stronger. As one Hanoverian volunteer, James Ray, was to write, 'happy it was for us that they stay'd so long with their Friends at Edinburgh; for had the Rebels, flush'd with Victory follow'd their Blow, whilst the Hearts of his Majesty's Subjects were dismay'd by General Cope's Defeat, and very few disciplin'd Troops in England, it is hard to say what would have been the consequence.'

The question of whether to go south came up again at the first meeting of Charles's newly-constituted Council. This now consisted of the grandees – the Duke of Perth, Lord George Murray, Lord Elcho, Lord Ogilvy, Lord Pitsligo, Lord Nairne, Lord Lewis Gordon; the chiefs – Lochiel, Keppoch, Clanranald, Glencoe, Lochgarry, Ardshiel; and Charles's inner circle of Sheridan, O'Sullivan and Murray of Broughton with the devoted, elderly Glenbucket. This unwieldy group met every day in Charles's drawing-room at Holyrood to deal with everything from major strategy to points of detail about how to govern Edinburgh.

The unfortunate dynamics within the Council were soon obvious, particularly the distrust between the Scots and the Irish. The Scots disliked the Irish contingent whom they viewed as adventurers along for the ride and, unlike the 'people of fashion', with nothing much to lose and able to cheat the gallows by claiming

French citizenship. They also saw them as a bunch of 'yes men'. Elcho later recalled how 'there was one-third of the Council whose principles were that Kings and Princes can never either act or think wrong, so, in consequence, they always confirmed whatever the Prince said.' An even more serious problem was Charles's growing dislike of Lord George Murray who was probably his most competent adviser and who was certainly not a believer in the infallibility of princes. The flames of this dislike were assiduously fanned by Secretary Murray, who saw Lord George as a threat and a rival.

It was to this diverse group riven by 'dissension and animosity' that Charles explained his passionate conviction that they must move quickly. His strong instinct was to attack General Wade at Newcastle where he was waiting to block off a Jacobite invasion. A second victory against Government forces would do immense harm to the Hanoverian's credibility and encourage Jacobite supporters to come out openly in support. However, the majority of the Council were against such a scheme and Charles yielded. He was subsequently criticised for this in the light of hindsight, but as the shrewd James Maxwell of Kirkconnell, who joined him in Edinburgh, observed, 'what would have been said of such an attempt had it miscarried?'

Charles settled into a routine during those weeks of waiting. He divided his time between Edinburgh and Duddingston where the bulk of the army was camped. Holyrood House saw a brief reflowering of its once dazzling court. 'There were every day, from morning till night, a vast affluence of well-dressed people. Besides the gentlemen that had joined or come upon business, or to pay their court, there were a great number of ladies and gentlemen that came either out of affection or curiosity, besides the desire of seeing the Prince. There had not been a Court in Scotland for a long time, and people came from all quarters to see so many novelties. One would have thought the King was already restored, and in peaceable possession of all the dominions of his ancestors, and that the Prince had only made a trip to Scotland to show himself to the people and receive their homage.'

Government spies were as active here as they'd been in Rome. One of these painted an interesting picture of Charles to his masters describing how he was 'always in a highland habit, as are all about him. When I saw him, he had a short Highland plaid waistcoat; breeches of the same; a blue garter on, and a St Andrew's cross, hanging by a green ribbon, at his button-hole, but no star. He had his boots on, *as he always has*.' The same spy noted that Charles practised 'all the arts of condescension and popularity', talking familiarly to the meanest Highlanders and making them 'very fair promises'.

It was not actually true that Charles always wore the Highland dress. Sometimes he took care to appear in 'a habit of fine silk tartan, (with crimson velvet breeches), and at other times in an English court dress, with the blue ribbon, star, and other ensigns of the Order of the Garter'. It was all carefully calculated to make the right impact. A later commentator wrote that as Charles moved to the sound of Scottish airs through the halls of his fore-fathers, 'an hundred of whom looked down upon him from the walls, that effect must have been something altogether bewilder-ingly delightful and ecstatic'.

Amidst all the splendour and magnificence Charles had a relent-less round of engagements. Every morning there was the Council meeting. After this Charles dined with his principal officers in public 'where there was always a Crowd of all sorts of people to See him dine'. After dinner he rode out attended by his life guards and reviewed his army. Again 'there was always a great number of Spectators in Coaches and on horseback'. After the review he returned to the Holyrood where he received the ladies of fashion in his drawing-room. Later, he supped in public and 'Generally there was music at Supper and a ball afterwards.'

However, Charles remained reflective in the middle of these gaieties. He knew the value of wooing the public but he was preoccupied with the task ahead. He managed to marry the two by making noble and lofty-sounding statements. When asked why he did not dance he made the grand reply, 'I like dancing, and am very glad to see the Ladies and you divert yourselves, but I have now another Air to dance and until that be finished I'll dance no other.' These words made a great impression and were repeated with admiration. Those closer to him were also impressed with his single-mindedness. O'Sullivan remarked that it was strange that a Prince of that age who had a passion for dancing and fowling never thought of any pleasures and was as retired as a man of sixty! Charles still showed no interest in women. When it was pointed out that the ladies of Edinburgh were at his feet he replied that frankly he would rather be with his brave Highlanders! 'These are my beauties,' he is supposed to have exclaimed pointing to a bearded Highland sentry.

He was probably more comfortable during the times he spent at the camp. Here there was a sense of martial purpose. Lord Elcho observed rather snootily that Charles often slept in the camp and 'never Strip'd'. However, even here he was not immune from the onlookers. Admirers and critics went to observe him. Mrs Hepburn, a Whig, wrote an enthusiatic account to a Miss Pringle about her visit to Duddingston. She described how Charles was sitting in his tent when she first arrived. The ladies made a circle around it and 'after we had Gaz'd our fill at him he came out of the Tent with a Grace and majesty that is unexpressible. He saluted all the Circle with an air of Grandeur and affability capable of charming the most obstinate Whig, and mounting his horse which was in the middle of the circle he rode off to view the men.'

He was the epitome of grace and nobility, dressed to kill in 'a blue Grogram coat trimm'd with Gold Lace and a lac'd Red Waistcoat and Breeches: on his left Shoulder and Side were the Star and Garter and over his Right Shoulder a very rich Broadsword Belt, his sword had the finest wrought Basket hilt ever I beheld all silver: His Hat had a white feather in't and a White Cockade and was trim'd with open gold Lace: his Horse furniture was green velvet and gold, the horse was black and finely Bred', and the lady noted that it had been 'poor Gardner's'.

She saw all the danger of such a young and charismatic figure, conceding that Charles 'in all his appearance . . . seems to be cut out for enchanting his beholders and carrying People to consent to their own slavery in spite of themselves. I don't believe Caesar was more engagingly form'd nor more dangerous to the Liberties of his Country than this Chap may be if he sets about it.' Mrs Hepburn also observed shrewdly that 'he will make a great noise and be much spoke of whether he win or lose. . . . Poor Man! I wish he may escape with his life. I've no notion he'll succeed.' So here was the fairytale in the making, the handsome young Prince born to charm but destined to waste himself in a doomed cause.

Charles added to his mystic appeal by apparently reviving the custom of 'touching for the King's evil', whereby the King's touch was supposed to cure this skin disease otherwise known as scrofula. Queen Anne had been the last monarch to carry out the ceremony and the Jacobites claimed that the usurping Hanoverians dare not 'lest they should betray their want of the real Royal character'. Charles now conducted the ceremony in the Picture Gallery at Holyrood. A little girl was brought to him and he 'approached the kneeling girl, and, with great apparent solemnity, touched the sores occasioned by the disease, pronouncing, at every different application, the words, "I touch, but God heal!"'. According to the tales precisely twenty-one days later the child was cured and she became an object of veneration to the Jacobites who no more doubted the efficacy of Charles's touch than his right to the throne.

Yet the pageant of life at Holyrood was just a passing phase to Charles. What mattered was attracting sufficient support to enable him to push on into England. Five days after Preston Pans he had despatched George Kelly to Versailles to tell Louis of the victory and to ask again for help. In fact help was already on its way before Kelly reached the French court. As a result of Antoine Walsh's lobbying, four small ships had sailed for Scotland at the end of September bringing volunteers and arms. The very day before the news of Preston Pans reached Louis he had ordered Lord John Drummond, the Duke of Perth's brother, to Scotland, with his Royal Scots Regiment amounting to one thousand men 'full of zeal and desire of shedding the last drop of their blood' and certainly well-armed and drilled.

Charles still hoped for a large-scale invasion. He had not forgotten the heady excitement and subsequent despair of those weeks at Gravelines. His spirits were lifted by the arrival in mid-October of an ambassador from Louis in the form of Monsieur du Boyer, Marquis d'Eguilles, aboard one of those four small ships. He interpreted this as a sure sign of Louis's good faith and exploited it to convince sceptics like Lord George Murray that the French would stand by him. D'Eguilles was 'vastly well received by the Prince and treated by every body with a Great deal of respect' as the 'French ambassador to his court'. The letters he brought from Louis were never shown to the Council but it was given out that Charles's brother was at Paris and was shortly to embark with a large French invasion force. These claims were to be the source of bitterness and accusations when the help failed to materialise but for the moment they buoyed up the Jacobites' spirits 'as they expected to hear of a French Landing daily'.

Charles had also been trying to rally support in Scotland. Macleod and Sir Alexander Macdonald received dulcet despatches assuring them that he perfectly understood their earlier unwillingness to commit themselves but suggesting that now he had beaten Cope they might like to join him. They did not. He also wrote to other powerful leaders like the Earls of Sutherland and Cromarty, Lords Reay and Fortrose and the chief of the Grants.

While he waited on these grandees his success elsewhere was mixed. In October Arthur Elphinstone, shortly to become Lord Balmerino, joined together with Lord Kilmarnock and Lord Nithsdale. So did Viscount Kenmure — briefly. Charles received Kenmure very graciously and dined with him, but the next morning he was gone. Murray of Broughton received a 'triffling letter' from his wife excusing Kenmure from joining Charles on the grounds that he was the only son left and if anything were to befall him asking what would happen to her and her child — his father had been executed at the end of the '15. Murray was exasperated at this sign of 'instability and weakness'.

Such nervousness was contagious. Lord Nithsdale, who had also dined with Charles that night, 'after he retired home from the palace was Struck with such panick and Sincere repentance of his rashness that he was confined to bed for some days ... where nothing but the most dreadful scene of Axes, Gibbets and halters presented themselves to his waking thoughts'. His father had been sentenced to death in 1715 but had escaped from the Tower, assisted by his mother who employed the standard device of dressing him in women's clothing. He too decided on a path of discretion rather than valour but not, as in Kenmure's case, with the agreement of his wife! Lady Nithsdale was 'so much ashamed of the pusilanimity of her husband that she Scorned to accompany him, but Stay'd in town, quite ashamed of his Cowardice. . . .'

Lord Kilmarnock remained loyal – the result of crippling debts and a fervently pro-Stuart wife as much as anything else. He was one of the few Lowland noblemen to join and soon received a rude reminder of how things had changed in the Lowlands since his father had rallied his people in the 1715 rebellion. His father had not had 'the slightest difficulty in raising a large regiment among his tenants and dependents, all of whom were at once willing to attend their baronial master'. By 1745, however, they were 'making fortunes by the manufacture of nightcaps, and had got different lights regarding feudal servitude'. All Kilmarnock apparently got out of them were some rusty old weapons.

Luckily there was some more solid support for Charles. Lord Elcho described how after Preston Pans 'a great many people of fashion joined the army'. For example, Lord Ogilvy now brought in some three hundred men. Old Glenbucket managed to rally a further three hundred clansmen from the north-east. Mackinnon of Mackinnon brought one hundred and twenty from Skye. True to his word the previously reluctant Macpherson of Cluny who was 'greatly beloved by his Clan' was able to raise three hundred fighters, while Lord Lewis Gordon, younger brother of the Duke of Gordon and reputedly 'more than a little mad', had gone north to raise the followers of his family. There were also encouraging accounts that the Frasers and Mackintoshes were in arms and ready to join the Prince; the former had been reluctantly raised by Lord Lovat's eldest son on his father's Machiavellian orders, and the latter by the twenty-two-year-old Lady Mackintosh, whose husband, chief of that name, was actually in the service of the Government.

Lady Mackintosh – or *la belle rebelle* or 'Colonel Anne' as she was variously known – was a remarkable young woman. An admirer wrote that 'it was through the influence of this heroine, endowed with [the] spirit and vigour of our sex, and all the charms and graces of her own, that the Mackintoshes took arms, not only without the countenance of their chief, a thing very rare among the Highlanders, but what is perhaps without example, against him.'

But it was a slow and frustrating process during those weeks in

Edinburgh. So many had deserted and showed no sign of wishing to return. The Jacobite Duke of Atholl, William, was trying without success to rally his men. Lord George Murray urged him to take desperate measures. 'For God's sake cause some effectual method to be taken about the deserters; I would have their houses and crop destroyed for an example to others, and themselves punished in the most rigorous manner.' Burning out was quite a common technique and even the 'gentle' Lochiel had threatened his Camerons with it. However, a Government official, Commissary Bissatt, snug in Stirling Castle, was able to report to the rival Duke James that 'The men are turn'd intirely obstreperous and . . . very Few will rise for him.'

However, the cavalry was taking shape under five leaders. Sixty-seven-year-old Lord Pitsligo arrived in Edinburgh with a contingent of horse and foot from Aberdeen and Banffshire. He was a 'little thin fair man' of a scholarly frame of mind but 'a worthy virtuous gent' known both for his courage and his humanity. Nobody doubted his sincerity when, setting out with his cavalry, he said simply 'O Lord thou knowest our cause is just. March gentlemen.' The much handsomer Lord Kilmarnock commanded the horse grenadiers. Murray of Broughton had his 'hussars' smart in plaid waistcoats and fur caps, while Lord Elcho was allowed to raise a very handsome company of Lifeguards composed of 'gentlemen of family and fortune'. As to be expected of this fashionable young man they made quite a splash in their uniforms of red and blue and were 'all extremely well mounted'. He would have been much affronted at a Whig allegation that they were just a rabble of men 'such as had no character to lose'. The fifth cavalry leader, Balmerino, was given the troop originally destined for the craven – or perhaps prudent – Kenmure.

Gradually the Jacobite force grew to some five thousand foot and five hundred horse. Yet despite this progress there was a long-running sore in Edinburgh. The Jacobites had failed to take the castle so that, while Charles was master in Holyrood, it could not be claimed that he had total mastery of the city. Two old Hanoverians, General Joshua Guest, aged eighty-five, and the bellicose fire eater General George Preston, aged eighty-six and scarcely able to walk, were sitting tight and firing at will on the city. Preston kept his guards on their toes by conducting regular inspections in his wheelchair. On 29 September Charles decided that he must bring this situation to an end and ordered a blockade. He was not prepared for the robust and unchivalrous response. Guest wrote to the Provost 'in a very blustering military Style, intimating that did the highlanders Continue to obstruct the Communication betwixt the City and the Garrison, he would ... be obliged to Cannonade the Town.'

He proved as good as his word, raining down cannon-balls – one of which can still be seen today in the side of a house – and killing and wounding a number of people. The streets were thick with bullets. Raiding parties stormed out of the castle and burned down nearby houses. This caused panic among the citizens who 'made the most hideous complaints against the garrison' and Charles, as a civilised man, had no option but to desist, leaving the castle to continue its mischief firing on the Highlanders. However, it taught him a valuable lesson for the future – that citadel as well as city must be captured.

Charles won the citizens' gratitude for his gentlemanly behaviour over the castle, but his measures to raise money were less popular in Edinburgh and the other Lowland cities. He levied taxes and customs in Edinburgh and asked the city for six thousand pairs of shoes, a thousand tents and a whole mass of other articles for his troops. Glasgow was asked to fork out fifteen thousand pounds – a sum later reduced to five thousand following vociferous complaints, but in Murray's view 'a very triffle to so rich a place'. Unfortunately, the town preferred to keep its money to raise troops to fight against Charles!

Despite these measures Charles remained very short of money and his enemies made propaganda out of it. Cope was told a story of two officers 'who chanced to be a little mellow, and in the most reproachful manner demanded arrears of their pay, which, as they said, were in arrears altogether except two guineas. He, [Charles] with sugared words, flattered them out, and then exclaimed, "Good God! what a slavery to have to do with these fellows!"' The story may be false but the problem was real enough.

As far as Charles was concerned things could not go on as they were. England, not Scotland, was his objective and he was in a fever of impatience to march south. There was no point waiting for further reinforcements either from France or the clans if every day his existing troops were deserting, bored by the enforced inactivity and suffering from his dwindling resources. On 30 October – while England was celebrating George II's birthday – he provoked a debate in the Council. Many of the chiefs showed their reluctance to leave Scotland at all. They said that 'they had taken arms and risked their fortunes and lives, merely to set him on the throne of Scotland; but that they wished to have nothing to do with England.' He had declared the Union at an end so why not just sit tight and force the Hanoverians to take the initiative? Charles explained why not. He had come to reclaim the crown of his ancestors not to hive off a single realm. According to Lord Elcho he was pretty blunt: 'I find, Gentlemen you are for Staying in Scotland and defending Your Country, and I am resolved to Go to England.'

The Scots in the Council were unhappy. It seemed to them that Charles 'was preoccupied only with England'. It was galling that 'he seemed little flattered with the idea of possessing a kingdom to which, however, the family of Stuart owes its origin and its royalty.' In the end, though, Charles won his point and the debate turned into a wrangle less about whether to invade England than about which route to take. Charles wanted to march for Newcastle and attack General Wade whose forces amounted to little more than the Jacobites. Lord George Murray pointed out that Wade was a wily and experienced old soldier and that the Jacobites would arrive exhausted by the long march and unfit for immediate battle. He proposed a compromise. Why not make for Cumbria which was mountainous and good fighting country for High-landers? Furthermore, the army would be well-placed to receive replacements from Scotland and to join up with the French when they landed. They would also be able to attract the large numbers of English Jacobites assumed (wrongly) to exist in the north-west of England. Charles was unhappy – it could look as if he was trying to avoid Wade.

The Council adjourned with the issue still unresolved. According to Secretary Murray, as soon as Charles had retired to his cham-bers he began to reflect that since most if not all the chiefs were for marching to Carlisle, forcing them to do the contrary would be unwise. He told them so the next morning and 'this condescention on his part, made in so obliging a manner, and as if proceeding from the Superior strength of their arguments seemed to give great contentment.' The Council agreed on a stratagem to deceive the enemy. This was that the army should divide for a time, with one column moving south-east towards Kelso to mislead Wade into believing that they were indeed marching for Northumbria.

On 1 November the Jacobite army marched out to seek its destiny. Of all the uncertainties that lay ahead the greatest was how the English would react. It was soon to become clear that Charles had grievously misunderstood the position. He was never to see Edinburgh again. For once that 'little ignorant school master' Henderson was spot on in his observations. 'Whom had he of the English Nation, or whom of the best part of the Scots?' he asked complacently,' . . . for now the Country is civilised: instead of being Soldiers, the People are Merchants and Traders. . . .' To many of the English Charles was an anachronism. They wanted peace and prosperity, not heroics, and they certainly did not want the 'handful of savages' following in his wake.

CHAPTER SEVEN

'WILD PETTICOAT MEN'

ENGLAND had become complacent again in the lull after Preston Pans. The Highlanders seemed a bit of a joke while they stayed north of the border. It was safe enough to mock them as in the raucous procession that wound through the streets of Deptford as part of George's birthday celebrations. This included 'a highlander in his proper dress carrying on a pole a pair of wooden shoes with this motto, *The Newest make from Paris*, a Jesuit, in his proper dress, carrying on the point of a long sword, a banner, with this Inscription in large letters "Inquisition, Flames and Damnation", two Capuchin friars properly shaved, habited and accoutred with flogging ropes, beads, crucifixes etc . . .', selling indulgences 'cheap as dirt, viz. murder, 9d. Adultery, 91/2d. Reading the bible, 1000£. Fornication, 43/4d . . . , and the Pretender, with a green ribband a nosegay of Thistle etc. riding upon an ass, supported by a Frenchmen on the right and a Spaniard on the left, each dressed to the height of the newest modes'. This exhilarating spectacle concluded with grand fireworks and a spirited rendering of 'God save the King'.

Horace Walpole took a similarly light-hearted not to say satirical view of things, fantasizing that 'The Dowager Strafford has already written cards for my Lady Nithsdale, my Lady Tullibardine, the Duchesses of Perth and Berwick and twenty more revived peeresses to invite them to play at whist, Monday three months' to celebrate a Restoration.' The chances of a real Restoration were seen as so remote as to be ridiculous.

Such levity had seemed a little premature when the news of Preston Pans broke. So did confidence in George's ability to keep the Popish threat at bay. The English Jacobites were an unknown quantity and much would depend on their reaction. Immediately after Preston Pans, John Hickson, the proprietor of the inn where Charles had stayed in Perth, was the slightly unlikely choice to be sent to tell them of 'the wonderful success with which it has hitherto pleased God to favour my endeavours for their deliverance', and to give them the glad tidings that 'it is my full intention, in a few days to move towards them, and that they will be inexcusable before God and man if they do not all in their power to assist me in such an undertaking.' However, Hickson was arrested at Newcastle and the Prince's letter was found concealed in his glove. He attempted suicide unsucessfully and subsequently turned King's evidence.

Charles remained convinced that a great body '. . . would join him upon his entering their Country', but the fact of the matter was that many were seduced by appeals in the Whig Press inviting them to consider whether it was 'worth fighting to change the name from George to James'. Even if the Hanoverians were not particularly popular, the economy was prospering. Most of the population were at best neutral towards the Jacobites, fearing the uncertainties and disruption that a change of king would bring.

The Jacobite army divided as planned. The main column under Lord George Murray, with the cannon and heavy baggage, went by Peebles and Moffat. The reaction of the Lowland Scots of Peebles was a taste of things to come in England. ' "There's the Hielantmen! There's the Hielantmen!" burst from every mouth, and was communicated like wildfire through the town; while the careful merchant took another look at the cellar in which he had concealed his goods, and the anxious mother clasped her infant more closely to her beating bosom.'

Charles led the second column composed of Elcho's Lifeguards and the clan regiments, making the agreed feint to Lauder and Kelso before veering off to Jedburgh where yet again he made a great impression on the ladies. It was quite a sight as the Lifeguards trotted by in their red and blue uniforms. The chieftains too looked magnificent, armed in the Highland fashion and fairly bristling with muskets, broadswords, silver-handled pistols, dirks tucked in their belts, targets of wood and leather studded with nails and with yet another dagger stuck in the garter of the right leg. They were quite a contrast to 'the undistinguished warriors of the rear ranks . . . in general armed in a much inferior manner, many of them wanting targets.'

As before Charles marched on foot, but it was nearly winter now and the lanes were dirty and the snow was deep. His endurance won him the admiration of the clans. People thought he would only walk for a mile or two to encourage the soldiers. They were amazed to see him continue all day, every day, setting a furious pace. 'It's not to be imagined how much this manner of bringing himself down to a level with the men, and his affable behaviour to the meanest of them, endeared him to the army,' wrote one of his admirers. Charles also rode back to encourage and round up stragglers.

On 6 November the force crossed the Tweed, apparently amid scenes of wild elation. The river was scarcely fordable but the story goes that the Highlanders plunged into the icy water 'expressing their delight by discharging their pieces and uttering cries of joy. Such was their humour, that they gave the horses which were taken from the enemy the name of General Cope, by way of expressing their contempt for the fugitive Englishman.'

On 8 November, Charles's column crossed the Esk. Murray of Broughton described a more subdued scene: '. . . the Highlanders without any orders given, all drew their Swords with one Consent upon entering the River, and every man as he landed on t'other side wheeld about to the left and faced Scotland again.' It was a poignant moment for them as they left their native land. According to one tale Lochiel drew his sword as he trod on English soil and cut his hand. It was seen as a bad omen. But if the Scots were dubious about what awaited them so was the local populace. According to young Lord Elcho, 'The people in England seemed mightily afraid of the army and had abanbon'd all the villages upon its approach.' The young sophisticate was startled by the story of one old woman in a house where some officers were quartered. After they had supped she apparently said to them, 'Gentlemen, I Suppose You have done with Your murdering today, I should be Glad to know when the ravishing begins.'

Ironically, it was in Edinburgh that barbarity had broken out. Murray of Broughton described indignantly how, no sooner had the Highlanders left, than the garrison fell upon the town 'like a parcel of hungry dogs, and without any Command or the least shew of order, discipline or humanity, ran into every house where either Soldier or officer had quartered, and pillaged, and destroy'd what they could not carry off, abused the poor house keepers where ever the highlanders had been quartered, and treated some of those that were left wounded in the most barbarous manner imaginable'. One poor man was dragged downstairs by his heels, his head striking every step and along the pavement until he died. But Murray added rather piously that he did not care to dwell on too many instances of this kind of behaviour for fear of appearing to complain too much.

However, the Jacobite army knew nothing of this as they marched south into England. On 9 November the two columns joined up again 'upon a vast heathery common in England, distant about a quarter of a league from Carlisle'. They had no idea what to expect from this border town. Matters were not helped the next day by a fog so dense that a man was hard put to it to see his horse's ears. The Duke of Perth together with O'Sullivan and some of the Atholl men penetrated the mist to within a pistol shot of the ancient walls. The fortifications looked strong but the reality was that the walls were crumbling away and the castle's cannon obsolete. The small garrison within its walls was composed of a company of eighty elderly men and several equally decrepit gunners under their gouty commander, Captain Durand. Durand was already anxious – the only other force under his command were the five hundred amateurs of the Cumberland and Westmorland Militia. As far as he knew General Wade and his regulars were still in Newcastle and unable to reach him in time.

Carlisle was 'a wealthy populous Place' as far as any English town apart from London and Bristol was populous at the time. The entire population of England and Wales was only seven million, with ten per cent of those living in the capital. Carlisle was noted for its neatly-paved streets and well-built houses. Perhaps Captain Durand took comfort from its reputation in times past as a bulwark against the Scots. The townspeople had their first good look at the Scots on Martinmas Saturday when fifty or sixty of Charles's cavalry rode in and coolly surveyed the town. The streets thronged with folk who had come in from the surrounding country and stared at the Jacobite horsemen, unsure what to make of it all. The clergy kept watch from their eyrie in the Cathedral tower.

The next day Charles sent a message to the town. His messenger was rather an unlikely character – a Mr Robinson who claimed he had been coerced. Charles called on the citizens to open the gates to him 'to avoid the effusion of blood' and the usual dreadful consequences for a town taken by force. The ultimatum was immediately taken to the Governor, the officers of the militia and the magistrates who agreed that no answer should be sent. When news came that the Jacobite army was moving off towards Brampton, some seven miles east of Carlisle they congratulated themselves on their firm stand. The acting Mayor, Alderman Thomas Pattinson, wrote a crowing letter to Lord Lonsdale claiming that: 'I told your Lordship that we would defend this city; its proving true gives me pleasure, and more so since we have outdone Edinburgh, nay, all Scotland.'

They had not. Charles had marched off to Brampton fired by the news that Wade was heading west from Newcastle with the express purpose of doing battle with him. But he had not forgotten Carlisle and the fact that the citizens had refused to open their gates to their rightful prince. When it became clear that Wade was not, after all, on his way but had been beaten back by thick snow, the siege began in earnest. It was surprisingly short-lived. Murray of Broughton described how trenches were dug and cannon brought up to batter the town walls more in hope than expectation. However, '. . . the dread the inhabitants had of a Siege, together with the Cowardice of the militia, made them hang out a white flag' on the evening of 14 November. What had clinched it was a message from Wade that he could do nothing to help them. Despite Durand's best efforts there had been mass panic with people climbing over the walls or forcing their way through the gates.

Pattinson and other civic dignitaries arrived to discuss surrender terms, wondering, perhaps, how they would explain this volte-face to Lord Lonsdale. At first they tried to bargain that Charles could have the town but not the castle, but after their experiences in Edinburgh the Jacobites knew better. After 'a good deal of reasoning on both Sides, it was agreed that the Castle Should be given up alongst with the Town'. The keys were then delivered up to Charles at Brampton by the Mayor and Corporation on their knees, but he returned them in 'a very obliging manner' assuring the citizens of his future favour and protection. So Carlisle was taken more easily than anyone had envisaged. The only Jacobite casualties had been one soldier and one officer. The officer – an Irishman named Dalton – had been rash enough to jump out of the trenches and jeer at the defenders who promptly shot him through the throat. Charles took possession of his first English prize on 17 November, riding into Carlisle on a white horse and preceded by a hundred pipers. But the watching crowd was sullen and unresponsive. Many stayed indoors, terrified about what was going to happen and expecting excesses of all kinds.

Murray of Broughton was taken aback by their lurid fears of child murder and cannibalism. 'To show how incredibly ignorant the Country people of England are, and industrious the friends of the Government were to impose upon their ignorance and credulity, in the little house where the Chevalier was quarterd after he had been for above an hour in the Room, some of the gentlemen who attended him heard a rustling below the bed, and upon Searching they found a little girl of five or six years old. The mother coming into the room to fetch something, seeing the Child discovered, called out for God's sake to Spare her Child, for She was the only remaining one of Seven she had bore. Upon which some of the gentlemen being curious to know what She meant, followed to the door and enquired what made her express herself in that manner. To which she answered that indeed She had been assured from Creditable people that the highlanders were a Savage Sett of people and eat all the young Children.'

The same terrors emerged at the christening of the Bishop of Carlisle's grandchild. Some Highlanders stumbled in on the ceremony and the family servants pleaded with them not to harm the baby. It was dealt with in a masterly way by Captain Macdonald. Hiding his astonishment at the idea that they would hurt a new-born infant he gravely gave them a white cockade to put in the baby's cap to protect her. The cockade was preserved with almost religious care and produced for the inspection of George IV when he visited Edinburgh seventy-six years later and met the old lady whose christening it had been.

Henry Fielding did not dwell on allegations of child-eating in the *True Patriot* but he invented other salacious tales to shock his readers, asserting that 'Our Accounts from Carlisle take Notice of the many detestable and shocking Villanies of the Highlanders during their Possession of that City, for not content with stripping several Families of all their valuable Effects, they scrupled not to make free with the Persons of several young Ladies there. . . .' He goes on with relish to describe how one poor man, having been stripped of everything, had the 'Misery to see his three Daughters treated in such a manner that he could not bear to relate it.' What, Fielding asked, did not this wicked Crew deserve?

The *London Gazette* picked up the refrain of wicked Highlanders looting and pillaging and spoiling. There was widespread disgust at the idea of these 'wild petticoat men' – 'the Southron [Englishmen] could see nothing but disgust, and express nothing but indignation, at having his domestic comfort invaded by a troop of persons whose manners were repugnant to him, and who so seriously injured his fortune.' But the reality was different. Charles and his chiefs were scrupulous about stopping looting and kept 'the most exact discipline in his army, paying for every individual thing they got'. They were largely successful in keeping order. A curate described with satisfaction how on finding that attempts had been made to force the door of the wine-vault belonging to his patron, Dr Waugh, he 'clap'd two more padlocks on the outside and was satisfied that all was safe within'. These measures would hardly have been adequate in the face of wholesale pillaging.

Murray of Broughton was quick to refute the 'false and Scurrilous accusation' that the Jacobites levied exorbitant sums from the towns they passed through. He wrote angrily that 'let it suffice here for once for all to say that the moneys said to have been levied at the different places, as well as here at Carlisle, are without foundation, save the public moneys due and such as shall be here mentioned, which at this place did not in whole amount to above

£60 pound, and not much above one hundred in most of the other places. . . .'

The unfortunate garrison at Carlisle came in for vitriol from all sides. The Whig papers expressed universal contempt for the fact that Carlisle had given in 'merely through Fear'. In London the centrepiece of the table at the christening of George II's baby grandson was 'the citadel of Carlisle in sugar . . . and the company, (which included Frederick Prince of Wales), besieged it with sugar plums'. The Jacobites were similarly scathing. Murray of Broughton noted that the defenders could have baffled all the Chevalier's efforts. A song described their feelings nicely:

> O Pattinson! ohon! ohon!
> Thou wonder of a mayor!
> Thou blest thy lot thou wert no Scot,
> And bluster'd like a player.
> What hast thou done with sword or gun,
> To baffle the Pretender?
> Of mouldy cheese and bacon grease,
> Thou art more fit defender!

Charles lodged in the house of a Mr Highmore, but there was no Highland hospitality here. True to his principles he paid twenty guineas rent but his lawyer landlord gave him not so much as a lump of coal or a candle. This domestic parsimony was symptomatic of the lack of enthusiasm for his cause. There had been no sign of the spontaneous rising Charles had so confidently expected on setting foot on English soil, merely 'sour faces' as the white cockades had flashed through hamlets and villages. Charles had expected his mere presence to be enough and had not been unduly concerned that his various attempts to communicate with the Jacobite leaders of England and Wales had so far failed.

He pinned all his hopes on the fact that in 1743–4 Lord Barrymore, Sir John Hynde Cotton and Sir Watkin Williams Wynn, the secret leaders of the Jacobite faction south of the border, had pledged themselves to bring levies to support Marshall Saxe's French invasion force. Charles still expected them to raise forces even though he was without that vital foreign support. His hopes were not entirely misplaced. On hearing of Charles's landing the three plotters had sent urgent messages to the French Court, arguing 'loudly and vehemently for a body of troops to be landed near London as the most effectual means to support the prince'. But that, as the Scots had suspected all along, was as far as their zeal went. Nothing would induce them to move without that support.

On closer inspection they were not the stuff of heroes. Like so many of those on whom Charles was relying, they were men whose heyday was past. Lord Barrymore was seventy-eight. He had been arrested as a spy during the 1743-4 invasion scare but released after a telling address to his inquisitors: 'I have, my lords, a very good estate in Ireland, and on that, I believe fifteen hundred acres of very bad land; now by God I would not risk the loss of the poorest acre of them to defend the title of any king in Europe . . .' Charles wrote to him just before the fall of Carlisle with the stern words that 'now is the time or never' and asked him to rally supporters to join him in Cheshire. The letter was delivered by mistake to Barrymore's son, a Hanoverian, and never reached him, but it might well have made no difference if it had.

Cotton was fifty-seven years old at the time of the '45 and was certainly not the stuff of heroes. He was 'one of the tallest, biggest, fattest men I have ever seen . . .' and supposed to be able to 'drink as much wine as any man in England. . . .' Sir Watkin Williams Wynn was in his early fifties and the most powerful landowner in Wales. However, his caution was as great as his wealth and he was determined not to make a move without French help. If, however, Charles would come to him in Wales he would certainly join him, he said. Charles had no intention of going to Wales.

What he wanted was to press further into England and as quickly as possible. Any delay would only benefit his enemies. It was obvious that they had been woefully unprepared to meet the Jacobite threat but they were now working feverishly to build up their forces. As well as despatching Marshal Wade northwards, the Government had recalled its troops from Flanders and they had been disembarking every day in the Thames. By the end of September seven British batallions and six thousand Dutch had landed to reinforce Wade. A second army under the command of Lieutenant-General Sir John Ligonier was sent north to intercept

Charles, and the Duke of Cumberland had arrived back from Flanders to be appointed Captain-General of the land forces. He was to take over from Ligonier, concentrating his forces around Stafford.

As Fielding had been urging, England was waking up. So were the pro-Government factions in Scotland. Edinburgh, Glasgow and Stirling were raising volunteers to fight with the Government and Gardiner's and Hamilton's Dragoons were back in Edinburgh. Lord Loudon had returned to Scotland after his ignominious flight in the wake of Preston Pans. Since mid-October he had been in command at Inverness, drilling the levies that Duncan Forbes had been diligently raising.

In this situation, with no sign of the English Jacobites, no sign of the French, and the growing military strength of his enemies, Charles must have known it would be difficult to bend his Council to his will. Many of the Scots had never wanted to come south of the border and they were not deceived by the ease of the capture of Carlisle. It had fallen but in the same way as a rotten plum at the first shake of the tree. If it was a victory where were the promised scenes of jublilation at the return of a lawful prince come to release his people from the yoke of oppression? Instead, they had found a people whose chief preoccupation was trade, whose chief interest was in political stability and whose chief fear was of them, the supposed liberators.

Charles's task was complicated further because he had fallen out badly with Lord George Murray. Charles had allowed the Duke of Perth to negotiate the surrender of Carlisle and this had not gone down well with Lord George Murray who resigned his commission. He wrote a letter to Charles bristling with resentment and announced that henceforth he would simply serve as a volunteer. The problem had arisen because Murray had refused to take command at the siege of Carlisle on the grounds that he knew nothing about siege warfare. Perth on the other hand had flung himself enthusiastically into the business of digging trenches, working side by side in his shirt sleeves with his men in the thick snow. It was a dilemma for Charles who had never liked Lord George but was only too aware of his influence over the clans. Murray may have been conceited but he was highly competent as a soldier in an army where military expertise was limited. He 'thought himself the fittest man in the army to be at the head of it; and he was not the only person that thought so. Had it been left to the gentlemen of the army to choose a general, Lord George would have carried it by vast odds against the Duke of Perth.'

So Charles was finding himself isolated. His judgement was also questioned for allowing Perth, as a Catholic, to receive the surrender of the Protestant city. This could only fuel popular hysteria about Charles being the puppet of the Pope. The Whig press was full of lurid reminders of the burnings of Protestants at Smithfield in Mary Tudor's reign, and gruesome speculaton about what the Inquisition would do once they had their blood-stained hands around England's throat.

The Duke of Perth, 'much beloved and esteemed', had the sense to see that he held the key to the problem. He maintained, probably quite truthfully, that 'he never had any thing in view but the Prince's interest, and would cheerfully sacrifice anything to it'. Consequently he insisted on being allowed to give up his command and was put in charge of the rearguard and the baggage. This left the field clear for Lord George Murray. Charles was forced to ask him to withdraw his resignation, but this spat left a bitter aftertaste. When Charles put his plans to the Council for continuing into England he found the Scots ranged against him. He needed a rabbit to pull out of the hat, and he had one – the Marquis d'Eguilles who was accompanying the Jacobite army as an observer. Asked to reveal his instructions from Louis, the Frenchman made it clear that Louis wanted to know the strength of English Jacobite support for Charles before fully committing France. This could only be achieved by marching on. Lord George had to agree but he was reluctant. All his instincts were for returning to Scotland and consolidating their position there. Charles, by contrast, was buoyed up, firmly believing in his destiny. He had hitherto had 'a wonderful run of success. He had great hopes of a French army landing, and of an insurrection in his favour'.

There were good reasons for agreeing to Charles's plans apart from his innate optimism and the blandishments of d'Eguilles. As Murray of Broughton explained: 'To have laid there any longer would have been both idle and dangerous; idle, having no prospect of a junction from his friends in those parts, and from the disposition that at that time seem'd to be formed by the Enemy, he must have been cooped up in that Corner by the Duke's army from the South. Mr Wade at Newcastle, and the 2 Regiments with the foot detached to Scotland on his left, so to prevent a junction of the D. and Mr Wade's armies, his only proper method was to march forward, that in case he came to action he might only have one army to deal with. . . .' It was decided to make for London on the Lancashire road but first the army needed to be reviewed.

This review revealed that the force was now reduced to some four thousand four hundred men. Two or three hundred were to be left behind to garrison Carlisle and about as many had deserted since the army had marched from Edinburgh. The smallness of the force was a worry, so was the question of how to cater for it. Loss of the tents on the way to the border meant that the men would have to be billeted each night in a town. It was bitterly cold now and not even the hardy Highlanders in their plaids would find it easy to survive in the open. To help with this it was agreed to advance in two columns. Lord George led the first with Elcho and his Lifeguards. Charles was to follow a day behind with the main army and the plan was to rendezvous at Preston.

Charles was glad to be on the move again, regaining the momentum of his quest. He reached Penrith on 21 November, where he lodged at the George and Dragon Inn, and made the long haul to Kendal on the 23rd. As before he led his men, marching at their head, and consciously picturesque. He was dressed in a light plaid with a blue sash and a blue bonnet on his head, decorated with a white rose. The bagpipes and drums played that stirring and much-used cavalier anthem 'The King shall enjoy his own again'. The clansmen carried banners bearing reassuring slogans about 'Liberty and Property, Church and King', but these failed to impress 'the cold spectators who beheld them with a corresponding enthusiasm'. It was physically exhausting in the snow and ice but Charles could not be persuaded to ride except when fording rivers. He was so worn out by the twenty-seven-mile slog to Kendal that he had to catch hold of the shoulder belt of one of his soldiers to stay upright. But he had a magnetic effect on some. One of the few Lancashire recruits, John Daniels, described how he felt when he first saw Charles 'the brave Prince marching on foot at their head like a Cyrus or a Trojan hero, drawing admiration and love from all those who beheld him, raising their long-dejected hearts and solacing their minds with the happy prospect of another Golden Age. Struck with this charming sight, and seeming invitation *"leave your nets and follow me"* I felt a paternal ardour pervade my veins. . . .'

Nevertheless, to Government supporters, this was no more than a rabble. Some were admittedly 'well mounted and accoutred with the Spoil of our Country . . . but for the most Part they were a very despicable Mob. . . . had it not been for the Arms they carried, it might well be thought there was a Famine in Scotland, and that they came to England to beg, but they soon undeceiv'd us letting us know they were sturdy Beggars, committing all Manner of Rapine as they ran along the Country.'

On 26 November the maligned army reached Preston – a place with an evil reputation in Highland minds. It had seen a Scottish defeat in 1648. It was also where 'the hopes of their party had been blighted in 1715, and their banners steeped in blood. The walls of Preston recalled to many of the volunteers of Lancashire the prison in which their fathers had died of fever, or starvation, or of broken hearts.' Many of those who had joined Charles were indeed the sons of those who had suffered in the '15. As a newspaper of the time observed nastily, 'Hanging is hereditary in some families.' Lord George was anxious not to let his men give in to this 'fright'. He hastily marched them through the town to the south side of the Ribble to debunk superstitious fears that a Jacobite army would never get beyond Preston.

But there was a growing spectre hanging over the little army. At every town where they stopped James was proclaimed King, but recruits remained few and far between. Some gentlemen did enlist – a Catholic Francis Townley from an old Lancashire Jacobite family and two Welshmen called Morgan and Vaughan. But only 'some few common people' joined them in Preston and not the large numbers that had confidently been expected. The sad truth was that, whatever their sentiments, people had too much to lose to want to follow Charles in his precarious quest.

Preston was a prosperous place doing very nicely out of trade in linen, yarn and cloth. Its streets were handsome, its balls and assemblies genteel and elegant. Its inns offered 'all kind of good Eatables, proper Attendance, civil Usage, and a moderate Charge; and where you may have all Things done after an elegant grand Manner, if required'. Such placid prosperity was not likely to produce revolutionaries and visionaries – especially if the risks looked high. The *True Patriot*'s warning that the Rebellion was 'putting an Entire Stop to all Trade' may have struck an ominous chord.

The army marched gamely on to Wigan but the picture stayed the same. 'The road betwixt Preston and Wigan was crowded with people standing at their doors to see the army go by, and they generally all that days march profes'd to wish the Prince's army Success, but if arms was offer'd to them and they were desir'd to Go along with the army they all declined, and Said they did not Understand fighting.'

On 29 November the Jacobites entered Manchester where surely, Charles reasoned, their fortunes would look up. After all, this was the heart of the traditionally Jacobite north-west and O'Sullivan was expecting at least fifteen hundred new recruits. In fact a bold attempt was already underway to rally support for the cause. Chevalier Johnstone described how one of his sergeants 'named Dickson, whom I had enlisted from among the prisoners of war at Gladsmuir [Preston Pans], a young Scotsman, as brave and intrepid as a lion . . . came to ask my permission to get a day's march a-head of the army, by setting out immediately for Manchester . . . in order to make sure of some recruits before the arrival of the army. . . .' Johnstone agreed and the sergeant set out with his mistress and a drummer. On his arrival in Manchester he immediately began to beat up for recruits for 'the yellow-haired laddie'. The populace was curious then angry. At first, believing the Jacobite army to be hard on the heels of the intrepid recruiter, they simply stood and gawped. Once they realised the force would not arrive till evening they mobbed Dickson, intent on capturing him dead or alive.

The Sergeant was prepared for them. He 'presented his blunderbuss, which was charged with slugs, threatening to blow out the brains of those who first dared to lay hands on himself or the two who acccompanied him, and by turning round continually, facing in all directions, and behaving like a lion, he soon enlarged the circle, which a crowd of people had formed around him. Having continued for some time to manoeuvre in this way, those of the inhabitants of Manchester who were attached to the House of Stuart, took arms, and flew to the assistance of Dickson, to rescue him from the fury of the mob; so that he had soon five or six hundred men to aid him, who dispersed the crowd in a very short time. Dickson now triumphed in his turn, and putting himself at the head of his followers, proudly paraded undisturbed the whole day with his drummer. . . .' And so, as a disgruntled Government volunteer put it, 'Manchester was taken by a Serjeant, a Drum and a Woman', but he consoled himself with the thought that the only recruits were people of the lowest rank and vilest principles.

These recruits were the kernel of the Manchester Regiment which was put under the command of Francis Townley, who was given a tartan sash to show his rank. The Regiment's fate was to be a tragic one, but this lay in the future. For the moment there was a mood of euphoria among Charles's new adherents. On 29 November he entered Manchester. The crowds huzza'd him to his lodgings, the town was illuminated and the bells rang out. This was more like it as far as Charles was concerned. 'There were several substantial people came and kis'd his hand, and a vast number of people of all sorts came to see him supp. . . .' But young Lord Elcho believed it was just so much flannel and that Charles was 'so far deceived with these proceedings of bonfires and ringing of bells (which they used to own themselves they did out of fear of being ill Used) that he thought himself sure of Success, and his Conversation that night at Table was, in what manner he should enter London, on horseback or a foot, and in what dress. . . .'

Elcho left a famous description of the growing dissent. So far Charles had managed to carry his Council with him, but the under-lying anxieties of the Scots were never far away. They were hard-headed practical men who believed in fighting at least on equal terms with their enemy. They did not share Charles's simple faith that his subjects would never take arms against him. 'The Principal officers of the army . . . met at Manchester and were of Opinion that now they had marched far enough into England, and as they

Prince Charles as a young man, by Antonio David

A race from Preston Pans to Berwick. Cartoon published on 21 September 1745

Prince Charles and the Highlanders enter Edinburgh after the battle of
Preston Pans. Engraving by J C Armytage
from a painting by T Duncan, A.R.A.

William, Duke of Cumberland, by David Morier (1705–1770)

March of the Guards to Finchley, 1750. Painting by William Hogarth

The Battle of Culloden, by David Morier (1705–1770)

Prince Charles
with Flora Macdonald

Prince Charles
disguised as Betty Burke

Flora Macdonald by
Richard Wilson

'Lochaber no more'. The
Farewell of Bonnie Prince
Charlie by J B Macdonald

had received not the least Encouragement from any person of distinction, the French not landed, and only joined by 200 vaga-bonds [an unfair comment – many were artisans and craftsmen, particularly weavers, and Elcho was a snob], they had done their part; and as they did not pretend to put a King upon the throne of England without their consent, that it was time to represent to the Prince to go back to Scotland. But after talking a great deal about it, it was determin'd to March to Derby, that so neither the French nor the English might have it to Say, the army had not marched far Enough into England to give the one Encouragement to Land and the other to join.'

So although Charles got his way, the Council meeting on St Andrew's Day, 30 November, was a highly-charged one. He needed the collective advocacy of Lord Nairne and the recently joined Welsh Jacobite lawyer David Morgan to win the argument. Morgan was one of only two Welshmen to join the army. As Charles was later to remark the Welsh had turned out to be no more than wine-glass Jacobites. He wryly promised to do for them all that they had done for him – drink their health. On 1 December the army moved out, but first Charles did a suitably princely thing. He ordered the repair of a bridge destroyed by the authorities on his approach. A proclamation told the good citizens of Manchester that 'His Royal Highness does not propose to make use of it for his own army, but believes it will be of service to the country; and if any forces that were with General Wade be coming this road they may have the benefit of it.'

He had done more for the supposed Jacobites in Cheshire than they had done for him. One of the few bright spots – and pathetic in its own way – was the case of old Mrs Skyring. She was said to have seen Charles II land at Dover when she was a little girl. A convinced Jacobite, she had been sending half her income anony-mously to James. She now sold her plate and jewels and gave the proceeds to Charles. Kissing the princely hand she is supposed to have declared, 'Lord, now lettest thou thy servant depart in peace.' She had her wish a few days later, dying of shock at the news of the retreat from Derby.

At Macclesfield – famous for its button-making – Charles received important news. Cumberland, who had taken over

Ligonier's command, was advancing, determined to engage Charles at the first opportunity. His forward troops were at New-castle-under-Lyme. A council of war was held and it was decided to try and outmanoeuvre Cumberland to get between him and London. Lord George Murray went ahead with the van towards Congleton to make Cumberland believe the Jacobites were about to attack him. He engaged Cumberland's advance guard whose commander, the Duke of Kingston, fled in such a panic he left his dinner to the enemy.

Lord George's men made another interesting discovery in a village two or three miles from Newcastle. They 'accidentaly Stumbled upon the house where Mr Weir, or Vere, who had acted the Spy, not only at Edr, but all the way upon the road, keeping a few miles before them' was about to have his supper. The 'obnoxious' Weir was immediately bundled off to Macclesfield to receive his just deserts. But Charles's 'humanity and good nature' saved him and instead of being hanged forthwith he was simply carried along with the army as a prisoner. As Murray of Broughton wrote, this was to have dire consequences: 'It was a pity that so humane an action Should have been followed by such fatal consequences as to have put it in the power of so vile a Creature to be a main Instrument in the Death of so many of his Servants.' Weir's evidence was to be the death warrant of many a Jacobite. Lord George Murray had wanted to have his own spy network but Charles had taken the view that it was too costly.

There was another Goverment spy hard on the heels of the Jacobites. Enter Captain Dudley Bradstreet, if he is to be believed. According to him the news of the rebels' entry into Manchester caused universal panic in London, with most people suffering 'the greatest Confusion and Consternation'. But not, of course, Captain Bradstreet and the Ministers of the Government. They sat down and coolly worked out a stratagem for obstructing Charles. Dudley proposed that he should 'go among the Rebels, and endeavour to make a Mutiny that might ruin the Pretender's Affairs, which I hoped to accomplish by their powerful Assistance; the first was, I would make large Promises to some distinguished Rebels, of Desperate Fortunes, to fire their Magazines, if possible, the Danger to be mine, the Success theirs. Another Scheme was, that I would take one of the finest Women in London with me, and, as the young Chevalier was reported to be a Man of Gallantry, she might perhaps get into his Confidence. . . .' In the end something less sensational was agreed upon. This was that Bradstreet should put himself into the hands of the rebels, try to gain the confidence of the Council, and find a means of delaying their advance. The arrangements for his departure were the stuff of novels. He went to Monmouth Street and equipped himself with a fine new suit of brown cloth richly laced with gold. It was difficult to get money because 'Matters were in so dreadful a Situation that Morning, that the Currency of the Bank of *England* was in a great Measure stopt.' But Bradstreet had been supplied with funds by his spy masters as well as with the necesssary passports. He made his will, buried a spare hundred pounds in his back garden and set out on his mission.

The Government was right to believe that the adventure was reaching its crisis. Lord George Murray had deceived Cumberland into believing that the Jacobites were making for Wales, and he withdrew. On 4 December the Jacobite army slipped past him and entered Derby. Charles was within a hundred and twenty miles of London and with Cumberland behind him the road was open. His fate and the fate of the kingdom seemed to onlookers to be teetering in the balance. The *Westminster Journal* had some advice for him: 'If thou hast any Regard to thy own Neck or the Necks of thy Followers, retire! before William comes too near with his Father's Vengeance.' But nothing was further from Charles's thoughts.

CHAPTER EIGHT

'. . . VERY ABUSIVE LANGUAGE'

DERBY was a Whig stronghold and all the charm in the world was not going to secure Charles a rapturous reception. Many of the leading citizens amongst its six thousand population had followed the example of the Duke of Devonshire and decamped towards Nottingham 'with the utmost precipitation'. Whig propaganda and disinformation had sown the seeds of panic and the appearance of the Jacobite army was not reassuring to the townsfolk. The vanguard may have looked respectable enough 'clothed in blue faced with red, and scarlet waistcoats with gold lace'. So did Elcho and his Lifeguards when they rode in with many of the chiefs, similarly attired and self-conciously 'the flower of their army'.

But when the main body marched in under the Duke of Perth, six or eight abreast with their banners flying and bagpipes playing, the spies and journalists gave free rein to their indignation. 'Most of their main body,' wrote one, 'are a parcel of shabby, lousy, pittiful looking fellows, mixed up with old men and boys.' He described their dirty plaids and dirty shirts and lack of breeches with disgust, and their plaid stockings reaching barely half way up their legs. Some were without shoes or next to none, and all were so worn out with the march that 'they commanded our pity rather than our fear.' Yet to most onlookers they were a despicable crew – short, wan, meagre and carrying their arms with difficulty. A gentleman wrote indignantly to the press, describing how the Gaelic tongue made them sound like 'a herd of Hottentots, wild monkies in a desert, or vagrant gipsies'. It was only in the field that their sneering critics discovered how terrifying these shoeless, stockingless warriors could be.

Before Charles arrived to claim the city, the ceremony of the Proclamation was enacted in the Market Place. Most of the city dignitaries obeyed the summons to appear in their robes, though some had fled and others pleaded rather lamely that they could not find their gowns. Charles entered at the head of the last body of the Jacobite force towards evening. As usual he was marching on foot and as usual he made an impression, even on a hostile audience. An eye-witness wrote: 'It is justice to say that he is a fine person, six foot high, a very good complexion, and presence majestic. He had a Scotch bonnet with a white silver rose. . . .' Another gentleman described him as 'tall, straight, slender and handsome, dressed in a green bonnet laced with gold, a white bob-wig, the fashion of the day, a Highland plaid and broadsword'.

His reception was warmer than he might have expected. O'Sullivan described how Charles was 'perfectly well received. Bonfires on the roads, the Bells ringing . . . it was really a fine sight to see the illuminations of the Town.' There are even tales that the ladies of fashion – always susceptible to Charles – were soon busy making white cockades. Some of them were to be castigated as the 'rebel sluts of Derby' but a verse captured Charles's attraction:

> If you saw him once . . .
> Do see him once! What harm is there in seeing?
> If after that there be not an agreeing,
> Then call me twenty rebel sluts if you
> When you have seen him, ben't a rebel too!

Followed by a lively and curious crowd Charles made his way to Exeter House which was to be his residence in Derby. Every other house in the surrounding streets was crammed with tired clansmen. After a supper of bread, cheese and ale they fell asleep where they could – some in beds but mostly lying on heaps of straw. Some of the very best accommodation was reserved for the handful of ladies who were travelling with the army, their carriage rumbling along with the marching clansmen. These included Lady Ogilvy, so young and beautiful that her husband had been afraid to leave her behind, knowing the morals of the age. There was also Murray of Broughton's wife, who had sat on her horse at the market cross in Edinburgh, handing out white cockades, and who probably insisted on coming. Unreliable rumours persisted that Jenny Cameron was also with them, delighting in administering soothing cordials to her lover the Prince.

As usual Charles was already considering the next step. That night at dinner his conversation was again about what to wear when he entered London – only ninety-four miles from his advance guard of some eighty men at Swarkston Bridge. Should it be High-land or Lowland dress, and would he would look best on foot or on horse-back? With untarnished optimism he predicted that 'the people of England, as was their duty, still nourished that allegiance for the race of their native Princes which they were bound to hold sacred, and that if he did but persevere in his daring attempt, Heaven itself would fight in his cause.' It also seemed as if the French might do the same. At Manchester Charles had received encouraging news from his brother Henry that 'the King of France was absolutely resolved upon the expedition into England . . . and that you might count upon it being ready towards the 20 December.' On arriving at Derby there were further optimistic signs – Charles heard that six French transports had slipped through the Royal Navy's net and successfully landed some eight hundred men of the Royal Scots and Irish Regiments of the French army at Montrose and Peterhead, commanded by the Duke of Perth's brother Lord John Drummond.

In the meantime invasion plans had been well under way in France. The indefatigable Walsh had been using his contacts to assemble the necessary shipping in the Channel ports. A nervous Government in London received reports that an invasion force of ten or twenty thousand troops was about to embark. The mood in the capital was already one of panic. The news that the High-landers had slipped past Cumberland and were between him and the city 'struck a terror into it scarce to be credited'. The *True Patriot* described the undignified scenes. 'On Friday last, the Alarm of the Rebels having given the Duke the Slip, and being in full March for this Town, together with the Express . . . from Admiral Vernon [that the French were embarking for invasion], struck such aTerror into several public-spirited Persons that, to prevent their Money, Jewels, Plate &c falling into Rebellious or French Hands, they immediately began to pack up and secure the same. And that they themselves might not be forced against their Wills into bad Company, they began to prepare for Journies into the Country; concluding, that the Plunder of what must remain behind in this City would satisfy the Victors. . . .' There was a run on the Bank of England and according to Fielding, in order to gain time, it paid out in sixpences heated up till they were too hot to handle.

However, there were plans for defending the capital, if it should come to that. The *True Patriot* rallied its readers with the news that 'While these fine Ladies, some of whom wear Breeches and are vulgarly called Beaus, were thus taking care of themselves, another Spirit hath prevailed amongst the Men, particularly in the City of London, where many Persons of good Fortune having provided themselves with the Uniform, were on Saturday last inlisted as Volunteers in the Guards.' These Guards camped out on Finchley common in readiness and some cavalry were stationed at Barnet. Tradespeople shut up shop and London held its breath.

But when the crisis came it was for Charles, not for the city on which he had set his sights. On the morning of 5 December, just as he was about to leave his lodgings, bonnet on his head, he received a visitor – Lord George Murray. According to an eyewitness Murray was brutally frank. He told Charles that it was high time to think about what they were doing. Charles asked him what he meant – was it not resolved to march on? Lord George replied that most of the chiefs were of a different opinion. He ushered Charles back into the house. The confrontation took place in the oak-wainscotted drawing room on the first floor and an impromptu council was called. Lord George asked the question that was on everyone's mind – was it prudent to advance any further?

The fears of the chiefs poured out – Cumberland was pushing on towards London by forced marches and might be at Stafford that very night; Wade was also pushing south by the east road; a third army was being formed near London; this would make thirty thousand Government soldiers; the tiny Highland force of five thousand would be encircled, overrun, massacred. The arguments for a retreat were 'unanswerable' the chiefs said apologetically. The only sensible course was to retreat to Scotland and join up with Lord John Drummond's forces. Charles did not agree. According to Lord Elcho he 'heard all these arguments with the greatest impatience, fell into a passion, and gave most of the Gentlemen that had Spoke very Abusive Language, and said they had a mind to betray him'. The rift between the Scots and the Irish had never been more apparent – Charles's 'Irish favourites' were for marching on and were heard to say that if they were captured the worst that would happen to them was a few months' imprisonment.

Charles could not believe that his dream was to be snatched away just as it was within his grasp, but it was difficult to dissuade the doubters. He could not produce any letters from Louis committing him unequivocally to an invasion of England. Nor could he be specific about what stage the French expedition had reached. Nor could he prove that the English Jacobites had any intention of doing more than raise their glasses to him. All that day he continued to insist on advancing, lobbying hard but without much success. Later that evening the Council reconvened. O'Sullivan and Murray of Broughton still supported Charles and the gentle Duke of Perth was all for an immediate attack against Cumberland. But ranged against them were the combined forces of Lord George Murray, grimly sure of his argument, and the influential trio of Cluny, Keppoch and Lochiel. They assured Charles that the Highlanders could easily march twenty miles a day. At that pace they could outstrip Cumberland. And if they met Wade on the road to Scotland they had no doubt that they could give him the same bloody nose as they had given Cope. The situation was on a knife-edge when that cheerful adventurer Captain Dudley Bradstreet claims to have stepped out from the shadows into history.

According to his own account Bradstreet had been enjoying himself hugely. He arrived in Derby coiffed and ruffled and belaced as befitted a gentleman of quality and mounted on a 'lovely and well-managed Charger'. He had laid his plans carefully with his hero Cumberland: his mission was to delay the Jacobites 'but twelve hours' to give the Government troops a chance to catch up. He announced himself as a man of quality come to serve the Prince Regent and was delighted to overhear the whispering clansmen hailing him as an English lord. He was conducted with great ceremony to Charles's lodgings where he met a number of the Jacobite leaders including Lord Kilmarnock and the Duke of Perth. Tossing down several glasses of fine wine he cheerfully told them a farago of lies. His *pièce de résistance* was to invent another army of eight or nine thousand men supposedly commanded by Hawley or Ligonier and waiting at Northampton to attack Charles. 'Observe,' he later wrote with glee, 'there was not nine Men at Northampton to oppose them, which shews that mighty Events are often effected by the smallest Causes; for this Report to them, I am as certain as of my Existence, was the only Reason and Motive for that fortunate and dreaded Army (until then) to retreat, from which Period date their inevitable Ruin.' He had set out to delay the Jacobites for twelve hours. If he is to be believed, he succeeded in delaying them forever.

The spy was brought before the Council and asked the same questions again. When he reached the part about an army at Northampton Charles knew that he was doomed – 'the Rebel Prince, who was in a Closet just by, opened the Door, and pointed at me, saying, "That Fellow will do me more Harm than all the Elector's Army;" and then directing himself to the Council, said, "You ruin, abandon, and betray me if you don't march on," and then shut the Door in a Passion.' The result of events that night in Exeter House was that Charles gave in. This decision was to prove the end of all his hopes and the point at which his life turned sour. Sheridan's sad comments were entirely accurate. 'It is all over,' he mourned, 'we shall never come back again.'

There have been many arguments about what would have happened if Charles had been allowed to follow his instincts and march straight to London. The real situation was nothing like as bad as the clan chiefs believed, even without Bradstreet's misinformation. In fact there were no more than some four thousand men between the Jacobites and the capital. Many contemporaries believed he had the throne within his grasp. Pitt the Elder told the House of Commons as much in 1749. Smollett agreed with him that 'Had Charles proceeded in his career with that expedition he had hitherto used, he might have made himself master of the metropolis, where he would certainly have been joined by a considerable number of his well-wishers, who waited impatiently for his approach.' Later generations thought so too. King George V remarked to the Duke of Atholl, 'Had Charles Edward gone on from Derby I should not have been King of England today.'

So it was fitting that 6 December was to become 'Black Friday' in the Jacobite calendar. The retreat began in freezing conditions. It was symbolic of what had happened that Charles now chose to ride rather than march at the head of his men. He had made his position quite clear to Lord George, '. . . in future I shall summon no more councils, since I am accountable to nobody for my actions but to God and my father and therefore I shall no longer either ask or accept advice.' In other words from now on he washed his hands of everything and Murray would have to sort it out. Observers described how Charles was so upset that he could hardly stand, which was 'always the case with him when he was cruelly used'. According to Bradstreet he had been weeping. This tragic figure hunched in despair on a suitably black horse was a different being from the Prince who had marched from Edinburgh to Derby at the head of his men, who was 'very strong, supped liberally, was often drunk, would throw himself on a couch at eleven o'clock at night without undressing' and be up again at three a.m.

A charade was enacted to conceal from the enemy that this was a retreat. A party of horse was sent cantering up the road to within a few miles of the enemy. Meanwhile the army retraced its steps to Ashbourne. Lord George knew he must also conceal what was happening from the clansmen. Only the day before they had been sharpening their dirks in eager anticipation of a battle. So powder and ball were handed out just as they would be before an action, and it was hinted that Wade was at hand. But the deception failed. When the Highlanders found themselves once again on the Ashbourne road they suspected the truth and were extremely dejected. 'All had expressed the greatest ardour upon hearing at Derby that they were within a day's march of the Duke of Cumberland; they were at a loss what to think of this retreat, of which they did not know the real motives; but even such as knew them, and thought the retreat the only reasonable scheme, could hardly be reconciled to it.'

Chevalier Johnstone described it even more vivdly: 'The Highlanders, believing at first that they were in march forward to attack the army of the Duke of Cumberland, testified great joy and alacrity; but as soon as the day began to clear in the distance, and that they perceived we were retracing our steps, we heard nothing but howlings, groans, and lamentations throughout the whole army to such a degree as if they had suffered a defeat.' The commanders thought of another artifice as the army marched gloomily on its way. It was given out that the reinforcements expected from Scotland were already on the road and had actually entered England; that Wade was trying to intercept them and that the Prince was marching to their relief. This was a plausible explanation and the suspicious clansmen brooded on it, but their officers noticed that they were sullen and silent the whole of that day.

It did not take long for the truth to dawn that this was a game of cat and mouse with the pursuing Goverment troops in the feline role. When he realised what was happening – and he was deceived for a short while – Cumberland gave chase. With Wade and Ligonier on his trail as well, Lord George's task was not an easy one. The army was demoralised and unsure of itself. The local people in the towns and villages they passed through were now actively hostile. And he had Charles to deal with – behaving like a glamorous but sulky schoolboy, uninterested in the problems and positively obstuctive. Lord George was depressed by this change in behaviour: 'His Royal Highness, in marching forwards, had always been first up in the morning, and had the men in motion before break of day, and commonly marched himself afoot; but in retreat he was much longer of leaving his quarters, so that, though the rest of the army were all on their march, the rear could not move till he went, and then he rode straight on, and got to the quarters with the van.' Part of Lord George's irritation was that he himself was commanding the rearguard.

Charles was dragging his heels. The idea that he was fleeing from his cousin weighed heavily. It did not help that Cumberland was virtually the same age and had grown up enjoying all the privileges that Charles believed should have been his own. Physically they could not have been more different. Charles was the fairy-tale prince – tall and slender. He would not have looked out of place holding a glass slipper in his hand. Cumberland – more of an ugly sister – was a vast young man. His portraits show a startling degree of embonpoint, and where he is mounted the horse is drawn similarly barrel-shaped. Their personalities were also very different. Charles saw himself as a model of what a young prince should be, humane and chivalrous even when it was to his disadvantage. Cumberland, by contrast, was a bruiser – fond of boxing and horse racing, loved by his men but harsh with them and without pity for his enemies. The brutality that was to earn him such a bad name in the aftermath of the '45 was already showing itself. He wrote to the Duke of Newcastle that 'There are, I believe, to the number of about fifteen or sixteen of their stragglers picked up who are sent to different jails. As they have so many of our Prisoners in their hands, I did not care to put them to death, but I have encouraged the country people to do it, as they may fall in their way.'

The country folk obeyed with a will. Lord Elcho described with disgust how 'They were quite prepared in case the army had been beat to have knock'd on the head all that would have escaped from the Battle. Whenever any of the men straggled or stayed behind they either murder'd them or sent them to the Duke.' He was not exaggerating. Two Highland stragglers were shot dead by a farmer and his sons on the road to Ashbourne. Lord George tried to find ways of rounding up the laggards, but it was difficult because the clansmen would only obey men from their own clans. He had to form a special unit of officers drawn from each of the clan regiments. All in all it was a desperate march. They were harassed by the locals who lit bonfires to signal the whereabouts of the rebel army, the militia played hit and run on their fringes, and it was bitterly cold. The discipline which the Jacobite army had displayed on its march into England began to break down. Some of the retreating Highlanders could not resist the temptation to help themselves to horses and other likely loot. Sometimes there was bloodshed. Two clansmen shot dead Humphrey Brown at Clifton near Ashbourne because he refused to hand over his horse.

As one report put it, the retreating army 'seemed to be extremely out of humour'.

The *True Patriot* gave Cumberland the credit for containing the mayhem the Highlanders would have inflicted if they had had the chance. It noted in approving tones, 'The great Expedition with which his Royal Highness the Duke hath pursued the Rebels, must have certainly prevented much Mischief to the Northern Counties, by forcing them to retreat with such Celerity: For when we consider the Temper in which the Rebels left Derby, incensed at their Disappointment, and the Ill-will which the Pretender and their Chiefs must have borne to their English Friends, from whom they received so little assistance, we must necessarily conclude, that had they had sufficient Leisure, they would not only have plundered every Place through which they passed, but have left the most terrible Marks of Cruelty behind them.'

So it was in a very different mood that the army was retracing its steps back through Ashbourne, Leek, Macclesfield, Stockport to Manchester. In Manchester they were now stoned by a hostile mob, and only extracted with difficulty the £2,500 they had levied on the town for its bad behaviour. An elderly Whig merchant was told to raise the money by a 1 p.m. deadline which sent him scurrying anxiously to the coffee house to consult his fellow-merchants. Between them they came up with the funds, but not without an extension of the deadline to 2 p.m. Even then the problems were not over. The party of Scots sent to collect the money were fired on as they crossed Salford Bridge and there were other signs of hostility. A sniper took a pot-shot at O'Sullivan from a garret window, mistaking him for Charles. Bradstreet, who was still with the Jacobites awaiting the opportunity to escape, later claimed that it was only his intervention which saved Manchester from being burned to the ground in revenge.

Bradstreet was continuing to undermine the Jacobites in any way he could think of. He had discovered his fellow spy Captain Vere in Ashbourne, 'tied with Ropes, after being kept starving a Day and Night'. The Duke of Perth wanted to hang him without further ado but Bradstreet persuaded Lord Kilmarnock to intercede. The result was that Vere was spared though kept crammed in a little closet. He was able to continue compiling his careful and damaging notes about the various Highland leaders. Before he took to his heels Bradstreet also had time to observe the rebel leaders at close quarters, which inspired some intriguing pen-portraits. 'Lord Kilmarnock was genteel in Person and Manners, the Duke of Perth was prodigious tall and thin . . . his Hair, when loose, came down to the Small of his Back; Lord Ogilvie was a young handsome Man; Lord Elcho was young, smooth-faced, inclined to Fat, and passionate, he commanded the Hussars, and wore a Fox Skin Cap with the Ears pricked up, which made him, when on Horseback at the Head of his Men, look very formidable; Colonel Sullivan was a fat, well-faced Man; Sir Thomas Sheridan was a drooping old Man; . . . the Duke of Atholl was old and infirm.'

Charles, meanwhile, was becoming increasingly stubborn about appearing to be fleeing from Cumberland and wanted to show the world 'he was retiring and not flying'. He would have been deeply upset by a 'stop press' in the *True Patriot* that 'The Highlanders are running away as fast as they can. . . .' In fact the papers had been very quick to pick up the true state of affairs. On the very day of the retreat from Derby the *London Gazette* received a despatch from Nottingham accurately judging what was happening. In Manchester Charles tried to persuade Lord George to stay an extra night and only gave up the idea after a struggle. At Preston he was quite determined. 'At Supper at Lancaster the Prince talk'd much about retiring so fast, and said it was a Shame for to go so fast before the son of an *Usurper*, and that he Would stay at Lancaster.' In the event they vacated Preston – with its fatal reputation for their cause – with only an hour to spare. There was a real prospect now that Cumberland would catch them before they reached the border. It was only a false report of a French landing on the south coast that stopped him by delaying him a day. But Charles was pleased that Cumberland was close. He wanted a battle and he said so to his commanders while they paused at Lancaster. Lord George Murray, Lochiel and O'Sullivan were sent off to find a suitable site outside Lancaster.

But in the event it was Wade's force, not Cumberland's, that came on the scene. Wade had sent an advance guard over the Pennines to try and intercept the Highlanders. There was a skirmish with Elcho's Lifeguards and some of the Government soldiers were captured. They gave the Highlanders the unwelcome tidings that both Wade and Cumberland would shortly be on them. This was too much even for Charles despite his 'fanciful taste for battles', and the Jacobite army set out post haste for Kendal. Lord George, with that air of superiority Charles found so irritating, could not resist saying to him as they left Lancaster: 'As Your Royal Highness is always for battles, be the circumstances what they may, I now offer you one in three hours from this time with the army of Wade which is only about three miles from us.' At Kendal, Murray tried to get O'Sullivan to substitute two-wheeled ammunition carts for the heavier four-wheeled wagons that were proving so difficult to manage on the poor country roads. But he found the Irishman at supper with Charles and enjoying some fine mountain Malaga. The only comfort the exasperated Murray received was 'a glass or two of it'.

The next hurdle was to cross Shap Fell, no easy matter, now or then, in snow and ice. Lord George proposed to Charles that the big guns should be left at Kendal. Charles refused, reminding him with some pleasure that at Derby he had promised to be in the rearguard during the retreat and to look after the baggage and artillery. Not a single cannon ball must be abandoned. Grinding his teeth Lord George had to agree. The consequence was that Charles, with the van of the army, managed to struggle across Shap Fell and reach Penrith. Lord George and the rearguard struggled on with the unwieldy carts, many overturning in the appalling weather. One fell into a stream rendering most of the contents useless. Lord George paid Glengarry's men sixpence a piece to carry over two hundred cannon-balls to Shap, some of them tying them in their plaids. Inevitably he became separated from Charles and the rest of the force. The Prince had reversed his policy of dragging his heels and was now going great guns. '. . . We had the cruellest rain that day, that ever I saw, we had several torrents to pass; the Prince was always a foot, and forded those torrents as the men did, never wou'd he get a' horse-back, & if it was not for the way he acted that day, I verilly believe we cou'd not keep half our men together.'

Murray was overtaken by some of Cumberland's dragoons and

mounted infantry. To his horror he heard 'a prodigious number of trumpets and kettle-drums'. A running battle broke out near the village of Clifton, with the cavalry attacking and the Highlanders repulsing them 'like lions'. Murray sent to Charles for orders – it seemed a good opportunity to go on the offensive before Cumberland's full force caught up – the numbers were 'pretty near equal . . . and the Ground was advantageous for foot to fight in'. Charles simply ordered him to retire to Penrith. Cluny Macpherson's regiment and the Appin Stewarts came to help Murray extricate himself but, as an increasingly sceptical Elcho remarked, it was a lost chance. He noted that 'As there was formerly a Contradiction to make the army halt when it was necessary to march, so now there was one to march and shun fighting when there Could never be a better opportunity got for it. . . .'

As it was, a short skirmish did take place an hour after sunset amid hawthorne hedges and stone walls. The sky was cloudy but, now and then, the moon shone through, picking out the bright clothes of the dragoons. The Highlanders moved towards them, invisible in their darker tartans, cutting their way through the hawthorne prickles which were 'very uneasy . . . to our loos'd tail'd lads'. They killed or wounded some forty dragoons, smashing their broadswords on the dragoons' newly-issued metal skull caps and enabling Lord George to secure his retreat. He rejoined Charles the next day in Penrith. The Prince's steward had managed to find him three bottles of cherry brandy and he was in an appropriately cheerful mood. Although they both knew the engagement had been against Charles's orders the Prince told the weary Murray that he was pleased with the night's work. They were not to know that it was in fact the last battle between rival armies on English soil. It also had a sinister aftermath. Cumberland wrote in his report that the rebels had cried, 'No quarter! Murder them,' and it was to be a forerunner of his own behaviour at Culloden.

On 19 December the army marched on to Carlisle. Charles was again marching on foot at its head and in renewed spirits. It was 'one of the darkest nights I ever saw, yet did his R. H. walk it on foot, and the most part of the way without a lanthorn, yet never stumbled, which many of us Highlanders did often'. However, it was now that Charles made one of the saddest and most controversial decisions of the whole campaign. He decided to leave a garrison behind, partly on the advice of O'Sullivan.

To the other leaders it looked like suicide. Lord George 'was clear for evacuating it' and had assumed that Carlisle would be abandoned and the castle and fortifications blown up. After all, the Jacobites knew better than anybody the real state of the 'crazy walls of the town and castle' – the fortifications were rotting. Johnstone realised that Carlisle 'could not hold out for more than four hours against a cannonade from a few field-pieces'. Not only that, but the population of the city was largely hostile. But Charles hoped to be back before long, reinforced with Lord John Drummond's troops from France and Lord Strathallan's Scottish forces, and he claimed to want to hold Carlisle to 'facilitate his entry into the kingdom' again. Retaining a toehold in England was also important psychologically. He could tell himself that his sortie into England had not been a failure.

Four hundred volunteers were left behind. These included the Manchester Regiment under Francis Townley together with a few men from the regiments of Gordon of Glenbucket, Lord Ogilvy, the Duke of Perth and Colonel Roy Stewart. There were also some hundred or so Jacobites in the service of the French but they knew that, if captured, they would be treated as prisoners of war not traitors. It was the Manchester men and the Scots who were to suffer the full weight of Cumberland's malice when he captured the town a few days later. The Duke wrote to the Duke of Newcastle with the grim comment that 'I wish I could have blooded the soldiers with these villains, but it would have cost us many a brave fellow, and it comes to the same end, as they have no sort of claim to the King's mercy and I sincerely hope will meet with none.' He had his wish.

Half of the officers including Townley were to be hanged, drawn and quartered and those other officers and men who survived the terrible conditions in the prisons and the hulks were transported to the colonies. But they did not realise the terrible fate that was so soon to overtake them as Charles thanked them for all they had done and suffered in his cause. He promised a speedy return with increased forces before the enemy could retake the town. Neither did Charles guess that in a matter of days his corpulent cousin would make a point of lodging in the same house and in the same bed that Charles had occupied. It was around this time too that Francis Strickland, one of the original seven men of Moidart, died of dropsy at Carlisle.

The army left Carlisle on Charles's birthday – 20 December (old-style) – and made for the border ten miles away. When they reached the river Esk at Longtown they found that the heavy rain had turned it into a flood. Government spies believed it to be impassable but they had reckoned without the courage and determination of the Highlanders. To the astonishment of the French envoy d'Eguilles, they formed a human barrier against the torrent: 'We were a hundred men abreast, and it was a very fine shew: the water was big, and took most of the men breast high. When I was near cross the river, I believe there were two thousand men in the water at once.' Charles played his part in this, relishing the opportunity for heroics and apparently saving one lad from drowning by grabbing him by the hair. The faithful O'Sullivan said, 'The men seeing the horses go over tho' with a great deal of difficulty, cried out that they wou'd pass it, as they did, which was one of the most extraordinary passages of a river that cou'd be seen. The Prince stopped them, & went in himself with all the horse we had, to break the stream, that it shou'd not be so rapid for the foot; this of his own motion. The foot marched in, six in a breast, in as good order, as if they were marching in a field, holding one another by the collars. . . .' According to him, the only losses were a couple of poor women 'that belonged only to the public' and who were swept away. Like others he thought it was significant that Charles should be in both England and Scotland on his birthday.

Extraordinary scenes took place on the Scottish banks of the Esk. Bonfires were lit, the pipes began to play and they danced Highland reels to get themselves dry. According to Lord George this did not take long, 'for they held the tails of their short coats in their hands in passing the river, so when their thighs were dry, all was right'. Lord George had dressed for the occasion as well. 'I was this day in my Phillibeg, that is to say without Breeches . . . and nothing encourag'd the men more than seeing their Officers dress'd like themselves and ready to share their fate.' In spite of all the hardships there was a sense of wild euphoria. 'They had carried the standard of Glenfinnan a hundred and fifty miles into a country full of foes; and now they brought it back unscathed, through the accumulated dangers of storm and war.'

Charles's enemies also understood what an extraordinary feat it had been, though they were more inclined to blame English lassitude than Highland daring. The *True Patriot*, while exulting in the retreat, asked '. . . can History produce an Instance parallel to this, of six or seven Men landing in a great and powerful Nation, in opposition to the inclination of the People, in defiance of a vast and mighty Army. . . . If we consider, I say, that this Handful of Men landing in the most desolate Corner, among a Set of poor, naked, hungry, disarm'd Slaves, abiding there with Impunity, till they had, as it were, in the Face of a large Body of his Majesty's Troops, collected a kind of Army, or rather Rabble, together. . . .' It was the beginning of the legend and Fielding stated angrily that it was England's fault as a 'sinful nation'. He even went so far as to call it 'our Sodom'.

There was great relief in England that the rebel army had crossed back into Scotland 'which to the generality here is the same as Norway'. As Horace Walpole wittily observed, 'No one is afraid of a rebellion that runs away.' The citizens who had been packing up their belongings and biting their nails vented their relief in some vicious pursuits. An apothecary surgeon in Macclesfield bought the body of a Highlander who had been overtaken and hanged at Cheadle. He paid 4s. 6d. 'to have had leather of the skin (worth his money) which he accordingly gave to a tanner to dress'. For whatever reason the tanning did not work, causing Jacobites to claim that the skin had mystical properties whereupon its ghoulish owner buried it. Another individual 'had a highlander flayed to make himself a pair of breech of the skin and sent it to three tanners to have it dressed'. Perhaps he had more success.

Words were as savage as deeds. Stories abounded of the repulsive habits of the Highlanders. 'Wherever they rested they had let fall their ordure all over the towns, and at people's doors, so caused the towns to stink intolerably; many of them also fouled their beds. . . .' An epigram on their disgusting behaviour 'during their flight' appeared in the *Newcastle Gazette*:

Such filthy farting, pissing, shiting
(From Nature be't or Fear of fighting)
Gives a shrewd proof, to make an end on't
Charles is a warming pan descendant
When thus he leads, from kindred clans
An Army of Scotch warming pans

But this warming pan army was not yet a spent force as events
would show.

CHAPTER NINE

'GOOD GOD! HAVE I LIVED TO SEE THIS?'

THE question was the familiar one – what next? It had been a spectacular achievement to bring the Highland army safely home, but without clear objectives the clansmen would simply melt away. Lord George was suffering from 'a most violent cold and cough' contracted a few days earlier and which had not been helped by floundering about in the freezing Esk. The whole army was exceedingly weary as it trudged on into Scotland. A contemporary verse sneered at the raggle-taggle force:

> And with joy they ran home,
> To the place whence they come,
> To Beggary, Oatmeal, and Itch.

The *True Patriot* also took the trouble to try to debunk the idea of Charles's personal charm. It carried a supposed letter from one young lady in the country to another in Edinburgh. It was not true, she declared, that Charles was a 'charming Man' with 'courtly, easy, winning, killing Behaviour', doing everything with 'an Air of Majesty and Charms'. She knew better, 'For I am informed by one who has seen him, that this Charmer is a black lanthorn-jawed Italian, and not to be compared with either of the Princes of the True Royal Blood, in Comeliness of Person.'

Meanwhile, on 21 December the 'Charmer' had reached Dumfries – 'a considerable town, full of fanatical Calvinists'. He lodged somewhat unromantically in what is now the Commercial Hotel. Remembering the citizens' previous lack of co-operation, he levied the excise and demanded two thousand pounds and two thousand shoes from the indignant citizens. The Highlanders meanwhile helped themselves to nine casks of gun powder, any arms they could lay their hands on and every house 'that could be found in town or country'. The *True Patriot* wailed about their wicked behaviour among these good loyal Lowland citizens: 'The Nastiness of these Savages is scarce credible. They may indeed be compared to Hogs, the same Stye in which they eat and sleep, serving them for every other Occasion of Life. These Wretches being now returned to Scotland, persist still in their Plunder.'

From Dumfries he marched to Drumlanrig where the Highlanders occupied the castle, seat of the Duke of Queensberry. His Grace received an agonised account of how the men laid straw in all his fine rooms to sleep on and defaced a portrait of William of Orange with their claymores. Even worse: 'They killed about 40 sheep, part of your Grace's, and part of mine, most of them in the vestibule next the low dining-room and the foot of the principal stair, which they left in a sad pickle, as they did indeed the whole house.' They drank all the Duke's spirits and most of his wine and were cheerfully making off with his bed linen until intercepted by the Duke of Perth who made them give it back. He was not the man to think lightly of the pillaging of a ducal home.

On Christmas Eve Charles arrived at Hamilton and lodged in its beautiful Palace. It must have been a strange Christmas. Only two years ago he had still been in Italy, eagerly awaiting his summons from Louis. That French help had not materialised, but he had not given up hope. In Dumfries he had assured his army that troops were on their way. He spent his first and last Christmas day in Scotland in one of his favourite boyhood pursuits – hunting – and rounded it off with a fine dinner of a turkey costing three shillings.

On Boxing Day afternoon the Prince entered Glasgow – one of Scotland's 'prettiest (but most whiggish)' towns – to the chagrin of its citizens. No one cheered, 'nor did the meanest inhabitants so much as take off their hats'. They knew that Charles meant to punish them for their former behaviour. Not only had they refused to help him but had raised a battalion against him. False reports that the Duke of Cumberland had defeated the Jacobites near Lancaster had brought them cheering onto the streets just a few days previously. So now they got their deserts as far as Charles was concerned. He forced them to cough up ten thousand pounds' worth of shirts, stockings, bonnets, waistcoats and shoes to clothe his ragged Highlanders.

However, the Prince still could not believe that these dour townspeople could really remain impervious to his charm. The reports describe how he sallied forth in his French garb, 'more elegantly, when in Glasgow, than he did in any other place whatsomever'. He held a ball but the Glaswegian ladies refused to attend and delivered the *coup de grâce* by declaring that he was 'not handsome'. Nevertheless, he had his devoted circle of Jacobite ladies which for a while is supposed to have included young Clementina Walkinshaw. She was from a fervently pro-Stuart family and her father had been a Jacobite agent. She had been named after Charles's mother who was one of her godmothers. She met Charles again a few days later at Bannockburn House where, according to some accounts, she first became his mistress. Whatever the case, she was later to be his mistress in exile.

At this stage Charles's mind was probably not on love. The situation in Scotland was quite different from the one he had left behind. Government troops now controlled Edinburgh, Lord Loudon held Inverness, and the Royal Navy was setting up a blockade on such a scale that it would be well nigh impossible for any French ships to slip through. In addition, Charles had now heard the dismal news of the fall of Carlisle. In the circumstances the best bet seemed to be to march north to rendezvous with his supporters at Perth and to besiege Stirling Castle. On 3 January the Highland army moved out of the Whig city 'in a handsome manner', to the beating of the drums, colours flying and pipes piping, and to the great relief of the townsfolk. At Stirling they met up with Lord John Drummond and his troops from France and with Lord Lewis Gordon. Lord Lewis was brother to the Duke of Gordon who, while sympathetic to the Prince, had prudently decided to keep out of things. Nevertheless, he had done nothing to stop his brother conducting a recruiting campaign in Gordon country. Lord Lewis had had mixed success and wrote a letter to the Duke of Perth which complained that both the gentry and the common people were 'more Remiss than I expected, and I am credibly informed . . . that their slowness is chiefly owing to Vile Presbyterian Ministers who abuse the Prince's goodness towards them by inculcating a Parcel of infamous Lies into the people's heads.'

However, Lord Lewis made some headway, mostly by threats, and raised a couple of well-equipped battalions. Other welcome reinforcements had arrived with Lord Strathallan bringing Frasers and Farquarsons. Lord Cromarty and Lord Macleod had raised the Mackenzies. Lord Cromarty was the target of one Whig account of the rebellion which claimed to be 'A Genuine Narrative of all that Befell that Unfortunate Adventurer [Charles] in the most Candid Manner and every fictitious Embellishment avoided'. The author went into gleeful and irrelevant detail about the unsavoury habits of the Earl as a young man. During one debauch he and some others apparently seized a man who was 'fix'd in a Posture proper for their purpose. They took a burning Candle, and applying it to the Orifice of the Anus, put the Man to the most horrid Pain. How they treated the fair Sex,' the writer primly observed, 'I do not chuse to mention; Tho' I have heard many Particulars on that Subject both in Ross and elsewhere.'

There were also the four hundred Mackintoshes rallied by Lady Mackintosh. Dressed in a tartan habit trimmed with lace, with a blue bonnet on her head and a pair of pistols at her saddle-bow, 'Colonel Anne' rode through her husband's country and succeeded in raising enough clansmen to form a battalion. This was the biggest Jacobite force yet assembled, despite the inevitable desertions which had plagued them since crossing back from England. Chevalier Johnstone recorded how the army found itself all of a sudden 'the double of what it was when we were in England'.

The town of Stirling fell to the Jacobites on 8 January due to the 'Pusillanimity, Disaffection and Cowardice of a few of the Inhabitants', or so the London Magazine announced disapprovingly. But the defenders of the castle were made of sterner stuff and defied the rebels. The protracted siege of the fortress was to prove a dangerous distraction from more fruitful activities. One factor in this was the arrival from France, in company with some

cumbersome artillery, of a French engineer Mirabelle de Gordon
– a man of awesome incompetence. Johnstone described the confidence placed in Mirabelle on the grounds that 'a French engineer,
of a certain age, and decorated with an order, must necessarily be
a person of experience, talents, and capacity; but it was unfortunately discovered, when too late, that his knowledge as an engineer
was extremely limited, and that he was totally destitute of judg-
ment, discernment and common sense. His figure being as whimsical as his mind, the Highlanders, instead of M. Mirabelle, called
him always Mr Admirable.' Neither he nor the artillery from
France were to have any effect on Stirling Castle which remained
untaken.

Meanwhile Charles had caught a fever and was being nursed
back to health at Bannockburn by Clementina, using the fashionable cinnamon treatment. Perhaps it was soothing to be able to
talk to her about Rome where she too had spent part of her
childhood. Whatever the case it seems that a bond was formed
between them. However, the period of calm did not last long. On
his second day at Bannockburn Charles received one of those visits
from Lord George Murray that he had learned to dread. Lord
George brought a petition from the chiefs asking him to convene
a council of war and containing an irritating list of all the things
which they believed would not have gone wrong had Charles been
prepared to call one earlier. In his fragile state this caught him on
the raw. So did the grumble that his men were volunteers not
mercenaries and that he ought to be more considerate towards
them.

Charles responded with his famous riposte that since this was
an army of gentlemen of rank and fortune he might have expected
more zeal, more resolution and more sheer good manners. He
concluded that his authority might be taken from him by violence
but that he would 'never resign it like an idiot'. The love affair
with his chiefs was clearly at an end. However, before the crisis
could develop the situation changed. News of an imminent French
landing sent Cumberland dashing back to London. Yet another
verse had been added to the national anthem to celebrate the
House of Hanover:

George is magnanimous,
Subjects unanimous;
Peace to us bring:
His name is glorious,
Reign meritorious,
God save the King!

Cumberland himself was celebrated in a special prologue added to performances of 'The Beggar's Opera'. The words combined loyalty with sugary sentiment:

O! Thou who dost o'er human Acts preside,
If Britain is thy care be WILLIAM'S GUIDE;
The noble Youth, whom ev'ry Eye Approves,
Each Tongue applauds and ev'ry Soldier loves;

Another change was that Wade had been replaced by the infamous Lieutenant-General Henry Hawley. This charming character, 'with no small bias to the brutal', had been amusing himself while he waited for reinforcements at Edinburgh by building gibbets on which to hang any prisoners. He also took the precaution of making sure that hangmen accompanied his army. He was hated by his men for his macabre cruelty. In Flanders he had hanged a deserter in front of his windows. He so enjoyed the spectacle that he was reluctant to sell the body to the surgeons for dissection. His solution was to ask for the skeleton back to hang up in the guard-room! His brigade-major, James Wolfe, the later victor over the French at Quebec, did not mince his words. He wrote that his men dreaded his severity and despised his military knowledge. Hawley, on the other hand, was immensely conceited. In the '15 he had fought at the Battle of Sheriffmuir on the victorious right wing and did not believe that 'these Rascalls' of Highlanders were anything to worry about.

So this was the man against whom Charles now pitted himself. Hawley advanced from Edinburgh. His battle-hardened army consisted of twelve battalions of regulars as well as some dragoons and the Glasgow Militia. This was a very different force from the nervous and inexperienced men chased off the field at Preston

Pans. They took Falkirk, and Hawley installed himself in great comfort at Callendar House, home of the Earl of Kilmarnock. Lady Kilmarnock was horrified to have such a brutish guest billeted on her. On 15 January the Jacobite army drew itself up in battle order on Plean Moor two miles south-east of Bannockburn and waited for an attack. And they did the same on the next day. And the next. But Hawley did not come.

Lord George Murray suggested that they should take the initiative and occupy the rough upland of Falkirk Moor two miles south-west of the enemy camp. This would put them in an advantageous position for an attack. To deceive Hawley he also proposed that Charles's standard should be left flying on Plean Moor and that a diversionary force under Lord John Drummond should be sent up the road to Falkirk. The scheme was then for the rest of the army to make for the river Carron. There were the usual arguments about tactics between Lord George and O'Sullivan. O'Sullivan was worried the Highlanders would be spotted by the enemy if they tried to ford the river in the daytime. Lord George dismissed this saying it was quite impossible for his men to sleep in the open that night and that the Government troops were too far away to pose a threat.

Murray was not entirely right about this. They were spotted, but Hawley's negligence meant that nothing was done to stop their advance. Hawley was revelling in the comforts of Callendar House where his hostess was now going to great lengths to keep him entertained and, no doubt, well-liquored. She was so successful that the bleary-eyed Hawley was in no mood to be disturbed. At the news that the Jacobites were on the move he reluctantly left the great log fires of Callendar and went out into the winter's cold. He surveyed the scene from the top of a small hill and saw nothing. That was enough for him. His arrogance was such that he did not believe Charles would dare to attack him. It was a sign of his contempt and his confidence that he did not even bother to send out cavalry patrols. Neither did he tell his men to get under arms. As far as he was concerned the Highlanders were 'the most despicable enemy'.

The unfortunate redcoats were taken unawares. The first they knew was when a man rushed into the camp with cries of

'Gentlemen, what are you about? The Highlanders will be immediately upon you!' They already had the jitters. When a hare ran through their lines one soldier 'more ready-witted than the rest, exclaimed "Halloo, the Duke of Perth's mother!" – it being a general belief that that zealous old Catholic lady was a witch and therefore able to assume the disguise of a hare. . . .' The awful truth had finally dawned on Hawley and he rushed to his men hatless and in a savage temper, his fine dinner uneaten and 'with the appearance of one who has abruptly left an hospitable table'. His mood was not helped by the fact that a storm was brewing and the light was fading. He made a desperate attempt to gain the high ground, ordering the cavalry followed by the foot and the artillery up towards the summit of the moor.

As his men struggled onwards and upwards Hawley's bloodshot eyes assessed the field of battle selected by his enemies. The hill rose steeply to a windswept plateau. Its face was a ripple of treacherous folds and ridges intersected by a deep gully. The three regiments of dragoons led the way followed by Hawley's frontline troops – the regiments of Wolfe, Cholmondeley, Pulteney, the Royal, Price's and Ligonier. (In those days regiments were known by the name of their colonel.) Behind them struggled the rear column, consisting of the men of Blakeney's, Munro's, Fleming's, Barrel's, Battereau's and Howard's.

The rival armies squared up to each other under a darkening sky. Lord George Murray knew – literally – which way the wind was blowing. It was gusting hard from the south-west and to make sure that it would be behind the Highlanders he had made a wide detour after crossing the Carron and then marched his two parallel columns in double quick time to the breast of the hill. The lie of the land concealed the dragoons hurrying to seize the high ground from the other side in what was effectively a race. It was only when both sides were almost at the summit that they saw each other. At first the Highlanders assumed that the dragoons were just scouts but quickly realised the truth: 'The Dragoons made several motions towards the front of Lord George's Column, and by coming very near often Endeavour'd to draw off the highlanders' fire but to no purpose, for they marched on until they came to a bog, and then the whole army wheel'd to the left. . . .'

There was then a pause in this strange ballet lasting a quarter of an hour. The Macdonalds advanced 'foot by foot' giving the other regiments time to come up on their left. Lord George, fighting on foot, walked up and down the line ordering the excitable clansmen to keep their ranks and not to fire until he gave the order. This was apparently carried out 'with as much exactness as was possible, and as sometimes one part of the line was farther advanced than the rest, they halted till the others came equal to them.'

The right wing of the army occupied the near level ground towards the summit while the centre and left wings cascaded down the hillside. Meanwhile on the Government side, the infantry were lagging well behind the dragoons. So was the artillery train. Captain Archibald Cunningham was in charge and having a miserable time with 'two of his biggest Guns in the front stuck in a Bog, which he could not disengage by any Endeavours he could at that time use, neither could he bring forwards any of the Guns that were behind except two 4 pounders & one 1½ pounder'. Hawley had already referred to him as 'such a Sot and so ignorant' that he could not see them agreeing for long. He was right. The action began before Cunningham arrived.

The dragoons continued their attempts to 'draw the fire, and ride in and break the Highlanders,' but the clansmen stood firm remembering their orders from Lord George. The storm broke as the last of the Government troops trudged up the hill 'running & quite out of breath [with] the fatigue'. The drenching rain soaked their cartridges so that when they came to fire their muskets one in four failed. Hawley's men took up their battle position trying to make out their enemy through the driving rain. The opposing lines of foot squared up to each other with a strange symmetry. The Government infantry on the left was outflanked by half the Jacobite front-line and on the right it was pretty much vice versa. Furthermore, the Government troops on the right faced the ravine which stopped them moving around the Jacobite left flank.

As the light faded on 17 January Hawley ordered his dragoons to attack. He had no doubt that his cavalry was more than a match for the scurvy band of bare-foot warriors and anticipated a speedy and victorious conclusion. However, as others with experience of Highlanders could have told him, this was not to be. Lord George Murray watched the dragoons advancing 'at full trot, in very good order' and when they were only about ten yards away raised his musket as the signal to fire. Some eighty dragoons slumped dead in their saddles. An observer recorded the carnage, especially how 'in one part of them nearest us I saw day light through them in several places'.

It had a devastating impact. Many simply turned and fled and Hawley saw for himself the folly of assuming that cavalry must be able to outmanoeuvre clansmen fighting on foot. Chevalier Johnstone described vivdly what happened next: 'The most singular and extraordinary combat immediately followed. The Highlanders, stretched on the ground, thrust their dirks into the bellies of the horses. Some seized the riders by their clothes, dragged them down, and stabbed them with their dirks; several again used their pistols; but few of them had sufficient space to handle their swords. Macdonald of Clanranald . . . assured me that whilst he was lying upon the ground, under a dead horse, which had fallen upon him, without the power of extricating himself, he saw a dismounted horseman struggling with a Highlander: fortunately for him, the Highlander, being the strongest, threw his antagonist, and having killed him with his dirk, he came to his assistance, and drew him with difficulty from under his horse.'

The sight of the fleeing dragoons was irresistible to some of the Highlanders. Ignoring Lord George Murray's command to hold their ground two of the three Macdonald regiments – Clanranald's and Glengarry's – hurtled after them. It had been a fine beginning but this anarchy on the field meant a wasted opportunity and cost the Jacobites dear. The Highlanders 'pursued the dragoons, others fell a plundering the dead; a considerable body that kept a just direction in their march, fell in with the Glasgow militia, and were employed in dispersing them'. They would have had far greater impact had they stayed on the battlefield.

Dramatic things were happening on the Jacobite left. Incapable of reloading and returning the fire they were now under, the Highlanders launched themselves on 'perhaps one of the boldest and finest actions, that any troops of the world cou'd be capable of'. They flung down their muskets and charged, swords aloft and

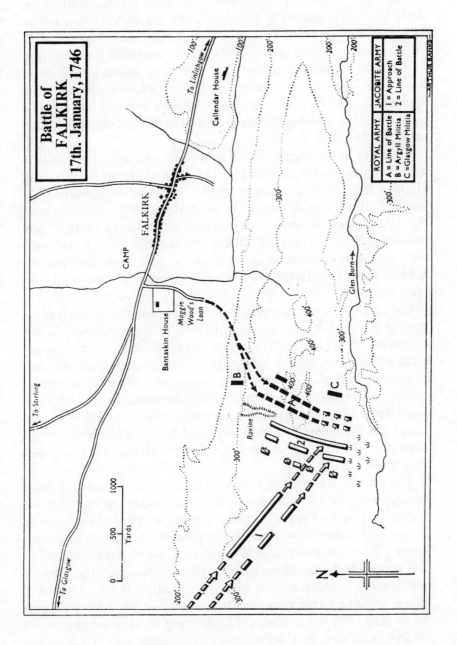

Battle of
FALKIRK
17th. January, 1746

To Linlithgow

Callendar House

FALKIRK

CAMP

Bantaskin House

Maggie Wood's Loan

To Stirling

Ravine

Glen Burn

To Glasgow

N

Yards
0   500   1000

ROYAL ARMY
A = Line of Battle
B = Argyll Militia
C = Glasgow Militia

JACOBITE ARMY
1 = Approach
2 = Line of Battle

—ARTHUR BANKS—

yelling their battle cry. This was too much for the soldiers of Wolfe's, Cholmondeley's, Pulteney's and the Royal – men who had seen and survived Fontenoy – and they ran, followed with little hesitation by the whole of the second line with the exception of Barrel's. Hawley was appalled. Someone asked him if there were any regiments still standing and if so where they were. The General apparently made no answer – or not one that was suitable to be recorded – and as the disorder and confusion increased, rode off down the hill.

Yet three of his regiments did stand firm and inflicted considerable damage. Moving up the hill they opened fire on the pursuing Highlanders, causing a panic made worse when Colonel Roy Stewart 'afraid lest this might be an ambuscade . . . called out to the Highlanders to stop their pursuit; and the cry of stop flew immediately from rank to rank. . . .' The bewildered clansmen were not sure whether to go on or stand still. Some even left the field and made for Bannockburn and Stirling with tales of a Highland defeat.

Lord George was managing things with more discipline, leading men of Keppoch's regiment and the Atholl Brigade down the hill 'in perfect good order'. His sights were on the stricken Government troops 'running off by forties and fifties to the right and left to get into Falkirk. . . .' However, even after calling for reinforcements, Lord George had no more than about six or seven hundred men. The rest were scattered right across the face of the hill and could not be rallied in time to support him. So he halted at the bottom of the hill and let the Government rearguard flee pell-mell into the darkness.

The official accounts of Hawley's retreat were somewhat economical with the truth. They explained smoothly enough that the excessive rain had made it more sensible to leave their camp in favour of Linlithgow where the troops could be put under proper cover. 'When we came to strike our tents, we found that many of the drivers had run off with the horses: upon which the General gave orders, that what tents were left should be burnt; which was done,' was one virtuous explanation. However, the truth was there to be seen. When the whooping, cheering clansmen ran into the abandoned camp they found most of the tents still standing and joyfully seized ammunition, waggons and a fine haul of 'three standards, two stand of colours, a kettledrum, many small arms, their baggage, clothing, and generally everything they had not burnt or destroyed'. To add insult to injury Charles entered Falkirk and ate Hawley's dinner, 'which he wanted very much'. O'Sullivan wrote an enthusiastic inventory of the 'great many hampers of good wines, & liqors & other provisions' found in the town. The Jacobites had advanced into Falkirk by torchlight to find the enemy gone and nothing but a few frightened stragglers to be dragged from their hiding places.

The Battle of Falkirk only lasted about twenty minutes. The Highlanders lost about fifty dead and sixty or seventy wounded as opposed to at least three hundred dead on the Government side, probably more. One of the most distinguished of the Government fatalities was Sir Robert Monro, 'who was heard much to blaspheme during the engagement, and as a punishment for which, his tongue was miraculously cut asunder by a sword, that struck him directly across the mouth' as one Jacobite recorded in self-righteous tones. The Whig Press described it rather differently, reporting that poor Sir Robert had been hacked to pieces in dastardly fashion. The Highland fallen were sometimes identified by the fact that they had bannocks and other food concealed under their left armpit. With amazing cheek Hawley claimed his losses at twelve officers and fifty-five men killed and a grand total of two hundred and eighty killed, wounded, and missing.

Charles behaved with his customary chivalry to his prisoners, who included a strange haul of bellicose Presbyterian ministers. Some had actually perished on the field like one who, 'seeing the danger he was in of losing his life as a Soldier, had recourse to his dignity, supposing that would be a cloak to save him. "Spare my life," said he to a Highlander, who was on the point of taking it, "for I am a Minister of My Master Jesus Christ!" To which the other ingeniously replied: "If you are a good one, your Master has need of you; if not, it's fitting that you go and take your punishment elsewhere!" – which dilemma was immediately solved by the Highlander's sword.' Charles also captured a clutch of Hawley's travelling hangmen. The latter were released on their parole. And broke it. Maxwell of Kirkconnell bewailed the morals of the age like a Fielding heroine: 'It is true, the decay of virtue and honour in our Island since the Accession is very remarkable, and the progress and barefacedness of vice astonishing. . . .' Hitherto, he mourned, a man's word of honour had been his bond.

The generosity with which the prisoners were treated, coupled with Charles's success in the field, were a seductive combination, causing one prisoner to exclaim, 'By my soul, Dick, if Prince Charles goes on this way, Prince Frederick will never be King George!' It was also noted that Charles's presence on the field, encouraging and praising his Highlanders, had had a visible effect on his men's morale. According to one account he had played an active role: 'The Prince, who was mostly in the center, and whose attention was turned to all parts, observing some regiments of the enemy's foot, and the remainder of the dragoons, marching up the hill, put himself at the head of the Irish pickets, and such of the scattered highlanders as were nearest to him, with a few gentle-men a horse-back, and advanced to attack them. But seeing the order of the pickets, and having a great storm of wind and rain in their faces, they fled precipitantly to their camp. . . .'

However, Charles suffered one unfortunate loss on his side. In the heat of the battle Macdonald of Tiendrish, the Major of Keppoch's regiment, mistook one of Hawley's regiments for Lord John Drummond's. He charged into their midst with the unfortunate injunction: 'Why don't ye follow after the dogs and pursue them?' The 'dogs' quickly made him their prisoner and nearly shot him as a spy there and then. He was reprieved but it did him little good as he was later executed at Carlisle.

Hawley, as usual, was not in a magnanimous frame of mind. According to the stories he smashed his sword against the Market Cross in Falkirk and retreated foaming at the mouth with 'rage and vexation'. Later that night at Linlithgow he sat down to write what must have been rather a difficult letter to Cumberland. It may also have made for confusing reading. 'Sir, My Heart is broke. I can't say We are quite beat today, But our Left is beat, and Their Left is beat. We had enough to beat them for we had Two Thousand Men more than They. But such scandalous Cowardice I never saw before. The whole second line of Foot ran away without firing a Shot. Three Squadrons did well. . . .'

And so Hawley, looking 'most wretchedly', was left to withdraw to Edinburgh and to vent his spleen on cowards and deserters – he employed himself with the hanging of thirty-one of Hamilton's dragoons for desertion and shooting thirty-two foot soldiers for cowardice. Poor Cunningham was cashiered. His sword was broken over his head, his sash cut in pieces and thrown in his face, and lastly the provost-martial's servant 'giving him a kick on the posteriors, turned him out of the line'. Neither were the Highlanders feeling particularly buoyant. Lord George was upset about the lack of discipline on the field that had caused them to miss the chance of following and really smashing the opposition. He was blamed in turn for his decision to fight on foot and for failing to bring up the right wing early enough.

While the respective sides weighed up the significance of Falkirk the news had a sobering effect in London, although Cope was said to look remarkably cheerful. He was rumoured to have bet £10,000 that the first general sent to Scotland would be beaten. Government sources tried to twist the truth and the Whig Press weighed in. The *London Gazette* carried a typical blend of fact and fiction reporting that: 'The Rebels, by all Accounts, lost many more Men than the King's Forces, and could not improve the Advantages they had at the Beginning of the Action, but were driven Back by, and fled before a Handful of our Army, and we remain'd Masters of the Field, tho', by the Inclemency of the Weather, and Want of Provisions, Night coming on, our Army was obliged to march to Linlithgow, and thereby abandon what Cannon and Tents they could not find Horses to carry off.' The *True Patriot* carried similar reports and bewailed the fact that the rebels were able to lay their hands on Hawley's cannon. Readers were able to temper their consternation by reading of disasters closer to home. One poor man, a plasterer apparently 'fell through a Necessary House into the River, and was drowned, as is Mr Monkwell of Wapping'. However, the seriousness of the situation trickled through – those itch-ridden laughable savages, the Highlanders, had beaten some crack troops. They were no longer an object of derision but a threat again, and public sentiment demanded action to extinguish 'so dangerous a Flame'.

Action was forthcoming in the corpulent form of the Duke of

Cumberland who now flew north 'like an arrow' to deal with his cousin once and for all. As he could hardly be allowed to set out on his quest without a poem or an ode or a song, a 'British Bard' composed the following lines 'upon his Setting out':

> Go, glorious Youth, belov'd of Britain, go,
> And pour Just Vengeance on the traitrous foe,
> William return'd with health and laurels bless'd,
> And curs'd Rebellion totally depress'd,
> Crush'd! Sunk! confounded! never to rise again,
> And let exulting Britains say – Amen.

The *True Patriot* noted the great number of cooks who were also sent up to Scotland to satisfy the royal appetite at Holyrood. 'Perhaps,' Fielding speculated satirically, 'it is intended to let these Cooks fall into the Hands of the Enemy, which would be no bad Stratagem, for could we introduce some of our Luxury among them, we should soon find it a much easier Task to beat them.' The Edinburgh populace took comfort from the knowledge that Cumberland was back in the saddle and the mere sight of him when he arrived in the early hours of 30 January apparently did 'the Business', 'banishing all Remembrances of the late untoward Accident, and the Troops shew'd uncommon Ardour to be led (Bad as the Weather was) into the Field again'. Bells and illuminations greeted the young hero.

However, the time for battle had not yet come. In the Jacobite camp the usual arguments had been going on about what to do next. Lord George wanted to march on Hawley and finish the job. Others argued for marching on London at once. There was also a powerful lobby in favour of continuing the siege of Stirling Castle and this prevailed with Charles. To Chevalier Johnstone it was a 'fatal resolution'. The Jacobites were putting all their faith in the ridiculous Mirabelle de Gordon and his wild promises that the castle could be reduced in a matter of days. As Johnstone pointed out, 'The possession of this petty fort was of no essential importance to us; on the contrary, it was of more advantage to us that it should remain in the hands of the enemy, in order to restrain the Highlanders, and prevent them from returning, when they pleased, to their own country, from the fear of being made prisoners in passing this Castle, for they were constantly going home, whenever they got possession of any booty taken from the English in order to secure it.' Desertion was, indeed, a growing problem. It was made worse when Glengarry's second son was accidentally killed by a stray shot in the streets of Falkirk – the clansmen were casual with their weapons. Although it was an accident, which the young Glengarry forgave on his deathbed, and although the unfortunate culprit was executed to stop inter-clan bloodshed, the Macdonalds of Glengarry were disheartened and began to fade away.

The Commander of Stirling Castle was adamant the Jacobites should not have it, whether it would be to their advantage or not. On receiving a summons to surrender, Major-General Blakeney sent the tart response that he had always been looked upon as a man of honour and that the rebels would find that he intended to die as one. Predictably enough it was difficult to pursuade the Highlanders to do manual work. The batteries were 'injudiciously errected, and the Highlanders shew'd a great Aversion for that Kind of Service, for which they are naturally unfit'. However, eventually three of the battery's six emplacements were ready. One 16-pounder gun and two 12-pounders were mounted and Mirabelle predicted the fall of the castle within eighteen hours of opening fire.

The cannonade began on 29 January, and 'M. Mirabelle, with a childish impatience to witness the effects of his battery unmasked it . . . and immediately began a very brisk fire . . . but it was of short duration and produced very little effect on the batteries of the Castle, which being more elevated than ours, the enemy could see even the buckles of the shoes of our artillerymen. As their fire commanded ours, our guns were immediately dismounted, and in less than half an hour we were obliged to abandon our battery altogether. . . .' The furious Highlanders began to wonder if Mirabelle had been sent amongst them as a saboteur.

Meanwhile news that Cumberland was on his way had given the clan chiefs the jitters. Not only that, but since Falkirk the Government forces had been joined by the artillery train from Newcastle and reinforcements of cavalry and infantry. A formidable force was collecting and would soon be at the Jacobites' throats. There then followed one of those events that Charles would always remember as a betrayal. Lord George Murray and the chiefs presented Charles with an address. This expressed their fears that they were in no state to meet the Government troops which would march as soon as the Duke arrived. There had been too many desertions from the Highland ranks. The only course was an immediate retreat to the Highlands to sit out the winter there and wait for the spring to come. The greatest difficulty they foresaw was over what to do with the artillery, particularly the heavy cannon, but the situation was so serious that it would be better to throw them into the Forth than risk either Charles or the flower of his army.

For Charles it was Derby all over again. He argued, stormed and raved. He 'struck his head against the wall until he staggered and exclaimed most violently against Lord George'. His bitter words were 'Good God! Have I lived to see this?' He predicted nothing but ruin and destruction, but the chiefs remained unmoved. He could not understand why they were willing to throw away the advantage so recently gained at Falkirk, and pointed out that a move north would destroy any hopes of major French aid – he had written to Louis after Falkirk appealing for help. Neither would it encourage any assistance from his friends in England which he still hoped for. It was no good. In the end Charles wrote to his chiefs agreeing to the retreat but saying that he washed his hands of consequences which he knew would be fatal.

The retreat began on the morning of 1 February, the day after Cumberland and the bulk of his force had marched into Linlithgow and his bivouacking troops burned down the ancient palace through carelessness. It had been agreed that the Jacobite force would rendezvous near St Ninians at nine in the morning, but this went wrong. Before daybreak the Highlanders were racing for the Fords of Frew in what looked like a complete panic, carts and cannon abandoned on the road. Even worse, the church in St Ninians was blown up by accident. It had been used by the Jacobites as a powder-magazine and the idea was to destroy the remaining powder by exploding it on waste-ground. However, the local people were busily pilfering it to sell to Cumberland's men. To put a stop to this freebooting a Highlander fired a warning shot and ignited a trail of spilt powder leading straight back to the church which was blasted to smithereens. Only the tower was left standing amidst the smoking rubble. Lochiel had narrowly avoided being hit by falling masonry and Murray of Broughton's wife was flung out of her chaise to lie senseless on the road until picked up by some village people. Lord George arrived, cursing furiously, to find this depressing scene and not a man in sight, despite all his carefully laid plans for an orderly withdrawal.

It was not surprising that the council of war held at Crieff on the evening of 2 February was bitterly acrimonious. According to one report, 'there never had been such heats and animosities as at this meeting . . .' – in the light of the rancour at previous councils this was saying something. Charles laid the blame for the disorder and chaos firmly on the shoulders of Lord George. Lord George blamed O'Sullivan and would hardly allow Charles to speak. In the end it was agreed that the army would divide. The cavalry and low country regiments would take the coast road to Inverness. The Prince and the clan regiments would take the Highland road. These were the high road and the low road of the songs. On 4 February the two forces went their separate ways but with Cumberland in hot pursuit. Like his cousin, Cumberland had an eye for an occasion. 'Shall we not have one song?' he asked and spurring his horse struck up with:

> Will ye play me fair?
> Highland laddie, Highland laddie

CHAPTER TEN

'LA BELLE REBELLE'

THE wintry weather matched Charles's mood as he marched through 'the cruellest snow that cou'd be seen' with his Highlanders. Meanwhile Lord George Murray struggled with the bulk of the artillery train. He tried to send cannon ahead to Blair Castle as Charles had asked, but the going was too difficult and fourteen of them had to be thrown into the Tay – a gift to Cumberland who fished them out again a few days later. However, Charles was this time able to subdue the small garrison at Ruthven with 'three Swedish pieces, & the Cannon he took at Falkirk'. From there his road lay via Aviemore where he crossed the Spey and made for Inverness. On 16 February he reached the welcoming walls of Moy Hall – home of Lady Mackintosh. This slender young woman had defied her husband, Aeneas Mackintosh, twenty-second Laird of Mackintosh, by herself calling out his men for the Prince after he had decided to throw in his lot with Hanover in return for 'half-a-guinea the day and half-a-guinea the morn'.

Charles was nobly entertained by 'Colonel Anne' who laid on an exceedingly 'plentiful and genteel' supper for his entire household of seventy-five. This was a welcome contrast to his stingy hostess of the previous night – Lady Dalrachny – who had charged the Highlanders for meal and said that she was glad to be shot of the lot of them: 'What a pack ye are! God let me never hae the like of you in my house again!' Yet the fine old house of Moy with its gracious hostess was no refuge. It did not take long for news of Charles's whereabouts to reach the Hanoverian Lord Loudon who was holding Inverness. Learning that Charles was at Moy he decided to try and capture him, lured both by the thought of the £30,000 reward and even more enticingly perhaps by the prospect of putting Cope's and Hawley's noses out of joint. The stories about what happened that night vary according to the teller, but what ocurred was probably something like this.

Delighted with his own cunning, Loudon threw a cordon around Inverness, reinforced the castle garrison and marched stealthily towards Moy with fifteen hundred of his men. His plan was to take Charles by surprise. However, fifteen hundred men cannot move unseen and unheard even on a cold February night in the Highlands. News of his scheme reached the dowager Lady Mackintosh in Inverness who shared her daughter-in-law's Jacobite, rather than her son's Hanoverian, sentiments. She despatched a young Mackintosh clansman with instructions to dodge through Loudon's patrols and get to Moy to warn the Prince. It was a hasty departure. He left the house with his bonnet on top of his nightcap, a somewhat ludicrous but heroic figure. Meanwhile young Lady Mackintosh had already taken the precaution of sending the Moy blacksmith, a massive man called Donald Fraser, and four others to camp out 'upon a moor, at some distance from Moy, towards Inverness' to keep watch.

Straining into the blackness, the blacksmith made out the shadowy figures of Loudon's advance guard and fired his piece, his four companions following suit. At the same time they bellowed their clan war-cries at the tops of their voices, and according to one account the blacksmith shouted, 'Advance, Advance, my lads, Advance!. . . . I think we have the dogs now,' which 'so struck Lord Loudon's men with horror, that instantly they wheel'd about, after firing some shots, and in great confusion ran back with speed to Inverness,' imagining the Prince's entire army to be at their heels. Lord Loudon wrote his own more dignified account but could not conceal that an army of fifteen hundred men had been thrown into 'the greatest confusion' by a blacksmith and four companions. The only casualty had been a piper – the famous Macrimmon, hereditary piper to the Macleod. He died at the blacksmith's first discharge and is reputed to have foreseen his end as befitted a man believed to have the second sight. Before leaving Skye he had composed a sad lament *'Cha til me tuille'*, meaning 'I'll return no more':

[169]

Macleod shall come back
But Macrimmon shall
never.

This inglorious episode came to be known as the 'Rout of Moy'
and established Anne Mackintosh in the first rank of Jacobite
heroines. Although the accounts of that night show a somewhat
distraught young woman 'in her smock-petticoat, running through
the close, speaking loudly and expressing her anxiety about the
Prince's safety', and even 'running about like a madwoman in
her shift' as O'Sullivan unchivalrously described her, it was her
presence of mind that saved Charles. Hearing that Loudon was
on his way, she had dashed into Charles's room where he lay fast
asleep. Charles instantly jumped out of bed 'and would have been
going down stairs directly, but Lady Mackintosh importuned him
to stay in the room till she should get him further notice and try
what could be done. . . .' However, Charles did not apparently
do as she bade. Instead, 'he run hastily out of bed to call up his
men, and as it was a keen frost contracted thereby such a cold as
stuck to him very long, and I may ev'n say endanger'd his life,
which was one great reason of his staying so much at Inverness
afterwards, to the great detriment of his affairs in other places.'
Certainly the freezing night air was too much for him, clad as he
was in dressing gown and slippers and his resulting illness put him
out of action for the rest of February. A Whig version of events
did its best to make him look ridiculous, describing him flying in
déshabille out of the house, running three miles and roaming
through the wilds till morning.

Whatever the effect on Charles, the whole experience proved
too much for some of Loudon's men. Next morning some two
hundred of them deserted. This led Loudon to decide that his best
course was to hurry across the ferry at Kessock to Easter Ross
which was relatively friendly to the Government and there await
the arrival of Cumberland. This enabled the Jacobites to march
to Inverness and take possession of the town without firing a shot.
It was one of those situations where the victorious army marched
in at one end and the defeated one hurried out at the other – in
this case retreating shambolically over the Ness Bridge. The castle

as well as the town quickly surrendered to its new masters and yielded some barrels of beef that were very welcome to the famished Highlanders. Charles insisted that the fortifications be blown up and it was unfortunate that the French artillery sergeant charged with the task blew himself up too, but it was apparently considered worth reporting, in typically British fashion, that a dog which was also caught in the blast 'received little Damage'!

If Charles thought the flight of Loudon and the capture of Inverness were an amazing stroke of luck, his cousin Cumberland was similarly astounded: 'I am really quite at a loss to explain all the contradictions I meet here from morning to night, for I am assured by people who should know the hills the best, that there are no places between the Blair of Atholl and Inverness where 500 man can subsist in a body, yet Lord Loudon has been driven across the Firth with 2,000 men which he said he had, and expecting a junction of 1,500 more, by that party of the rebels alone which marched from Blair with the Pretender's son, and which I could never make, by the best account I had, above 600 men. . . .'

Charles chose several comfortable establishments for his recuperation. One of these was Culloden House some five miles from Inverness and the home of the Lord President, Duncan Forbes. Forbes had been working to thwart him from the outset and although Cumberland dismissed him as an 'old woman', he had been effective in raising troops and containing the rebellion by discouraging wavering chiefs. So there was a fine irony in enjoying his comfortable house and the hogsheads of claret in his cellars. Even in Captain Burt's day, Culloden House had been famous for its hospitality so that 'few go away sober at any time' and some were incapable of going anywhere. Forbes himself, sober or not, had fled with Loudon just the day before.

Charles was joined soon after by Lord George Murray, who complained bitterly about the fatigue and trouble he and his men had undergone. One of these men, John Daniels, left a moving account of their journey: 'When we marched out of Aberdeen, it blew, snowed, hailed, and froze to such a degree, that few Pictures ever represented Winter, with all its icicles about it, better than many of us did that day.' He described men covered with icicles, their eyebrows and beards encrusted with ice, stragglers lost in the deep snow drifts and driving snow and cutting hail making it impossible to see more than a few yards ahead. Lord George's companions had not been lively company. He had been rejoined on the march north by the love-sick Lord Ogilvy who had left his pretty young wife, his 'angel', at his father's house because he feared the cold would kill her. He also feared a rival might take her away from him and was sunk in gloom. Lord Balmerino, on the other hand, bearing out a description of his 'warm disposition and blunt deportment,' was getting more and more short-tempered at what he saw as Murray's bossiness. 'Let us do what we are ordered. It is vain to dispute,' he told his men. 'A time will come when I shall see things righted at Lord George's cost and mine. But at present he is my superior, and we must obey for the good of the Prince.' All in all it had been a trying expedition.

Murray had sensibly left garrisons behind at Elgin and at Nairn to hinder Cumberland's advance and stop him joining up with Loudon, but Cumberland was having problems as well in the bitter conditions. Before he could face a Highland winter he had to have supplies. This meant he had no option but to remain at Perth until 20 February when he at last was able to begin his march to Aberdeen. His vanguard reached it three days after the Jacobites had left. He also had trouble with the six thousand or so Hessian troops who had arrived at Leith on 8 February with their Prince Frederick, married to George II's daughter Mary. The Hessians were a chivalrous group and not much impressed with the blunter manners of Hanover. In particular, they were disgusted by Cumberland's attitude towards Jacobite prisoners whom he insisted on treating as rebels, undeserving of any code of conduct towards them. The Hessians refused to fight without such a code and the Prince of Hesse found a good way of expressing his contempt for Cumberland. While the young Duke was away campaigning, the Prince gave a series of balls in Edinburgh to which 'none but Jacobite ladies were invited'.

In Aberdeen Cumberland was again forced to give his attention to laying in supplies. He seized a supply of Spanish arms and ammunition from Corgarff Castle in Jacobite country. His own behaviour and that of the charming Hawley was that of an army of occupation in hostile territory. They lived completely free for six weeks at the end of which Hawley departed with several hundred pounds' worth of his hostess's belongings. They also tried to suppress the distribution of pro-Jacobite 'Libels dropp'd about the Town by the Rebel Party' by checking the handwriting of suspected authors, 'but it proved ineffectual'. A far better use of time was Cumberland's efforts to train his troops to counter Highland tactics. The Whig newspapers raged against the Highland fighting style, implying it was not only wild and unorthodox but somehow unfair.

According to one contemporary, the tactic of the Highlander 'when descending to battle, was to place his bonnet on his head with an emphatic "scrug", his second, to cast off or throw back his plaid; his third to incline his body horizontally forward, cover it with his target, rush to within 50 paces of the enemy's line, discharge and drop his fusee or musket; his fourth to dart within 12 paces, discharge and fling his claw-butted steel locked pistols at the foeman's head; his fifth to draw claymore and dirk at him!' Another account described how the Highlanders 'stooped below the charged bayonets, they tossed them upward by the target, dirking the front-rank man with the left hand, while stabbing or hewing down the rear rank man with the right; thus, as usual in all Highland onsets, the whole body of soldiers was broken, trod underfoot, and dispersed in a moment'.

Cumberland decided to do something about this. His orderly-book recorded his view that 'The manner of the Highlander's way of fighting' was 'easy to resist, if officers and men are not prepossessed with the lyes and accounts which are told of them'. He devised and taught his men a new bayonet exercise. Basically this relied on each man lunging at the Highlander to his immediate right rather than his own direct assailant. It was an effective tactic and the troops became so expert 'that the whole Spell of the Highlander's irregular way of fighting was broken, as appear'd afterwards in the battle of Culloden', as one smug account put it.

None of this boded well for the Jacobites but at least it gave them a breathing space, and while Charles recuperated at Culloden House, the chiefs devised a Highland strategy dear to their hearts. They wanted to keep Cumberland holed up in Aberdeen and retain a grip on the coastal supply line in case aid should arrive from

France. They also wanted to reduce the Goverment's Highland forts, to disperse Lord Loudon's army, and to repel any Government reinforcements that tried to sneak up through the central Highlands. Lord George cheerfully envisaged a guerilla campaign lasting several years which would force the English to come to terms. What Charles, lying on his sick-bed, thought of all this is unknown.

At first the strategy had some success, as Maxwell of Kirkconnell later described: 'The vulgar may be dazzled with a victory,' he wrote in lofty tones, 'but in the eyes of a connoisseur, the Prince will appear greater about this time at Inverness than either at Gladsmuir or at Falkirk.' Fort Augustus on Loch Ness surrendered on 5 March after a two-day siege when a shell landed in the powder magazine. Its subsequent sacking was a traditional Highland affair with pillaging on a grand scale. However, Fort William, strategically placed at the head of Loch Linnhe as a reminder to the Jacobite clans of Lochaber to toe the line, was not such easy pickings. Neither was the siege so well directed. The director of operations, one Grant, was killed by a stray cannon-ball and the 'senseless' Mirabelle was again allowed free rein. He was no match for the fort's determined and competent commander Caroline Scott, a Lowlander, who was later to achieve an entirely deserved reputation for sadism for the way he hunted down fugitives after Culloden. Not surprisingly the siege declined into stalemate.

However, the anti-Loudon campaign was effective enough. In his flight from Moy, Loudon had seized as many boats as he could find. These enabled him to flit backwards and forwards across the Dornoch Firth, dodging his Jacobite pursuers. The Duke of Perth decided this must stop. He rounded up a fleet of fishing boats and embarked his men. They sailed across the Firth in a thick fog, surrounded Loudon's nervous army and scattered it to the winds. Loudon, Forbes and the other leaders were forced to flee to Skye. In the aftermath a number of prisoners were taken and these included Aeneas, husband of 'Colonel Anne'. On Charles's orders he was handed over to his wife at Moy where 'he could not be in better security or more honourably treated'. His wife greeted him with 'Your servant, Captain', to which he is said to have replied, 'Your servant, Colonel.' Charles was continuing with his policy of treating his prisoners humanely and causing his own men to grumble. One of these, a Mr Peter Smith, 'who had always very singular ideas', suggested cutting off the thumbs of their right hands to stop them from holding muskets. But this did not find favour with Charles.

On 15 March Lord George marched out with his Atholl men. His sights were set on the Government's thirty military block-houses that dotted the Atholl landscape. Together with Cluny Macpherson's men he orchestrated a series of early morning raids on 17 March which were so successful that every single blockhouse was taken without the loss of a single Highlander. The victorious raiders returned with three hundred dazed prisoners who had no idea what had hit them. Inspired by this Murray moved on to the siege of Blair Castle, which belonged to his brother, and occupied a strategic position, but this campaign was not a success and, according to an eye-witness account later published in the *Scots Magazine*, had its farcical side. The castle was being held for the Government by Sir Andrew Agnew, a man of such fearsome repu-tation that no Highlander would agree to carry the summons from Lord George calling on him to surrender. In the end they decided to send the maid-servant from the inn at Blair who, 'being rather handsome, and very obliging, conceived herself to be on so good a footing with some of the young officers, that she need not be afraid of being shot, and undertook the mission. . . .'

However, her powers of advocacy were not what she had hoped and she was glad to escape from Blair with her life. Agnew promised to shoot the next such messenger through the head but was denied the pleasure when Government reinforcements arrived to help him, including some of the Hessians. Lord George requested twelve hundred extra men to support him, Charles turned him down, and that was that. He said that he did not have that number of men in Inverness. This led Murray to try to treat with the Hessians on his own, knowing that their Prince was still declaring that he had no wish to risk his subjects in a fight between the Stuarts and the House of Hanover. What he hoped to achieve was an end to the rising with a negotiated settlement. However, Charles saw this as nothing less than betrayal and from that day forward had Lord George even more closely watched. All the stories he had been told about Murray's friendship with Duncan Forbes and former allegiance to the house of Hanover returned to haunt him.

However, Murray's soldiers captured a Hessian hussar during the siege. Murray conversed with him in Latin, their only common language, before sending him back with a letter addressed to Prince Frederick asking to know 'upon what footing Your Highness proposes making war in these Kingdoms' and whether the Prince would like to have some sort of reciprocal arrangement about the treatment of prisoners. The Hessian Prince's answer would have been an unequivocal 'yes' but he had to consult his portly commander. Cumberland's response was predictable – and sinister in what it implied. He marvelled at 'the insolence of these rebels, who dare to propose a cartel, having themselves a rope round their necks'. This was enough for the Hessian who refused to move his men north of Pitlochry, and Cumberland was thus deprived of their support at Culloden.

Murray's exploits in Atholl may have lifted Jacobite morale but they had also strengthened Cumberland's resolve to deal with Charles once and for all. For a while the two rival armies dodged and feinted around each other, but the advantage seemed to be with the Jacobites. They knew the terrain and how to fight in it. They retreated across the Spey believing that a vast force under Cumberland was on the move towards them. Yet as soon as it became clear it was just a reconnaissance, they counter-attacked and won a swift-fought battle against their old enemies the Campbells in the churchyard at Keith. It seemed in those heady weeks that Charles was in the ascendant and that there would be a long campaign with everything to play for. However, as so often in this tale, just when success seemed to be within reach it was snatched away again. . . .

Not that the young Prince was really in a fit state to judge his chances of success. He had got over the bout of pneumonia that had struck him down after Moy, thanks to the care of the dowager Lady Mackintosh but he was still weak. On 11 March he set out to tour the Jacobite defences on the Inverness side of the Spey but in Elgin he fell dramatically ill with 'a spotted fever' which was probably scarlet fever. There was very real concern that he might not recover but in spite of the best efforts of the surgeons who bled him rigorously he survived. It is part of the folklore that on 20 March he insisted on getting up, asserting that if he had to die he would rather do it on horseback fighting Cumberland than lying about in bed sipping gruel, and that people were only ill if they thought themselves so! The sight of their Prince 'caused a joy in every heart not to be described' but everything was about to go wrong.

For one thing Charles was 'in great distress for want of money'. A consignment of treasure from France aboard *Le Prince Charles* – formerly the Government sloop of war *Hazard* – failed to reach him through a series of misadventures. Chased by a British naval squadron, the captain had been forced to beach his ship in the Kyle of Tongue. Knowing how much Charles was depending on the gold, he and his men struggled to carry it along 'frightful roads' in hostile territory. They surrendered at last near Ben Loyal having tossed twelve thousand pounds into the heather to keep them out of Government hands. However, this was small comfort to the Jacobites. Maxwell of Kirkconnell described how 'This last misfortune soon took air . . . and disheartened the army.' What it meant was that the Highlanders were reduced to receiving their pay 'mostly in meal, which they did not like and very often mutiny'd, refused to obey orders, and Sometimes threw down their arms and went home. . . .' The *London Magazine* reported with glee that the enemy camp was beset with 'Confusion and Mutinies'. Government supporters were delighted. They read in the papers that the most valuable part of the sloop's cargo had been a cask of consecrated beads to be distributed by the priests, and rejoiced at the thwarting of yet another Popish scheme.

Another misfortune was that Murray of Broughton had also fallen ill at Elgin at the same time as Charles. He had to be replaced by the manifestly incompetent Hay of Restalrig who was hopeless at organising provisions. Nothing was done to ensure adequate supplies for an army engaged in an arduous campaign in a remote and impoverished part of the country. Without food it was inevitable that men would desert. In addition news began to filter through that 'the embarkation from Boulogne, which had amused the world so long, and even that from Dunkirk, were entirely laid aside. . . .' No military aid was coming from France after all.

Perhaps it was to forget such bleak thoughts that in those last weeks before Culloden Charles threw himself into a round of feverish gaieties. He went hunting, shooting and fishing. He gave frequent balls for the ladies of Inverness and danced himself which, as Maxwell of Kirkconnell pointed out, 'he had declined doing at Edinburgh in the midst of his grandeur and prosperity.' Of course, Inverness was very different from the capital where he had held court. According to one of Cumberland's men, it was 'a small, dirty, poor Place'. While it was the capital of the Highlands this was not saying much when the average Highland town was just 'composed of a few huts'. In the eyes of some the only thing to recommend it was its handsome women. Life was so impoverished there that an onion or carrot was a rarity and when a tailor made a suit of clothes for a gentleman everything, including the thread and buttons, was weighed before him and woe betide if the weight of the finished garments and leftover scraps did not correspond exactly. However, Charles needed to reanimate that sense of romantic destiny that had driven him in the early stages of his campaign.

The period of dalliance ended with the news that Cumberland was on the move at last. He had left Aberdeen on 8 April, apparently marching on foot with his men as Charles had been so fond of doing. By the time the news reached Charles on 13 April, Cumberland was already over the Spey. It was one of the many mistakes in what was becoming a tragedy of errors that nothing had been done to stop him. The so-called Jacobite 'Army of the Spey' which Perth and his brother had boasted would stop Cumberland crossing did nothing to stem the 'verminous tide of red coats' as one Highlander described it. The swollen waters had receded and Cumberland's men forded it in three places without opposition and with the minimal loss of one dragoon and his wife, who fell off their horse 'lovingly together', and three women. According to some accounts they were in good spirits. One Government volunteer recorded with gusto how they marched through a village 'noted for a famous Bawdy-House, kept by an old Woman and her two Daughters', cheerfully stringing up suspected spies.

At least the period of waiting was over – the Highland army had been at Inverness for two months suffering all the disadvantages of privation and uncertainty. On 14 April Charles 'ordered the drums to beat and the pipes to play to arms. The men in the town assembled as fast as they could, the cannon was ordered to march, and the Prince mounted on horseback and went out at their head to Culloden House, the place of rendezvous; and Lord George Murray was left in the town to bring up those that were quartered in the neighbourhood of Inverness. . . .' He joined up with Charles later that day. On the following day, Lord John Drummond met up with them as well, and 'the whole army marched up to the muir, about a mile to the eastward of Culloden House, where they were all drawn up in order of battle to wait the Duke of Cumberland's coming'.

This 'muir' lay at the north-western edge of a great expanse of upland country known as Drummossie Moor between the Nairn and the Moray Firth. The verdict of many eye-witnesses was that it was a pretty poor place for the Jacobites to do battle. It was probably O'Sullivan's choice but that was not the only reason Lord George disliked it. He later described his feelings with all the bitterness of hindsight: 'I did not like the ground, it was certainly not proper for Highlanders. I proposed that Brigadier Stapleton and Colonel Ker should view the ground on the other side of the water of Nairn, which they did. It was found to be hilly and boggy; so that the enemy's cannon and horse could be of no great use to them there.' Culloden, on the other hand, was a disastrous choice. 'Not one single soldier but would have been against such a field had their advice been askt. A plain moor where regular troops had . . . full use of their Cannon so as to annoy the Highlanders prodigioulsy before they could make an attack.'

However, this is where the Jacobite army stood to arms on that cold spring day of 15 April, scanning the heather and straining their ears for the first enemy drumbeat. Yet Cumberland did not come. It was his birthday and he was celebrating it snug in his camp at Nairn where his men munched cheese and toasted 'the youth who draws the sword of liberty and truth' as one ghastly birthday poem describe him – in half a pint of brandy. Charles's men shivered on the open moorland, cold and hungry. Their food, the meal which was their payment, had been left at Inverness due to the ineptitude of John Hay. His only response when challenged by a furious Lord George was to bleat 'Everything will be got! Everything will be got!' All the men did get on being stood down was a biscuit a piece.

Lord George was also worried by the fact that the army was anyway below strength. There would be little chance of success in a pitched battle, particularly given the terrain of Culloden Moor. The more he surveyed it the gloomier he became. Nothing was more likely to favour the fighting tactics of regular troops. This persuaded him to agree to lead an attack on the Duke's camp some twelve miles away at Nairn, provided it was at night and not, as Charles had suggested, at dawn. Cumberland's men would, he reasoned, be 'drunk as beggars'. Charles was delighted. For a while he forgot all his grievances against Lord George and embraced him like an old friend. O'Sullivan described how he took him by the hand and placed his other one around his neck, telling him that the glory of the idea was his alone, that by it he would deliver the kingdom from slavery and that he and his father the king would never forget the service he had done. Lord George appears to have been unmoved by all this eloquence. He took off his bonnet, bowed stiffly and said not a word.

Charles's euphoria was short-lived. The army set out in two columns – the van led by Lord George with his Athollmen, Lochiel's Camerons and the Appin Stewarts. They were guided over the treacherous ground by members of the clan Mackintosh whose territory this was. The second column was led by Lord John Drummond with Charles and the French troops in the rear. The plan was that the first column should make a detour around Nairn and attack Cumberland's camp from the east and north. The second column was to launch a simultaneous assault from the south and east. However, it was not until eight o'clock in the evening that the army finally set out. By then many men had deserted, desperate for food. 'When the officers who were sent on horseback to bring them back came up with them, they could by no persuasion be induced to return again, giving for answer they were starving; and said to their officers that they might shoot them if they pleased, but they could not go back till they got meat.'

It was dark and visibility was made worse by a thick fog. Even more men slipped away across the boggy terrain to search for food, unseen by their commanders. Others flung themselves on the ground, too exhausted to move. Inevitably the first column began to lose touch with the second one which lagged further and further behind, the heavily equipped French troops soon floundering in the 'trackless paths, marshes, and quagmires' where 'men were frequently up to their ankles, and the horses in many cases extricated themselves with difficulty'. The exercise was too much to ask of weary men and it soon became clear that they could not possibly reach Nairn before daylight. There are many accounts of what happened next, as conflicting messages and orders passed up and down the line. According to one eye-witness it was Lochiel who first realised that it was hopeless. He had an urgent conference with Lord George who saw the force of his argument and began the retreat. 'The day is coming and I have taken my decision,' he said.

Charles was never consulted. The first he knew of it was when he came across some of the Duke of Perth's men heading back towards Culloden. '"Where the devil are the men a-going?"', he demanded and then, 'Some positively say that he cry'd out, "I am betrayed. What need I give orders when my orders are disobey'd?" . . . He was very keen for sending orders to Lord George to return; but being told that Lord George was already so far on his way back that it would be impossible to bring up the army with time enough to execute the intended plan, he said with an audible voice "'Tis no matter then. We shall meet them and behave like brave fellows".' One suspects he may have said a great deal more than that. But the net effect was the same – he knew the plan had failed.

It was an exhausted and hungry army that limped back towards Culloden in the dawning light. It was also a disgruntled one: 'The fatigue of this night's march, join'd to the want of sleep for several nights before and the want of food, occasion'd a prodigious murmuring among the private men, many of them exclaiming bitterly ev'n in the Prince's hearing, which affected him very much. Many of them fell asleep in the parks of Culloden and other places near the road, and never waken'd till they found the enemy cutting their throats.' They had walked some twenty miles and some of them had had nothing to eat for two days but a biscuit and some water. It was not surprising that morale was low but there was little that could be done to remedy the desperate situation. After the return from Nairn Charles had tried to get a meal for his men but time was simply running out. Moreover, 'everybody seemed to think of nothing but sleep.' Exhausted clansmen lay everywhere, in the fields and the ditches, dead to the world and the pangs of hunger. Charles returned to Culloden House and fell asleep – as Cumberland had done that night – in his boots.

Oblivion was short-lived. The news came that nemesis – in the form of Cumberland's army – was marching towards them. He was only four miles from Culloden and advancing quickly. There was panic as the drums began to beat. The pipers struck up with the clan rants and men tried to force themselves awake some 'quite exhausted and not able to crawl'. Charles ordered cannon to be fired to assemble the clansmen. Riders dashed to Inverness to sound the alarm. Those that could made their way to the site chosen by O'Sullivan and formed up as they had the previous day, swaying with weariness and straining to catch their first glimpse of Cumberland's men. Charles rode to the moor on a grey gelding at the head of the Camerons, an excited but determined figure in tartan jacket, buff waistcoat and a cockade in his bonnet. He tried to rally their spirits, talking of the glories of Preston Pans and Falkirk. ' "Go on my lads" he said "the day will be ours and we'll want for nothing after". He took a sword from one of the clansmen and tested its edge saying "I'll answer this will cut off some heads and arms today!" ' All that was needed to see off a dispirited enemy was 'a brisk attack'. O'Sullivan thought him truly princely at that moment.

This view was not shared by all. Some – like the French envoy d'Eguilles – had tried to reason with him that it was madness to confront Cumberland in this weakened state and that they should withdraw. Charles was deaf to such arguments, still convinced of his destiny and tired of hesitations and delays and sideshows. 'He could not bring himself to decline battle even for a single day,' wrote the exasperated Frenchman who hurried off to Inverness to burn his papers and to think about how to save any French troops fortunate enough to survive the coming catastrophe. Others had taken over where d'Eguilles had failed, urging Charles to shun a battle or seek a more favourable site. Lord George Murray and Lochiel had pleaded for a withdrawal across the water of Nairn, but he was not to be moved, listening only to his 'favourites' – the Irish – who encouraged his optimism and flattered his ego as Lord Elcho believed. A servant heard him exclaim, 'God damn it, are my orders still disobeyed?' Brigadier Stapleton, Commander of the Franco-Irish Picquets, threw his pennorth in by remarking, 'The Scots are always good troops till things come to a crisis.' This was a like a red rag to a bull to the touchy Highland chiefs. According to Lochiel, 'I do not believe that there was a Highlander in the army who would not have run up to the mouth of a cannon in order to refute the odious and undeserved aspersion.'

This was the mood of bitterness and uncertainty on that chilly April morning. What they were all about to witness was not only the last battle on British soil, but the last time the attacking cry of 'Claymore' would be heard against a Government army and the destruction of the Jacobite dream.

CHAPTER ELEVEN

'NONE BUT A MAD FOOL
WOULD HAVE FOUGHT THAT DAY'

WEDNESDAY 16 April 1746 was a cold and misty day. Sleet and a bitter wind scoured the faces of the Prince's exhausted men. By eleven o'clock in the morning the two armies were face to face and just two and a half miles apart. Cumberland marched another half mile forward then drew up his men in battle order. His own Highlanders, mainly Campbells, were on the flanks – men so nimble that:

> With Kingston's Horse as spies and van,
> From hill to hill they skipt and ran

To Cumberland's pleasure his men manoeuvred 'without the least confusion.' He was firmly convinced that they would 'fight better on empty bellies'. Besides, eating first would be tempting fate – he remembered 'what a dessert they got to their dinner at Falkirk'. Perhaps he reminded Hawley, now commanding his militia and cavalry, of this. He rode amongst his men, a portly but imposing figure urging them to rely on their bayonets. 'Let them mingle with you,' he exhorted them, 'let them know the men they have to deal with.' Neither could he resist a grand speech. His redcoats were fighting for King and country, religion, liberty and property. Any man that wanted to retire could do so with a free pardon because he would rather lead one thousand brave and resolute men than ten thousand tainted with cowardice. Whatever their feelings his men were wise enough not to put this offer to the test.

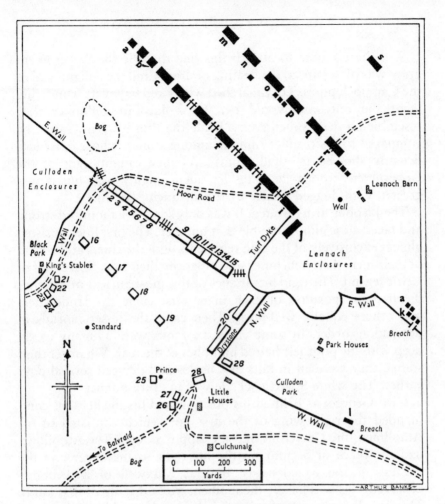

BATTLE OF CULLODEN

Jacobite Army		*Royal Army*	
1 Glengarry	15 2nd Batt Atholl Bgde	a Cobham's Dragoons	o Fleming
2 Keppoch	16 Irish Piquets	b Kingston's Light Horse	p Bligh
3 Clanranald	17 Royal Scots	c Pulteney	q Sempill
4 Duke of Perth	18 Foot Guards	d Royal Scots	r Ligonier
5 Glenbucket	19 Ld L. Gordon	e Cholmondeley	s Blakeney
6 John Roy Stewart	20 Ld Ogilvy	f Price	
7 Farquharson	21 Hussars	g Royal Scots Fusiliers	
8 McLean and McLachlan	22 Perthshire Horse	h Munro	
9 Mackintosh	23 Stonywood	i Barrel	
10 Fraser	24 Bannerman	j Wolfe	
11 Appin	25 Balmerino's Life Guards	k Ld M.Kerr's Dragoons	
12 Cameron	26 Ld Elcho's Life Guards	l Campbells	
13 1st Batt Atholl Bgde	27 FitzJames Horse	m Battereau	
14 3rd Batt Atholl Bgde	28 Avuchie	n Howard	

The Duke of Cumberland's position is marked by the small solid square between and in advance of Howard's regiment and Fleming's (*n* and *o*). The small solid squares between and in advance of Fleming's regiment and Bligh's (*o* and *p*), and to the left of Ligonier's (*r*), represent the cohorn mortars.

With barely time to absorb this fine rhetoric the Government army was off again, to the beating of drums and the defiant wail of the Campbell pipes. They marched with fixed bayonets wondering what the outcome would be. To a Jacobite onlooker they resembled a deep sullen river, 'while the Prince's army might be compared to a streamlet running among stones, whose noise sufficiently showed its shallowness'. As they caught sight of the Government troops the clans let out a mighty roar but it was greeted with dogged silence by the advancing red line.

The Jacobite army waited. It was only some five thousand strong and faced a foe almost double that number. The first line consisted almost exclusively of the clan regiments with the chiefs at the head of their men, their henchmen and pipers by their side, figures out of Celtic legend. The rigid hierarchies of this most ancient of societies dictated the position of each man. First came the landowners and others equally well-born. Then came the lesser mortals in descending order. In some clans the ranks were as many as six deep with the poor felt-haired humblies at the rear. Whatever their status, they were all in kilts as Charles had decreed several days earlier. The white Stuart cockade was in every bonnet.

Lord George, as befitted his position and his inclination, commanded the right wing of the first line which consisted of his Athollmen, the Camerons and the Appin Stuarts. The Athollmen had the place of honour on the far right to the anger and the distress of the Macdonalds, but, as Maxwell of Kirkconnell observed, this was hardly the moment for 'a dispute of that kind'. The Athollmen's right flank grazed the edge of the Culwhiniac enclosure. There had been sharp arguments about the stone enclosures of Culloden Park. Lord George saw this one as a hindrance and wanted it pulled down. O'Sullivan on the other hand thought its dry stone walls would provide excellent cover for the Jacobite right flank. As usual his arguments held sway with Charles and as usual they proved fallacious.

The Camerons – some seven hundred strong – stood to the left of the Athollmen. Their bloodthirsty pibroch could be heard loud and clear: 'You sons of dogs, of dogs of the breed, O come, come here on flesh to feed!' The Appin Stuarts to their left were commanded by their chief's tutor since the chief was only a child.

Lord John Drummond was in command of the centre with the Frasers and some five hundred men of the Clan Chattan, an ancient confederation of tribes that included the men raised by 'Colonel Anne'. They were led by the huge Alexander MacGillivray, 'a clean pretty man' over six foot tall with red hair and a white skin. The battlefield was close to Clan Chattan's traditional burial places and it was said with irony that those who perished were 'much obliged to the soldiers, for by their means many of them died on a spot nearer by one half to the usual place of their burying than if they had expired in the arms of their wives'.

To their left stood a collection of smaller clans, each with their own proud history and traditions like the Chisholms. This particular family was divided, like so many, between the two sides as a way of hedging their bets. Two of the chief's sons were with Cumberland while his youngest son Roderick Og was for the Prince. His piper stood at the youngster's shoulder holding the mystical black chanter of the Chisholms known as 'The Maiden of the Sandal'. The Chisholms were Catholics and had brought it from Rome. It was believed to have strange powers and that if a member of the chief's family was about to die not a single note could be coaxed from it. Young Roderick Og waited in the heather and scanned the enemy lines for his two brothers who were with the Royal Scots on the right of Cumberland's line. He must have been wondering what it would mean if the chanter failed to sound. Would it be heralding his death or his brothers'?

The Duke of Perth commanded the Jacobite left. The first line consisted of the Macdonald regiments, muttering angrily at finding themselves fighting in this position. Perth tried to inspire them with the idea that 'If you fight with your usual bravery you will make the left wing a right wing,' and promised that if they did well he would change his name to Macdonald from that day forward. Such sophistry did not move the thousand or so men of Clanranald's, Keppoch's and Glengarry's regiments.

Chevalier Johnstone had forgotten that he had never got to bed in Inverness the preceeding night and was preparing to fight at the side of his friend Donald Macdonald of Scotus, one of Glengarry's captains. It was soon to become clear to him and to others that the Jacobite frontline was uneven. The right wing was only some five hundred yards or so from where Cumberland's forces had finally halted, but the left stretched back more than eight hundred yards – a misalignment which was to have desperate consequences.

The Lowlanders made up most of the second line behind the clans. Cavalry made up a kind of third line, grouped around the Stuart standard, but by now many were without horses like Kilmarnock's regiment, Pitsligo's Horse and Baggot's Hussars. Their last surviving beasts had gone to strengthen Charles's Life guards and FitzJames's Horse. They were hardly, as Cumberland nastily observed, what one generally understood to be cavalry. Neither was Charles's artillery up to much. It was, as it had always been, a liability rather than an asset, poorly served and consisting of an odd assortment of cannon.

At first there was a sense of unreality as the two expectant forces faced each other. The Highlanders were ready to leap to the attack as soon as the command was given, but there was nothing but the sound of the pipes and that silent solid wall of red clearly visible through the sleet. At last, just after one o'clock, the battle began. The Jacobite batteries in the centre of the line delivered the opening salvoes – seeking Cumberland, or so the story goes – but the shots went wide. The Government artillery, ably commanded by thirty-four-year-old Brevet Colonel William Belford, responded, the dull boom of their massed three pounders crescendoing across the sodden fields. To eye-witnesses it looked as if their gunners were in turn firing on the Stuart Prince: 'The battle being now begun, the whole fury of the enemy's artillery seemed to be directed against us in the rear; as if they had noticed where the Prince was . . . seeing the imminent danger from the number of balls that fell about him, he was by the earnest entreaties of his friends forced to retire a little off. . . .' Charles had a close shave when his groom, Thomas Ca, was decapitated by a cannon-ball and he was spattered with his blood. Minutes later his horse was hit in the flank, forcing Charles to dismount from the terrified animal and find another. Lord Balmerino's men escorted him to a safer place, but it gave him a less clear view of what was happening which was more than unfortunate given that he was in personal command.

Meanwhile Cumberland's gunners were wreaking havoc, 'making a great slaughter house of the rebels' battery'. As a new rainstorm burst from the blackening sky, the Hanoverian artillerymen switched their attention to the front of the Jacobite line. It was the first time that Charles's men had faced disciplined and professional artillery fire. Its influence was crucial. Cumberland was pleased to note that the artillery was 'rapidly thinning the Jacobite ranks without experiencing any loss in return'. Their next tactic was to switch to grapeshot which swept over the fields 'as with a hail-storm' and scythed through the Highlanders like corn as they waited exposed and impotent for their officers to sound the attack. This was truly the day when the Jacobites' luck ran out. Murray begged Charles to order the attack. Charles did so but his messenger was felled by a cannon-ball which took off his head. Another messenger – Brigadier Stapleton – had to be found, but the delay proved too much for some of the clansmen. With a blood-curdling yell of 'claymore' the Athollmen on the right charged without waiting for the niceties of Stapleton's say-so. The Macdonalds on the other hand refused to budge from their position on the left when Sir John Macdonald passed on Charles's orders. Neither would they respond to the Duke of Perth and his brother. The disastrous consequence was that the Jacobite right went forward alone.

It was a brave and strangely beautiful act, the last great Highland charge in Scotland. The clansmen 'came up very boldly and fast, all in a cloud together, sword in hand'. They attacked with all the ferocity that was their birthright, 'like Wildcats cutting and hacking and hewing'. Clan Chattan reached the enemy first, their mighty, red-haired, white-skinned colonel, MacGillivray, at their head, but as they charged they swerved to the right seeking firmer ground. The centre joined with the right, 'and in a sort of mob, without order or distinction of corps, mixed together, rushed in and attacked'. The clansmen were so tightly packed that they could hardly wield their broadswords. Also the stampede to the right had the effect of exposing the flank of the charging centre clans directly to the fire of the Hanoverian centre. The Athollmen charged forward almost at once to support them but got jammed between the swerving centre and the park wall and became target practice for the men of Barrel's, Monro's, Wolfe's and Campbell's. Some of the Hanoverian troops, including the Campbells, had now got into the enclosures to the right of the park wall and poured in further flanking fire, resting their muskets on the stone walls.

Maddened by the fierce musketry, the smoke-blackened High-landers fought and clawed their way through the ranks of Barrel's and Munro's regiments to the second line, MacGillivray still in the lead. Bligh's and Sempill's fought them off with well-drilled volleys and cold steel. Most of the Highlanders who penetrated to the second line were bayoneted, MacGillivray – pretty no longer – crawling off to die face down in a puddle as he tried to drink. Cumberland's training was paying handsome dividends. 'We gave them an English reception,' boasted one officer 'and plied them with continual fire from the rear and fixt bayonets in front.' Barrel's claimed that after the battle the regiment had not a bay-onet 'but was either bloody or bent and stained with blood to the muzzles or the musket'. Their Lieutenant Colonel Rich tried to parry a broadsword and instead lost both hand and sword. Still he stood and encouraged his men, taking six sword cuts to his head, his face one bloody mess. Lord Robert Ker supposedly ran through the first Cameron Highlander, but was killed immediately afterwards, 'his head being cleft from crown to collarbone' by Gillies MacBean of Clan Chattan.

Lord George lost his horse, his hat, his wig and his sword during the desperate assault of the right, and his coat was rent with bayonet slashes, but he found another weapon and stormed back through the ranks of his own men searching desperately for reinforcements. He found some of Lord Lewis Gordon's men and Lord John Drummond's Royal Scots and led them back into the eye of the battle. They advanced in good order giving and receiving 'several fires' but it was too late, 'the day was irrevocably lost; nothing could stop the Highlanders after they began to run'. Dynamic in attack, they were equally unstoppable in flight. For a few moments Clan Chattan held their ground, hurling stones and defiance at Cumberland's men. Then they too turned and ran and limped back through the sulphurous black smoke, but not without their yellow and blue standard. The original bearer, a young Mackintosh, had fallen early in the charge. Now a private soldier held it aloft until the clan began to retreat. Then he ripped the silk from its staff, wound it about his body and fled. Carrying it

safe home to the glens he came to be known as *Donuil na Braiteach*
– Donald of the Colours – and his sons were called Angus and
Charles of the Colours. Roderick Og, the young leader of the
Chisholms, was dead, wounded early by one cannon-ball and
killed by another when being carried from the field by his brave
henchman. The Chisholms charged the Royal Scots, among whose
officers were Roderick's two brothers. Later when these two found
his body among the dead of their clan they washed it and protected
it from mutilation.

The Camerons and the Stewarts ran too. Lochiel had been
wounded in both ankles by grapeshot and was helpless. His men
hastily scooped him up and carried their chief with them as they
ran, but as the Highlanders fled past the park wall they were fired
on by the Campbells who had been lying in wait and now took a
bitter toll of their enemies. They drew their swords with cries of
'Cruachan!' and, jeering at their foe, advanced onto the moor,
hewing and hacking at the stragglers. The Campbells later claimed
the distinction of having been 'the only foot who pursued, and
that the regular foot did not advance a step after the action'.

The Jacobite left, on the other hand, never really attacked. The
commanders of the left pleaded with the Macdonalds to charge
but they were still some twenty or so paces from the Government
lines as the right began to fall back. Keppoch was so ashamed of
the behaviour of his men that he charged alone in one of the last
great heroic acts of the campaign. He is said to have cried out, 'O
my God, has it come to this, that the children of my tribe have
forsaken me!' and was shot down almost at once, his red and
black tartan crimsoning with his own blood. He was later carried
from the field by his son and grieving clansmen but died soon
after. Clanranald was badly wounded in the head just as he seemed
to have won his clansmen round to the charge. Stung to action, the
Macdonalds advanced 'firing their pistols and brandishing their
swords' and daring the enemy to come out and fight.

Chevalier Johnstone was with them and saw the disastrous
consequences. The Hanoverian troops simply picked them off as
they stood there yelling their defiance. 'As far as I could distin-
guish, at the distance of twenty paces, the English appeared to be
drawn up in six ranks [actually three]; the three first being on

their knees. They kept up a terrible running fire on us.' His friend Scotus of Glengarry's was cut down at his side. Although the Macdonalds showed the 'greatest resolution' they could not stand up to this for long and began to fall back without ever having reached the enemy line. 'What a spectacle of horror!' Johnstone wrote. 'The same Highlanders who had advanced to the charge like lions, with bold and determined countenance, were in an instant seen flying like trembling cowards in the greatest disorder.' For a while they were given cover by Stapleton's Franco-Irish force who took up positions behind the walls of the Culloden enclosure and kept up a barrage of flanking fire. Stapleton was to die a few days later of wounds he received in this gallant holding action which cost half his men their lives.

Meanwhile, Cumberland had seen his chance.He sent his cavalry down on the centre of the Jacobite second line and nearly managed to encircle the Royal Scots. On the right he came close to out-flanking the retreating Jacobites. The jubilant Campbells had breached the west wall of Culloden Park, leaving a space wide enough for the cavalry to pass through three abreast. They were nearly up with the Jacobite rear when Lord George Murray realised the danger. In the nick of time he ordered Elcho's Life-guards and FitzJames's Horse to face the pursuing dragoons. It was not an equal contest. One hundred weary and bedraggled Jacobites on famished horses faced five hundred well armed sturd-ily-mounted dragoons. Even so, it was more than ten minutes before the dragoons found the courage to attack. Although Elcho and his dogged little band could not hold out for long, they enabled the remnants of the right wing of the Jacobite army to escape in reasonable order.

It was plain that the game was up. 'The men in general were taking themselves precipitately to flight; nor was there any possi-bility of their being rallied,' wrote one survivor. O'Sullivan came galloping up with a cry of 'You see, all is going to pot' and urging that Charles be forced off the field. There are many accounts of those last frantic moments. According to some, Charles was contemplating one last mad act of bravado. He shouted over the roar of the battle that he'd never be taken alive and seemed about to spur his horse forward. Seeing this, Lochiel's uncle, Major

Kennedy, lost no time in grabbing the Prince's horse by the bridle and taking Charles away. Charles later claimed that he was 'forced off the field by the people about him'. Whatever the case it was a dreadful moment for him. He had pinned his faith on two things – the invincibility of his Highlanders and his conviction that Cumberland's men would never fight against their lawful Prince. He had been proved wrong on both counts.

His Italian valet Michele Vezzosi described his sheer disbelief, how he saw 'with astonishment these troops which he had looked upon as invincible, flying before the enemy in the utmost disorder and confusion. In vain did he strive to reanimate and persuade them to return to the charge; the mouths of murdering cannon spoke a louder and more persuasive language than all his promises and entreaties could do, though uttered in the most moving terms, such as these: "Rally, in the name of God. Pray, gentlemen, return. Pray stand with me, your Prince, but a moment – otherwise you ruin me, your country and yourselves; and God forgive you."' Stirring words, but for once his pursuasive powers failed utterly. One of the problems may have been that the Gaelic-speaking clansmen could not understand a word he was saying.

There was farce in the midst of the disaster: 'While he was in this confusion and endeavouring to stop the torrent of his men's flight, his wig and bonnet blew off; the last it's said was taken up by one of his friends and presented to a gentlewoman of the Roman Catholick religion, who kept it as a sacred relic. . . . His wig he recovered as it was falling from the pommel of the saddle.'

Charles was in a state of shock. With a small escort that included the faithful Sheridan he galloped towards the ford of Faillies over the Nairn. Halting under a tree he could hear Cumberland's men cheering. Elcho and O'Sullivan joined him at the ford. Elcho claimed Charles was 'in a deplorable state' and completely paranoid about the Scots, convinced they meant to betray him. As more and more Scots arrived, Charles 'ordered them to go away to a village a mile's distance from where he was, and he would send his orders thither'. Elcho also accused Charles of only worrying about the fate of his Irish companions and being quite callous about the fate of the Highlanders. In his eyes Charles had fallen from grace and this bitterness characterised Elcho's feelings about

Charles for the rest of their lives. According to one account, he had actually shouted at Charles as he left the field, 'There you go for a damned cowardly Italian.'

Charles set off towards Fraser territory, hoping for assistance from Lord Lovat, and ordered the officers to proceed to Ruthven and await further instructions. Meanwhile, Lord George Murray was conducting the retreat of the Jacobite right 'with the greatest regularity', pipes playing. Cumberland's cavalry treated them with considerable circumspection. During their retreat they encountered a party of dragoons who 'appeared as much embarrassed as the Highlanders; but the English commander very wisely opened a way for them in the centre, and allowed them to pass at the distance of a pistol shot without attempting to molest them or to take prisoners.' According to Chevalier Johnstone, one officer thought otherwise and decided to take a Highland prisoner. He selected his man and advanced a few paces, only to be cut down by the contemptuous Scot who 'stopt long enough to take possession of his watch, and then decamped with the booty'.

Such coolness apparently won him the admiration of the English commander who 'could not help smiling and secretly wishing the Highlander might escape on account of his boldness, without appearing to lament the fate of the officer, who had disobeyed his orders'. A bit of wishful thinking on the Chevalier's part perhaps, but it shows the healthy respect of seasoned soldiers for those Jacobite units that were still intact. Cumberland's men preferred to devote their energies to 'sabering such unfortunate people as fell in their way single and unarmed'. When he reached Faillies, Lord George took the road for Ruthven and wondered what to do next.

The retreat of the left had been rather different. According to one Government soldier: 'A few royals [mortars] sent them a few bombs and cannon balls to their farewell, and immediately our horse that was on the right and left wings pursued them with sword and pistol and cut a great many of them down so that I never saw a small field so thick with dead.' The cavalry were relentless, riding down and sabering the exhausted Macdonalds on the Inverness road. There was no mercy and the killing went on to within a mile of the town. Weary clansmen who had sought a few hours' sleep after the night march were murdered in the bothies and ditches where they lay. Fugitives from the battle were burned alive in the huts where they had taken shelter. Non-combatants were also slain, such as two poor old weavers and a man and his young son murdered by troopers in a ploughed field. 'The Troops were enraged at their Hardships and Fatigues during a Winter campaign; the habit of the enemy was strange, their Language was still stranger, and their mode of Fighting unusual; the Fields of Preston and Falkirk were still fresh in their Memories.'

The actual clash of arms had only lasted half an hour, but Culloden was the beginning of a new and greater nightmare. Cumberland's men were already showing that they were more than victors on the field – they were a merciless army of occupation. Some poignant scenes were acted out. Maclean of Drimnin tried to return to the field – by now a grisly blood-soaked, limb-strewn piece of ground – to search for his two sons. Two troopers tried to stop him. In his rage and desperation he shot one and wounded the other, only to be hacked to pieces by their comrades. Schoolboys like little Archie Fraser, younger brother of the Master of Lovat, had played truant from school to watch from the heather as their fathers and brothers marched out to face Cumberland and had carried the news of the defeat to their homes. Women came to search anxiously among the slain, risking their own lives to find loved ones or help the suffering. Whisky and oatcakes were administered as the last sacraments to dying men. Mrs Stoner, Mrs Leith and the latter's maid Eppy set out from Inverness on the day of the battle to tend the wounded, left to lie among the corpses in retribution for Charles's supposed treatment of Cope's men after Preston Pans. Some wounded Highlanders had managed to crawl from the field only to be found and bayoneted. Others took extreme measures to treat themselves and keep on the move. Mrs Macdonald of Culwhiniac was startled in her kitchen by a Highlander who ran in and thrust the bleeding stump of his severed arm onto the red-hot griddle on which she was baking bread to cauterize the wound. One local witness trapped in the rout saw to his horror 'a woman stript in a very indecent posture and some of the other sex with their privities placed in their mouth'. He also saw a twelve-year-old boy dead with 'his head cloven to his teeth'.

There were many such stories, like the tale of the dragoon who grabbed a new born child from its fleeing mother, Elspeth McPhail, and twirled it round by its thigh before releasing it.

Cumberland was delighted with his men. 'You have done the business!' he congratulated them and if that business included murder he was not concerned. The rebels deserved it and it had his personal seal of approval. Riding across the blood-sodden moor he noticed a wounded Highlander, the twenty-year-old Fraser of Inverallochy. He asked Fraser what was his allegiance. When he answered 'To the Prince', Cumberland ordered Brevet Major Wolfe to shoot him. To his credit Wolfe refused but the order was carried out by someone less squeamish. One of the great lies perpetrated in the war of words was that Charles had ordered no quarter to be given to Government troops. Cumberland even produced a forged document. It gave a cloak of respectability to a slaughter which would have happened anyway, 'since the time was now come to pay off the score, our people were all glad to clear the reckoning and heartily determined to give them receipt in full'.

Lords Balmerino and Kilmarnock were taken on the field and were lucky not to have been shot out of hand. As a rule of thumb only those whose uniforms showed them to belong to the French army were spared as prisoners of war. Old Lord Balmerino had preferred surrender to flight, but poor Kilmarnock was taken prisoner when he mistook the Government horsemen for his own. He found himself face to face with his own son James, Lord Boyd, who was fighting for King George and who held a hat in front of his father's face to hide his tears.

The business done, Cumberland's infantry lunched on biscuits and cheese on the battlefield and then marched to Inverness, many wearing the hats and coats and bonnets of their slain enemies as trophies. Some were still covered in blood. A Hanoverian officer admitted, 'The moor was covered with blood and our men, what with killing the enemy, dabbling their feet in the blood, and splashing it about one another, looked like so many butchers rather than Christian soldiers.' They created such a spectacle that the inhabitants of the town thought that every chief and man of rank in Charles's army must have fallen, and quaked with fear. The volunteer James Ray described their consternation with pleasure: 'The Rebels had order'd the Inhabitants of Inverness to provide all the Oatmeal they could spare, and with it bake Bannocks for their Suppers, against their Return from the Victory; but their Disappointment was very pleasing to us, who came to eat it in their Stead.' Ray had worked up a fine appetite by cutting the throats of a couple of clansmen he had discovered hiding in the town. It was not long before the execution squads were being sent out from Inverness to kill any survivors they could find, shouting 'Billy' as they marched.

There was pandemonium as the jails of Inverness were thrown open and Government soldiers were released. Their place was taken by new Jacobite prisoners, including the Royal Scots and some of the Irish picquets. More were brought in every hour and the church and other buildings were turned into temporary jails. Cumberland, arriving at Inverness at four o'clock, made himself comfortable in old Lady Mackintosh's sandstone house in Church Street. He seemed to enjoy sleeping in the same quarters as his cousin. His elderly and acerbic hostess was less than pleased, particularly as he had her locked up and put on a diet of meal and water. This unchivalrous usage caused her to remark that she had had 'two king's bairns living under my roof in my time and to tell you the truth, I wish I may never have another'. She had her wish but for now her immediate fears were for her beautiful daughter-in-law who was soon to be a prisoner in Government hands. She was arrested and brought to Inverness where her youth and loveliness captivated many of Cumberland's officers, though not, of course, Hawley. 'Damn the woman,' he is said to have roared over the dinner table, 'I'll honour her with a mahogany gallows and a silken cord!'

Meanwhile, the Stuart 'bairn' had made for Gorthlick some twenty miles from the battle-field where he sought the dubious hospitality of Lord Lovat. The old man was in a lather of anxiety and could hardly get rid of Charles quickly enough. 'Chop off my Head, Chop off my Head, the old Lord cryed out to the unhappy Fugitive: My own Family, with all the great Clans are undone. . . .' All the comfort he gave him was two or three glasses of wine, and tradition has it that Charles's tears mingled with the vintage. Still hedging his bets, Lovat reminded him of Robert the Bruce who lost eleven battles but won Scotland by the twelfth, and offered more help from the Frasers. However, he was plainly anxious for Charles to be off, giving him some cold chicken to put in his pocket. He was later to say that none but a madman would have fought that day.

The Prince was in despair, convinced that the best thing he could do was to flee to France. He received a message from Lord George to the effect that his Highlanders were full of animation and ardour, and eager to be led against the enemy again, but Charles did not respond with similar passion. Instead, he sent a message that everyone should 'look out for the means of saving himself as best he could'. This struck a chill into the hearts of the Highlanders. They had never imagined their Prince would abandon them, neither could they understand the justification for it. Surely they were strong enough to fight another day?

Instead, here was an end of an enterprise that had begun so curiously but had struck so much fear into the hearts of the Scottish Lowlanders and the English. Greater decisiveness, less bickering and clearer objectives might have won Charles the prize without which his life would become meaningless – the paradox was that it was the only battle Charles ever lost and the only battle Cumberland ever won. Charles had not given up completely. He believed that if he could get back to France he could rally more support for another attempt. However, he did not appreciate that he was leaving his Highlanders to a similar fate to the one which overtook the gallant little garrison at Carlisle. Even if he did return he would not be in time.

Lord George realised something of this. He sat down and wrote a famous letter to Charles burning with reproach and criticising him for ever having raised the standard without proper assurances from the French. He thundered against the 'gross incompetence' of O'Sullivan and the stupidity of Hay in failing to get adequate food for the army on the eve of Culloden. The letter ended with his resignation, but it changed nothing. Charles did not respond directly but wrote a general letter to his chiefs justifying his actions. He said he had only ever desired their good and their safety, and he saw 'with grief I can at present do little for you on this side the water'. There is no record that they ever received the letter, but they already knew that the end had come.

Chevalier Johnstone described the last poignant moments of the Jacobite army. Charles's message had been a 'sad and heart-breaking answer for the brave men who had sacrificed themselves for him'. It was 'a most touching and affecting scene' as they said their 'eternal adieus'. The Highlanders knew the fate that would soon be upon them – they would be ravaged 'and themselves and their families reduced to bondage, and plunged in misery without remedy'.

South of the border the mood was different. 'Fame, like an Eagle, carried the News of the Defeat upon her Wings.' News of the Government victory reached London before the arrival of Lord Bury who had been despatched with the glad tidings, but he was able to restore King George's peace of mind about Cumberland. '"What's become of my son?" George is said to have cried. "He is very well", answered Bury. "Then all is well to me" replied the King, and unable to speak for Joy, he withdrew for a little, and ordered Bury 1,000 Guineas.' As the news spread through the city there was open rejoicing. 'The Joy upon publishing the News was as universal as the Illuminations (the most splendid ever seen) were general and delightful, forming but one continued Blaze.'

The *True Patriot* was quick to trumpet about the superior brav-ery of the English troops. 'His Royal Highness has subdued the Highlanders,' it wrote joyously, 'and the Highlanders themselves will soon be civilised.' It also accused Charles of cowardice, asserting he 'stood an idle Spectator of the Battle, at a safe Dis-tance, and took the first Occasion to preserve by Flight, a Life perhaps more worthless and miserable than that of the meanest of those Wretches who had been the Followers of his Fortune, and were now, at a great Distance, the Followers of his Flight.' The *London Evening Post* made similar jibes, while the *London Magazine* compared the two Princes and made some insinuating remarks about Charles: 'He lov'd the Men better than the Women; and yet, which is wonderful, the less he courted the Ladies, the faster they followed him.'

Culloden was hailed as the extinction of the rebellion. It was also the excuse for an orgy of humble addresses, loyal reflections, admiring odes to the 'much accomplish'd Youth! Britannia's pride!', and earnest proposals for the erection of statues to the stout young victor. The panic of late 1745 was forgotten. The Highlanders resumed their place in the popular imagination as benighted savages rather than the formidable warriors who had been within an ace of marching on London. And their Prince, instead of being a sinister pawn of Rome and Spain, was simply a fugitive on the run.

During the next five months Charles was to read about his supposed exploits in the Whig Press. Perhaps it brought home to him that to most of the English, and many of the Lowland Scots, he had seemed more adventurer than saviour. It was to the Highlanders that he must look for salvation, trusting to their fidelity and forgetting his suspicions. John Roy's lament – written from his hiding place in Strathspey – expressed the curious place that Charles held in their hearts in spite of the débâcle: 'All pleasure has departed me, my cheek is frosted with sorrow, since at present I hear no glad tidings about my beloved Prince Charles, rightful heir to the crown, who knows not which way to turn.'

CHAPTER TWELVE

'O MISS, WHAT A HAPPY CREATURE
ARE YOU. . . .'

T HIS was the beginning of Charles's life as a fugitive. It was
also the beginning of those wild and romantic adventures
which, far more than Culloden, were to fix him in the
popular imagination and inspire a whole folk tradition. What
could be more appealing than a young prince fleeing for his life
and saved by his faithful Highlanders without a thought for their
own safety or, indeed, the thirty thousand pounds on his head?
What could be more glamorous than a brave young girl – Flora
Macdonald – sailing with her prince over the sea to Skye? As the
weeks passed, an increasingly sympathetic press carried detailed
accounts of 'the unhappy Fugitive' and his adventures, whetting
their readers' appetites with promises of further instalments, so
that by the time Flora Macdonald was brought to London as a
prisoner she found she was almost a national heroine. Yet what
really happened during those five months after Culloden? There
was heroism and romance, certainly, but there was also squalor
and hardship and, for many, a bitter legacy.

Charles was a wanted man from the moment he left the battlefield. After quitting Lord Lovat he made for Fort Augustus in the
hope of news, but the clansmen had melted away and there was
not 'any mortel that cou'd give him any accounts'. The atmosphere
was menacing and fearing capture at any moment, he and his
small band hurried on to Invergarry Castle where their reception
was a cheerless one – there was no welcoming laird to order a
feast to be spread and fires to be lit. The castle was silent, empty
and 'without meat, drink, fire or candle'. It could provide no

entertainment for a wandering prince or even any food until the resourceful Highlander Ned Burke, an ex-Edinburgh sedan chair carrier who was acting as Charles's guide, went fishing and caught two salmon 'which furnished an ample repast'. The fugitives washed it down with some wine and discussed what they should do.

Nervously they decided that the best course was for the group which included Sheridan, Alexander Macleod, O'Sullivan, Felix O'Neil, Allan Macdonald, a priest, and John Hay of Restalrig to split up. It was not safe for the Prince to travel with so many men. There would be eyes everywhere and he must be as inconspicuous as possible. O'Sullivan, Macdonald and Burke would be his only companions and he took the precaution in case of capture of changing his tartan doublet for Burke's worn old coat. They set out on foot for the west coast in the hope of finding a French ship. The country was rugged and the weather bitter as the men trudged along.

On 17 April they reached the house of Donald Cameron of Glenpean on Loch Arkaig and Charles was able to sleep properly for the first time since before Culloden. But the next day they were off again, through Glen Pean to Loch Morar by 'the cruelest road that cou'd be seen'. Here they waited for a boat but as night drew on and nothing appeared they were forced to seek shelter in 'a small sheal house near a wood' where their Macdonald host fed them butter, milk and curds. On 20 April Charles moved on to claim shelter in the house of Alexander Macdonald of Borrodale. He recouped his strength on meals of meal, lamb and butter and slept on a bed of straw.

However, there was no sign of any French ships off Borrodale. As it seemed dangerous to linger on the mainland Charles decided on his flight to the isles. He still believed that those wily grandees of Skye, Sir Alexander Macdonald and Macleod of Macleod, would help him and he summoned the elderly Donald Macleod – who had been chosen to pilot him to Uist – in the hope that he would take them a message. Their conversation has become part of the folklore: 'The Prince, making towards Donald, asked, "Are you Donald Macleod of Guatergill in Sky?" "Yes," said Donald, "I am the same man, may it please your Majesty, at your service.

What is your pleasure wi' me?" "Then," said the Prince, "You see, Donald, I am in distress. I therefore throw myself into your bosom, and let you do with me what you like. I hear you are an honest man, and fit to be trusted."'

When Macleod later recounted this tale to Bishop Forbes the tears ran down his aged face. At the time he was touched and flattered by Charles's appeal but refused to take messages from the fugitive Prince to known Government supporters who 'were then, with forces along with them, in search of him not above the distance of ten or twelve miles by sea from him. . . .' However, he agreed to help Charles escape and went to look for a suitable boat. By the time he had found a stout one, together with enough competent and willing boatmen, four pecks of oatmeal and a cooking pot, a storm was brewing. He advised Charles to wait but the Prince was 'anxious to be out of the continent where the parties were then dispersed in search of him'. News had come that a detachment of Cumberland's men was closing in. As the skies blackened he and his small band, which included O'Neil again, climbed into the boat 'in the twilight of the evening' and trusted to fate. It must have crossed Charles's mind that this was the very spot where he had landed so full of hope only a few months ago.

It was not long before he realised that the old pilot had been right to advise him to wait. Their little craft rolled and bucked in the swell. Shouting above the thunder and the driving rain, Charles asked Donald to return to shore – he would rather 'face cannon and muskets than be drowned in such a storm as this' – but it was too late. If they tried to turn back they risked being dashed against the rocks and their only hope was to ride out the storm. O'Sullivan described the furious waves that broke over the boat throwing the Prince from side to side and Charles crying out, 'There is no hurt, there is no hurt.' It was a long and terrifying night. 'But as God would have it, by peep of day we discovered ourselves to be on the coast of the Long Isle,' as Donald later recounted.

A miserable, cold, sodden group of men found themselves in the dawn light off Benbecula, the middle island of the Long Island of the Outer Hebrides which belonged to Clanranald. They landed at Rossinish in a wind so strong they could scarcely stand up and 'all wet from head to foot & black wth cold'. Charles took stock of this new world. It was a place of barren desolation and they were lucky to find a hut where they could shelter from the rain. They lit a heather fire to dry their clothes and Charles managed to sleep for a while on an old sail spread out on the ground. Food was a problem but 'there were Cows about the house', and they shot and cooked 'one of the fattest' which, in keeping with the rules of Highland hospitality, Charles paid for. After a couple of days the weather eased and they decided to sail on to Stornaway. Charles hoped to find a ship there to take him to Orkney and then to Norway and eventually France. They set out on 29 April but again a storm blew up pushing them off course to Scalpa. This bleak rock of an island looked unpromising, but the weary little party found a kind host in Donald Campbell, a friend of Donald Macleod. He was let into the secret of Charles's identity and took pity on the bedraggled group which 'cou'd really pass for peoples that were Shipracked for we were in very bad equipage, all the Princes clothes were a Vest, Coat & breeches, that he got made before he parted from the main land, of an old Riding Coat he had ... & every stitch they had as stiff as buckrum from the salt water.'

Despite his name, Campbell was loyal to the Prince and soon proved his devotion to the tradition of Highland hospitality. A boat bristling with armed men and led by the Rev. Aulay Macaulay – grandfather of Lord Macaulay the historian – landed on Scalpa 'with a determined resolution to seize the Chevalier and secure the bribe offered by the Government'. However, Campbell 'scorned the bribe' and told the reverend gentleman to be off since 'he himself would fall in his cause, rather than give up the man that intrusted him with his life, or entail shame on his posterity'. Charles and his companions had been ready to give MacAulay 'a hot reception' but he slunk away with his cronies, 'ashamed and disappointed at the loss of the money, which they already had devoured in their thoughts, and divided to every man in his due proportion'.

Donald Macleod went on alone to Stornaway in Campbell's boat – 'a fine, light, swift sailing thing' – to try and hire a vessel to take Charles to the Orkneys. A few days later, Charles set out to join him, at first by boat but then overland through 'the wildest country in the universe, nothing but moors & lochs, not a house in sight, nor the least marque of a road and path, walking all night with a continual heavy rain'. He and his companions got lost and arrived cold, wet and exhausted. The first thing Charles did was to send for a bottle of brandy. According to O'Sullivan he 'was in a terrible condition' with his shoes disintegrating and tied to his feet with cords and his toes 'quite stript'. The news which greeted him did not improve his temper. The men of Stornaway had guessed who the boat was for and, fearful of 'losing both their cattle and their lives', were refusing to let him have it. As far as they were concerned, Charles was as welcome as the plague and should leave at once for the continent 'or anywhere else he should think convenient'.

Crestfallen and anxious, Charles and his little party made their way back to Scalpa, only to discover that their host of a few days ago was now away skulking. There was barely time to digest this before they were sighted by a man-of-war, forcing them to put out to sea and make for Benbecula again. All they had to eat on their perilous journey was meal and salt water – a new experience for Charles. He 'ask'd them whether it tasted better than it look'd, they answered if he would only try it, he would be as well pleased with it as what they were, whereupon calling for a little of it, he eat it as contentedly as the most delicate dish that ever was served upon his table, saying at the same time that it tasted pretty well, considering the ugly appearance it made'. Again they were sighted by a man-of-war and the Prince rallied his crew with the words, 'If we Escape this Danger my Lads, you Shall have a handsome reward; if not, I'll be Sunk rather than taken.' Luckily for them the larger vessel was becalmed and could not follow their 'nimble little boat'. As soon as they landed on Benbecula, Charles sent for Clanranald who arrived with wine, beer, biscuits and trout. As O'Sullivan cheerfully remarked, 'Never a man was welcomer to be sure.' Clanranald also sent Charles some shirts, together with some shoes and stockings which must have gone some way to alleviate the problems of those 'stript toes'.

The result of this fruitless and dangerous junketing around the Hebrides meant that Charles had missed a very real chance of rescue. The instincts that had driven him to the west coast had been sound – Antoine Walsh had been making plans, even before the news of Culloden had reached the ears of the French court. As early as March he had been writing to Maurepas that 'the Prince's fortunes could so decline that he would have no alternative to seeking refuge in the hills, and this could make him think of returning to France.' He had accordingly arranged that two privateers should make sail for the west coast of Scotland. On 30 April the *Mars* and the *Bellona* were in Loch nan Uamh where their crews learned of Culloden and congratulated themselves on their timely arrival. In the event, though, it was not Charles they rescued. Other Jacobite fugitives came flocking on board – the Duke of Perth, now very ill, Lord John Drummond, the despondent and bitter Lord Elcho, fond old Sheridan, feverish with anxiety about the Prince, Hay of Restalrig and many others, but not Charles.

There were rumours that the Prince was in the Hebrides and it was agreed that a message should be sent, summoning him back to the mainland. However, before this could be done, the Royal Navy's twenty-four gun *Greyhound* and the sloop *Baltimore* alighted on the *Mars* and almost crippled her and her sister vessel. They were forced to limp back to France, leaving the most wanted Jacobite of all behind to the mercy of an increasingly efficient military search operation. The other disaster from Charles's point of view was that the French ships had brought some 35,000 *louis d'or* packed in six cases. Coll MacDonell of Barrisdale – a great fair-haired goliath of a man, later accused by Charles of betraying him – had the welcome task of unloading it, but when the royal navy ships appeared much of it had to be buried at Loch Arkaig for safekeeping. Its subsequent fate was the subject of much debate and ill-feeling, but whatever the case it could be of no immediate use to the Prince.

As yet, though, Charles knew nothing of these missed opportunities. Neither did he know that the first rumours of the defeat at Culloden had reached France on 13 May to be confirmed a few days later. This had convinced Walsh that whatever the fate of the *Mars* and the *Bellona* yet more ships must be sent. As June broke other French vessels slipped past the Royal Navy and began to comb Lochs Broom, Ewe and nan Uamh for the royal fugitive.

Sadly, Charles was still in the islands and his patience was wearing thin. There had been an abortive attempt to find him a hiding place in a grasskeeper's hovel on Benbecula about three miles from Rossinish but he had drawn the line at this 'little hut of a house . . . the entry of which was so very narrow that he was forced to fall upon his knees, and creep in upon his belly, as often as he entered. This habitation not pleasing him, he begged of Clanranald to send him into some Christian place wherein he could have more . . . freedom and ease, for in that monstrous hole he could never have satisfaction, which he said the devil had left because he had not room enough in it.'

A more 'Christian place' was found by the long-suffering Clanranald – this was the delightful Coradale, 'a little pleasant glen' on South Uist in the shadows of the mountains of Hekla and Benmore. It was a good hiding place. Having sent Donald to the mainland with letters to Lochiel and Murray of Broughton and instructions to bring back information, money – and that increasingly necessary commodity brandy – Charles settled down to life in a house 'which he swore look'd like a palace in comparison of the abominable hole they had lately left'. The weather had turned fine and he spent an agreeable few days fishing and shooting. His spirits, which had been 'very low' according to the sympathetic O'Sullivan, began to revive and he was delighted with a new companion sent to him by Clanranald. This was Neil Maceachain, a young schoolmaster about the same age as Charles who was struck by the Prince's cheerfulness. He 'was so hearty and merry, that he danced for a whole hour together, having no musick but some highland reel which he whistled away as he tripped along'.

There was serious carousing when local Jacobites came to call. Boisdale arrived too late for one party. He was 'received by the Prince with open arms, and found some of the gentlemen of the country who came to see him the day before . . . lying in their bed, very much disordered by the foregoing night's carouse, while his royal highness was the only one who was able to take care of the rest, in heaping them with plaids, and at the same time merrily sung the De Profundis for the rest of their souls'. Charles plainly had the constitution of an ox and Neil wrote approvingly of how he 'took care to warm his stomach every morning with a hearty bumper of brandy, of which he always drank a vast deal; for he was seen to drink a whole bottle of a day without being in the least concerned.'

Clanranald visited him again and this time brought Charles a complete suit of Highland clothes. O'Sullivan left a lively description of Charles's pleasure. When he put them on he became 'quite another man. "Now," says he leaping, "I only want the Itch to be a compleat highlander".' Charles would shortly have his wish but does not seem to have been much disturbed by matters of fastidiousness. According to O'Sullivan the only thing that 'repugned him' was having to drink out of a common vessel 'for he is not delicate in any thing else'. Clanranald offered him sheets to sleep in but he said he was perfectly content to roll in his plaid like a Highlander. Bishop Forbes recorded in *The Lyon in Mourning* how Charles was also quite happy to clean himself up by rubbing his legs and belly with his plaid, though he wondered if it was quite proper to describe such an unroyal approach to cleanliness.

When he wasn't roistering Charles had time to reflect on events for the first time since the battle. According to Neil Maceachain, 'his ordinary conversation was talking of the army, and of the battle of Culloden, and the highland chieftains whose lamentable case he deplored very much.' He fretted over his decision to allow the Athollmen and others to fight on the right 'merely by the persuasion of my Lord George Murray, and several others', and paid tribute to the courage of the Macdonalds on the field. Underlying everything was his bitter condemnation of Lord George Murray 'as being the only instrument in losing the battle. . . .' He comforted himself by looking out to sea in the belief that the ships which could be seen in the distance were French vessels. He still seemed confident that the French would send an invasion force to England under his brother Henry.

To an extent Charles was living in never-never-land during those golden days of summer at Coradale and they could not last. The Government was determined to capture him and the net was drawing tighter. News came that troops were sweeping the glens in his direction, forcing him back into the arms of that unreliable ally, the sea. He and Neil went into hiding on Benbecula before Donald and O'Sullivan reached them by boat and took them off. Not that there was anywhere to go – in desperation they made in mid-June for Loch Boisdale on South Uist, hoping that Boisdale would help them, only to learn that he was now a prisoner in the hands of the sadistic Lowlander Captain Ferguson. His house had been ransacked and his wife tied up. The situation needed a miracle: 'We were never a day or night without rain, the Prince was in a terrible condition, his legs and thighs cut all over from the briers; the midges or flies which are terrible in that country devoured him and made him scratch those scars which made him appear as if he was cover'd with ulcers.' Not only that but Charles was suffering from a 'bloody flux' which they treated with treacle, apparently successfully. However, it was clear they could not go on like this.

They decided to split up, with Charles heading north with Felix O'Neil and Neil Maceachain and the others – O'Sullivan, Macleod and Ned Burke – left to fend for themselves as they thought best. It was a sad parting between Charles and the faithful O'Sullivan, at least according to the Irishman's account. Charles took him in his arms and held him for a full quarter of an hour while tears poured down O'Sullivan's weatherbeaten face. Neil Maceachain recorded how O'Sullivan was 'left under a rock with the best part of the prince's baggage'. And so they parted. It was not long before O'Sullivan was rescued and whisked off to France with tales of the Prince's plight but for Charles another bizarre episode was about to begin.

Enter the most famous Jacobite heroine of them all, Miss Flora Macdonald. As Maxwell of Kirkconnell put it, 'Now it was a young lady that was most instrumental in extricating him out of this, the greatest of all the difficulties he had hitherto been in.' At first glance Flora was an unlikely heroine. Hers was not the romantic fervour of a Colonel Anne. Neither was she a beauty though she was 'of a fair complexion and well enough shap'd'. Flora was a sensible young woman of twenty-four who needed a lot of convincing before she agreed to help the fugitive Prince.

However, she was an undoubted Jacobite both by birth and inclination. She had grown up in the islands amid deep memories of past risings and avid speculation about future ones. She later told Bishop Forbes that her step-father, one-eyed Hugh Mac-donald, had been the first clansman to kiss Charles's hand when he landed on the mainland. Hugh had not come out for Charles for fear of offending his chief, Macdonald of Sleat, whose factor he was. Indeed, he had been appointed captain of one of the companies raised by Sleat for the Government, but his influence was critical in the dangerous days that lay ahead for his step-daughter. Flora was also helped by the fact that she could travel without rousing suspicion. Her brother managed the family farm at Milton on South Uist while her mother and step-father lived on Skye. As such she was a frequent traveller between the isles.

Gaining her consent was a delicate operation and the ground-work was done by Felix O'Neil. He met Flora at Clanranald's house and hinted that she might see the Prince. She was suitably thrilled saying that '. . . a sight of him wou'd make her happy, tho' he was on a hill and she on another.' She was to have her wish. It was a Hebridean custom for the young girls to take the cattle up into the high pastures in the summer months. Flora went with her brother's herd up to Sheaval, a seven-hundred-and-fifty-foot hill behind Milton. She was asleep in the 'shieling' – a sort of shelter – when she had a royal visitor. She barely had time to pull on 'the half of her clothes' when Charles appeared in the doorway. While she stood there dazed, he told her of his plan to go to Skye disguised as a woman and asked for her help.

Flora's first reaction was dismay. It seemed a crazy plan which would put herself and her family at risk. 'With the greatest respect and loyalty', she turned him down. Felix did his best, promising her that if she agreed she would gain 'an immortal character'. He even said that if she were worried about her reputation he would marry her. However, all this eloquence counted for nothing until Charles made a passionate appeal with all the charm he was cap-able of. He would, he said, always retain a sense of 'so conspicuous a service' if she would only help him. He talked to her of Hugh, her stepfather. He coaxed and cajoled her irresistibly and against all her better instincts she gave in. It was agreed that they would meet in a few days at Rossinish, and Flora set out in some trepida-tion for Clanranald's house to enlist Lady Clanranald's help and to prepare Charles's female disguise.

Flora's problems began almost at once. Government troops were on the look-out for anything suspicious and she was arrested by the militia as she crossed the ford between South Uist and Benbecula because she had no permit to travel. The soldiers began to question her, but she kept her head and demanded to know who their captain was. To her relief she discovered that it was her step-father. When he arrived next morning he was able to order her release and save her from interrogation. However, just as she was breakfasting with him, more soldiers burst in with Neil Maceachain. Frantic with impatience, Charles had sent him to find out what had happened to Flora and he had fallen right into their hands. Hugh was able to save him as well and he quickly made his way back to Charles to reassure him that all was well. It was difficult – by now Charles was cold, wet, hungry, suffering from scurvy and tormented with sores. Life among the rocks and the rain did not suit him and he gave vent to 'hideous cries and complaints' about the midges. It was a squalid predicament for a young hero and not the sort of thing the songs and poems would dwell on.

Meanwhile, Flora and her stepfather laid their plans with care. He gave her travel passes for herself, a manservant and a woman – Betty Burke – and she set off for Lady Clanranald at Nunton. Soon the women were busily sewing a costume for Charles because there was nothing in the house big enough for him. Fingers and needles flew as they made a quilted petticoat, a calico gown with sprigs of lilac flowers, a white apron, a dun-coloured cloak 'after the Irish fashion', with a capacious hood and a cap designed to hide Charles's face. They also got together some stockings, some blue velvet garters and some shoes for their gawky female impersonator.

At last everything was ready. On 27 June Neil Maceachain brought Flora, Felix O'Neil, Lady Clanranald and other loyal helpers to a rendezvous with the midge-ridden prince. They sat down to a meal of roasted offal but were interrupted with the frightening news that at that very moment General Campbell had landed close to Nunton with fifteen hundred troops. According to Maceachain, 'All run to their boat in the greatest confusion, every one carrying with him whatever part of the baggage came first to his hand, without either regard to sex or quality'. The party fled across to Loch Uiskevagh, a sea loch to the north, but messages came from Nunton that General Campbell was demanding the return of Lady Clanranald and threatening to destroy the house. Not only that but other troops were on their way. It was clear that no time must be lost in putting the plan into action.

Hugh had given Flora a letter addressed to her mother on Skye to act as her passport. It was later destroyed but according to Flora it read:

My dear Marion,

I have sent your daughter from this country lest she should be in any way frightened with the troops lying here. She has got one Bettie Burke, an Irish girl, who, she tells me, is a good spinster. If her spinning please you, you may keep her till she spin all your lint; or if you have any wool to spin, you may employ her. I have sent Neil MacKechan along with your daughter and Bettie Burke to take care of them. I am, Your dutyful husband,

Hugh Macdonald

There was no mention of Felix O'Neil or any alias for him which meant that he must be left behind. Charles begged and pleaded for him to come but this was no time for sentiment and the clear-headed Flora refused on the grounds that 'she could more easily undertake the preservation of one than of two or more.' As soon as the rest of the party had gone Charles struggled into new attire helped by Flora, 'but could not keep his hands from adjusting his headdress, which he cursed a thousand times'. He wanted to conceal a pistol under his petticoats but again Flora would not hear of it and it sparked a wry response from Charles. 'Indeed, Miss,' he is said to have remarked, 'if we shall happen to meet with any that will go so narrowly to work in searching as what you mean, they will certainly discover me at any rate.' However, she allowed him to keep his cudgel.

The plan was to make a dash across the open sea under cover of darkness so they hid until nightfall. There were a few moments' panic when five wherries full of armed men sailed by, but they did not spot the Prince's small craft in the shadow of the shore. After sunset the small group embarked on their famous journey 'over the sea to Skye'. At first the weather was calm but towards midnight a westerly gale blew up and they were engulfed in a thick mist 'as robbed them of the sight of all lands'. The rowers heaved and sweated and the boat pitched and rolled in the teeth of the wind. Exhausted by the events of the last few days, Flora drifted into sleep and Charles guarded her, 'lest in the darkness any of the men should chance to step upon her'. These were the hours which established Flora as one of the heroines of Scottish history and earned her the envy of many a Jacobite lady. What could have been more desirable than sailing to Skye with the handsome young Prince she had plucked from the jaws of danger and who now tenderly guarded her while she slept? The fact that Charles was dressed as a woman, smelled to high heaven and was covered with lice has never been allowed to dull that shining image.

Flora's own account was to feed the legend. She later described how 'Happening to wake with some little bustle in the boat she found the Prince leaning over her with his hands spread about her head. She asked what was the matter? The Prince told her that one of the rowers being obliged to do somewhat about the sail behoved to step over her body . . . and lest he should have done her hurt either by stumbling or trampling upon her in the dark . . . he had been doing his best to preserve his guardian from harm.'

While the boatmen argued about which course to take, Charles, who was in high spirits, sang 'pretty songs' to divert her, including one of his favourite airs:

> For who better may our high sceptre sway
> Than he whose right it is to reign
> Then look for no peace for the wars will never cease
> Till the King shall enjoy his own again.

He shared the milk which Lady Clanranald had given him with his boatmen, drinking from the same bottle 'jock-fellow like', his erstwhile fastidiousness forgotten. However, he reserved the half-bottle of wine he had left for Flora, 'lest she should faint with the cold and other inconveniences of a night passage'. When, as a prisoner, she told these stories to the ladies who visited her they caused a sensation and cries of 'O Miss, what a happy creature are you who had that dear Prince to lull you asleep, and to take such good care of you with his hands spread about your head when you was sleeping! You are surely the happiest woman in the world!' 'I could,' says one of them, 'wipe your shoes with pleasure, and think it my honour so to do, when I reflect that you had the honour to have the Prince for your handmaid. We all envy you greatly.'

When morning broke, Charles, 'who was not in the least discouraged' by the appalling weather, urged the boatmen on, offering to row himself as they were 'almost ready to breathe out their last'. They had been blown off-course in the night and were dangerously close to the Macleod country in the north-west of Skye. The 'cold' Macleods were out hunting for Charles as good servants of King George and it was doubtful whether they would take such a flexible view of things as the Macdonalds of the Long Island. The boatmen hastly pulled away from the shore but at the next place they tried to land they were spotted by militia men who fired on them. At last, having rowed 'for dear blood', they managed to bring the craft safely into shore on the Trotternish Peninsula. They made for a small beach still called Prince Charlie's Point and landed 'within a cannon shot' of Macdonald of Sleat's house of Monkstat. Demure in her lilac sprigged gown Betty Burke was confident of a loyal reception.

CHAPTER THIRTEEN

'THE CAGE'

F LORA set off for Monkstat accompanied by Neil to seek the help of Lady Margaret Macdonald, the Chief of Sleat's wife. They had left strict instructions that, if anyone approached, the boatmen were to say that Charles was Flora's maid and to curse her for a lazy jade for not attending her mistress. Sleat himself was away, apparently waiting on Cumberland. However, his wife had other company which made Flora's arrival particularly unwelcome. She was entertaining Lieutenant Alexander Macleod 'a sneaking little gentleman' in charge of the militia guarding that particular stretch of coast. Luckily for Flora, Macdonald of Kingsburgh, one of Sleat's factors was also there. While Lady Margaret and Kingsburgh conspired urgently, Flora had to go and make polite conversation to the objectionable lieutenant in the dining room. She dealt coolly with his questions, explaining that she was on her way home to her parents at Armadale and had called on Lady Margaret to pay her respects. Her 'close chit-chat' as she later called it disarmed the lieutenant who had no suspicions.

Flora was rather more in control than Lady Margaret, who foresaw nothing but ruin for herself and her family if she helped Charles. She was 'in the greatest perplexity', mentally and physically wringing her hands. This was a very different matter from admiring the Prince from afar and sending graceful gifts and loyal messages, and now she wished Charles anywhere but at Monkstat. She and Kingsburgh were joined by Donald Roy, one of the few of her husband's men to come out for the Prince, who had fought at Culloden and been wounded. Between them they agreed that

Charles must not come to Monkstat – it was far too risky. Instead, it was decided that Kingsburgh would take the Prince to his own house from where he could travel overland to Portree and on to the isle of Raasay.

Donald Roy left at once to find out whether Raasay was safe. Meanwhile, Neil had returned to Charles to guide him to a safe place while plans were finalised. He found the Prince in an intractable mood. When he suggested that Charles carry a bundle of light clothes 'as if it had been some of Miss Flora's baggage' to give an air of authenticity to his disguise, Charles soon threw it down, 'saying that he had carried it long enough' and told Neil to carry it himself or leave it. When he realised he had left a set of knives in the boat he insisted Neil should return for them and spoke like a true autocrat. 'I must absolutely have it, so no more words.' He was, as poor Neil observed, 'quite out of humour and ready to fly in a passion'. Cold, hunger, diarrhoea and uncertainty were taking their toll and Charles could not sustain the sort of princely behaviour that Flora experienced.

It was a relief to everyone when an hour before sunset they set out. Charles walked with Kingsburgh and Neil, loping along in his unlikely disguise and making little attempt to behave in a demure or subservient way. Flora rode behind with Mrs Macdonald of Kirkibost and her maid. Her worst fears were confirmed when she heard what the locals were saying about the 'impudence and assurance of Miss Burk'. They were frankly amazed by her – 'what terrible steps she takes, how manly she walks, how carelessly she carries her dress' and a hundred such-like expressions fell on Flora's anxious ears.

Not that very high standards were expected. A few years earlier Captain Burt had been struck by the unprepossessing ways of Scottish maidservants: 'They hardly ever wear shoes . . . but on a Sunday; and then, being unused to them, when they go to church they walk very awkwardly: or, as we say, like a cat shod with walnut-shells . . . I have seen some of them come out of doors early in a morning, with their legs covered up to the calf with dried dirt, the remains of what they contracted in the streets the day before: in short, a stranger might think there was but little occasion for strict laws against low fornication.' Nevertheless,

Flora was convinced that Charles's capture was imminent. There was a particularly nasty moment as they crossed a ford. Without thinking Charles yanked his skirts high and Neil called out, 'For God's sake, Sir, take care what you are doing!'

Kingsburgh decided to cut across country so that the ungainly Betty Burke would attract less attention, while Flora went on by road having to endure Mrs Macdonald's chatter. When they arrived at last at Kingsburgh's house, everyone had gone to bed. A servant was sent to wake his wife with the news that the master was come home with company which included Flora Macdonald. However, she was sleepy and while she said that Flora was welcome to the run of her house she was not going to come down. The first intimation she had that something strange was going on was when her daughter Anne burst in on her exclaiming, 'O mother, my father has brought in a very odd, muckle, ill-shapen-up wife as ever I saw! I never saw the like of her, and he has gone into the hall with her.' Kingsburgh himself then appeared and told her to dress and prepare food for his visitors though he would not say who they were.

Since her daughter was still having the vapours about the 'odd muckle trallup' with her 'lang wide steps', Mrs Macdonald was forced to enter the room where Betty Burke was sitting to fetch her keys. As she did so the great gaunt creature rose and saluted her. Her suspicions were thoroughly roused by now and she rushed back to Kingsburgh to demand an explanation. 'Why, my dear,' he told her, 'it is the Prince. You have the honour to have him in your house.' Her response was one of fear rather than gratification and she said they would all be hanged if they were caught. Kingsburgh merely told her to go and get some food. With trembling hands she produced a meal of 'roasted eggs, some collops, plenty of bread and butter' and some beer, worrying that this was no fit meal for a prince. After supper Charles poured himself a large glass of brandy and drank to the health of his hosts, saying proudly, 'I have learn'd in my skulking to take a hearty dram.' He sat up far into the night with Neil and Kingsburgh, smoking and drinking punch.

The next morning while the rest of the household was up and about Charles slept on, enjoying the novelty of clean sheets, but

Flora was anxious. The boatmen had been sent back to South Uist and, as Kingsburgh's wife pointed out to her, they were likely to be seized by the militia who would torture them until they told what they knew. She tried to persuade Kingsburgh to wake him but he did not have the heart to rouse the exhausted young prince. Later, when Charles was up, there is a story that Flora came and asked for a lock of his hair at the request of Kingsburgh's wife. 'When Miss came in he begged her to sit down on a chair at the bedside, then laying his arms about her waist, and his head upon her lap, he desired her to cut out the lock with her own hands in token of future and more substantial favours.' Flora kept one half of the lock for herself and gave the other to Mrs Macdonald according to Bishop Forbes. Charles was already assuming something of the character of a saint. Among the other 'relics' were the sheets from his bed which were put away unwashed. Kingsburgh's wife decided she wanted one of them for her shroud and so, apparently, did Flora.

The ribbon Charles had worn about his head was even to inspire an ode by an admiring lady:

> Most honoured ribband, of all else take place,
> Of greens and blues, and all their tawdry race.
> Thou wast the laurel the fair temples bound
> Of Royal Charles, for greatness so renown'd.
> Thee I'll reserve, as Heav'n reserves his crown,
> Till his rebellious foes be overthrown.
> Then in thy place a diadem shall shine
> His by his virtues, as by right divine.

The object of all this veneration was preparing to go on with his journey. He left the house still dressed as Betty Burke. Anne had had to help him because, she claimed, he was so useless at dressing himself he could not even put in a pin without help and 'was like to fall over with laughing'. Once out of sight of the house he stopped and changed into a new suit of clothes. Kingsburgh had advised him to get out of women's clothes as soon as possible because 'he was very bad at acting the part of a dissembler' and his airs were 'all so man-like'. The awful journey of the previous day with Betty Burke was burned into Kingsburgh's memory. The dress was later retrieved and used as a bedcover and Flora was given Betty Burke's apron.

Charles hurried on to Portree with only a boy to guide him across the boggy ground. It was raining hard and by the time he arrived at the inn at Portree and met Flora, Neil and Donald Roy, he was soaking. Donald Roy was worried about him but Charles replied that he was more sorry that 'our Lady [as he called Flora] should be abused with the rain'. Donald tried to get Charles to put on his own kilt and shirt which were dry but the Prince refused to change in front of Flora and said he would eat first. He also called for a dram as the best way to keep out the cold and seems to have ordered a bottle or two. The innkeeper MacNabb had a shrewd idea of who his guest was. He told Donald Roy that Charles looked 'very noble' but when questioned by the ferocious Captain Ferguson a few days later he swore he had no idea who his visitor had been.

Charles and his 'fair conductress' parted in the early hours of 1 July, eleven days after they had first met. According to Donald Roy he kissed her hand and said, 'For all that has happened I hope, Madam, we shall meet in St James's yet!' Her reply is unknown but she was to feel the effects of those eleven days for the rest of her life. In fact she was about to be arrested, and if the stories are true Charles had a premonition of this. He had some sugar in his pocket and said to Donald Roy: 'Pray, Macdonald, take this piece of sugar to our Lady, for I am afraid she will get no sugar where she is going.' He was right. Within ten days of their parting Flora had been arrested and General Campbell knew every detail of Charles's escape down to the lilac sprigs on Betty Burke's dress. Many others who had helped him were also to pay a high price. Kingsburgh was taken. So were the boatmen who, as Kingsburgh's wife had foreseen, were brutally dealt with.

North of the border such suffering only added to the power of the legend. South of the border the legend was also quick in the making. It was not long before readers of the *London Magazine* were being enthralled by accounts of Charles's escape 'under the Disguise of a young Lady's Maid', and their appetites whetted by promises of further accounts of his 'adventures'. Even the spiteful

Horace Walpole was intrigued: 'he is concealed in Scotland and devoured with distempers: I really wonder how an Italian constitution can have supported such rigours!'

These rigours were not over yet. After parting from Flora, Charles had to face another ten weeks on the run. He set off for Raasay, ever hopeful, with a bottle of whisky tied to one side of his belt and a bottle of brandy and a cold hen on the other. His saviours now were the young men of the laird of Raasay's family, in particular Captain Malcolm Macleod, who had agreed to help Charles make the crossing. However, the island had been thoroughly pillaged with most of the houses burned down and the animals wantonly slaughtered, and could offer little shelter. Charles found refuge in 'a mean, low hut', so low, in fact, 'that he could neither sit nor stand, but was obliged to lie on the bare ground, having only a bundle of heath for his pillow' and relying on the young laird of Raasay to bring him food 'viz., a lamb and a kid in the nook of his plaid. . . .' He pondered on what he had seen of Cumberland's revenge on the Highlanders: 'Surely that man who calls himself the duke, and pretends to be so great a general, cannot be guilty of such cruelties. I cannot believe it,' was his horrified reaction.

Charles returned to Skye in fierce gales, with the faithful Captain Macleod and others of the family. When the crew begged to turn back again he urged them on 'with a merry Highland song'. Back on the island he had so recently left he decided to head for Mackinnon country with Malcolm Macleod as his guide. Once again it was a time for disguises with Charles pretending to be the Captain's servant, using the name Lewie Caw. He was becoming tired and dispirited and was still suffering from the flux and from lice. He told Macleod he had removed some four score of them but 'the fatigues and distresses he underwent signified nothing at all, because he was only a single person; but when he reflected upon the many brave fellows who suffered in his cause, that, he behoved to own, did strike him to the heart, and did sink very deep with him.' He was in an introspective mood, wondering whether he had been put on earth for a purpose and not inclined to take advice on practical things. He had an interesting exchange with Macleod about drinking cold water when he was hot. Macleod told him not to, but Charles was adamant: 'If you happen to drink any cold thing when you are warm, only remember Macleod . . . to piss after drinking and it will do you no harm at all.'

They managed to make contact with the Mackinnons. Charles was looking so appalling with 'a dirty white napkin' tied on his head that 'With hands lifted up [they] wept bitterly to see him in such a pickle.' It was only with difficulty that Macleod had dissuaded him from blacking his face. The dirty napkin was a compromise to try and conceal Charles's 'odd remarkable face' but was no real disguise. He was lucky to evade detection as they continued their dangerous journey – Charles was a bad play-actor. However, he had other trials to face as well. At one house a serving wench was instructed to wash his muddy feet and legs but 'offering to wash his Thighs a little too high' an alarmed Charles instructed Macleod in English to tell her to stop at once.

He had a fraught voyage back to the mainland he had left ten weeks before, with his companions just managing to outrow a boatload of 'blood-thirsty pursuers'. Now Charles was confronted with further ample evidence of what had been going on, and he was 'struck with horror at sight of the devastation and solitude he observed as he went along'. He heard how the homes of Lochiel, Kinlochmoidart, Keppoch, Cluny and many others had been burned to the ground; how women and children had been stripped naked and turned out into the cold to fend for themselves; how the cattle had been driven off and the crops destroyed, how the Highlanders were 'starving in their lurking holes'. This ruthlessness heightened his resolve to escape because he suspected that if he was captured by Cumberland's bloodhounds he was likely to be killed out of hand. The Mackinnons shared his sense of danger and tried desperately to find another clan to help. It was like a dangerous game of pass the parcel.

Old Clanranald refused to take him, so did Macdonald of Morar who was living in a hut since the loss of his house, although his wife, Lochiel's daughter, greeted the Prince with tears and a dish of reheated salmon. The stakes were simply too high and it was a sobering experience for Charles to realise that he could not rely on all his 'brave Highlanders' to risk life and limb for him anymore. Their own circumstances were too desperate.

However, Angus Macdonald of Borrodale was prepared to shoulder the burden and took Charles to the cave where he was skulking. This was the begining of a twilight life. There were too many redcoats in the glens for him to move by day so it was under cover of darkness that his helpers moved him on from place to place, leading him over the heather and guiding him across deep ravines and hidden gullies. There were some close shaves, but he managed to evade the net. This went on until 24 July when the exhausted young Prince met the eight Glenmoriston men. They had risen for Charles and subsequently turned to a life of banditry, delighting in raiding redcoat patrols. They were not quite in the Robin Hood mould but undoubtedly loyal to Charles. They took a famous oath to him: 'That their backs should be to God and their faces to the devil; that all the curses the Scriptures did pronounce might come upon them if they did not stand firm to the Prince in the greatest dangers', and they meant it. They offered him comforts that seemed to him miraculous: 'making a bed for him, his royal highness was lulled asleep with the sweet murmurs of the finest purling stream that could be, running by his bedside, within the grotto, in which romantic habitation his royal highness pass'd three days, at the end of which he was so well refreshed that he thought himself able to encounter any hardships.' Charles seems to have enjoyed the camaraderie as they hunted together by day and sat around the fire at night, all in the same disreputable old clothes. According to the accounts, Charles was wearing a dark coat, a tartan vest, plaid and trousers, a saffron-coloured shirt, a scarf around his neck, an abominable wig and bonnet and his shoes were tied together with string. Not the sort of garments to inspire an ode.

However, news came that the militia were drawing closer and the Glenmoriston men had to leave their cave for the greater security of the mountains. Charles went with them but he was anxious to keep in touch with news from the coast. He was sure the French would be looking for him and a bizarre game of hide-and-seek began, with French officers trying to dodge the militia to find the Prince. As they discovered it was not easy. Maurepas put it in a nutshell writing in mid-June: 'It seems certain that the Stuart Prince is in one or other of the small islands of the north of

Scotland. But he is so well concealed from his enemies and from those who would help him, that both seek him with the same lack of success.' Charles's return to the mainland did not make things any easier.

By 13 July the fact that he had left the islands was known to the Government who unleashed five hundred redcoats and the Highlanders of the Munro and Mackay Independent Companies who began to move westwards to block off the passes and hill tracks from Loch Hourn to Glenfinnan. The cordon was closing and Charles's only hope was to make contact with his rescuers. As he moved on with the Glenmoriston men through the remoter fastnesses, they tried to learn what was happening in the wider world. What French ships were at hand? Were any French agents seeking the Prince? It was hard to get any clear intelligence and for the Prince it was like trying to play chess without being able to see his opponents' moves. For much of the time he and his protectors could only guess at where the redcoats were, although there were other occasions when they picked up useful information from the newspapers which were reporting the chase with gusto.

Charles's wanderings with the Glenmoriston brotherhood brought him at last to Lochiel's country. He had not seen Lochiel since Culloden when the chief had been carried from the field, his ankles shot through with grapeshot. His handsome house at Achnacarry where Lochiel had been planting trees when he heard of Charles's landing had been destroyed. The Cameron chief was reduced to skulking some twenty miles away in Badenoch but was anxious to see his Prince. He sent his brother Archibald Cameron and Mr John Cameron to seek him out. The two Camerons set off and a bizarre sequence of events took place. Almost at once they encountered the messenger sent by Charles to Lochiel, but in this suspicious world of spies and secret agents he was only prepared to reveal Charles's whereabouts to Lochiel himself. So the party returned to Lochiel and Charles was sent for. After various alarms he and Lochiel were at last reunited in early September. John Cameron described his un-Princely appearance: 'He was then bare-footed, had an old black kilt coat on, a plaid, philabeg and waistcoat, a dirty shirt and a long red beard, a gun in his hand, a pistol and durk by his side. He was very cheerful and in good health, and, in my opinion, fatter than when he was at Inverness.' Perhaps the large amounts of brandy he consumed helped Charles keep his weight up during his months as a fugitive.

It was an affectionate if rather jumpy reunion. Cluny Macpherson's youngest brother Donald left a vivid description: 'the joy at the meeting was certainly very great and much easier to be conceived than express'd. However, such was his Royal Highness circumspection that when the other would have kneeled at his coming up to him, he said, "Oh! no, my dear Lochiel," clapping him on the shoulder, "you don't know who may be looking from the tops of yonder hills, and if they see any such motions they'll immediately conclude that I am here, which may prove of bad consequence."' However, this was followed by a hearty feast 'with plenty of mutton newly killed, and an anker of whiskie of twenty Scotch pints, with some good beef sassers made the year before, and plenty of butter and cheese, and besides, a large well cured bacon ham. . . .' Charles was in excellent spirits and 'took a hearty dram, which he pretty often called for thereafter to drink his friends healths; and when there were some minch'd collops dress'd with butter for him in a large sawce pan that Lochiel and Cluny carried always about with 'em, which was all the fire vessels they had, he eat heartily, and said with a very chearful and lively countenance, "Now, gentlemen, I live like a Prince," tho' at the same time he was no otherwise served than by eating his collops out of the sauce pan, only that he had a silver spoon.' The whisky no doubt went down even better with them all. As Captain Burt had observed on his travels, 'Some of the Highland gentlemen are immoderate drinkers of whisky, – even three or four quarts at a sitting; and in general, the people that can pay the purchase, drink it without moderation.'

This reunion lasted for two days when it was judged safer for Charles to move on. While he was with Lochiel he had met two French officers who had been nervously scouring the hills for the Prince but their own ship had been captured and there was no news of any other vessels. So it was decided that the capable Cluny Macpherson would now take charge of Charles. The last leg of his extraordinary journey was to be a fitting end to all his adventures and features large in the folklore. Cluny decided that the safest place for his royal charge was his 'cage', the refuge he had built high on Ben Alder after his graceful colonnaded house had been burned down by Government forces. It 'was really a curiosity, and can scarcely be described to perfection', wrote Donald Macpherson who nevertheless did his best. 'Twas situate in the face of a very rough high rockie mountain called Letternilichk, which is still a part of Benalder, full of great stones and crevices and some scattered wood interspersed. The habitation called the *Cage* in the face of that mountain was within a small thick bush of wood. . . . This whole fabrick hung as it were by a large tree, which reclined from the one end all along the roof to the other, and which gave it the name of the Cage. . . .' It could hold six or seven people, 'four of which number were frequently employed in playing at cards, one idle looking on, one becking, and another firing bread and cooking.'

Charles spent some ten days in this 'very romantic comical habitation' hidden from the eyes of the world, but it was only a temporary solution. Lord Loudon's army was a mere ten miles away and it could not be long before news of his whereabouts began to leak out despite all the precautions. Cluny was already preparing him a 'subterranean house' in which to face out the winter, if it should come to that, but escape was the real objective. Charles's heart leapt at the news that two French ships had landed on the west coast and he set out on foot 'even though at that very time he was troubled with a looseness or flux'. Two privateers from St Malo, *L'Heureux* and *Le Prince de Conti*, had slipped into Loch Boisdale on South Uist in early September. After various fruitless enquiries they switched their attention to Loch nan Uamh across the Minch from where contact was at last made with the Prince through a chain of intermediaries. This last stage of his journey was fraught with danger. Again he was travelling by night. He and his companions who included Lochiel had to cross the River Lochy by moonlight in a 'crazy' leaky old boat, but their spirits were raised by copious amounts of brandy, all the more palatable because it had come from Fort Augustus. Lochiel said, ' "Will Your Royal Highness take a dram?" "O" said the Prince, "can you have a dram here?" "Yes," replies Lochiel, "and that from Fort Augustus too" Which pleased the Prince much that he should have provisions from his enemies. . . .'

The next night took them to the ruins of Lochiel's house at Achnacarry, spectral in the 'fine moonshine'. The burned-out shell of the once lovely house symbolized the destruction of all their hopes, but there was little time for introspection if the small band of fugitives was to reach the coast in time. Luckily for them the Government had switched their attention to the east coast where an embargo had been laid on all shipping from the ports. So on 19 September they reached their journey's end without incident. Charles thankfully boarded the *Prince de Conti* and then transferred to *L'Heureux* with Lochiel, his brother Dr Cameron and other 'skulking gentlemen'. In all some 'Twenty-three gentlemen and a hundred and seven men of common rank' apparently set sail with him in the two vessels. One newspaper reported the scene and how 'the gentlemen, as well as the commons, were seen to weep, though they boasted of being soon back with an irresistible force.'

What were Charles's feelings? They are not recorded but must have been a strange mixture. There was relief at being rescued but the fact remained that he was a vermin-infested fugitive whose quest had failed, rather than 'the daring Youth that but a little before made the whole Island of Great Britain tremble at his Motions, and shook the very Throne of one of the greatest Princes in Europe'. This was not the end he had imagined in those summer days of 1745 when he had threaded his way through the western isles to begin the rising. Neither was it the end he had forseen at Glenfinnan, when the standard fluttered proudly in the breeze to the cheers of the Highlanders, or when he entered Holyrood Palace to the acclaim of the mob, or when he stood victorious on the fields of Preston Pans and Falkirk, or when he crossed into England and penetrated its heartland. As *L'Heureux* weighed anchor, and slipped out into the Atlantic in the hours before dawn, the 'rude grandeur' of Loch nan Uamh and its surrounding hills stood out in the moonlight. Over time the once-bright images of rivers and mountains and glens would become shadows in his memory. Whatever he may have hoped in those last moments as the ship creaked and rolled out into the open sea, his glory days were over and would not come again. His cause was finished and the way of life of the Highlanders was already vanishing as surely as the coast of Scotland was fading from his view.

'Will ye no' come back again?' the songs would plaintively ask, but he had had his chance and lost.

EPILOGUE

'What can a bird do that has not
found a right nest?'

O N 29 September 1746 the wanderer returned at last to
France. Charles went ashore at Roscoff to a twenty-one
gun salute, a ragged, weather-beaten figure rather then
the handsome Prince of popular imaginings. However, it was not
long before, bathed and scented, he was off to Versailles to present
himself informally to Louis and plead his cause. The sentiments
with which he was greeted were balm to his wounded spirits – he
was Louis's '*trè cher Prince*' and hailed as the embodiment of
everything a hero should be. These gratifying meetings were followed by his formal reception at Versailles in a coat of 'rose-
coloured velvet embroidered with silver and lined with silver
tissue'. Again he was caressed and flattered and it was all highly
acceptable, except that Louis would make no firm commitments.

Charles tried to ignore the suspicions he had always had about
French motives and decided to remain in France and wait on
events. He settled down to a sybaritic existence in a smart part of
Paris, very different from the 'hole' he had complained about in
1744. He was soon the darling of French society, cossetted by the
nobility and cheered by the crowds when he went to the opera or
the theatre. Ladies of quality fought for the ragged garments he
had been wearing on his voyage from Scotland which were treated
like holy relics. One lady insisted on having Charles's wig which,
as O'Sullivan testified, was 'a most abominable one'. He was
amused that 'She was told it wou'd infect her, that it was full of
vermine, as really it was, & never such a one was set to frighten
Crows away, but she got it. . . .'

However, days turned into weeks and weeks into months and nothing happened. It was not long after his return to France that Charles began to quarrel with his family and friends. There had been an initially affectionate reunion with his brother Henry, but soon, prompted by George Kelly, he was accusing him of not having done enough to pursuade the French to send an invasion force. James intervened to defend his younger son only to find himself the target of Charles's anger. Charles also argued with his father about whether or not to accept a pension from Louis, setting his face against charity from the ally who should be giving him military help. To Charles it was 'a most scandalous arrangement', but to James any refusal would be 'unchristian, unprincely and impolitic'. He was reaching the end of his tether: '*Enfin*, my dear child, I must tell you plainly that if you don't alter your ways I see you lost in all respects . . . I have been already too long in hot water on your occasion. . . .' As well as this, Charles was falling out with that most faithful friend Lochiel who was urging him to accept French proposals for a small force to be sent to Scotland, rather than the wholesale invasion of England on which he had set his heart.

Charles's hopes received a truly mortal blow in the summer of 1747 with the news that Henry had taken the purple of a Roman Catholic Cardinal. Charles described it as a dagger to his heart, much worse than anything Cumberland could have inflicted on him. After all his careful work to demonstrate religious tolerance the next Stuart heir was now a Catholic prelate and celibate. Not that any heirs were likely to have been forthcoming – Henry was a homosexual with a liking for good-looking young clerics. However, Charles felt betrayed on all sides – his father, brother, Louis and the Pope had all colluded to deceive him and this was something he could never forgive. His disturbed childhood had left its mark and Henry's act enhanced his feelings of insecurity.

Charles's life became a rapid rake's progress. The more disillusioned he became the more he flung himself into a life of debauchery. He took mistresses whom he treated with a jealous obsessiveness entirely in character. He had a highly-charged sexual relationship with the young Louise de Montbazon, insisting on his right to visit her whenever he wished – day or night – and demanding her promise not to sleep with her husband. When she failed to live up to his standards he flaunted a new amour, the glamorous and highly accomplished Princesse de Talmond, ten years his senior and cousin to the Queen of France.

Charles began to see himself as some kind of 'noble savage' who need not be subject to normal constraints. The ideas of the Paris '*philosophes*' he met in the salons combined nicely with his experiences with the Highlanders to produce this romantic self-image. His excesses were given a fillip when the War of the Austrian Succession came to an end and France and England made peace at the Treaty of Aix-la-Chapelle. For Charles this was his final betrayal by France. The English would only agree to the peace if France would agree to exile the Stuarts. They would. 'Furious and obstinate in everything', Charles refused to leave gracefully and the débâcle came in December 1748 – just two years after the return of the '*cher prince*' – when Louis signed an order expelling him. Charles was arrested on his way to the opera, tied up with silken cords and bundled out of France to Avignon. Here he managed to alienate the Archbishop by introducing boxing and prize-fighting. When the British applied pressure the exasperated cleric had no compunction about ordering Charles to leave.

This was the beginning of a rootless and peripatetic existence. Sometimes Charles dropped out of sight altogether, to his father's despair. Now and then rumours of wild schemes reached his ears but he had no influence over his wayward and unhappy son. Charles's life had become a caricature of his flight through the isles, devoid of dignity and far from heroic. His Highlanders would not have recognised in this petulant, disillusioned, but still young man their 'Tearlach' – the cheerful young prince who had marched at their head and shared their hardships. But what, as he himself demanded, 'can a bird do that has not found a right nest'?

In 1750 Charles made a brief and clandestine visit to London in the hopes that the English Jacobites were at last planning to do something. Once again he was travelling in disguise, according to one account 'in an Abbé's dress with a black patch over his eye and his eyebrows black'd'. He later told Gustavus of Sweden that he actually inspected the defences of the Tower of London. He also took the opportunity to be received into the Church of England which was probably as much a blow at James and Henry as an act designed to rally support. He attended a gathering of some fifty Jacobite grandees in Pall Mall, the last time such a formal meeting ever took place to discuss a Stuart Restoration. George II was apparently informed of his presence in the capital but was so little disturbed by it that he simply said: 'I shall do nothing at all, when he is tired of England he will go abroad again.' He was quite right. Charles was soon 'convinced he had been deceived' and departed to pursue his peripatetic life in a twilight world of spies and intrigue.

In 1752 came the Elibank plot – a half-baked scheme to attack St James's Palace and murder the royal family. Charles is unlikely to have approved of it, and it was anyway betrayed by that curious mole in the Jacobite camp, 'Pickle the Spy'. Dr Archibald Cameron, Lochiel's brother, was arrested on the Scottish border for his complicity and executed. What he was actually hanged for was his part in the '45, giving him the dubious distinction of being the last Jacobite to be executed for taking part in the rising.

As Charles's grip on reality weakened, he continued plotting busily with Antoine Walsh, writing to him that 'assurances are requisite from this old aunt Ellis . . .', 'Aunt Ellis' being his rather disrespectful codename for Louis XV. He still believed in his destiny and his duty to pursue it. 'No, Sir,' he wrote, 'The poor girl in question [himself] does not live a soft life, that will never be his choice. . . .' The hero of Culloden was turning increasingly to the bottle and his instability, drunkenness and paranoia were driving away his supporters. To these unpleasant characteristics he added another – that of wife-beater. By 1752 Clementina Walkinshaw, the gentle freckled girl who had nursed him at Bannockburn House had become his mistress. At first the relationship was a happy one and Pickle was reporting that 'The Pretender keeps her well and seems to be very fond of her.' In 1753 she gave birth to a little daughter, Charlotte. However, his obsessive jealousy of Clementina became such that, as she later confided to Lord Elcho, 'he would surround the bed in which she slept with chairs perched on tables, while on the chairs he would put little bells which would sound if anybody approached during the night.'

In 1760 Charles received a particularly bitter blow when George

III ascended the throne to popular acclaim. He was the first of his line to be seen as an Englishman born and bred and he was proud of it. The days of foreign rulers whose hearts were in Hanover rather than England were over, together with any realistic hope of a Stuart Restoration. In his heart Charles must have known it although there is a romantic myth, repeated by Sir Walter Scott in *Redgauntlet*, that he attended George's coronation in 1761 and let fall a white kid glove from the balcony in challenge.

Whatever the case, his violence towards Clementina had become so intolerable that in 1760 she fled with her little girl to a convent. Charles's response was that he would sack every convent in Europe until he found them. He never forgave her for this, as he never forgave anyone else who he considered had let him down. He still included his father in this bracket of 'betrayers' and it was only on James's death in 1766 that he returned to Rome. He was at last reconciled with his brother on whom he now relied for financial support. Henry generously gave him half the pension he himself received from the Pope, together with money James had left him in his will. Charles began to go out in Roman society and seems to have tried to put a break on his drinking, 'the nasty bottle' as Henry called it, but the handsome young prince of the '45 was long gone. He was 'bloated and red in the face' – a fat, middle-aged man with protuberant eyes and uncertain temper.

Charles did not redeem himself in the years that followed. He made embarrassing scenes at various fashionable resorts and continued to involve himself in fruitless intrigue. In 1772 it seemed as if his life – and the fortunes of the House of Stuart – might have reached a turning point when he married the young and worldly Louise of Stolberg in order to produce an heir. Yet it was not long before 'The Queen of Hearts' as she was known was being unfaithful to her fat, unattractive husband. He probably deserved it, having made little attempt to temper his behaviour. As one Englishman wrote anonymously to Charles: 'All my countrymen who return from Italy are surprised that your amiable consort stays with you: there is not a single person who would not go to any length to deliver her.' The final breach came in 1780 when she accused Charles of rape and sought sanctuary in a convent by tricking Charles. As one amused commentator put it: 'The mould for any more casts of the Royal Stuarts has been broken, or what is equivalent to it, is now shut up in a convent of nuns.' Not that Louise stayed in the convent for long. She soon ran off with her lover the Italian playwright Vittorio Alfieri.

Charles declined into old age, all passion spent, but his last years were cheered by his daughter Charlotte. She forgave him his abuse of her mother and his neglect of her and came to live with him in the Palazzo Muti in Rome. His relationship with her was probably the only stable one he ever had with a woman. She protected him both from himself and his memories. When a visitor pressed Charles to talk about the '45 he fell in a fit on the floor. 'Oh, Sir, what is this?' Charlotte is said to have chided the visitor. 'You have been speaking to him about Scotland, and his Highlanders. No one dares speak about such things in his presence.' According to the stories Charles died in Charlotte's arms on 30 January 1788. There was no special star in the sky to mark his passing. It was just the death of a disappointed old man in a crumbling palace haunted by the past.

But what of those others whose lives and destinies had been so closely linked with his? The fate of the Scottish chiefs and grandees had been mixed. Lord George Murray had escaped to the continent after Culloden. He came to Paris in 1747 hoping to see Charles, but the Prince, convinced of his treachery, refused any interview and sent a message to his former commander to be gone. Lord George returned to exile in Holland where he died in 1760 without ever seeing his beloved Scotland again. One of his sons inherited his Hanoverian uncle's title of Duke of Atholl, another became a British general and a third became an admiral. The Duke of Perth died on board the ship bearing Lord Elcho, Lord John Drummond, Maxwell of Kirkconnell and other fugitives to safety. Lord Ogilvy hid in Angus until he too made his escape to France where he obtained a commission in the French army. The beautiful Lady Ogilvy joined him after escaping from Edinburgh Castle disguised as her own maid. Cluny Macpherson remained skulking in Scotland for a number of years, perhaps motivated by thoughts of the buried treasure at Loch Arkaig, and later fell out bitterly with Charles. The faithful Lochiel who had boarded *L'Heureux* with Charles was given a regiment in the French army by Louis but, like Lord George, was a very reluctant exile from Scotland. He died of brain-fever in 1748. Chevalier Johnstone also escaped after many adventures disguised as a Scots pedlar, and eventually became aide-de-camp to General Montcalm, fighting against Wolfe at Quebec as he had fought against him at Culloden. Neil Maceachain lived in France and his son became one of Napoleon's most famous generals.

Of the 'seven Men of Moidart' who had accompanied Charles on his historic voyage to Scotland in 1745, O'Sullivan made his escape back to France after parting from Charles on South Uist, but eventually fell foul of him, married a rich widow and died in about 1761. William, Duke of Atholl, was captured and died in the Tower of London in July 1746, while his Prince was still a fugitive in the Highlands. Aeneas Macdonald, the banker, had been absent in Barra collecting Spanish money at the time of Culloden. He was later captured, tried and eventually released only to perish in the French Revolution. Francis Strickland, the only Englishman, had already died of dropsy in Carlisle thereby escaping an even nastier fate at the hands of Cumberland. Poor old Sir Thomas Sheridan died of an apoplectic fit in 1746 after being ordered to Rome to give an account of Charles's doings to James and apparently being rebuked by the King for giving the Prince bad advice. George Kelly, the parson and intriguer, had been sent to France to spread the news of Charles's victory at Preston Pans. He later rejoined Charles in Paris but quarrelled with him and died in 1762. Sir John Macdonald surrendered after Culloden, claiming protection as a French subject and was subsequently exchanged for English prisoners.

Lords Balmerino, Cromarty and Kilmarnock were tried by the Upper House in July 1746 and condemned. Charles read the accounts of their trials in the newspapers while hiding in the heather. Cromarty's wife managed to secure her husband a reprieve by swooning dramatically at the feet of George II. However, Balmerino and Kilmarnock went to the block and both of them impressed the watching crowd. Balmerino tested the sharpness of the axe with his thumb and made a defiant speech absolutely denying Cumberland's claim that Charles had ordered no quarter to be given at the battle of Culloden. Lord Kilmarnock behaved with such dignity that even the executioner was in tears and had to be given a strong drink.

Lord Lovat was impeached by the Commons in March 1747. He had never actually taken up arms for Charles, but his double-dealing had finally caught up with him and he had been arrested while hiding in the trunk of an old tree – quite a feat for a man in his late seventies. His correspondence with the Jacobite leadership was disclosed at his trial by his own secretary and by Murray of Broughton who had turned King's evidence after his capture. Murray was in such a state that before testifying he drank a whole bottle of wine 'and would have had brandy if it had been to be come at'. Lord Lovat was found guilty and it did not surprise him. There is a story that as he was being taken back to the Tower one day an old woman leant in through the window of his coach and shouted, 'You'll get that nasty head of yours chopped off, you ugly old Scotch dog'; to which Lovat snapped back, 'I believe I shall, you ugly old English bitch.' At his execution one of the stands collapsed killing several spectators and it caused him some amusement. 'The more mischief the better sport,' he commented wryly before extending his wrinkled old neck to the axeman. His son, the Master of Lovat, whom he had sent to join the Prince, was pardoned and later served in the British army with his regiment of Fraser's Highlanders, fighting at Quebec under his former opponent General Wolfe and elsewhere in the Americas.

Murray of Broughton had fallen ill at Elgin shortly before Culloden. While he could have escaped to France he opted to remain in Scotland only to be betrayed by a cowherd. He saved himself by turning King's evidence but his beautiful wife left him and he was hated and despised by many Jacobites. There is a story that one night he visited Sir Walter Scott's father on business and drank a cup of tea. After he had left Scott threw the cup out of the window, telling his astonished wife, 'Neither lip of me or of mine comes after Murray of Broughton's.' Paradoxically Charles seems to have forgiven Murray, but his former secretary died in a mad-house in 1777.

The rebel ladies of the '45 suffered their own hardships and indignities though none were executed. Lady Mackintosh of Moy was arrested after Culloden and wounded by a soldier's bayonet as he tried to rob her. She was taken to Inverness along a road strewn with dead and dying Highlanders. Although Hawley had nurtured fantasies of hanging her with silken cords, she was eventually released and in 1748 visited London where she was 'caressed by Ladys of Quality'. There is a story that she danced with Cumberland at a ball to the tune of 'Up And Waur Them a', Wullie!' but then called for the next dance to be 'The Auld Stuarts Back Again'. Reunited with her husband she lived until well into her sixties, an enduring symbol of the romance and heroism of the '45. A number of other ladies were also imprisoned like the famous Jenny Cameron, portrayed in the newspapers as Charles's mistress. Of the ordinary Highland women, a number fell into Cumberland's hands and some of these were eventually transported.

Their fates are largely unknown, but this is not true of Flora Macdonald whose conduct after her arrest won admiration on all sides. Flora had known the risks she was running when she reluctantly agreed to help Charles. She was betrayed under torture by one of the boatmen who had rowed her and the Prince to Skye. The vile Captain Ferguson of HMS *Furnace* was soon on her trail, questioning the Kingsburghs about what had happened the night Charles had lodged in their house in his maid's disguise. Had they 'laid the young Pretender and Miss MacDonald in one bed,' he asked pruriently. Kingsburgh's wife replied, 'Sir, whom you mean by the young Pretender I shall not pretend to guess; but I can assure you, it is not the fashion in the Isle of Skye to lay the mistress and the maid in the same bed together.' This robust response did not stop Ferguson from arresting Kingsburgh who later admitted Flora's involvement in Charles's escape.

Flora was arrested and imprisoned in the *Furnace*. Conditions on board for the ordinary prisoners were appalling. The captives were kept below deck, given half rations in 'foul nasty buckets' and the smell of ordure was everywhere. Flora was kept apart from the others and was questioned not by Ferguson but by the more humane and gentlemanly General Campbell. She was calm and courageous, answering as truthfully as she could without incriminating others, and he ordered she should be treated with respect. While taking the air on deck she encountered Felix O'Neil, also now a prisoner. She is said to have slapped his face lightly and observed: 'To that black face do I owe all my misfortune.'

These misfortunes were not to end for some time. Flora was kept prisoner in various places including aboard the HMS *Bridgewater* which was moored for a while at Leith. She was not allowed ashore but could receive visitors, and found herself lionised by Leith and Edinburgh society. The ladies were enchanted by the tales of Flora's days with the Prince. Lady Mary Cochrane even begged the honour of sleeping in Flora's bed with her. After a while she was sent to London where she was eventually put under a kind of house arrest and allowed considerable freedom. By 1747 the anti-Jacobite mood was easing and she found herself a celebrity. Pamphlets were written about her, dwelling on her physical charms rather than her 'treasonable practices'. Later that year an amnesty was declared and she was released and able to travel north to Scotland. Her companion on her journey was Malcolm Macleod who had been arrested after helping Charles on Raasay. Many years later he told Boswell and Johnson how surprised he had been – 'I went to London to be hanged and returned in a post-chaise with Miss Flora Macdonald.'

Although Flora had her freedom again, her life was always to be coloured by her fame as the heroine who had saved the Bonnie Prince. In 1750 she married Kingsburgh's tall handsome son and the *Scots Magazine* reminded its readers that she was 'the young lady who aided the escape of the young Chevalier!' Her fame was also to follow her across the Atlantic. Like many others she and her husband began to find life in the Highlands too hard and joined the great wave of emigration to the American colonies. She sailed to Cape Fear, Carolina, to be hailed as the 'symbol of Highland bravery and independence'. It was a bad time to arrive. There was a rising climate of rebellion, but Flora and her family were not revolutionaries. It was ironical that, like many of the other Highland emigrants, they found themselves ranged firmly on the side of Good King George. This made for uncomfortable times. When the fighting broke out Flora's husband was captured and Flora and her daughters suffered all kinds of harassment.

This period was a further strange chapter in a life that had already had more than its share of drama. Flora was to face many trials and tribulations before she and her husband were at last reunited again on Skye. Towards the end of her life Flora allowed the story of her life to be set down in writing and in 1790 she died. Her funeral was a fitting one for the Prince's guardian angel. According to one eye-witness there was a mile-long cortège, and the pipers played 'the usual melancholy lament for departed greatness'. He also noted that some three hundred gallons of whisky were consumed. She was buried less than two miles from the point where she landed with Charles.

Flora Macdonald's journey to Skye is the cornerstone of the legend of Bonnie Prince Charlie. She is without doubt the most famous Highlander associated with the events of the '45 and she suffered for her role. However, for many hundreds of ordinary people a much worse fate awaited. Their collective woes are what give the story of the '45 such a powerful emotional appeal, together with the fact that Culloden marked the end of the Highland way of life.

Cumberland may have disliked Scotland in general, but he left no doubt that he loathed and despised the Highlands and its people in particular. He ordered the extermination of the wounded at Culloden and this was the beginning of a campaign of suppression. Bishop Forbes wrote a moving account from the Jacobite perspective: 'In several parts of the Highlands the soldiery spared neither man, woman, nor child. The hoary head, the tender mother, and the weeping infant behoved to share in the general wreck, and to fall victims to rage and cruelty by the musket, the bloody bayonet, the devouring flame, a famishing cold and hunger.'

Cumberland set about his task of subduing the Highlands from his headquarters at Fort Augustus. Martial law was imposed, fugitives were hunted down and indiscriminantly hanged and shot. Houses and cottages were razed to the ground and the clansmen's cattle slaughtered or driven off to be sold to the Lowland and English dealers who flocked to Fort Augustus sensing a bargain. His brutal methods led to protests from even such loyal Government supporters as Duncan Forbes, whom he afterwards referred to contemptuously as 'that old woman who talked to me about humanity'. What concerned Forbes were the numerous reports of murder, arson, rape, torture and looting in the Highlands and islands. Many of those who suffered had had little or nothing to do with the rising, like a blind girl raped on Rona. It was a particularly favoured practice to rape the women in front of their burning homes, also to strip them and leave them to fend for themselves quite naked and without food like the wife of Cameron of Clunes. The driving off of the cattle deprived many of the clans of their only means of subsistence. Some of them were reduced to begging to be allowed to lick up the blood of their own slaughtered animals.

Nearly three and a half thousand men, women and children were taken prisoner and their plight was pitiful. Over six hundred died in captivity of starvation, disease and abuse. The conditions aboard the prison ships were particularly dreadful. The stench from these hulks was so great that it deterred all but the most avid sightseers who rowed out to take a look while they were moored at Tilbury. A letter to Bishop Forbes described how the prisoners were 'lying between decks like fish in a pond and everyone had a twig in his hand, to defend himself from the attacks of his neighbours lice'.

Some one hundred and twenty were executed, including Captain Francis Townley of the Manchester Regiment and fellow members of that gallant little garrison left to defend Carlisle when Charles retreated north. Some of these suffered the traitor's death of hanging, drawing and quartering. The newspapers gave lurid reports of the executions. For example, the *London Magazine* described to its readers how when some prisoners had 'hung ten Minutes, the Executioner cut them down, laid their bodies on a Stage, and stripped them naked'. He then cut out their hearts, 'throwing them into the Fire with cries of "Gentlemen, behold the Heart of a traitor". . . .' Over nine hundred were transported to the American colonies and a further one hundred and twenty or so banished 'outside our Dominions'. As one Jacobite lamented, 'Woe is me for the host of the tartan, scattered and spread everywhere. . . .'

However, the real blow to the 'host of the tartan' was the policy of de-Gaelicizing the Highlands and destroying the ancient clan system. Everything that had distinguished the old clan ways was swept aside. The chiefs lost their hereditary powers of jurisdiction over their people – the rights of 'pit and gallows'. Their clansmen were no longer allowed to bear arms on pain of death. Neither were they permitted to wear their traditional clothing. In August 1747 it was decreed that 'no man or boy within Scotland . . . shall on any pretence whatsoever, wear or put on the clothes commonly called highland clothes, that is to say, the plaid, philebeg or little kilt, trowse, shoulder-belts, or any part whatsoever of what particularly belongs to the highland garb. . . .' The penalty for a repeated trangression was transportation.

The previous year, fears about celebrations to mark Charles's birthday had led to the ludicrous situation of Government soldiers being ordered to arrest any woman found wearing a tartan gown, stockings, sash or cape in Leith. All they found was one old woman in her dotage, Mistress Jean Rollo, who happened to be wearing a tartan gown and knew nothing of any ban. However, there was nothing farcical about the legislation which was a very real nail in the coffin of the Highlander's way of life. By the time tartan was legitimised again in 1782 it was as a romantic and whimsical gesture to a bygone age. Tartans were 'reinvented' and attributed to the different clans but had little to do with the old ways. By then many of the young men had anyway left the glens to wear the uniform of the Highland regiments of the British army and fight for the expanding Empire.

But what of the instigator of all this misery? Despite a letter from a fellow military man written shortly after Culloden saying, 'Return as soon as you please. No lady that prides to the name of an Englishwoman will refuse you,' Cumberland stayed at Fort Augustus until July 1746. He spent his time making thorough arrangements for the subduing and government of the Highlands. Only then did he joyfully leave the task of finishing what he had begun to the Earl of Albemarle.

Cumberland arrived in London to a hero's reception: mobs ran after his coach; there was a service of thanksgiving in St Paul's at which he arrived dressed to kill in scarlet, blue and gold; Handel wrote 'The Conquering Hero' in his honour, and mock battles were enacted in Hyde Park. A flower was named Sweet William in his honour (though, when news of this reached the Highlands, a particularly noxious weed was christened 'Stinking Billy' in retaliation). A new ballet was staged at Sadlers Wells which, unlikely as it may seem, promised its audience 'an exact view of the battle accompanied by a prodigious cannonade'.

However, it was not long before the more thinking citizens began to be concerned by the reports of the savage suppression of the Highlands. Letters in the papers described what some of the officers had seen and questions began to be asked about why so few prisoners had been taken at Culloden. Cumberland's shining image was becoming tarnished and when it was suggested he should be made an honorary member of a city guild one wry suggestion was 'Let it be of the Butchers'. This was the genesis of the soubriqet 'Butcher Cumberland'.

Culloden was Cumberland's high spot, and as much as his cousin Charles, his later life was disappointment and anti-climax. He returned to the wars in the Low Countries against Marshal Saxe, but Culloden remained his only personal victory. In 1757, defending Hanover with a German army against the French, he was defeated at Hastenbeck and signed the convention of Kloster-Zeven under which he unwisely agreed to disband his army. His actions were condemned by his father and public opinion, the convention was repudiated and he resigned his military appointments. He died unmarried at the age of only forty-four, loved by his soldiers, despite his harshness, but not much mourned elsewhere.

Cumberland's accomplice in the suppression of the Highlands, the explosive General 'Hangman' Hawley, died in 1759 leaving characteristically blunt instructions that he was to be buried with 'no more expense or ridiculous show than a poor soldier (who is as good as any man)'.

The 1745 Rebellion was the turning point of their lives for many who took part, Jacobite or Whig. It also saw the last flowering of the old Highland ways. Yet it is an interesting postscript that at the Normandy landings nearly two hundred years later, Lord Lovat stormed ashore on Sword Beach accompanied by a piper in full rant. He ordered the piper to keep playing as his commando brigade advanced up the beach, which so amazed the German snipers that they held their fire, believing he must be insane. Lovat may not have had henchman and bladier by his side as well, but it was a reminder that some Highland traditions survived that cold April day at Culloden field in what is still called 'Charlie's Year'.

BIBLIOGRAPHY

NEWSPAPERS AND PERIODICALS 1745–46

Caledonian Mercury
Gentleman's Magazine
London Evening Post
London Magazine
True Patriot

PUBLISHED PRIMARY SOURCES
(PUBLISHED IN LONDON EXCEPT WHERE INDICATED)

BLAIKIE, W. B., *Origins of the Forty Five* (Edinburgh, 1916)
BRADSTREET, D., *The Adventures of Captain Dudley Bradstreet* (1755)
BURT, E., *Letters from a Gentleman in the North of Scotland* (1818)
CHAMBERS, R. (ed.), *Jacobite Memoirs of the Rising of 1745* (1834)
ELCHO, LORD, *A Short Account of the Affairs of Scotland in 1744, 1745 and 1746*, ed. E. Charteris (1907)
FORBES, BISHOP R., *The Lyon in Mourning*, ed. H. Patton, 3 vols (Edinburgh, 1895)
HENDERSON, A., *History of the Rebellion 1745–1746* (1753)
HOME, J., *The History of the Rebellion in the Year 1745* (1802)
JOHNSTONE, CHEVALIER DE, *A Memoir of the '45* (1820)
MAXWELL OF KIRKCONNELL, J., *Narrative of Charles Prince of*

Wales's Expedition to Scotland in the year 1745 (Edinburgh, 1841)

MURRAY OF BROUGHTON, J., *Memorials*, ed. R. F. Bell (Edinburgh, 1898)

RAY, J. A., *Compleat History of the Rebellion* (1752)

DE LA TREMOILLE (ed.), *A Royalist Family Irish and French (The Walshes) 1689–1789 and Prince Charles Edward*, translated by A. G. Murray MacGregor (Edinburgh, 1904)

TAYLER, A. and H., *1745 and After* (contains O'Sullivan's account) (1938)

TAYLER, H., *The Stuart Papers at Windsor* (1939)

—*Jacobite Epilogue* (1941)

—*Anonymous History of the Rebellion in the Years 1745 and 1746* (1944)

—*Two Accounts of the Escape of Prince Charles Edward* (Oxford, 1951)

—*Jacobite Miscellany* (Edinburgh, 1948)

Woodhouselee MSS (Edinburgh, 1907)

SECONDARY SOURCES

BLACK, J., *Culloden and the '45* (Stroud, 1993)

BLAIKIE, W. B., *Itinerary of Prince Charles Stuart from his Landing in Scotland July 1745 to his Departure in September 1746* (Edinburgh, 1897)

CHARTERIS, E., *William Augustus Duke of Cumberland* (1917)

DAICHES, D., *Charles Edward Stuart* (1973)

DOUGLAS, H., *Charles Edward Stuart, the Man, the King, the Legend* (1975)

—*Flora MacDonald The Most Loyal Rebel* (1993)

DUKE, W., *Prince Charles Edward and the Forty-Five* (1938)

—*In the Steps of Bonnie Prince Charlie* (1953)

—*The Rash Adventurer* (1952)

EARDLEY-SIMPSON, L., *Derby and the Forty-Five* (1933)

ERICKSON, C., *Bonnie Prince Charlie* (1993)

FORSTER, M., *The Rash Adventurer* (1974)

GIBSON, J., *Ships of the '45* (1967)

JARVIS, R. C., *Collected Papers on the Jacobite Risings* (Manchester, 1972)

LANG, A., *Prince Charles Edward Stuart* (1903)

LENMAN, B. P., *The Jacobite Risings in Britain 1689–1746* (1980)

LINKLATER, E., *The Prince in the Heather* (1965)

MACKENZIE, C., *Prince Charlie's Ladies* (1934)

MACLEAN, SIR FITZROY, *Bonnie Prince Charlie* (1988)

MACLEAN, KYBETT S., *Bonnie Prince Charlie* (1988)

MONCRIEFFE, SIR IAIN, and HICKS, D., *The Highland Clans* (1967)

MCLYNN, F. J., *The Jacobite Army in England 1745* (Edinburgh, 1983)

—*The Jacobites* (1985)

—*Charles Edward Stuart – A Tragedy in Many Acts* (1988)

MILLER, P., *A Wife for the Pretender* (1965)

—*James* (1965)

MOUNSEY, G. C., *Carlisle in 1745* (1846)

PETRIE, SIR CHARLES, *The Jacobite Movement – The Last Phase* (1950)

PREBBLE, J., *Culloden* (1961)

SCOTT-MONCRIEFF, L. (ed.), *The '45 – to gather an image whole* (Edinburgh, 1988)

SPECK, W. A., *The Butcher – the Duke of Cumberland and the Suppression of the Forty-Five* (Oxford, 1981)

TERRY, C. S., *The Forty-Five – A Narrative of the last Jacobite Rising by Several Contemporary Hands* (1900)

TOMASSON, K., *The Jacobite General* (Edinburgh, 1958)

TOMASSON, K., and BUIST, F., *Battles of the '45* (1962)

URE, J. A., *Bird on the Wing* (1992)

VINING, E. G., *Flora MacDonald* (1967)

INDEX